BIMBOS &
ZOMBIES

BIMBOS & ZOMBIES

including

BIMBOS OF THE DEATH SUN

AND

ZOMBIES OF THE GENE POOL

Sharyn McCrumb

GARDEN CITY, NEW YORK

BIMBOS OF THE DEATH SUN

AUTHOR'S NOTE

MORE THAN TEN years ago, when I was a struggling graduate student in the Virginia Tech English department, the university science fiction club sponsored a short story contest, to be judged by a colleague of mine, English instructor John Nizalowski. As a practical joke, I slipped an outrageous manuscript into the pile of story entries and waited to hear John's scream when he read it. The spoof was entitled "Bimbos of the Death Sun."

When John had recovered from reading a manuscript in which his dog and his officemate were depicted as evil aliens in a parody of *Moby Dick*, he returned it to me saying, "You know, that title is really too good to waste on a practical joke."

"I know," I said, "but I could never write the book that went with that title."

I tucked the idea away in a few spare brain cells in the math section of my cortex and went back to writing the Elizabeth MacPherson novels, which were "Jane Austen with an attitude"—definitely not science fiction.

A few months later, I had an idea that fit the title. What if one of the university's engineering professors wrote a hard science fiction novel about the effect of alien sunspots on computer circuits, and what if he sold that novel to a cheap paperback house, and they changed the title to *Bimbos of the Death Sun*? I pictured the professor going to a small regional SF convention to promote his book and trying to keep his students from finding out that he was the author of the paperback with the lurid bikini-clad girl on the cover. *That* book I could write, I thought.

I completed the first two chapters for fun, drawing on a local science fiction convention called Mysticon for inspiration—and on my observation of my husband's war-gaming friends. Writing those chapters was cheaper than therapy. Still, this wasn't the sort of book that I was writing for my New York editor, Joe Blades, so I put the pages in a drawer and went back to writing term papers on the Brontës and chronicling the adventures of Elizabeth MacPherson.

Then the science fiction club had its own convention. It was being held one weekend at the Blacksburg Econo-Lodge, and the club had raised enough money to bring one—*one*—author in to star in about eight hours of programming. Even as out of touch with reality as they were, they realized that this poor author would need to be given a recess every now and then, so they cast about for other ways to fill the day.

One of them hunted me up on campus. "You! You're a published writer!" he said accusingly.

"Well . . . not anything you guys read," I murmured.

"Doesn't matter. The real author will have to eat, and so on. Why don't you come and do a one-hour session? A reading, maybe."

I didn't get many offers to give readings in those days, so I accepted the invitation, but I knew the science ficiton club wouldn't care for my usual work. Then I remembered those ten pages of *Bimbos of the Death Sun*. I dug them out of the file cabinet and took them to the Econo-Lodge.

The guest author stayed for the reading, laughed harder than anybody, and asked for a copy of the manuscript. I photocopied the pages for her, thinking that she wanted to pass them around the office when she got home. She did—but the office was that of her publisher.

Six months later, I received a phone call at work from a strange man who said, "We want to buy your book."

I said, "What book?"

The rest is history. I agreed to write the rest of the novel in fewer than eight weeks, so my memory of that autumn is a blur of computer screen and exhaustion, but I did finish it. *Bimbos of the Death Sun* was published in the spring of 1987, and it went on to win the Edgar Award that year for Best Paperback Original Mystery. That's when I realized that the joke was on me. I had envisioned a professor haunted by his paperback with its garish cover—and that is exactly what my novel looked like. My cover was *his* cover, and for a long time I would be known as the author of *Bimbos of the Death Sun*. Try living that down!

Then the book proceeded to have a life of its own.

At book signings in Hollywood, cast members of science fiction television programs turned up with battered copies of *Bimbos of the Death Sun*. "We use it as a survival manual," one of them told me. "It's the best way to explain to guest stars what they'll experience when they go to a fan convention."

SF fandom discovered the book, and readers either loved it or were outraged by the description of fandom. Panel discussions debated the issues raised in the novel. I felt like the Salman Rushdie of science fiction. People from all over the U.S. and Canada would tell me that they recognized their friends in the book—people I had never heard of. And I was able to keep track of which authors in the genre were being difficult by who Appin Dungannon was reputed to be. His identity kept changing in the popular mind-set.

Bimbos of the Death Sun was intended to be an observation of the culture of fandom, and a gentle warning. Science fiction writers build castles in the air; the fans move into them; and the publishers collect the rent. It's a nice place to visit, but please don't try to live there.

That said, welcome to Jay Omega's castle. Read on . . .

—Sharyn McCrumb
October 1996

CHAPTER 1

THE VISITING SCOTTISH folksinger peered out of the elevator into the hotel lobby. When he pushed the button marked "G," he naturally assumed that he would arrive at the ground floor of the building. Now he wasn't so sure. Things were different in America, but he hadn't realized they were *this* different. Perhaps "G" stood for Ganymede, or some other intergalactic place. Who were those people?

A pale blue blonde wearing a green satin tunic stepped on to the elevator, eyeing his jeans and sweatshirt with faint disapproval. "Going up?" she said in her flat American accent. She looked about twenty, he thought. The elevator was moving before he realized that he'd forgotten to get out.

"You here for the con?" she asked, noticing his guitar case.

"No. I'm a tourist." He liked that better than saying he was on tour; it prevented leading questions that ended in disappointment when the American discovered: 1) that they had never heard of him, and 2) that he didn't know Rod Stewart. "What are you here for?"

She grinned. "Oh, you mean you don't know? It's Rubicon—a science fiction convention. We're practically taking over the hotel. There'll be hundreds of us."

"Oh, right. Like Trekkies." He nodded. "We have some of your lot back home."

"Where's home?" she asked, fiddling with the key ring on her yellow sash.

"Scotland." At least she hadn't tried to guess. He was getting tired of being mistaken for an Australian.

As the elevator doors rumbled open on the fifth floor, the departing blue person glanced again at his jeans. "Scotland, huh?" she mused. "Aren't you supposed to be wearing some kind of funny outfit?"

"Is Diefenbaker here yet?" asked Bernard Buchanan breathlessly. He always said things a little breathlessly, on account of the bulk he was carrying around, and he was always clutching a sheaf of computer printouts, which he would try to read to the unwary.

Miles Perry, whose years of con experience had made him chief among the wary, began to edge away from the neo-fan. "I haven't seen him," he hedged.

"I had a letter from him on Yellow Pigs Day, and he said he'd be here," Bernard persisted. "He's supposed to be running one of the wargames, and I wanted him to look at my new parody."

Miles swallowed his exasperation. It was, after all, the first hour of the convention. If he started shouting now, his blood pressure would exceed his I.Q. in no time, and there were still two more days of wide-eyed novices to endure. Diefenbaker *would* encourage these eager puppies; he brought it on himself. Miles had a good mind to post a notice in the hotel lobby informing everyone of Diefenbaker's room number. Maybe a few dozen hours of collective neo-fans, all reading him fanzine press at once, would cure him of these paternal instincts. Really, Diefenbaker would write to *anybody*. Just let someone in Nowhere-in-Particular, New Jersey, write in a comment to Diefenbaker's fan magazine, and Dief would fire back a friendly five-page letter, making the poor crottled greep feel liked. More comments would follow, requiring more five-page letters. Miles didn't like to think what Dief's postage budget would run. And this is what it came to: post-adolescent monomaniacs waiting to waylay him at cons to discuss Lithuanian politics, or silicon-based life forms, or whatever their passion was. If he weren't careful, he'd get so tied up with these upstarts that he wouldn't have time to socialize with the authors and the fen-elite. Miles would have to protect Dief from such pitfalls, for his own good.

"I don't think he's due in until tomorrow," he informed the anxious young man. "Of course, you might look around the exhibition rooms and see if you can spot him."

"But I don't know what he looks like!" wailed Buchanan, but Miles Perry was already disappearing into the crowd.

"Miles, I must speak to you!" In a green turtleneck sweater and medallion, Richard Faber looked like a champagne bottle; he could be equally explosive as well.

"Why, hello, Richard. How nice to see you." Richard and Miles were fellow players in an otherworld Diplomacy game called Far Brandonia, in which players became heads of state of mythical countries, and engaged in war or diplomacy, all meticulously recorded in a mimeographed fan magazine called *Brandywind*.

At the moment, Miles and Richard were in détente, which called for scrupulous politeness and as little communication as possible. "Have you signed any treaties with C.D. Novibazaar?" Richard demanded.

"Why do you ask?" countered Miles pleasantly.

"Because he has an army sitting on my southern border, that's why! I thought he was going to lend it to me, but now I'm not so sure. Is Clanton here? What about Diefenbaker?"

Miles noticed a crowd around the registration table. Wendy would be needing some help. "Perhaps we can get together later when the chaos subsides, Faber."

"Novibazaar still has the Seal of Corstorphine, hasn't he? Have we decided yet whether that gives him control of the railroads through Gondal?"

Miles closed his eyes for dramatic effect. That was just the trouble with Faber, in the game and out of it. No patience and no tact. "Richard, I will get back to you when—oh, good lord, it's him!" He began to run toward the registration table, having just glimpsed a white cowboy hat bobbing about five feet above the floor.

Miles Perry parted the crowd with less than his usual smoothness, and bent to shake hands with the figure beneath the bobbing Stetson. "Mr. Dungannon, what an honor to have you here!"

"The pleasure is entirely yours!" snapped Appin Dungannon, sounding for all the world like a peevish elf. His narrowed piggy eyes darted from one autograph seeker to another, and finally cantilevered upward to glare at Perry's plaster smile. "Are you going to get me out of here?"

"I'd be happy to escort you to your room, and we can discuss the schedule." Miles turned to the pack of fans, waving Appin Dungannon paperbacks. "You can catch up with him later, people," he told them. "Let him get settled in first." Picking up Dungannon's leather bag and computer case, Miles steered the guest author toward the elevator, talking soothingly of complimentary liquor and bulk orders of his books. Perhaps by the time they reached his room, Dungannon would have calmed down sufficiently for Miles to ask him about judging the writing contest.

Behind them, an unfortunately loud voice exclaimed, "*He* writes Tratyn Runewind?" The elevator doors sealed out a chorus of "Shhhhs" from the surrounding fen. That sentiment, seldom so untactfully voiced, was one of the great common experiences in fandom: the shock of discovering that the chronicles of the golden Viking warrior Tratyn Runewind were written by a malevolent elf with a drinking problem. Part of fen lore, to be imparted to promising newcomers, was the lecture on How to Deal with Appin Dungannon. He was susceptible to flattery; willing to autograph books (even second-hand copies—signature only); but he would not discuss future

Runewind books, and if questioned about details on the old ones, he was likely to know less about the book than the fan did. He had probably not read it as often. The one cardinal rule of Dungannontry was: never, never approach the author while wearing a Tratyn Runewind costume. He had once hurled an entire stack of hardbacks and a water carafe at a Runewind imposter. Still, he was internationally famous, and his appearance at a con was a guarantee of good attendance, so con organizers suffered him gladly; besides, his atrocities made good anecdotes to recount at later cons.

"And we were hoping you'd judge the costume contest later this evening," Miles was saying to his scowling charge. "Just a brief little event."

Dungannon grunted. "Especially if you're male."

Wisely choosing to ignore this, Miles continued, "And for dinner tonight, I thought you might like to join me and Walter Diefenbaker. You remember Diefenbaker, perhaps, from Mysticon?"

Dungannon made a sound that might have been assent or the sound of a Kyle-dragon swallowing a village. "Anyway, we thought we'd take you to dinner, and then you can sign autographs or whatever until costume time. There'll be filksinging in Room 211."

"I am indebted to you for the warning," said the author with a little bow.

"Oh, one other thing. There is another guest author coming to the convention. Perhaps we ought to ask him along to dinner as well."

"Who?"

"He's a local guy, a professor at the university. Just had his first SF novel come out in paperback. Would you like to meet him?"

Dungannon produced a fanged smile. "Let him wait in line with the other groupies," he said, giggling.

Miles Perry sighed, sensing a nasty Dungannon legend in the making.

CHAPTER 2

DR. JAMES OWENS Mega looked again at the empty registration desk, and then at the inhabitants of the lobby, trying to decide whom to ask for help: the green pirate, the robot, or the giant insect. None of the above. Further inspection revealed an even more interesting individual: a portly, pleasant-looking fellow who reminded him of Winnie-the-Pooh. The interesting thing was that the fellow wasn't costumed as Winnie the Pooh; he was wearing rimless glasses and an ordinary tweed suit, but he looked like a Milne character anyway. He must have been born middle-aged, Mega thought. Probably in his mid-twenties now, but he'll still look that way at fifty. Not entirely a bad thing, though. Mega, an engineering professor, had the opposite problem: he was thirty, but librarians still mistook him for an under-graduate. At least I don't look out of place here, he thought. He looked again at the giant insect. But, then, who would?

"Winnie" had noticed his bewilderment and ambled over to chat. "Hello," he said, offering what Mega couldn't help thinking of as a pink paw. "Our registrar has gone to the ladies' room. Perhaps I can sign you up. Are you preregistered?"

"I'm not sure," stammered Mega. "That is, I'm expected."

The bear was all smiling patience. "You sent in your fee?"

"No, I'm James Mega." He waited for a beam of recognition, but none was forthcoming. Mega managed a modest smile. "I'm the guest author."

The smile turned to stricken consternation. "Dungannon can-celled?"

Mega winced. "Sorry. I should have said I'm *one* of the guest authors. I believe Appin Dungannon is still scheduled to appear." He had a sudden premonition of what the weekend was going to be like.

"I'm afraid I've been a bit of an oaf." The bear smiled. "My name is Diefenbaker, and I'm sure I'll like you better than *anybody* likes Dungannon. Let me just get you a name tag. James Mega, did you say?"

"Well, I have sort of a pen name," Mega murmured diffidently. "It's my initials, really. You see, I'm an engineering professor at

Tech, and I got this idea for a problem involving the effects of sunspot activity on computers . . .'' He felt as if he were taking his orals again, and that he'd never stop worrying the explanation. A few stray conventioners had assembled within earshot and were looking curiously at him, as if trying to decide if he were someone or not. Mega plunged on into the explanation. ''I couldn't do the thing as a research project, because the conditions were purely abstract, so I decided to write it up as fiction, and a paperback house liked it. . . . I just sent it in for fun . . . and—''

''I know you!'' cried a ferrety-looking youth in a green turtleneck. ''You wrote *Bimbos of the Death Sun!*''

Dr. Omega hung his head. ''Yes,'' he sighed.

There it was: his pride, his fictionalized exercise in pure reason concerning the effects of sunspot activity in relation to polymer acrylic on capacitive interaction among high-frequency microcomponents in thick film circuits. He had known that when Alien Books bought it, there would have to be some commercialization, but he hadn't bargained on being heralded as the author of something called *Bimbos of the Death Sun*. And the cover art! A female bodybuilder in a fur bikini sprawled in front of a computer terminal, clutching the leg of a white-coated man holding a clipboard.

Dr. Omega lived in fear that some undergraduate student in engineering would figure out who he was and bruit the news around campus. As it was, he checked all the book stores in town once a week to make sure that no copies had been slipped onto the local author rack. His pen name, which he'd been so pleased with at the time, now seemed entirely too obvious.

''So you're Jay Omega?'' smiled Diefenbaker, shaking his hand again.

''Er—yes. Short for James Owens Mega.''

''It has a good sound to it. Does it signify anything? I seem to remember something about *omega*.''

''Oh, yes? Have you studied engineering?''

Diefenbaker waved his hand. ''I pick things up here and there.''

''It was a good guess. Jay Omega is an electrical engineering term for frequency times the square root of negative one. It's the *imaginary* part of an inductance, you see, and since I was doing a work of fiction . . .''

''Oh, very clever!'' beamed Diefenbaker. ''I should love to read it. Did we order copies for the con?''

Jay Omega reddened. ''Well, actually . . . my publisher's publicity department doesn't pay much attention to me, and I couldn't persuade them to send any, but I got the local bookstore to order some copies for me from the warehouse.'' He glanced down at the large, bulging canvas suitcase propped up against the registration table.

"I see," said Diefenbaker faintly. He smiled again. "Well, I shall tell everyone to come and get an autographed copy from you. In fact, I'll buy the first one myself after we get you signed in.''

"Thanks very much. Do you think you could tell me what I'm supposed to be doing?''

"This is your first con, isn't it?''

"Yes. It wasn't my idea, really, but a friend of mine . . . she teaches science fiction in the English Department , , ,'' And I'll get her for this if it's the last thing I ever do, he finished silently. He could picture Marion perched on the arm of his sofa, saying, "Your job is only half done when you finish the book. Nobody will read you if they've never heard of you. So, publicize!" She found out about Rubicon from one of the sophomores in her science fiction class, and before he knew it, "Jay Omega" was a featured guest—paying his own way, of course.

"Why don't I show you around a bit, and then we can see where they're going to put you for the autographing.''

Jay Omega looked again at his tweed-clad companion. "Why aren't you in costume?''

Diefenbaker looked surprised. "But I'm a wargamer!" Seeing that this reply had not proved enlightening, he explained. "The world of fandom is divided into several subgroups, mainly into hard science fiction—people who would read your book, for example—and fantasy folk, who are into Tolkien, Dungeons & Dragons, and—''

"Appin Dungannon?''

"Exactly. They're the ones in cloaks and broadswords. The rest of us settle for small tokens of resistance.'' He pointed to a button on his lapel: REALITY IS A CRUTCH FOR THOSE WHO CAN'T HANDLE SCIENCE FICTION. "Do you play wargames, by any chance?''

"Ah . . . on the computer?''

"No. Board games. Strategy between players. *Diplomacy. Kingmaker. War in the Pacific.* No, I see you don't. How about SF? Who do you read?''

Omega thought hard. "I read something I rather liked once. About an alien spaceman who was stranded on the moon and was trying to get to what would have been prehistoric earth. Can't remember who wrote it. What was it called?''

After a few seconds of polite silence, Diefenbaker sighed. "*Inherit the Stars.* James P. Hogan. He's an engineer, too.''

"Oh. I don't have much time for reading fiction, really. When I'm not doing my research, I'm usually in my garage taking a car apart." Usually Marion's car. He could never convince her that the Christian Science approach was not a viable one to auto mechanics: the car would not heal itself if left alone. You had to fix it.

Diefenbaker had an inspiration. "I bet you'll like the technical displays. We have a room of computer set-ups, air ionizers, and various other high-tech toys."

Omega grinned. "Lead the way."

"All right. Oh, by the way, Miles Perry, one of the con organizers, and I are supposed to have dinner with your fellow author. Would you like to join us?"

"With Appin Dungannon? Sure, I guess so." Even people who couldn't read had heard of Appin Dungannon. His characters had been borrowed for a Saturday morning cartoon series called *Dungannon's Dragons*, and cardboard displays in every drugstore and supermarket hawked the Runewind books. "I hope he won't expect me to have read his stuff, though."

Diefenbaker smiled. "Don't volunteer the information. He never talks about his work, anyhow."

The front doors of the hotel swung open, and a gaunt young man with matted black hair and burning eyes marched into the lobby. He was dressed in a floor-length navy-blue overcoat, with a guitar slung over one shoulder. Rasputin, thought Omega. A mixed crowd of turtlenecks and satin cloaks converged on the new arrival, chanting, "Monk Malone! Monk Malone!"

Omega admired the modest but genial attitude the young man took toward his admirers. He made a graceful celebrity, signing his name with a flourish on a couple of Rubicon programs. "What does he write?" he asked Diefenbaker. "Or is he an actor?"

Diefenbaker stopped in mid-wave. "Monk Malone? He's a BNF. I thought everybody had heard—oh, no, I guess you wouldn't. BNF stands for Big Name Fan. He goes to all the conventions, knows all the filksongs, contributes to a dozen fanzines. He's a household word."

Omega was still puzzled. "But what does he *do*?"

"You mean in mundane terms? When he isn't at cons? I think he's still a custodian at the hospital. He works every weekend that there isn't a con, so they're pretty good about letting him off to come to them."

Omega shook his head. A hospital custodian was posing for pictures with various costumed princesses. It still didn't make sense. "But what's he so famous for?"

"He's a fan," said Diefenbaker gently. "And he's very good at it."

The elevator doors opened just then, and Miles Perry shot out like the White Rabbit in Wonderland. He halted for breath in front of Diefenbaker and Omega, and pointed in the direction of the upper floors of the hotel. "Do you know what he wants?" he demanded.

"Dungannon?" asked Diefenbaker.

Perry nodded vigorously. "Who else?"

"Well . . . what does he want?"

"I don't know!" wailed Perry. "Something called Smarties and Yorkies. Drugs, I expect."

"No, Miles. It's British candy. Smarties are like M&Ms, and a Yorkie is a chocolate bar." Being a Canadian gave Diefenbaker an occasional cultural advantage over his more insular American colleagues.

Miles Perry slapped his forehead. "Great! Where am I supposed to get British candy on five minutes' notice?"

"Just tell Dungannon it can't be done," said Omega reasonably.

They both looked at him as if he were tap-dancing on a mine field. Miles turned back to Diefenbaker. "But, seriously, Dief, what am I going to do?"

Diefenbaker shrugged. "Mass appeal, I guess." Cupping his hands to his mouth, he bellowed out across the lobby, "We need some British candy, folks! Anybody got any? All help will be appreciated."

A wave of shrugs passed through the clumps of people, but after a few moments of silence, a blonde girl in a green tunic and blue body-paint approached them. "British," she said shyly to Diefenbaker. "Like . . . does that include Scotland?"

Diefenbaker hastily changed a snicker into an encouraging smile. "Yes, Kathy. Indeed it does. Why?"

She twisted her yellow sash and shifted from one foot to the other in an effort of concentration. "Well . . . like I met this guy today, you know, in the elevator, and he said he was from Scotland, but he wasn't dressed up or anything. He was just in regular old jeans. I'd say he was a mundane. But he might like candy!"

"I'll find him if I have to mind-meld the desk clerk!" cried Miles, hurrying away.

Diefenbaker thanked the blue lady with grave politeness and sent her on her way. "You see what I mean about Appin Dungannon?" he said to Jay Omega. "He probably doesn't even want the candy. I expect he's looking forward to the tantrum he's going to pitch when he doesn't get it."

Jay Omega smiled. "I was just thinking how nice it would be to be famous enough to be difficult."

The Scottish folksinger picked up another magazine. Suppose you didn't want to fix gourmet meals in minutes, lose ten pounds in two weeks, or redecorate your kitchen? What did you bloody read in the States? Magazines that were sold in brown paper wrappers, he supposed, but those were a bit of a bore as well. He thought of turning the television back on, but there'd be nothing at that hour except the soaps. When he had first arrived in the U.S. for his folksinging tour of the East Coast, he'd planned on being quite a dedicated tourist, dutifully spending his days on bus tours and consulting guide books. After a while, though, all the cities became as indistinguishable as the hotel rooms, and he stopped going out at all. He had thought of doing some sightseeing in Washington, D.C., since he was so close. But he was thirty miles away from D.C., with no car, dependent on a ride to the gig, stuck in another of those bloody hotels; the view out of his window looked like every other place he'd been: gas stations, fast food joints, and an endless stream of four-lane traffic. He still sent postcards off to Margaret in Glasgow, of places he hadn't bothered to go and see, but he spent his afternoons reading magazines or watching telly, until it was time to get ready for his evening performance. Bloody boring it was, too. Didn't the Yanks ever get tired of "Auld Lang Syne"?

He decided to have a quick look over the arrangement of his opening song, but a knock on the door saved him the trouble.

"Yes?" he called out. "Who is it?" You never knew about crime in the States, even in good hotels—which this one wasn't, not with Martians in the lobby.

"Mr. McRory!" More tapping.

"I'm Donnie McRory!" he yelled back. "I asked who *you* were!" He decided to open the door. It wasn't likely to be autograph hunters in this godforsaken—"Well?" he demanded of the burly young man on the threshold.

Miles Perry nearly lost his nerve, but the thought of Appin Dungannon's tiny face, purple with rage, spurred him on. "I'm sorry to bother you, sir, but I'm one of the organizers of the science fiction convention, and we had a sort of emergency come up. I . . . I was wondering if by any chance you had some British candy with you?"

Donnie McRory narrowed his eyes. "Would it be a scavenger hunt?"

"Oh, no! Our guest author at the convention has asked . . . demanded, really . . . that we get him some Yorkies and Smarties, and we were wondering if . . . if . . ." Miles realized how inane all of it must sound to someone not faced with Appin Dungannon's malevolent presence. "He's a very *famous* person."

Donnie McRory sighed. A very famous person. *He* played to sell-out crowds at the Glasgow City Hall, packed them in at every Edinburgh Festival for the last five years, had a couple of specials on the BBC . . . but this writer bloke was a "very famous person," and *he* was somebody to borrow candy from. The United States could be very bad for one's ego. He looked again at Miles Perry's anxious face. "Well," he said, shaking his head, "I can let you have a couple of Yorkies. Didn't bring anything else with me. Why don't you get him some M&Ms? They're pretty similar."

Miles accepted the chocolate bars as if he had just pulled them from a stone in suburban Camelot. "Oh, thank you! You've saved my life! Listen, if you'd like to come to the con . . ."

Donnie McRory waved him away. "Thanks all the same, but I'll give it a miss." Ah, well, he thought, closing the door, it will make a fine story to tell back home. "What did you do in America, Donnie?"—"I loaned chocolate bars to the Martians."—Ah, well. He picked up a magazine: LEARN TO SAY NO WITHOUT GUILT. Perhaps he ought to have a look at that.

CHAPTER 3

JAY OMEGA TRIED to stand still as Diefenbaker patted an adhesive name tag onto the pocket of his blazer. Out of the corner of his eye, he could see a mousy young girl in a harem costume talking earnestly to an Imperial Storm Trooper.

"Interesting outfits," he remarked to Diefenbaker.

"Much of a muchness," said Dief, shrugging. "All the girls who weigh less than one-twenty wear as little as possible, and the rest of them put on cloaks and medieval dresses to conceal their bulk. You get used to it. I'd invite you to judge the costume contest, but we're using that honor as a sop to Dungannon."

"I don't know anything about costume design, anyway," murmured Omega.

"Neither does Dungannon. He lets his gonads do the judging, which means that the Galadriel with the best cleavage will win. Oh, dear, I think you're about to be put on the spot as guest author."

Jay reached into his pocket for his felt-tip autographing pen, but before he could fish it out, he realized that the pudgy young man who had just walked up was holding a sheaf of computer printouts, not a copy of *Bimbos of the Death Sun*. He managed a weak smile, hoping that this was not a Tech sophomore who had tracked him to the con with a Drop-Add form.

"Really glad to meet you, Jay Omega," wheezed the fan. "I've read your book."

Walter Diefenbaker glanced at the name tag, winced, and began to edge away.

"I'm a fellow writer, and I thought we could talk a little shop."

"What have you written?" asked Jay Omega. As soon as he said it, he realized that he might be talking to Stephen King, in which case he had just committed the worst blunder in con history, but instinct told him that this could not be so. Stephen King's presence would be heralded nonstop if he should so much as stroll through the lobby, and besides, Jay Omega was sure that if he ever did meet Stephen King, he would not be greeted as a fellow writer and invited to talk shop.

Bernard Buchanan began to rifle through his papers. "I publish a fanzine called *Apa-Lling*, and beginning in this ish, I have a parody of Tratyn Runewind, called "Scratchy Woodwind," and instead of a magic sword, he has an enchanted oboe. Get it? Woodwind?" He thrust a Coke-stained page into Jay Omega's hand. "Now in this one, he offers to give the Demon Emperor a blow job. Get it? Like the Pied Piper!"

Jay Omega flipped through the pages of *Apa-Lling*, because it seemed preferable to actually talking to the crazed being in front of him.

The fanzine, a grainy photocopy of a computer-generated document featured on its title page a still from *The Day the Earth Stood Still*. In front of the Washington Monument, Michael Rennie as Klaatu stood with his robot, Gort, but the photo had been altered so that Gort had the face of Ronald Reagan. The caption, serving as the fanzine title, was: "Now That's APA-LLING!"

Omega turned to a page at random. The words PERSON TO PERSON were hand-lettered at the top in magic marker, and the rest of the page consisted of two columns of short messages, addressed to a name or a set of initials. Still trying to make sense of the page, he read a few:

"John and Pat: Hope you're no longer croggled by all the mundanes in 'Frisco. Remember, the Force is with you."

"Chip Livingstone: Thanks for your letter; great as always, but writing letters is such a hassle. Why can't you call? If bread is a problem, call me at work, and I'll call you back on the WATS-line. It would be easier to settle things without having to rely on the Post Offal."

"M.P.: Don't forget that in the British election of 1859, Italy was one of the few issues that solidly united the British Left. The Workers liked Garibaldi as a popular leader with an army; the Liberals liked bigger trading partners and the principles of nationality; and the Whig Lords approved of the climate. I know Browning wrote: 'Oh, to be in England now that April's here!' but he was in Italy at the time— and a good thing, too, since most Aprils in Britain are solid fog and rain. No wonder they conquered India!"

"Never mind that," said Bernard, peering over Jay's shoulder. "Read my parody. Chip Livingstone says it's brilliant."

Jay Omega blinked. "Who's Chip Livingstone?"

Bernard Buchanan looked shocked. *"You've never heard of Chip Livingstone?* Why he's a super-fan! He's a major contributor to a dozen fanzines, and he's ranked third in the wargamers' poll, and I've heard that he is a *personal friend* of Robert Silverberg!''

"Jay Omega is an author," said Diefenbaker gently. "You can't expect him to know fan politics."

"What is this stuff?" asked Jay Omega, still staring at the page of non sequiturs.

"APA's are soap boxes for people who can't get anyone to publish them," murmured Diefenbaker. "These are messages to individual subscribers."

Jay Omega blinked. "Then why don't they just write personal letters to each other?"

"Would you like to keep that copy?" Bernard persisted. "I was saving it for Walter Diefenbaker, but I can't find him anywhere."

"Perhaps he'll turn up later," Dief assured him, grasping Jay Omega firmly by the elbow. "We have to dash."

When they had put several clumps of warriors and slave girls between them and Bernard Buchanan, Jay Omega looked again at the grubby print-out. "I still don't understand what this is."

"Think of it as a chain letter for disturbed children," said Diefenbaker soothingly. "I doubt if you'll find Bernard's parody very entertaining, so you can either lose that copy or be prepared to dodge him for the rest of the weekend. Unless, of course, you fancy telling him the truth about his work."

Jay Omega slid the papers into an R2-D2 trashcan.

"Wise move." Diefenbaker nodded approvingly. "Let's hide out in the art gallery until he latches on to someone else."

"Did he want advice about his writing?" asked Jay, still trying to make sense of it.

"Not advice, really. Praise. And then he'd have wanted the name of your agent, and your editor's phone number, and a letter of recommendation to both."

Diefenbaker led the way out of the hotel's lobby, a marble-floored rotunda dotted with red plush couches and potted palms, and into a corridor which connected a cluster of meeting rooms used for conventions within the hotel. Small white cards attached to the hotel's printed map, labeled the Pocahontas Room HUCKSTERS, the adjoining Powhatan Room ART GALLERY, and the Thomas Jefferson Room at the end of the hall was marked HIGH TECH, indicating the computer display area. Past the vending machines and the rest rooms, a smaller meeting room, the Patrick Henry Nook, had been labeled PRIVATE, and was reserved for the use of Miles Perry and his fellow convention officials.

"These rooms are for the permanent exhibits," Dief explained. "The seminars and gaming sessions are scattered throughout the hotel in smaller meeting rooms, and tomorrow night's banquet will be upstairs in the auditorium. You'll find a map on the back of your program in case you need it."

He led the way into the art room, where six free-standing partitions had been set up, each holding a collection of paintings and sketches, which were framed or mounted, and bore the artist's name on an index card below.

Jay stared up at a picture of *Star Trek*'s Mr. Spock changing into a werewolf on a chessboard in space. Not Salvador Dali, he decided.

"I like this one," Diefenbaker remarked, pointing to an oil painting of a unicorn beside a waterfall. "My taste in art is rather Victorian, I fear."

Jay Omega was staring at an orange spaceship arching above a red and silver planet. "I don't think the perspective is quite right on that one."

"Probably not. It's one of Eric Bradley's, and he's only fourteen. But very promising, don't you think? Part of the proceeds from Rubicon go toward an art scholarship."

"Umm." Jay Omega thought they might do well to invest in some psychiatric counseling as well, but he reminded himself that if he had any fans, these were they, and that charity was in order.

"Sometimes we have a professional artist come to the con as a special guest. Of course, we can't afford Boris Vallejo, but we did try to get Peter Seredy. He did your cover, you know. His style is unmistakable."

Omega nodded. Certainly is, he thought, but my book advance won't cover the price of a hit man.

After a long and thoughtful inspection of the metal-band sculptures, the Yoda soap carvings, and the pen-and-ink sketches of dragons, Jay Omega followed his guide into the more commercial sphere of . . . he had heard the term *fandom*, but could one say *con-dom*? He snickered. One had better not.

"Hucksters' room," announced Diefenbaker with a wave at the chaos before them. "This is where you feed your habit—or wear it," he added, as a monk-robed individual brushed past them.

The guest author solemnly contemplated the colorful chaos of weapons displays, movie posters, comic books, and a thousand lurid paperbacks scattered across a dozen metal tables, each surrounded by an assortment of elves and aliens.

"I thought you said there were electronics exhibits," he said at last.

"Different room. We'll get there. I thought you might like to see if any of the dealers have your book. It would be kind of you to autograph their copies."

"I never know what to write," sighed Jay Omega.

"Oh, just a signature would do," Dief assured him. "But it would be very kind of you to put their names and the date in as well. Of course, I've never written a book, but if I did, I think I might write 'Thank you for reading me.' If anyone ever asked me to autograph it, that is."

Jay Omega thought it over. " 'Thank you for reading me.' Yes . . . that would be good." He remembered Marion's stern lectures about publicity. He certainly hadn't received any promotion help from Alien Books. Even the mall in his parents' town hadn't been told about him. Marion said that Alien Books ought to be in charge of national defense, because they were so good at keeping secrets.

He edged his way past a Dorsai and said to the first book dealer, "Do you have any books by Omega?"

"Matheson," said the dealer promptly, pulling out a hardback.

"I beg your pardon?"

"Richard Matheson wrote it. *The Omega Man.* A movie starring Charlton Heston. They changed the ending, though. The original title was *I Am Legend.* This is a first edition."

"No, that's not it."

"Hmmn. Kane Omega, *Cosmic Sex*, Lyle Stuart, 1973."

"No. That's not it, either."

"I see you have my Runewind series," said a solemn voice behind him. "Shall I autograph these for you?"

Jay Omega turned around with outstretched hand. "Appin Dun . . ." His voice trailed away.

The young man behind him, a few inches taller than Omega himself, wore a white satin tunic and a wool homespun cloak. His bone-white hair fell to his shoulders, and his green eyes burned with intensity. He stood spread-eagled in white tights and scuffed leather buskins, one hand resting on his broadsword, and smiled benignly at the mortals in his path. With graceful dignity he accepted Omega's outstretched hand, which was still dangling in the air as he gaped.

"No," he smiled gently. "I am not He Who Writes the Saga, but He Who Lives It. I am Tratyn Runewind, Lord of the Eildon Hills,

Wielder of the Red Gold Sword of Cu Chulainn, son of Aiofe and the Runewolf—''

"Dog meat if Dungannon sees you," Diefenbaker remarked. "You know how he feels about people impersonating his character, Cliff."

The Presence lifted his chin and endeavored to look noble. "The Scribe's envy is an affair for his soul, not mine," he intoned.

"He threw a water carafe at you at World Con," the bookseller pointed out.

"He once chased a Runewind down three flights of steps with a battle-axe!" said the Dorsai.

"Of course, he did!" snapped the Rune Warrior. "That was an imposter!"

"If he hears that you've been offering to autograph his books, you'll probably die from the aftershock of his rage."

"Well, I may change after the costume competition," the warrior conceded.

Diefenbaker was about to continue the discussion, but at that moment Miles Perry appeared, waving two packs of Reese's Pieces and three Yorkie bars, "I got them!" he announced breathlessly. "The Scotch guy said this would work."

Diefenbaker frowned. "I think some of the colors are different."

"Which ones?"

"I'd have to think about it."

"Come on, then. You get to sort them out. He wants them in twenty minutes."

Diefenbaker cast a helpless look at Jay Omega, as he was being dragged away. "I'll be back! Perhaps someone else could show you the gadget room . . ."

Left unattended, Jay Omega decided to spare himself the further humiliation of inquiring after his book. Instead he would find the gadget room on his own. A poster-sized map taped to a pillar in the hucksters' room provided reasonably clear directions. A large red arrow in the lower right-hand corner was labeled YOU ARE HERE. In the lower left-hand corner, a facetious physicist had penciled in, YOU MAY BE HERE. WERNER HEISENBERG. Omega smiled. After so much uninterrupted bewilderment, it felt good to get the joke. He took this as a hopeful sign that things would make more sense among the computers.

"Dr. Mega!"

Among the computer displays, air ionizers, and laser models sat Joel Schumann, a junior from last semester's microprocessing class. Omega groaned inwardly. He should have known that this would happen. One of his students had turned up at the con, and would soon discover the professor's guilty secret: *Bimbos of the Death Sun*. He might be able to swear Joel to secrecy, though. Omega took the offensive. ''Er, what are you doing here, Joel?'' the professor asked innocently.

The lanky blond grinned and tapped a computer monitor. ''I came to look after these babies. They're on loan from the campus computer center. I volunteered because I thought it might be fun to come to this thing. See a couple of old sci-fi movies, watch the goings-on, and swap information with other hackers. What about you, Dr. Mega?''

Jay Omega managed a weak smile. ''It's a long story, Joel.''

CHAPTER 4

APPIN DUNGANNON STARED at the vacant gray screen of his computer terminal, as if he were waiting for the darkness to roll up on one side and reveal glowing letters of wisdom on the other. He tapped out $c = 1/\sqrt{\mu_0 \varepsilon_0}$ while waiting for other inspiration to occur, but the exercise did not make him feel any closer to creation.

Beginning a stint of typing was always the most difficult part of writing a book. Once he got going, his brain projected a mental movie of the action onto the computer screen, so that he was not so much inventing as recording what he visualized. He could do maybe fifty pages a day on automatic pilot once he got going, but it was the getting going that was the hardest part. The early chapters of the book were like trying to carve the Gettysburg Address on Mount Rushmore with a toothpick; by the denouement, which was his current fixation, he had pretty much lost interest in what the story was about anyway, so it was even harder, if that is possible, to get it up for the task. He sighed inwardly, wishing, as always, that he hadn't already spent his publisher's advance.

Maybe it would help if he threw something.

Appin Dungannon had written twenty-six books about Tratyn Runewind. Or maybe he had written one book about Tratyn Runewind twenty-six times. He could no longer remember why the series had seemed like a good idea to him, or how he had felt about the first half dozen. It was as if he'd awakened one day to find himself manacled like Marley's Ghost with garishly covered paperbacks, a line of Runewind action figures (for which he received a percentage that was obscenely low), and a loathsome cartoon series, of which his cut was so meager that he'd fired his agent for the insult.

He was rich enough, according to his accountant—certainly his tax bill seemed to bear that out; and he supposed he was famous enough. He got fan letters in Elvish, and execrable unsolicited manuscripts to "please recommend to your publisher." He used those under his cat's dish, and by the phone for scratch paper.

Appin Dungannon was not as happy as perhaps a legend ought to be. His books were best sellers in the genre, but beyond that they went unread. He could expect, at best, a paragraph in *Publishers Weekly*, and he was always bypassed for the major SF awards. Dungannon fiddled a bit with the brightness knob on the monitor. He would have traded ten thousand costumed autograph hounds for one gilt-edged monograph on "Dungannon's Use of Celtic Mythology in Contemporary Fantasy."

At the moment, though, he didn't feel much like a synthesizer of Celtic mythology: he felt like Milton's God in *Paradise Lost*, and his Satan had him by the throat. Tratyn Runewind, Tratyn Goddamn Runewind, with the flowing white locks and the clean-chiseled features of a sea hawk. Dungannon scowled. It must have been some kind of sick fantasy, he decided. The five-foot-one schmuck with the Mickey Rooney face writing Viking bullshit. He was sure that the vermin discussed its psychological implications endlessly behind his back. There wasn't much he could do about that, except to cordially despise them, but, by God, he could make them keep out of his sight with their infernal Runewind get-ups. The very sight of some faggoty adolescent in tights and tunic made his hands itch for something to throw.

Dungannon glanced at his watch.

Someone was taking him to dinner soon, he thought. He supposed they'd expect him to talk to them. He reached for the bottle of Chivas Regal, and poured himself half a glassful. That ought to fuel a couple of paragraphs. It just wasn't *fun* anymore. The first books had been carried by his curiosity about the folklore, and when that ran out, he'd enjoyed putting his editors and his ex-wife in the manuscripts as monsters, but even that became dull after a while. Now he wrote out of inertia, and because they kept waving money at him. And the letters kept coming: scrawls of praise for the series, and pathetic little drawings of "Tratyn Runewind," but he went on writing, anyway. Because he couldn't turn down all that money; because he was afraid that stopping would dry up the gift of words; and because the serious novel in the typing-paper box wouldn't sell to anybody. He couldn't give it away. But for Runewind they would pay the earth.

Appin Dungannon took a stiff swallow of Scotch and stabbed a wavering finger at the keyboard. With a giggle of defiance he pressed ESCAPE.

No one had come back to claim Jay Omega for any con-related duties, but he was quite happy to be left to his own devices. In this case, the devices were various pieces of computer software which he and Joel Schumann were trying out one by one.

"These disks with burned protection sectors are a pain to copy," Joel remarked, tapping a few keys.

Jay Omega looked over at the screen to see if anything had happened, but a large, familiar brown suitcase was suddenly positioned between him and the monitor. Near the handles, where the zipper wouldn't close, copies of *Bimbos of the Death Sun* leered at him from their canvas confinement.

"I thought I'd find you here. *These* were chucked under the registration desk, quite abandoned. So was the smaller suitcase containing your clothes. I had that sent up to your room."

"Hello, Marion," said Jay, hoping he didn't look as foolish as he felt.

"I might have known you couldn't be trusted in the same building with gadgetry," she sighed. "But have you done *anything* to promote your book?"

"I asked the booksellers if they had it."

"And did they?"

"Er—no."

"And did you offer to provide them with some autographed copies? . . . I didn't think so. Well, perhaps we ought to find somebody who knows what guest authors are supposed to do." She grinned up at him. "How do you like my costume?"

Jay Omega eyed her warily. This type of question wasn't his forte. Let him compliment her new hairstyle, and it would turn out that she'd changed shades of lipstick. At present, Marion was wearing her dark hair in some sort of smooth flip style—he was sure that was different— and she was clad in a black jumpsuit. He was about to risk further humiliation by asking if it *were* a costume when the penny finally dropped. *"The Avengers!"* he cried. "You're Mrs. Peel."

Marion was pleased. "Not much resemblance to Diana Rigg," she said, shrugging. "But she was always my idol. I guess while other girls my age wanted to be Mary Tyler Moore, keeping house in New Rochelle for Dick Van Dyke, I wanted to be Emma Peel, going off with some terribly clever man who treated me as an equal, and having adventures."

Jay Omega pointed to the milling crowd of spacemen and Middle Earthlings. "Will this do?"

She handed him the battered suitcase. "Thank you, Mr. Steed. It will."

Marion led and Jay followed, which was pretty much the way it had been since that day eighteen months ago, when a shy young man in jeans and sneakers had appeared in the English Department with a spiral-bound computer printout, asking to speak to someone about science fiction.

Dr. Marion Farley, who had been in the office checking her mailbox, had given him a disinterested once-over, and said, "Sorry. The class is full. Tell your advisor to put you down for spring quarter."

The young man had quietly explained that he really didn't need the course, since he was already an assistant professor in electrical engineering, but that he would like to talk to someone about his book.

Before Marion had finished apologizing, he had invited her out to lunch, and over a couple of roast beef sandwiches at Bogen's, he explained to her that he had written a novel, based on a theoretical problem in engineering.

"You see," he'd said, finishing off the last of her potato chips, "the story involves a sun that emits rays causing slow but steady brain damage. But it affects only the women at the research station."

Marion, one of the more outspoken members of the Women's Network, gave him a wary nod. "Go on."

"The really important thing is that it affects the computers. What I'm actually concerned with is the effects of sunspot activity in relation to polymer acrylic on capacitive interaction among high-frequency microcomponents in . . ."

"The really important thing?" said Marion. "The really important thing is the *machines*, not the women?"

Sensing that he had said something wrong, he halted his narrative. "Well . . . from an engineering standpoint, I mean. What do you think?"

What did she think?

Marion thought that James Owens Mega was an ugly duckling who had not noticed his transition to swandom. She was sure that he had been a runty undergrad who had spent all his free time rewiring circuits, and who made good grades because he'd had no social life to distract him. She recognized the type from her own student days, when she'd hung around the wargames club, where it was okay for a woman to be smart and not pretty. Thank God she'd outgrown her pariah phase, she thought, adjusting one amethyst earring. Substituting aerobics classes for lit classes had done her a world of good. She'd gotten out of a miserable marriage to a fellow outcast who was going to remain in grad school forever, and, freed of the guilt of surpassing him, she'd earned her Ph.D. in two years. Now, in a new job at the English department at Tech, Marion had finally reached the stage of accepting herself as both smart *and* pretty.

She looked at her lunch partner, who was unselfconsciously finishing off a butterscotch ice cream cone. He must have filled out a bit since his scraggly adolescence, and the contact lenses he'd gotten "for better peripheral vision" did wonders for his dark eyes. He'd probably worn safety glasses before, she thought, and he'd have looked like a mosquito in them. Marion looked at his hair, the color of the butterscotch, and at the fine bone structure of his face. He's adorable, she thought. And he hasn't been notified.

"Are you still thinking about the plot?" he asked again.

"What? Oh, the plot. Why don't you leave the novel with me, and I'll read it and let you know. Actually, the idea of women getting progressively stupid is pretty exciting from a publisher's standpoint. It feeds the male hostility toward the competitive modern woman." She looked at him closely. "Did you do that on purpose?"

He blushed. "No. I just threw that in because I realized that some diseases are sex-linked, and it seemed plausible. My main concern was the computers."

Marion sighed. "It would be."

By the time Marion had tinkered with the characterization in his novel, and advised him through rewrites, chapter outlines, and query letters, he had become used to her, in much the same way that a stray cat gets used to belonging to someone. Marion had used a similar method of "taming": no sudden moves, a calm and friendly manner, and regular offers of food. She hadn't completely conquered his shyness, though. Marion sometimes felt just before they kissed that he was gearing up for it as one might approach the high-dive—with careful planning and much trepidation. She thought he was making progress, though. And his diffidence was certainly preferable to the first-date lunges of other professors she'd been out with, the post-divorce swingers.

Marion told herself that she was too happy in her newly won independence to be comfortable playing second fiddle to a male engineer earning three times her salary. Anyway, what if one of them got tenure and the other didn't? Marion had seen too many academic couples break up over tenure problems. If the university denied tenure to a professor, he or she had one year's grace period, and then it was: find another job. If your specialty was Chinese art or mining engineering that next job might not be anywhere close by. Usually in a relationship, if she got tenure and he didn't, you could kiss the marriage goodbye; the male partner's ego usually saw to that. Anyway, when faced with a choice between a lifetime of job security or a marriage with no guarantees, most people chose the job. She didn't want that kind of pressure built into her relationship with Jay. And maybe in two years, she would know what she wanted.

So marriage wasn't discussed. They didn't talk about the future, but neither of them dated anyone else, either. She didn't want to do or say anything that might change what they had. Marion knew that she often acted brisk and bossy, and that her tendency toward sarcasm made her seem tough and self-sufficient. She was afraid, though, despite her best efforts, that Jay Omega knew how much she loved him.

In the hospitality suite, Diefenbaker was just finishing the last of the yellow Reese's Pieces. They had been removed from the candy dish, because Smarties did not come in that color. Dief thought it was an exercise in futility anyhow; surely Dungannon would notice that there weren't any pink or purple candies in the dish, a dead giveaway that they weren't Smarties, and even if he failed to notice, one bite ought to give the game away. No one could mistake a peanut butter filling for a chocolate one. In any case, said Miles Perry, the Great One barely glanced at the ersatz British candy once it was rushed into his presence. No doubt he had a dim recollection of demanding it.

The hospitality suite television was showing a videocassette of *Forbidden Planet*, but no one was there watching. Most of the convention guests would not arrive until early Friday evening, and those who had come already were busy checking in, looking up old friends, or visiting the exhibits and game rooms. Toward the wee hours of the morning, when there were no competing sessions, a few of the faithful would gather to watch *Star Trek* episodes, and the couches would be taken by crashers who hadn't booked a hotel room. Diefenbaker occasionally allowed floor space in his room to an impoverished friend, but this time he'd decided to hold out for peace and quiet. He was going to be besieged by people as it was, what with so many Far Brandonians in attendance.

Since Diefenbaker lived in Ontario, most of his fellow gamers had to rely on correspondence and a severely limited phone budget for contact with him. Rubicon, his yearly foray into the U.S., was their only opportunity for a face-to-face meeting, and, to the limits of his civility and endurance, they were determined to make the most of it.

"Aha, I found you!" said Richard Faber, blocking the doorway. "That only leaves Chip Livingstone."

"You make it sound like a scavenger hunt." Diefenbaker smiled.

Faber began spreading photocopied maps over Diefenbaker's table. "There's an army on my southern border," he announced.

"I know. I put it there."

"I know, but—"

"You asked me to."

Faber turned crimson. "That was before I found out that C.D. Novibazaar was acting as minister of state for Emily of Gondal. That changes everything!"

A teenage boy with the word NOMAD scrawled on his forehead walked into the room just then. "Who's C.D. Novibazaar?"

The only thing Richard Faber liked better than to argue was to lecture. With a missionary gleam in his eye, he rounded on the new-comer. "Cambrecis Desmoulins (de) Novibazaar was a Hungarian refugee who held various posts in nineteenthcentury French govern-ment. Just before the Peace of Campo-Formio, when Napoleon's ar-rival in Vienna seemed imminent . . ."

Having now received enough information to know that Novibazaar could not be read, smoked, or played on a PC, "Nomad" tuned out the rest of the explanation and returned to his original errand. "Miles Perry said you'd know what to do with these," he said, handing a stack of papers to Diefenbaker.

Dief looked at the top sheet. " 'The Verdant Moon of Milos.' Entries in the Rubicon Writing Contest?"

"Right. Cover sheets with the authors' identities are stacked on the bottom. You gotta get 'em judged so we can announce it after the costume contest tonight."

"I thought Appin Dungannon was judging these. Didn't Miles ask him?"

"No. He was planning to bring up the subject when he showed Dungannon to his room, but after the Smarties and Yorkies tantrum, he lost his nerve."

"Oh, more's the pity," said a disappointed Dief. "I don't suppose it would have done any good to ask. Judging a writing contest is such hard work and, um, Dungannon does rather prefer the sexual possibilities of a costume contest. All right, I think I know someone who will judge the manuscripts. Where is Miles, anyway?"

"Orbiting the hotel, more or less, trying to be everywhere at once. He said something about meeting you for dinner. Didn't say where."

Diefenbaker looked at his watch. Just over five hours to get the manuscripts read and judged, Dungannon to entertain for dinner, and a hundred other minutiae to accomplish in between. He wondered if he ought to take a pill now, or wait for the headache to arrive.

"Richard, I really must go," he said, scooping up the manuscripts.

"Why don't you talk to Bonnenberger?" He nodded toward an inert form on a straight chair near the window.

Joseph Bonnenberger, shirt buttoned up to his chin, four pens in his pocket, and 10W40 hair, sat squinting at a Rubicon brochure, apparently in preference to actually attending any of its events. Eventually his obsession with the Diplomacy game would force him from his lair into actual interaction with others of his species, but a breakthrough of this magnitude was still hours away.

Faber gave Dief a look of horror. "Talk to Bonnenberger?" he hissed. "The guy's a remora!"

Most people knew better than to talk to Joseph Bonnenberger, because he was indeed like the remora, a fish whose dorsal fin is a suction disk allowing it to attach itself more or less permanently to larger creatures. No one was willing to risk being civil to Bonnenberger, because it might result in their having to struggle through the rest of the weekend, dragging the bloated personality of the human remora in their wake. With Bonnenberger, it was best to limit oneself to pleasantries; anything more than that could be fatal.

"I'd rather drink Falstaff!"

Diefenbaker smiled pontifically. "Yes, Faber, but you deserve each other."

Before Faber could think up a reply, he was gone.

Not much had changed in the lobby. Diefenbaker noticed that "Filksinging with Monk Malone" had been chalked in on the announcement board for eleven P.M. He decided to let Miles handle the hotel management on that score. His own primary concern was to unload the contest manuscripts before he had to read them himself. He was about to set off for the computer room when he spotted a dark-haired woman seated off in a corner behind a small mound of *Bimbos of the Death Sun*.

When he approached the table she seemed so pitifully glad to see him that he bought a copy just to spare her feelings. "I was really looking for Dr. Omega," he said.

"He went in search of a Coke machine," Marion told him. "If you want him to autograph your book, leave it here, and you can drop by for it later."

Diefenbaker hesitated. Surely he couldn't just dump the manuscripts without getting Omega to agree to do them, but a glance around the lobby had shown three people waving frantically for his attention. As quickly as he could, he explained the problem to Marion, who smiled encouragingly, and assured him that Jay Omega would love to judge the writing contest. More reassured than perhaps he should have been, Diefenbaker scurried away.

Miles Perry had been cornered in the hall by a *Star Trek* officer and a heavy-set young woman with a serenely pretty face.

"We need to talk to you about the wedding," said the blue-shirted young man.

Miles blinked, trying to summon up a Rubicon program from his memory circuits. "Er—ah?"

The couple glanced at each other uneasily. "It's all set, isn't it?"

"What?"

"We are going to get married tomorrow night after the banquet in a *Star Trek* ceremony."

Miles Perry looked at the young man's dark hair, cut square across his forehead. "Spock and . . . ?"

"Saavik," said the bride. "We'll put our ears on later. Anyway, we wrote to ask about doing this, and we got a letter from Chip Livingstone saying it would be okay." Her voice quavered. "It is, isn't it?"

Miles Perry frowned. No one had bothered to notify him about any of this. He wondered if Diefenbaker were playing godfather to this. This Chip Livingstone business was getting out of hand! Still, it would provide a bit of drama, and perhaps some local publicity for the convention—not a bad thing. He studied the careful copy of the *Enterprise* science officer's uniform, and wondered if the bride would be similarly attired—in which case she might be mistaken for the planet Venus.

"Uh . . . Do you have a minister?"

"Yes. One of the campus chaplains has agreed to come over and perform the ceremony dressed as Captain Kirk."

"Splendid!" Miles wondered if the local paper would send someone on short notice.

"And my bridesmaids will be dressed as Yeoman Rand and Nurse Chappell."

"Best man?" asked Miles Perry, fascinated in spite of himself.

"Ensign Chekov," said the groom. "We couldn't find an Oriental, but my roommate is a *Bullwinkle* freak, and he does a great Russian accent. Boris Badenov."

"Okay, let's see if I can find you a room for that hour," said Miles. "Is that all you need?"

They glanced at each other again. "Well," said the bride softly. "There is just one thing missing."

Miles Perry nodded. "I think I can help."

CHAPTER 5

As JAY OMEGA opened the door to his room, a bound manuscript hit the wall near his head, and slid to the floor in front of him. "I didn't realize hotel rooms made you so jumpy," he remarked to Marion, who was sitting in the middle of his bed surrounded by papers. Most of the floor was covered with typed pages as well, he noticed.

"Idiot!" muttered Marion, consulting a clipboard. She scribbled furiously for several seconds before looking up to see Jay Omega, still in the doorway, poised for flight. "Oh, hello," she said. "I'm becoming dangerously homicidal."

"Yes, but your aim is bad."

Marion grinned. "Come in. You're safe. At least, unless you wrote one of these."

"I hope not. What are they?"

"They're the entries in a short-story competition they want you to judge. I thought I'd have a look at them. After all, I *teach* science fiction." She glared at him defensively, as if she expected him to object.

He nodded at the papers strewn on the floor. "Interesting grading system. What do you think of them so far?"

"The ones that landed near the bathroom are Bad Tolkien imitations or transcripts of a D&D adventure; bad Herbert, Heinlein, and Asimov are below the television; and these on the bed are the ones whose authors I want to hunt down personally and slap." She extracted a laser-printed manuscript in Gothic lettering from a pile on the pillow. "Listen to this . . .

> *Starwind, with her flaming hair about her shoulders and a red harem costume of sheerest Polarian silk, looked as seductive as any of the Rigelian slave beauties Hawker had seen in* Astro-Porn Magazine.
>
> *She tugged at her purple belt of passion. "My father, the president of the galaxy, said that I should make you welcome, Hawker-of-Earth."*

"Bad color sense," said Jay Omega, trying not to grin.

"Shut up! You know exactly what's wrong with this! It's a throw-back to the Thirties teenage space-opera stuff. It's a stroke book!"

"Would you mind reading it again?"

Marion ignored him. "Or how about this one? It's called—are you ready for this?—'Goron: Alien Mercenary', and it's set three thousand years in the future. Listen:

> Goron was grim as he faced the President of United Earth. 'This came in the mail yesterday,' he told her, setting the envelope and check on her desk.
>
> The blonde picked up the check and looked at the signature. 'Warlord Yoon! I thought he was dead!' She tore the check into tiny pieces. 'I wouldn't want the cleaning woman to find this.'"

Jay Omega blinked. "Three thousand years in the future?"

"That's what the author says," nodded Marion, tapping a line of typescript.

"And they still get mail? We don't even do that on campus. I leave messages for people on the computer mainframe, and they just check their file once a day. Electronic mail. Instantaneous."

"You don't send messages to me like that."

"No, just to other engineers, mostly. But eventually the English Department will catch on, and I don't think it will take three thousand years. Two thousand, tops." He ducked another manuscript.

"Did you hear what he called the 'President of United Earth'? *The blonde!* I'd like to use that kid's vertebrae for wind chimes!"

"His technology is absurd, Marion. Checks? Direct deposit banking is becoming a way of life now. Three thousand years in the future there's no telling what they'll be using, but it won't be paper checks."

"Did you notice the bit about the cleaning woman?"

"Good point. Machines should be doing all the maintenance work by then. I don't think he's thought out his civilization very carefully."

"I don't think he's ever met any women," grumbled Marion. "Too bad your book got titled *Bimbos of the Death Sun*. It's the perfect name for half these stories."

"I think it's too bad about the title, too," said Jay Omega softly. "Do you think my book is chauvinistic?"

Marion sighed. "Of course not. We've been through that before. The title isn't your fault."

"It's strange to be the author of something called *Bimbos of the Death Sun*, with pictures of female barbarians on the cover." He shuddered. "If the campus chapter of Women in Engineering ever finds out . . ."

Marion touched his arm. "It's a good book. For hard science fiction, that is. It's scientifically sound; it isn't pretentious; and I made damn sure it isn't demeaning to women. That's saying a lot for this genre. People who read it will know it isn't trash, no matter what stupid title they give it or what the cover art looks like. Science fiction is notorious for that kind of thing, anyway."

He nodded. "What are Appin Dungannon's books like? Have you read them?"

"They're thrust upon me. Sophomore computer science majors with bad skin and zero interpersonal skills are always wanting to do theme papers on Tratyn Runewind. They're not fiction, they're wet dreams. But don't tell him I said so at dinner tonight."

"Oh, Lord! Dinner! Should I change?"

Marion smiled. "Not unless you brought shining armor."

Appin Dungannon narrowed his piggy eyes as he contemplated the menu. The stuffed trout was expensive enough, but nauseatingly wholesome, and he was on the lecture circuit too much to ever order chicken voluntarily. What did that leave? Prime rib . . . the local specialty: peanut soup and Virginia ham . . . He didn't want them, either.

His nearest table partner, that Diefenbaker person, leaned over the menu and said, "Don't worry about time. The costume competition doesn't start until nine."

Appin Dungannon grunted. "The costume competition doesn't start until I'm *there*. However, I am ready to order. I think I'll have the trout. White goes with fish, you know. It'll go with my vodka." He held up his glass in a mock toast to them and giggled.

Diefenbaker and Miles Perry exchanged worried glances. The Eminent Pro had shown no signs of mellowing out as the evening wore on. His eyes glittered more as he talked, and he kept smiling in a none-too-reassuring way, but he still reminded them of a pinless hand grenade, and they couldn't be sure how many seconds were left.

Across the table Jay Omega and Marion were smiling nervously, and acting as if they were at the birthday party of a hyperactive child. Conversation was forced.

Dungannon had dismissed his fellow author by saying, "Haven't read your paperback. Doubt if I'd like it."

Once the orders had been given to the hovering waiter, he turned his attention to Marion. "Aren't you a little old for a femmefan?"

Marion's eyes narrowed. "I teach science fiction at the university."

Dungannon looked pleased. "Who's required reading?"

"Clarke, Brunner, Le Guin—"

"Heinlein?"

"The early works. And in the fantasy course, we teach C. S. Lewis, Tolkien—"

"Tolkien! Ah, so you do mythology? What about British myths?"

"Yes, of course. There's an excellent book based on Celtic lore. The students love it."

Appin Dungannon smirked. "Which Runewind is it? *The Singing Runes? The Flag of Dunvegan?*"

Marion raised her eyebrows. "No. As a matter of fact, it's *The Mists of Avalon*, by Marion Zimmer Bradley."

Dungannon took a hefty swallow of vodka, and everyone else at the table began talking hurriedly about the next *Star Trek* movie/Carl Sagan's novel/ and the rumor that the PC would soon be obsolete. Marion went back to her salad with the air of one who has performed an unpleasant task only to discover that she enjoyed it.

Jay Omega, who had never managed to feel like an author anyway, felt no sense of kinship with his fellow writer. He could think of nothing to talk about, and the idea of provoking Dungannon's ill-concealed wrath made him even less likely to talk than usual.

Miles Perry, who would have liked to have discussed convention business with Diefenbaker, felt compelled as host to keep up a flow of bright chatter. He had launched into a long and pointless account of Far Brandonian weaponry, to which no one listened, but the drone of his voice was soothing, and relieved everyone else of the obligation to talk.

Diefenbaker turned to Marion. "Is Dr. Omega one of those terribly sane and steady engineers, or does he have writer's quirks?"

Marion thought about it. "You mean like Balzac having to wear a monk's habit and write by candlelight? Jay isn't temperamental at all, but I don't know about engineers being sane and steady. The first time I went to his house, I found a radio in the refrigerator."

"There was a perfectly good reason for that," said Jay Omega. "Sometimes there's an intermittent problem in the radio, something that goes away when the unit heats up, and those problems are very difficult to detect. If you put the radio in the refrigerator, the problem will usually become permanent, and then you can fix it."

"Sounds reasonable," Diefenbaker conceded.

"Yes, but he also has lemons in there that are old enough to vote."

Jay Omega smiled. "I eat out a lot."

Appin Dungannon, apparently deciding that the attention had strayed from him long enough, announced to the table in general: "I think the roots of human behavior lie in the distant past, not on some silly planet out in deep space. In the heroic sagas like Beowulf, Elric of Melnibone, and of course, Tratyn Runewind, there are metaphoric implications . . ."

And all the women are cheeseburgers, thought Marion, spearing a piece of asparagus with her fork.

Dungannon's harangue continued for several more minutes, while everyone concentrated on cleaning their plates, occasionally nodding fervently to maintain the illusion of interest. Finally Dungannon wound down, noticing that his dinner was almost untouched. Taking a last swig of his vodka martini, he leered across the table at his fellow author. "Well, that's enough about me!" he declared. "Now let's talk about you. Which one of my books did you like best?"

The Scottish folksinger propped one buskined foot on the bed and studied his reflection in the mirror. His dark suede trousers and laced linen shirt made quite a swashbuckling costume, quite in keeping with his repertoire of traditional Celtic tunes. People were always asking him why he didn't wear a kilt. "Because I'm not Harry Bloody Lauder!" was his invariable reply. Nobody seemed to realize that the whole kilt business was thought up in the early nineteenth century, and that it was the Englishmen who'd been given Scottish peerages who wore them. Perhaps he ought to say a word or two about it in his patter between songs.

He was scribbling a reminder on the song list taped to the guitar neck when he heard the tapping on the door. Donnie McRory glanced at his watch. An hour before show time. No reporters had asked for an interview. He hadn't ordered room service. Having run out of guesses, he flung open the door.

"Not the bloody Martians again!"

A blue-shirted Trekkie with pointed ears stood clutching the hand of a behemoth in a white tulle gown. Both were smiling up at him with an anxious cheerfulness. About twenty-three, he decided. Too old to be parading around in dress-up.

"Ooh, I love your costume!" said the girl. "Who are you supposed to be? Tratyn Runewind?"

Donnie McRory's jaw tightened. "I am not a part of your perishing convention! Now, was there something you wanted?"

They nodded solemnly. "It will take a little explaining," said the boy. "May we come in?"

Donnie McRory waved them toward the bed. He didn't suppose they had brought back his Yorkies. "Well?"

"We're getting married this weekend."

"Oh. That's magic, innit? Well, all the best. Here's luck, and all that. Decided which planet you'll live on yet?"

The bride frowned. "We were hoping you'd do us a big favor. It's very important to us."

Donnie McRory smiled expectantly, but he was thinking: Does he need help to carry you over the threshold, dear? I should think six blokes ought to do it, same as pallbearers.

The smile froze into place as they described their *Star Trek* wedding, with Chekov for best man and the minister dressed as Captain Kirk. "And the one thing we need to make the wedding absolutely perfect is—"

"*Beam me up, Scotty!*" cried McRory, suddenly remembering. "It's that phony Scot on the program you're wanting me to impersonate, isn't it? The one with the vaudeville Glasgow accent?"

"He's from Aberdeen," said the groom.

"Aberdeen Proving Ground, maybe. He's not a Scot!" McRory insisted.

"Yes, sir, but you are, and it would be so wonderful if you would just come and be him for the ceremony. It's a short little ceremony, really . . ." They looked up at him pleadingly, like demented puppies.

He scowled at them. "When is it?"

"Tomorrow night! You mean, you will?"

I'll dine out on this one, thought Donnie McRory. But it did beat reading the stupid American magazines or watching the telly. Tonight's concert was the usual one-nighter and he was booked into this bleeding hotel for the entire weekend. "I don't have to do anything else, but just be there?" he asked menacingly.

"Well . . . do you play the bagpipes?"

"Do you own a kilt?"

The social hour preceding the costume contest seemed to Jay Omega to be a cross between a worship service and a Senate investigation. As a relatively small fish in the literary pond, he had ample opportunity to observe Appin Dungannon in intellectual combat.

Dungannon, his ego weatherproofed with vodka, held court in front

of a table of Dungannon paraphernalia: hardbacks, paperbacks, Runewind posters, action figures, and game spinoffs. The transactions
involving these items were managed by a clerk, whose existence was
beneath Dungannon's notice.

The encounters did not often go as Jay Omega had expected. As
a new author, he had pictured public appearances in which faithful
readers, their faces shining with admiration, would approach the author shyly and murmur what a wonderful book he'd written. The
actual author/reader dialogues fell far short of his fantasies.

"You Dungannon?" asked a tall red-haired youth in armor.

"Correct," said Appin Dungannon, without bothering to look up
from his autographing.

"Well, I just finished your last book and I don't think you ought
to have killed Beithir in the last battle. I mean, sure, he threw the
Sword of Ossian into Black Annis' Well, but he did save Tratyn
Runewind from the Gabriel Hounds, and—"

Appin Dungannon skewered the fan with an arctic stare. "What's
the matter with you, pinhead? Don't you have a life? If you enjoy
meddling, join the Peace Corps!"

Another fan turned up with a stack of Dungannon novels. "Would
you sign all these, please? Just a signature is okay."

"There are a few people behind you. Doesn't it bother you to be
so selfish?"

The fan shrugged. "Not particularly. I figure this is my big chance
to get your autograph."

"You have three copies of the same book in here."

"Right. Someday you'll be dead, and I'll be rich."

The crowd moved back a little in order to dodge flying hardbacks,
but the outburst was not forthcoming. With a grim smile, Dungannon
signed each book in the stack. When he had finished, the speculator
snatched his copies and hurried away.

Two signatures later, just as a scrawny youth in G.I. camouflage
was criticizing Dungannon's last book, a howl went up from the other
side of the lobby.

"You little creep!" roared the guy with the stack of books. "You
ruined my books!"

Dungannon leered at him. "You said signature only!" he yelled
back.

"Look at this!" wailed the fan, holding out a book for the bystand-
ers to see. "He signed 'J.R.R. Tolkien' on every goddamned one of
them!"

"Who's next?" purred Dungannon.

No one wanted to discuss plot mechanics with Jay Omega. No one seemed to have heard of the book. Several fen ambled up to the table and examined the cover, which always made the author profoundly uneasy. "Er—it isn't really like that," he murmured to a young woman in a harem costume with a worried frown.

She tossed him a coy look. "Dirty old man!"

Even worse were the people who approved of the book, based only on its cover. One pizza-faced youth gazed longingly at the amazon in the cover art, and whispered hoarsely, "I think I'm going to like this one. Is it really raunchy?"

Marion snickered.

"No," said Jay Omega earnestly. "It's really very scientific."

"No explicit sex?"

"Not even close," Marion assured him. "Jay's idea of a stag movie is *Bambi.*"

The young man wandered away, and several more fen, like browsing cattle, edged up to the book table.

"Do you make a lot of money writing paperbacks?" asked a Dorsai.

"No," said Jay Omega. "Hour for hour, the Seven-Eleven pays better."

"Do you have an agent?"

"Uh. Yeah." Her husband was from the same hometown as his college roommate; but only Marion had been trusted with that secret of how he got his big break in publishing.

"And what's your agent's name and phone number?"

Jay Omega was still wondering how Appin Dungannon would have fielded this question when Marion leaned over and said, "Never ask an author that, unless you want to be taken for a complete jerk!"

"Well, I have this great manuscript . . ."

Marion turned to Jay Omega. "What's your consulting fee in engineering?"

"For companies? Two hundred and fifty dollars a day, but—"

"Fine." She smiled up at the would-be author. "He'll read your stuff for two hundred and fifty dollars. In advance. Next!"

Joel Schumann, on a break from the computer displays, pulled out his wallet. "Is this your book, Dr. Mega! Hey, great! Would you autograph it for me? Boy, I can't wait to tell the guys in the lab that—"

"No! You can't do that!" gasped Jay Omega. "Look, Joel, what if I give you a book, autographed and everything. Will you not tell anybody I wrote it?"

He blinked. "Well, sure, I guess, Dr. Mega. If that's what you want."

"It is, Joel. It really is. Here, take the book. Now, is that 'Schumann' with two 'N's?"

"Yes. Say, Dr. Mega, are you coming back to the computer room?"

"Tomorrow for sure," he promised, avoiding Marion's disapproving glare.

"You're hopeless," sighed Marion, when Joel was gone. "All you want to do is play with your high-tech toys. You ought to hire someone to be Jay Omega for you."

"Someone like that?" asked Jay Omega, nodding toward his fellow author.

Marion looked at Appin Dungannon, who was posing for a Polaroid photograph with two barbarian maidens in leather battle garb. "Forget I mentioned it, Jay."

CHAPTER 6

THE RUBICON COSTUME Contest, held in the hotel ballroom, was the social event of the evening. Since no audience participation was required, except lust, which was optional, even sociopaths like Bonnenberger chose to attend. Wargamers, Dungeon Masters, NASA freaks, comic book junkies, and other assorted fen, costumed and otherwise, sprawled in metal folding chairs facing the stage and waited for the pageantry to begin.

As official judge of the competition, Appin Dungannon was given a seat of honor in full view of the stage, and a small table with refreshments and a yellow legal pad, on which he might make notes about the various contestants. At the moment, however, he seemed more interested in the lint on his cowboy hat than he was in the proceedings at hand.

Miles Perry, who was master of ceremonies, clutched his notecards in a sweaty fist, and glanced toward the wings. "Are they ready yet?" he mouthed at Diefenbaker.

Dief shook his head vigorously, and made a little sign that meant "Stall them."

Miles tapped the microphone. "Ah ... hum. Can you hear me out there?" An electronic shriek accompanied his voice, sending two technicians scurrying for the sound system. "First of all, I'd like to thank ... I'D LIKE TO THANK ... Testing."

"The costumes are really works of art," whispered Marion to Jay Omega. "It's rather sad, really."

"Why? I think it would be nice to have such ... talent," he said almost enviously.

"I was thinking of how they use it, Jay. Imagine working for six months on a costume that you'll only get to wear once or twice a year, instead of going into dress designing or some other profession related to that skill, where you could actually accomplish something."

Jay Omega smiled. "Not everyone has a tenure-track mind, Marion."

"I still think it's a waste." She looked up at the stage where the first contestant had made her entrance. "And that is particularly a waste."

The costume was impressive: yards and yards of green velvet, carefully embroidered with gold thread and artificial pearls. A leather cummerbund with crisscrossed laces cinched the waist, and the white satin bodice stopped quite abruptly to expose two aggressively prominent breasts. The effect of this medieval artistry would have been pure enchantment, had the ensemble been ten sizes smaller, and had it not been battened on to a fierce-looking redhead who might have outweighed the average calf.

"This . . . ah . . . this is Brenda Lindenfeld of Annandale, portraying the Welsh goddess Arianrhod." Miles Perry's voice made little puffing sounds in the microphone as he leaned over his notecards.

The audience waited in polite silence—or perhaps weary indifference. No catcalls rang out from the darkness, and even Appin Dungannon remained solemnly bent over his legal pad, although the time he had spent evaluating the costume could be measured in milliseconds.

"I'm glad nobody laughed," murmured Jay Omega.

"Oh, no, they wouldn't," Marion assured him. "These guys know what it's like to be outcasts; they are very tolerant indeed. Except intellectually. Besides, look around you."

Jay Omega glanced toward the rows behind them, wondering what he was supposed to notice. "Yes? Looks like one of my engineering classes to me."

"It would," grinned Marion. "Mostly males. Women are at a premium in this hobby, and therefore even the plain ones are prized. That poor creature up there could pick up six guys by Sunday if she chose. I expect she'll settle for one."

Jay Omega peered at Brenda Lindenfeld, who was rotating slowly to show off her hooded cloak. "Any six guys?"

"No, silly. Any six losers. You know, the terminally shy guys who have no idea how to talk to a woman; the runty little nerds that no one else wants; and the fat intellectuals who want to be loved for their minds. She can take her pick of those."

"That's nice. I guess."

Marion shook her head. "I find it very frustrating. It seems to me that they all cluster together like sheep with their backs to the wind, when they would be a good deal better off coming to terms with the world."

"They seem happy enough," said Jay Omega, wishing somebody would laugh or applaud to prove his point.

"Sure, they've moved their egos into fictional bodies on the paperback rack so that they can ignore the rejection in real life. I teach science fiction, Jay! I know these people."

The second contestant, an Imperial Stormtrooper in a homemade uniform of cardboard and white Styrofoam clumped onto the stage. He pointed his laser-gun at the audience, leered menacingly through the white face mask, and bowed to Appin Dungannon. The judge's salute turned into a stifled yawn, and the Stormtrooper marched back into the wings.

Miles Perry leaned into the microphone. "And that was contestant number two. Chip Livingstone, as Sanyo the Stormtrooper." He clapped a couple of times half-heartedly, but the audience response was weak.

Marion turned back to Jay Omega. "I knew a guy once—Brian Something-or-Other—who had read every single book we covered in the science fiction course. He had also read every other book by the same authors. And do you know what grade he got in the course? An F. He didn't come to class half the time. He even missed the mid-term. He was off role-playing and dragon-slaying."

Jay Omega frowned. "That doesn't make sense. It's an elective course, and he knew the material. Why would he blow an easy A?"

"Beats me. I never could figure it out. A's don't mean much to a dragon-slayer."

"And yet . . . dragon-slaying does have its charms, even for that rare integrated personality in the universe," said Jay Omega.

Marion looked at him like, who was he kidding? He was kidding her.

"You're right," she sighed. "I guess it bothers me so much because as an adolescent, I used to be one of these misfits. And in some ways, I guess I still am."

Jay Omega patted her hand. "You mean well, Marion, but you have the soul of an Old Testament prophet."

Walter Diefenbaker hurried down the steps at the side of the stage and scooted across to the empty chair beside Jay Omega. "I think things will take care of themselves backstage," he whispered. "So I thought I'd sneak out and watch."

The next contestant might have stepped off a book cover. It took the audience a moment's thought to realize that the perfect elf boy on the stage must really be a thirteen-year-old girl. Her smooth, dark hair was shaped to her head like a cap, and her slender body and small, pointed features suggested equally pointed ears beneath the hair. Her costume, vaguely reminiscent of Robin Hood, consisted of a puffed-sleeve shirt, leather jerkin and breeches, and fringed knee-length boots. Tied to her forearm was a stuffed satin dragon, positioned for flight.

Cameras flashed.

"This is Anne Marie Gregory of Reston, as a Dragonrider," Miles Perry informed the crowd. This time the applause was generous.

"She's excellent!" said Marion. "For once, a face that fits the costume."

"Quite talented, too," nodded Diefenbaker. "She makes those dragons herself. There are some on display in the art room."

Marion glanced in the direction of Appin Dungannon, who seemed no more interested than usual. "I suppose she'll win?" she asked Diefenbaker.

Dief reddened. "Well, she certainly has a good costume, and she shows a lot of talent, doesn't she? We must hope for the best. Of course, judging is purely subjective, and—" His voice trailed away to the sound of two hands clapping—Appin Dungannon's hands, in fact.

A simpering little blonde of normal weight had wandered up to center stage and was smiling uncertainly across the footlights. Her long golden hair was crowned with a garland of silk flowers, and the elegant white dress was a wedding gown rescued from the Goodwill. She was the personification of cotton candy.

Miles Perry looked anxiously at the applauding judge, and then at the vision in white. "Ah . . . we have here Miss Brandy Anderson as the lovely Galadriel from *The Lord of the Rings*."

Marion scowled at Diefenbaker. "Do you mean that this is going to turn out to be a beauty contest? Does it matter whether you made your costume, or how original you are?"

"Well," said Diefenbaker. "Sometimes it does."

"The blonde didn't make that costume. She just brushed her blonde curls and threw on a wedding dress!" Marion had spent too many years as an ugly duckling herself to approve of beauty winning out over merit.

"You mustn't rely too much on the judge's objectivity," stammered Dief. "Still, the Dragonrider was well done, and I find that I'm never much good at predicting what people will do."

The next two contestants, a Gandolf in a velour bathrobe and a high-school-varsity version of Conan the Barbarian, drew a ripple of polite applause from the audience, but their appearances hardly disturbed anyone's conversation. Probably the most original costume of the evening was a tentacled alien, glistening with plastic slime, and belching smoke from his navel. He received loud applause from the audience, and a standing ovation from his roommates, but Dungannon waved him off with a sour smile. A short person in a monk's robe and a rubber Yoda mask drew some cheers from favoritism, but he rated no more than a glance from the judge.

"That was Matt Simpson from Laurel, Maryland, as Yoda the Jedi Master in *Star Wars*," said Miles Perry, as if anyone needed to be informed. "Our next entrant is Clifford Morgan, costumed as . . . oh, dear!" With a stricken look, Miles Perry dropped his notecards and fled behind the curtain.

In the ensuing fascinated silence, the audience could hear a murmur of voices rising from backstage, building to an occasional crescendo of shouting. After several moments of muffled argument, the curtains parted, and a tall, slender youth with a homespun cloak and snow-white hair appeared at center stage.

The audience gasped and whispered, as the contestant drew his sword and raised it in a salute to Appin Dungannon. "Writer of the Saga!" he cried. "Tratyn Runewind salutes you!"

Appin Dungannon looked as if he had just sat on Excalibur. He glared at the posturing figure on stage with the look of a fire dragon about to belch forth a wave of fire and sulphur: eyes bulging, nostrils flared, and face an apoplectic shade of purple.

With the possible exception of the immortal Rune Warrior, nobody breathed. All eyes turned to Dungannon. After an interval of suspended animation that felt to Marion long enough to do one's taxes in, the tableau exploded.

Appin Dungannon snatched up the nearest empty folding chair and hurled it at the stage. "You impudent maggot!" he roared, hoisting another chair over his head. "Out of my sight! Out of this con!"

"Tratyn Runewind" continued to smile as he dodged folding chairs, comforted perhaps by the knowledge that he had now become a legend in the annals of Fandom. Years from now, oddly dressed misfits would hunch over their Cherry Cokes, and between rolls of the eight-sided dice, they would tell the novices how Clifford Morgan had suffered abuse and risked untold real-life hit points from projectile folding chairs, in defense of the integrity of his player-character, Tratyn Runewind.

Fortunately, Appin Dungannon eventually ran out of chairs, and in the lull from bombardment, Miles Perry crept back on to the stage and half-dragged Clifford Morgan behind the curtain.

"But I wanted to ask him about his new book!" Morgan protested as he vanished from sight.

Appin Dungannon took his place behind the table as if nothing had happened. "Proceed," he said, pointing his pencil at the stage.

The Klingon admiral who appeared from behind the curtain was showing considerably more emotion than his race is purported to have. He stood white-faced and rigid before the footlights, as if anticipating a firing squad. When Appin Dungannon flashed him a benign smile and waved him off, the Klingon bolted for the wings, a performance that was, as Mr. Spock would say, "Highly illogical."

The remaining contestants strutted and fretted their minute upon the stage, barely noticed by anyone, except when Miles Perry, whose notecards were out of order, referred to a Batman impersonator as "a character who manages to be strong and yet beautifully feminine at the same time." The next contestant, Wonder Woman, hurried onstage, but the giggles and references to Robin and the batpole continued for several minutes.

Finally Miles Perry announced that the contestants had all been seen, and that after a few moments of deliberation, the judge would make his rulings known. Appin Dungannon pulled his cowboy hat over his eyes, and propped his boots up on the table.

"Do you really think he'll pick the blonde?" hissed Marion.

"I don't think he'll pick Tratyn Runewind," said Jay Omega.

Diefenbaker smiled nervously. "It isn't important. All the winner gets is an autographed copy of a Dungannon first edition and a gift certificate from Pizza Hut."

"It's the principle of the thing," grumbled Marion.

Jay Omega consulted his program. "It says they're showing movies in here after this. Want to stay for them?"

"That depends," said Marion. "What's playing?"

"I'm not familiar with them. There's one called *Robot Monster*."

"That's a man in a gorilla costume and a diving helmet pretending to be an alien. And he keeps contacting the mother ship on a Jacob's Ladder from a high school science lab," said Diefenbaker.

"Fifties. Low budget," added Marion.

"Okay. How about *The Thing*? It says James Arness is in it. I liked him in *Gunsmoke*."

"Well, you won't recognize him here. He plays a giant asparagus who crash lands in the arctic."

"Hmm. *Plan Nine From Outer Space . . .*"

"Oh, no!" cried Marion and Dief together.

"Cardboard tombstones!"

"Hubcap flying saucers!"

"Bela Lugosi died while they were making the picture, and they kept the footage he was in, but they finished the movie with a replacement who looked nothing like him.''

Jay Omega looked hopeful. Visions of the computer room danced in his head. ''Well,'' he said, ''I guess we don't have to see that.''

Marion grinned. ''Of course we do! It's so bad you won't believe it.''

All entrants of the costume competition except the offending Runewind had lined up across the stage awaiting the judge's decision. Batman and Wonder Woman held hands, while Conan and the Klingon scowled at the audience. Yoda chatted with the Dragonrider.

Appin Dungannon pushed back his Stetson and took his feet off the table, nodding to Miles Perry that he was ready. Perry rushed over to receive the results, but Dungannon waved him away, and ambled toward the stage himself. The audience cheered loudly.

After adjusting the microphone some four inches downward, Dungannon smirked at the audience and motioned for silence. ''Can it, you sleaze-puppies!'' he said cheerfully. ''Nothing you think could possibly make any difference to me. In fact, it would be news to me that you *did* think. Are there any Libertarian assholes out there?''

A few wargamers raised their hands.

''That's right. Raise your grubby little hands. You should all be belled, like lepers. Where was I? Oh, yeah. To keep from having to say this two hundred more times during this con while you grovel for my autograph: yes, I am working on the new Tratyn Runewind. In fact, I expect to be finished with it tomorrow, and since I am over deadline as usual, my editor will be coming here to pick it up.''

Several members of the audience began to look alert.

Appin Dungannon sneered. ''Stop salivating, vermin! You have all the creativity of a Spellcheck disk! I have told my editor not only to avoid you at all costs, but also to disinfect his overcoat after he leaves, in case some of you brush past him in the halls.''

''I don't believe this!'' whispered Marion. ''He's alienating his fans.''

Diefenbaker shook his head. ''He's always like this. People expect it.''

''Can you tell us about the new novel?'' yelled a guy in the fifth row.

''No, pinhead. Your attention span isn't that long. Besides, I want all of you to save the quarters you receive for casual sexual encounters in the men's room, and buy the book. And after you have finished reading it, with your lips moving no doubt, I want you to write me a nice long letter saying exactly what you think of the plot, the characters, and every little detail—and use it for toilet paper! Because I don't want to hear from you morons! None of you can spell *litera-ture*, much less recognize it!''

"Who won the costume contest?" someone called out.

"See what I mean about your attention spans? Shut up, cretin, I'm vilifying you. When I have finished abusing you, I will announce which of these poor afflicted sociopaths gets a free pizza to encourage his delusions." Dungannon shaded his brow with his hand and leered across the footlights at his captive audience. "A pizza! You people need pizzas like TWA needs terrorists."

Murmurs rippled through the audience.

Dungannon looked pleased. "I've wounded you? That's a promising sign. You're too stupid to leave, but at least you know when you're being insulted." He beamed at them. "By the way, I see according to tomorrow's schedule that some of you will be staging your own pathetic D&D variant at an ungodly hour, running all over the hotel pretending to be elves and things." He shook his head. "Isn't ridicule enough for you? Must you have contempt as well?"

The costumed fantasy fen booed gently.

"Oh, spare me your whines! I wish I could arrange for cannibalistic orcs to lurk in the halls and eat the lot of you, but—contrary to your delusions—that is not possible. So let me just warn you that any asshole who dares to disturb me during your morning antics, while I'm writing, will have an IBM keyboard for a suppository!"

Dungannon answered the catcalls and cries of "The plane! The plane!" (an oblique comparison of his size to that of Herve Villechaize) with a tip of his cowboy hat. When the hissing died down, he consulted his legal pad. "Now about the costume contest. May I suggest that next year's prize be a lifetime of therapy and the sedative of your choice? I came up with several possible categories of merit. Most Likely to Be Mistaken for a Dirigible . . ." He nodded in the direction of the velvet-gowned Brenda Lindenfeld who reddened and scowled. "Most Sexually Ambiguous. Most Ludicrous. Most Pathetic. An outstanding bunch; the competition was fierce. —But not for first place. That choice was quite simple. The winner is Miss Brandy Anderson as Galadriel."

The blonde in the wedding gown clapped her hands and rushed forward to hug Appin Dungannon amid faint applause.

"I don't believe it!" hissed Marion. "That old satyr!"

"I'm afraid it was no surprise to the rest of us," Diefenbaker reminded her. "Remember, it's only a pizza."

Marion nodded. "Didn't you say that the Gregory girl had stuffed dragons in the art show?"

"Yes, you can bid on them during the auction Sunday."

"Fine. I'll bid what I think the piece is worth *plus* the price of a large pizza! Somebody has to see that justice is done."

Jay Omega grinned. "Thank you, Mrs. Peel!"

"We said that we were going to announce the winner of the writing contest tonight," Dief reminded them. "Are you ready?"

Jay looked at Marion. "I think so."

"Give us a few minutes to confer," Marion told Dief.

When he had gone to alert Miles of the delay, she and Jay put their heads together. "Okay, I eliminated all the garbage and the written accounts of D&D episodes. Do you remember the three stories you read?"

"I remember what they were about, I think. I didn't have much time," said Jay.

Marion handed him a piece of paper. "I wrote down the titles and authors to refresh your memory. 'The Prodigies' is about the group of kids with ESP."

"Oh, right. That was pretty well-written. It looked like a lot of work was put into it."

Marion sighed. "Fiction shouldn't look like a lot of work was put into it. It should flow. But the story was okay."

"Which one was 'Memory Awake?' The computer that had killed the ship's crew?"

"Yes. The title is a line from Emily Dickinson: 'Remorse is memory awake.' "

"That's okay, isn't it?"

"That's wonderful, Jay. It shows a glimmer of literacy. And the grammar is better than the rest of them."

"I thought the technical material in that one was well done. Some of the details I'd quibble with, but it held my attention."

"That's because it was hard science fiction. Your genre. But you're right. It was a good story. The last one is 'Elfsong.' It's fairly standard fantasy, but the author handles description beautifully. The writing is very strong, but the story is so-so."

Onstage, Miles Perry had finished presenting Miss Anderson her pizza certificate, and after urging a final round of applause for all the contestants, he gripped the microphone and looked inquiringly at Diefenbaker. Dief pointed to Jay Omega and nodded.

"One last award to be given tonight, folks. Our other guest author has very graciously agreed to judge the short story contest, and I'd like to get him up here to announce the winner. He's here as Jay Omega, author of *Bimbos of the Death Sun*. Let's have a big hand for Dr. James Owens Mega of Tech's own engineering department!''

Jay Omega stopped in mid-stride, looking stricken. The audience was cheering louder than ever, and Marion was motioning for him to go ahead. Oh, well, he thought, maybe I could make a living repairing sports cars in a specialty garage. He wished Appin Dungannon would throw a folding chair at Miles Perry. How did he know, anyway? Of course, Marion must have explained it all to the con organizers when she arranged for him to come as a guest; apparently his preference for anonymity had not been made clear enough.

He joined Miles Perry onstage. "Thanks very much for the introduction," he said, trying to smile. "As Miles told you, I judged the short story contest, and there was certainly a wide range of entries."

Marion nodded. Bad Herbert, bad Tolkien, bad Stephen King.

"Choosing a winner was really a tough decision." I wouldn't paper-train a dog on most of them, Marion had declared. "I know you're all very serious about your writing, and that you put a lot of work into writing and rewriting your fiction." He grinned. "I know I do.

"Anyway, before I announce the winner, I want to wish all of you luck with your writing endeavors and to tell you to keep trying."

Because they need all the writing practice they can get, Marion finished silently.

Jay Omega consulted his list. "This year's short story contest winner, for 'Memory Awake,' is Diana Gentry."

Gasps and buzzes of conversation swept the audience. Finally, a cherubic fourteen-year-old boy in tights and tunic approached the stage.

Jay Omega took all the time allowed by the youth's approach trying to think of a diplomatic way to ask. No inspiration was forthcoming, and when the kid joined him onstage, Jay Omega blurted out: "You're Diana Gentry?"

He blushed. "No. She's my mom, and she's not here tonight. She teaches English at the junior high. You said the contest was open to anybody."

Jay Omega handed the boy a gift certificate from Blue Ridge Books. "Accepting on behalf of his mother . . ."

Marion shrugged. "An English teacher. It figures."

CHAPTER 7

"DID YOU KNOW that there's going to be a wedding at this con?" Miles Perry asked Diefenbaker.

"Mark and Linda? Somebody mentioned it to me. Their player characters are getting married in a D&D episode run by Jerry Larson tonight. Why? Do you want to go?"

Miles shook his head. "Not them. Somebody's having a *Star Trek* wedding tomorrow night after the banquet."

"Oh. Well . . . surely they cleared it with you, Miles. You're director of the con."

"No. They say Chip Livingstone gave them the go-ahead."

Diefenbaker looked over his shoulder with a frown. "That is very strange."

"You're telling me," said Miles. "I guess I should have asked to see the letter."

"Yes," agreed Dief. "I hope they don't expect him to show up at the nuptials."

"I trust not, though it seems everywhere I turn these days, I trip over the name of Chip Livingstone!"

Dief permitted himself a snicker. "He's becoming quite the BNF, isn't he?"

"He certainly is! I heard a couple of neofans boasting that they were going to have breakfast with him!"

The laughter was louder at that.

"I should like to be there for that," said Dief. "And how about the *Star Trek* wedding—did you manage to work out the details?"

Miles nodded. "Yes, I have no objections. In fact it ought to be good publicity for the con. Maybe we'll make the front page of the city section this year."

"I'm glad you're pleased. I just hope there aren't any more surprises in the works. Appin Dungannon is quite enough spontaneity for one con."

Jay Omega had spent another half hour at his autograph table, thus earning at his present royalty rate another thirty-six cents in book sales, while Marion toured the hucksters' room. Presently she returned, pinning a calligraphy button to the pocket of her jump suit. It said:

IF THEY CAN SEND
A MAN TO THE MOON,
WHY CAN'T THEY
SEND ALL OF THEM?

"Don't take it personally," she told Jay. "I just thought it was cute. It will sustain me through the cheeseburger fiction I have to read from the more chauvinistic male writers."

"I don't have the energy to be insulted," said Jay Omega. "Bewilderment is taking all my concentration. I keep hearing snatches of conversation as people walk by, and trying to make sense of them. 'Life on a breathable gas ring...'"

Marion nodded. "They were discussing a book by Larry Niven."

"Oh. I thought they were talking about a contaminated stove. How about this one? A 'real Monty Haul campaign'?"

"Dungeons & Dragons. Monty Hall hosted a giveaway show called *Let's Make a Deal*. Gamers use the term to mean an adventure in which players get lots of treasure and easy victories."

"Good evening," said a young man in a broad-brimmed floppy hat, edging past them.

Jay stared at the young man's costume—a long, many-pocketed overcoat, and at the twenty-foot scarf dangling at both ends. "Who was that?"

"Quite correct," grinned Marion. "It was, indeed. Now, would you like to look in on the filksinging? It's nearly eleven."

He yawned. "Gee, is it eleven, already? Shouldn't we plan to turn in, since we have a lot to do tomorrow?"

Marion's face fell. "Oh, are you really tired? I was sort of looking forward to the filksinging."

"But you keep saying how ridiculous all this is."

She sighed. "Old habits die hard, I guess. I can remember sitting around singing defamatory *Star Trek* parodies until the wee hours of the morning.—Years ago, that is," she added hastily.

"And you keep saying how glad you are that you outgrew it," Jay reminded her.

"It might be fun," said Marion wistfully. "We don't have to stay long."

Jay Omega reflected guiltily on the times he'd made Marion spend an hour in the auto parts store, and of keeping her waiting twenty minutes for lunch while he did "just one more thing" on the computer.

"Okay," he said, "I suppose we could just stop by."

Stashing his books in the canvas suitcase, he followed Marion into the elevator. Its other occupant, a stocky teenager, was wearing army fatigues and a button reading:

> BAN THE BOMB!
> SAVE THE WORLD
> FOR CONVENTIONAL WARFARE

Jay Omega decided that this was one of the wargamers Diefenbaker had been talking about.

"Where is the singing? Back in the auditorium?"

"No. It isn't a concert—just a sing-along. They'll probably have it in Monk Malone's room."

Jay remembered the Rasputin character who was "very good" at being a fan. "Yes, I've seen him," he said. "A sing-along, huh? Will we know the songs, do you think?"

"In a way," smiled Marion. "I guarantee you'll know the tunes. And the words will be passed around on mimeographed sheets." Seeing Jay's disconcerted expression, she added, "We won't stay long."

They emerged on the fourth floor, and threaded their way past a corridor D&D game. A stern-looking DM, surrounded by piles of reference books, was flipping through something called a *Monster Manual*. Five players sat in a circle, whispering among themselves. Two of them were in medieval costume, and a third wore a button that read:

> I'M NOT STUPID
> I'M NOT EXPENDABLE
> AND I'M NOT GOING!

Jay Omega decided that the young man's player character must be a low-ranking member of the expedition.

"I still say we ought to try the holy water!" hissed the player in the brown cloak.

"Can't my character see through that wall?" another demanded.

Farther along the passage Marion pointed to a door with a DO NOT DISTURB sign looped on the doorknob, and a larger one in calligraphy taped to the door: DO NOT DISTURB! TRESPASSERS WILL BE VIOLATED. "Appin Dungannon's room."

"I don't see how he can write at a convention," said Jay Omega.

"They pay him well," said Marion. "You, on the other hand, make more from teaching summer school than you will ever make from *Bimbos of the Death Sun*, so you lack motivation."

Jay Omega wisely decided against replying. The discrepancy between the salaries of engineers and those of English professors was a sore point, and one that Marion could not discuss in modulated tones for more than two minutes. He noticed a piece of paper under Appin Dungannon's door, and thought that it must be nice to have such ardent admirers that they slipped mash notes under your door.

"Fan mail," sniffed Marion. "Not that he deserves any. That was quite a performance tonight."

"I think it was all part of the show," said Jay Omega. "I got to thinking how outrageous someone would have to be to attract any attention in this crowd, and I think Dungannon has hit upon one of the few ways to stand out."

Marion scowled. "He's an odious man. And the worst part of it was that most of the time I agreed with him!"

Jay had stopped walking, and seemed to be listening to something in the distance. A moment later, Marion heard it, too: the sound of Sixties folk music came wafting down the hall to meet them. They walked toward the sound and found the door to room 467 ajar. A few feet of floor space remained in one corner of the room, but the area around the double bed was thick with costumed adolescents. Monk Malone, in a Nehru jacket and Levi's, sat curled up on the bed, clutching an old Gibson guitar. Around him, mimeographed pages rustled, and the impromptu choir sang to the tune of "The Sloop John B":

So put up the Enterprise's *shields*
Recharge the phaser banks,
Beam up the captain on board,
And let us go home . . .

Jay Omega seemed to remember a Kingston Trio version of that song, having to do with a sailboat in the Caribbean. This version seemed to be about *Star Trek*. He eased down into the empty floor space next to Marion, wondering if the room had fallen into a twenty-year time warp.

* * *

It couldn't be the beer. Donnie McRory was certain of that. If you sent American beer out to be analyzed, the lab would probably phone up and say, "Your horse has diabetes." Anyway, he hadn't had more than a pint or so. He lay on the bed, still dressed, listening to his headache and wondering if reading would make him drowsy. It seemed a bit early to call it a night, but he hadn't felt like staying around in the bar after he'd finished his set. Too many mellow and friendly Americans wanted to talk to him, but that always seemed to involve a discussion of American versus British tax plans or an offer of things he didn't want, usually illegal things. He'd decided to give it a miss.

Very tiring, being a tourist. Very lonely. Phoning Margaret was out of the question, too, because it was five in the morning in Glasgow.

As he lay on the bed in the darkness, faint familiar strains materialized in his head.

> *"And it's no, nay, never!*
> *No, nay, never no more . . ."*

In spite of his headache Donnie McRory chimed in, *"Will I play the wild rover; no, never, no more."* He sat up, wide awake. Hallucinating in an American hotel, was he? Nobody else was in town, he was sure of it. By "nobody else," he meant the Clancy Brothers, the Chieftains, the Corries, or any of a lesser-known assortment of blokes in white fisherman sweaters billed as Celtic folk groups. But who else would be singing "Wild Rover"? Somebody was singing it. He was awake enough now to be sure of that.

Donnie McRory grabbed his guitar and his room key and headed out to investigate.

In Monk Malone's room on the fourth floor, the filksingers swayed in time to the music, and someone was slapping a tambourine to punctuate the chorus of the song: *"And it's oh,* (crash) *no,* (crash) *never . . ."*

The Cossack on the bed nodded approvingly. "Well done, my children. Now, one more time for Gordy."

> *"I've been a wild Dorsai for many a year,*
> *And I spent all my money on Saurian beer . . ."*

"I don't get it," whispered Jay to Marion.

"No," she replied. "And unless you are willing to read about two hundred science fiction novels, you never will."

Jay Omega sighed. "Tell me again why we're here."

Marion patted his hand. "It's a new experience for you! Don't be such a stick in the mud. Anybody who can sit through the entire graduation ceremony year after year, in his cap and gown, ought to be able to endure an hour of this. Besides, Jay, who knows? Maybe someday they'll compose a filksong about one of your books."

"Yeah, and it'll probably be *Bimbos*. I can imagine what they'd pick. *'Wait 'til the sun shines, Dummy.'* "

The last strains of "The Wild Dorsai" had just ended for the second time when Donnie McRory appeared in the doorway. "The Martians," he muttered. "I might have known."

Monk Malone looked up at the newcomer, still in the leather Celtic costume from his act. "Nice costume, man," said the Monk. "Are you a Scadian?"

"No. I'm a Scot."

"I knew a Scadian Scot once. I think he was The Black Douglas. Anyway, his specialty was medieval Scottish warfare."

Marion whispered to Jay, "Scadian. Member of the S.C.A.—Society for Creative Anachronism."

Donnie McRory began to back away. "Yes, well, I just recognized the song you were singing, and came down to see what you were on about." Even American beer might be preferable to spending an evening with someone who thought he was The Black Douglas.

"That's a nice guitar, too," said one of the rug rats. "Do you play?"

After a moment's frosty silence, Donnie McRory decided that he couldn't pass up the challenge. That's your trouble, Donnie, Margaret would say. You're an incurable show-off.

"Off the bed w'ya," he said, shooing Monk Malone into the corner by the television. After a few experimental strums on the guitar, and the adjusting of a string or two, Donnie played the intro to "The Wild Rover."

Obediently the filksingers ground out: *"I've been a wild Dorsai . . ."*

The strumming ceased. "What was that rubbish you came out with?" he demanded. "Have you been monkeying with the words?"

Sheepishly they nodded.

"Right. Well, here's another tune. This one's about your friend Doug," he said to Monk Malone. He sang the first verse of "The

Lammas Tide'' amid a respectful silence. "There," he said, glaring
at them when he'd finished. "Does anybody have any Martian words
to that?"

Fifty negative replies.

"Right, then. Let's start again, you lot. In the key of G.

> *Now it fell about the Lammas tide . . .*
> *When the muirmen whin their hay . . .''*

Diefenbaker had been run to earth in the wargamers' conference
room by Richard Faber, Bernard Buchanan, and two people he didn't
recognize, but who would turn out to be Far Brandonian correspondents, he was sure.

"I'm really glad I found you," said Bernard Buchanan, still clutching his sheaf of computer printouts. "My parody is really coming
along. In fact, I was hoping you might show it to Appin Dungannon . . ."

"Novibazaar!" said Richard Faber in his most nonnegotiable
voice.

"I have a question about the term 'Brudhorc,' " said one of the
strangers.

Diefenbaker tried to look patient. "I don't have any of my Brandonian files with me at the moment . . ." he murmured.

"Are you free for breakfast?" asked Bernard Buchanan.

Dief was prevented from expressing the conviction that starvation
would be preferable to dining with Bernard by the agitated appearance of Bill Fox in the doorway. "Dief, man, you gotta come now!
Somebody's yelling their head off in one of the upstairs halls, and
it's going to disturb half the hotel."

The hostage was so relieved to be rescued from Far Brandonian
politics that he nearly forgot to ask what the difficulty was, but at
the last moment it occurred to him that the information might prove
useful, and he inquired.

The messenger shrugged. "Beats me. Somebody on fourth is yelling about somebody having been murdered. They sent me to get
you."

CHAPTER 8

As DIEF HURRIED out of the elevator on the fourth floor, he saw that Miles Perry and most of the crowd from filksinging had already congregated in the hall. The central attraction was a shouting match between the cloaked D&D player and another member of the party. Off to one side a forlorn young woman in a white tunic and slacks was clutching a packet of tissues, and sobbing loudly.

"You killed him!" shouted the D&D player. "I can't believe that. And they let you!"

Walter Diefenbaker, wise in the ways of cons, did not spare a glance in search of a lifeless body. Edging his way through the spectators, he planted himself between the two combatants, and waited for silence. When the recriminations had trailed away into a sullen silence, he said, "Do you realize that you could get all of us tossed out of this hotel?"

Behind them, the sobbing continued unabated. Dief glanced over his shoulder. "Will somebody go and buy her a Coke?"

Marion slipped out of the crowd and put her arm around the girl's shoulders. "Come on," she said. "You'll feel better if you talk about it."

The girl allowed herself to be led toward the elevator. "I didn't know what they were going to do," she sniffled. "But Mark is never going to believe that."

"What did they do?" asked Marion.

"Well, Mark and I were going to get married tonight."

"Your player characters?"

"Yes, of course. We'd been planning it for ages, and of course everybody who was in the game with us knew about it, and so did Jerry. He's the Dungeon Master. So tonight when we started the ceremony, Daciano the Red Dwarf—that's Phil Castellow's player character—killed Wolfgang Bartok, who is Mark."

Marion nodded sympathetically. "And you didn't know."

"No! But everybody else did. Phil must have been on the phone for hours setting all this up, and the DM had to have helped him. Before the ceremony, Daciano crept into Wolfgang's room and killed him, and then, using the Shapechanging Talisman from an NPC cleric named Laurence Talbot, he assumed Wolfgang's appearance.''

"Did you know about it before the ceremony?''

The 'widow' frowned. "I did, of course, because as a player I hear Larry describing everything to us, but the point is that my character, Arianna of the Golden Wood, couldn't know that a switch had been made, so she had to go through with it in good faith. You have to play your character according to how they'd really act . . .''

Marion nodded as she thought, "And this, above all, to thine own self be true . . ." She didn't think a handy quote from Shakespeare would be very comforting, though, so she didn't mention it.

Dietenbaker was still talking soothingly to the recently deceased bridegroom, and the crowd, giving up hope of a fistfight, began to drift away.

"It was fair in the game,'' erstwhile dwarf Phil Castellow insisted. "He should accept it as the will of the gods.''

"You are slime, Castellow!'' hissed the late Wolfgang Bartok. He had come dressed for his "wedding'' in a gold tunic and matching tights, and a short blue velvet cloak, all of which clashed with his red tear-streaked face.

Jay Omega, deciding that Marion would come back to the filk-singing to look for him, wandered back to Monk Malone's room, where a band of faithful Celtophiles, mostly Scadians in medieval dress, still clustered around Donnie McRory. He had worked his way through "Annie Laurie'' and "The Lewis Bridal Song,'' and was just beginning "The Skye Boat Song,'' when Anne Marie, the elfish Dragonrider, piped up.

"Do you have any songs about fantasy? We're kind of into that.''

The others nodded. "You know. Dragons, fairies, ghosts.''

"Oh, aye?'' said Donnie McRory. "Just average Yanks, I thought you were.'' Still, after years of performing, he saw an audience's preferences as law, so he gave it a moment's thought. As he looked up for inspiration, Jay Omega slipped in the door.

"What was that din down the hall?'' McRory wanted to know.

Jay Omega reddened, hoping that he wasn't about to be mistaken for a Martian. "Two of the fantasy gamers were arguing because one killed the other in the game.''

"Ah. Character assassination.'' McRory grinned at his own joke. "Now getting back to this song you wanted. We have one about a soldier in the army of Bonnie Prince Charlie's, and he's on the point of death. Dying in England, far from his home in Scotland. So he tells his mate to go off without him, but that he'll be the one home first, because he'll be taking the way of the dead, the fairy route, which can be traveled in the twinkling of an eye.'' He paused for effect, pleased at the rapt attention of his audience. ''We call that fairy way the low road.''

''The low road,'' murmured the circle of listeners, shivering under the spell.

''Right. And here is the song about it.'' He strummed the guitar. '' *'You take the high road, and I'll take the low road . . .'* Well, before we go into that one, would somebody go and get me a beer?''

Elsewhere in the hotel, Richard Faber's hands felt like the bottom of a beer bottle—cold, wet, and glassy—but his throat was dry. He was attempting the frightening and unfamiliar: a conversation with a human female approximately his own age. Brenda Lindenfeld was not, however, Richard Faber's own weight: she could have made two of him, and would still have had enough flesh left over to construct a standard-sized tapir. At the moment, this entire mountain of femininity was gazing at Faber with respectful attention, suggesting that it had been her life's ambition to hear a detailed account of the Battle of Leningrad.

Still dressed in her velvet gown from the costume competition, Brenda was an impressive, if not attractive, figure. She spent most of her time in the wargames room, which was too monotonous for other women to bother with, and the lack of competition prevented unfavorable comparisons. Besides taking care to be the only woman in the room, she smiled a lot. She had decided that Richard Faber had potential; he was, in real estate terms, a real fixer-upper, a bargain for anyone willing to put a little effort into the project. His hair looked like the floor of a service station, and his clothes would have been rejected by a reputable charity, but these flaws were easily corrected, she thought, with praise and successful management. The fact that Richard Faber was an obnoxious bore was more worrisome, but even that could be an advantage. There was considerable security in the knowledge that no one else could possibly want him.

Brenda Lindenfeld felt that security should be valued, if not above rubies, then at least above pleasant companionship. She endured more trauma on a daily basis than the Hershey Chocolate Company could ever hope to assuage. Children stared at Brenda when she passed on the street; people made remarks about her in public, seeming not to care if she heard them. They seemed to think they were giving her constructive criticism, or perhaps alerting her to a hitherto overlooked fact—as if it had somehow escaped her notice that she weighed two hundred and sixty-seven pounds.

Brenda Lindenfeld knew, all right. Her mother managed to mention it at least once at every meal, and her grandmother sent diet articles from *Family Circle* in her letters. Jobs other than those paying minimum wage, out of public view, were not open to her. People in high school hadn't wanted to be seen in her company—nobody's ego is secure enough in high school to allow a friendship with the class leper; guilt by association is the law of the teenager. So she cordially hated everyone in her class, and she ate to make up to herself for all the injuries she endured; and instead of having a social life, she read.

Brenda had discovered that reading is as close as you can come to teleporting. By identifying with the plucky elfin princess in a fantasy novel, Brenda achieved her own version of astral projection: she left the tank of flesh behind her, and lived for the duration of the book in free form, in a world where problems could be solved by magic and by swordplay, rather than by painful and boring exercise courses and diets of boiled rice.

When she turned twenty-three, still living at home and taking the occasional course at the community college to postpone Life Itself, as she thought of it, Brenda made another momentous discovery: a social life was possible. There were others like her. A hotel in Richmond had advertised a science fiction convention, featuring as special guest her favorite fantasy author, so Brenda had invented a speeding ticket to get the registration fee from her parents, and off she went.

The weekend had been a revelation. No one laughed. People in the fantasy seminars seemed to judge her by what she said, rather than by her looks. Brenda was inspired. She had stayed up late in the conference room, listening to a discussion of group marriage as described in Heinlein's book, *The Moon is a Harsh Mistress*. When she read it later, she realized that the boy who defended it had completely misunderstood the concept, and she wondered how the author would have felt about his book being prized as a rationale for promiscuity. But that night Brenda agreed enthusiastically, even reverently, with the speaker's premise; she was thinking maybe he would like to get laid. She didn't expect to have too many other chances.

That first encounter had been rather clammy and uncomfortable, and no relationship had come of it, since they had forgotten to exchange their real names, but Brenda knew that she was on the right track as far as life was concerned. Now work and the community college were simply time-killers between cons, a sop to her parents' expectations. She kept changing majors so that no one could be sure when she was supposed to graduate. This term it was Day-Care Management. It ensured parental good will and free room and board, leaving Brenda considerable spare time to establish her real life, as the goddess Arianrhod in the world of Fandom.

Brenda's latest project, Richard Faber, would pose no particular acquisition problem; and she was well aware of his other liabilities. As he continued to drone on about some stupid battle or other, she had sized him up sexually, and pronounced him not so much gay or straight as "ambidextrous"—in the literal sense of the word. It was the only option that had thus far afforded itself in Faber's nonexistent social experience. Unless she miscalculated—and practice with other members of his species made that unlikely—Faber was an over-eager but terrified virgin, who should be good for about two minutes of frenzied but uninspired coupling, and for an infinite amount of gratitude and devotion thereafter. Brenda didn't particularly enjoy sex, since all her experience thus far had followed this pattern, but like any pusher, she realized the value of the drug to the addict, and she profited from the affection that followed the high. It was quite amazing to her that such an inconsequential, messy little act could result in so much dependence and emotion. Quite magical, really. The goddess Arianrhod gloried in her mystic powers.

Thank God he knew so much about tactical warfare and diplomacy, Richard Faber was thinking. His explanation of the Battle of Leningrad had really fascinated this intelligent creature. At last, someone who respected him for his knowledge, someone who shared his interests. He grew more confident as he went along. She hadn't questioned a single one of his theories! He had patted her hand once when she'd said, "How interesting," and she hadn't pulled it away. In the back of his mind Faber knew that he should be trying to track down Walter Diefenbaker to settle matters about Novibazaar, but he couldn't bring himself to leave. Really, when you got up very close and looked into her large brown eyes, she wasn't bad at all.

Finally, with more courage than it took to aim your Zero at an aircraft carrier, Richard Faber managed to say, "We could continue this discussion in my room if you like." His palms felt like the sides of an aquarium.

For form's sake, Brenda Lindenfeld hesitated. The less experience she permitted to show, the better the spell worked. "Well," she said. "I suppose we could. I wouldn't want us to disturb anyone out here, but I just have to hear the rest of this. It's so interesting!" She hoped he wouldn't expect her to know which war he was talking about.

Faber sighed with relief. He'd done it! The conquest had been made. Another couple of hours and she might let him kiss her.

Brenda was thinking that it was about time he'd got around to asking her, and wondering when she should go and get her belongings from behind the curtain in the video lounge. Hotel rooms were expensive, and of course she hadn't booked one. She thought she could put up with another half hour of this drivel, and then she had to get him laid so that she could get some sleep. Late nights made her puffy.

Appin Dungannon was back in front of his computer monitor scowling at the words TRAIYN RUNEWIND. The evening had not been altogether unpleasant. He had tossed and gored several obnoxious fans, and he had quite enjoyed the exercise of heaving folding chairs at an incarnation of his cretinous Rune warrior. He had been in quite a venomous mood that evening, probably because of the chapter he'd been working on before dinner, but now it was time to write the most hackneyed part of a Runewind book, the ending. He should be able to knock it off in an hour or two, and that would leave the early morning for proofing and final corrections, which need not be too extensive. Some post-teen English major enslaved to the publisher to proof copy could go through and make sure that Runewind's horse was not black on one page and brown on another. Really, he didn't know why they bothered. The demented fans who read the series had hours of fun devising plausible explanations for his sloppiest screw-ups. They would churn out endless articles in their unreadable mimeographed excrescences trying to explain why Runewind's sword changed lengths or why his mother was known by two different names. So far, the two likeliest explanations—apathy and Chivas Regal—had not been suggested.

He felt almost virtuous to be slaving away at the keyboard in the small hours of the morning, especially considering that he'd had other offers. Several of the less grotesque femmefans had hinted at a willingness to add a night with an Eminent Pro to their list of celebrity memorabilia. Dungannon usually declined these offers for a variety of reasons: proofs of age could be faked, and lawsuits were a nuisance; some of the girls might carry the Andromeda Strain as well as having read it; and, most daunting of all, he could never go through with such an encounter without imagining the evening written up in a grubby fanzine. "Is Runewind's Sword a Dirk? A Blow-by-Blow Account of Appin Dungannon's Bedside Manner." The very thought of such an article could cripple his strongest lust. And since the fen had no more privacy sense than a bee and no knowledge of copyright, such an article once written would be reprinted by every 'zine in fandom. It would be harder to kill than the ax man in *Friday the Thirteenth*. Sleep alone, thought Appin Dungannon, safety first. He hated the fen too much to give them such a weapon. Might as well give a chimp a hand grenade.

Tratyn Runewind gazed down at the mighty Runesword in his scarred left hand. At his feet, the gold-tressed warrior princess cowered, awaiting the inevitable blow. She would not plead for her life. Hers was a proud race, one that died with lips bubbling laughter and froths of heartsblood. She was very young.

With a sigh of regret for the death-tide that flowed between them, Tratyn Runewind sheathed the red-tipped blade. "Live to fight again, my fair one," he said, pulling her to her feet.

The girl-general narrowed round blue eyes in suspicious disbelief. What could the Celtic dog mean to do with her? Did he not know that she would grasp her own death gladly before she would submit to such as him?

Runewind gave her a gentle push in the direction of the dragon-prowed longships. "Perhaps we will meet again in the woof of time. Go now."

Fingering the hilt of his Runesword, Tratyn Runewind watched his enemy scramble down the path like a frightened and bewildered child.

When she reached the bend in the rock cliff, she turned and looked at him, hesitantly lifting her small white hand.

"Another time," whispered the warrior.

There were corrections to make, and other details to be attended to, but they could wait until he was sober. Appin Dungannon retrieved his disk, yawned, and watched the monitor screen go dark.

And so to bed.

Marion yawned. "Well, what did you think of your evening in Middle Earth?"

Jay Omega finished arranging the contents of his pockets on the dresser top. "Well, I wouldn't want to live there." He grinned.

"No. I don't suppose you would. But then you happen to be particularly well suited for this planet, lucky for you." She sat down beside him on the bed and began to rub his back.

"You seem to get along pretty well yourself," he pointed out, arching a shoulder blade.

"Just like my cat," she laughed, scratching the shoulder. "Are you going to purr?—I suppose I do get along well these days, but it was an acquired skill. In high school I was too smart and too puppy-fat to be anything but miserable. That was what made the SF group so appealing: we were all outcasts together. Even after all these years it stays with me. I can't help feeling that I get along in the world only because I learned what was expected and how to go about things. Like Marco Polo in China—functioning, but not really belonging. You, on the other hand, seem to have been born knowing how to cope."

Jay Omega nodded. "Like an IBM computer with BASIC built into its ROM. No programming for it necessary."

"Whatever that means." Marion frowned. "I suppose so. You enjoy all the things that other people consider necessary evils—yard work, meetings, teaching undergrads. I used to think you were a saint, but after knowing you a year, I've decided that saints aren't saints, either. They are just people who happen to enjoy doing things the world approves of. And sometimes I think to myself that if we'd gone to high school together you wouldn't have asked me out, and it annoys me—still!"

"I'd have been afraid to. You can be rather fiercely feminist sometimes."

"At the moment, I don't feel that way at all. Are you sleepy?"

"Not any more," said Jay. "In fact, I think I'll go down to the video room. I heard they were going to show *War Games* at midnight. It has a lot of computer technology in it. Want to come?"

Marion shook her head. I'll just stay here and take a cold shower, she thought grimly.

CHAPTER 9

MILES PERRY COULD open one eye just wide enough to see a six and a four on his digital alarm clock. That meant he had been allowed at most three hours of sleep. He groped for the shrieking telephone, and managed to find it without making further demands on his eyes.

"Huh—what?" he croaked into the earpiece.

The responding voice advanced him three levels toward wakefulness.

"Yes, Mr. Dungannon! Good morning!—You want what?—Oh. Room service. I'm sure the hotel has it. Would you like me to give you that number? I could look it up."

He sat up now, wondering where the phone book would be hidden. "What's that, sir?—Well, no, I don't suppose the hotel room service would go to Burger King to get you an egg and cheese croissant. —Oh. I see. Yes, sir. It'll take me half an hour to get dressed. — Fifteen minutes, yessir. Fifteen minutes to get dressed. —And I should tap on your door to let you know it's there. —Certainly, sir. I'm on my way."

To a madhouse, thought Miles Perry, hanging up the phone. Why had he agreed to supervise this con? It was going to be the longest weekend of his life. He just knew it. Of course, he knew exactly why he had agreed to run the con. It would make him very important among the area fen, gain him prestige with the national organizations, and it made him feel delightfully important, something he never felt while managing the grocery produce section at Food Lion. It was an ego trip—but it took its psychic toll.

Marion had almost been awakened by the sound of the shower, but she discovered that if she put her head under both pillows, she could ignore it enough to go on sleeping, incorporating a Tahitian waterfall into her last dream.

Jay Omega pulled back the bed covers. "Wake up, sunshine!" he said, tickling her foot. "Time to commute to fairyland."

Marion groaned. "May an orc eat you for breakfast."

Jay Omega pushed a copy of the Rubicon program under the pillow. "Lots of things to do today. No time to sleep."

"My God," she moaned, stretching and making a grab for the bedspread. "Not only do you have a Ph.D. in engineering and the ability to fix cars, you're also a morning person. Or a morning android. The possibility that you are human gets remoter all the time."

"Flattery will get you nowhere. Get up or it's the wet washcloth on your neck."

She looked at him curiously. "Are you that anxious to get to the con?"

"No. It doesn't start for another two hours. That will give us time to eat breakfast and to visit an auto parts store I know that opens at eight. I need a master cylinder for my clutch. Then, if you insist, we can go to the con."

Marion threw a pillow. "Shut up, Android, or I'll unplug your surge protector."

Jay Omega grinned. "I think you already have."

"Really?" She sat up, smoothing her hair. "I think we have time for that."

"Too late. I've already showered." He started to rummage in his suitcase. "Hurry up, will you? I'm starving!"

Marion yawned and ambled to the bathroom. Maybe he really is an android, she thought.

In the video lounge those pulling an all-nighter were watching as the credits to *The Day the World Ended* rolled up the screen.

"Man, I knew the rain was going to kill the mutants," said Bill Fox, flipping off the television. Because of his status as a mechanical engineering major at Tech, Fox, a member of the Rubicon steering committee, was in charge of the video room.

The six people sprawled on chairs and couches throughout the room went on sleeping. Two other video junkies yawned and stretched. "I thought that was a lot scarier last time I saw it," one remarked.

"How old were you then?"

"About eight."

Joseph Bonnenberger, still in his lair in the corner, looked up to see why the sound had stopped. "Television," he said.

"Breakfast time," said Bill. "Knock off till nine. Gotta go get something to eat." He watched Bonnenberger dump his change on the end table. "Candy machines are in the hall next to the lobby, man."

"Anybody got a program handy?" asked a sleepy Star Fleet officer, uncurling out of a lounge chair.

"Yeah," said Bill. "Usual stuff starts at nine. Videos, wargames, art show, hucksters. Then at ten, there's a live-action D&D game that begins in the lobby. Real weapons strictly forbidden. And the art pro will have a seminar also at ten."

"Is Dungannon talking today?"

"One o'clock in the auditorium. Anything else you need?"

"Just a toothbrush."

"Use your finger." Bill Fox scooped up the videos and started out the door, nearly colliding with Brenda Lindenfeld in the hall.

She was still wearing her velvet gown, but her expression had softened considerably from the fierce scowl of the night before. She was escorted by a scrawny young man in a green turtleneck who walked beside her when hallway space permitted it.

Bill Fox turned back to the video lounge. "Hey! Who was that guy with Brenda Lindenfeld?"

Bonnenberger looked up from his book. Since he and Bill were alone in the lounge, he decided to venture a quip. "Her lunch," he said.

You always got more of Bonnenberger when there was no one else around.

Walter Diefenbaker hoped the registration clerk would be back from breakfast soon. He should have asked someone to bring him something from McDonalds. Now he had a choice between peanut butter crackers from the vending machine or missing the live D&D game. Dief was not a fantasy person, but he did allow himself an occasional frivolity, and the role-playing sounded like a lark. Today his tweed jacket sported a button reading:

IS THERE REALLY A CANADA,
OR ARE ALL THOSE GUYS JUST KIDDING?

He should check with Miles, though, to see if he could be spared for the duration of the game. If one of the staff volunteers failed to show up, Miles would need someone to pitch in. Where was Miles, anyway? He hadn't been around all morning.

"Hello!" said Marion, leaning over the registration desk. She had changed her *Avengers* costume for a preppy-looking navy blazer and canvas skirt. "Jay has gone upstairs to get his books. When would you like him to set up?"

Dief shrugged. "Whenever. How long can he stand to autograph? We did want to talk to him, though. The local physicist who was going to lecture on quasars at eleven has canceled out, and we were hoping that Dr. Omega might be willing to conduct a writing seminar."

"I don't know. Surely Appin Dungannon . . ."

"Surely *not* Appin Dungannon."

"I'm not sure Jay would have much to say to a writing seminar," said Marion. "He's not very chatty about his work, and he doesn't subscribe to *Writer's Digest* or anything like that. You can ask him, of course."

"I'll see if Miles has managed to come up with anything else. There's always the *Star Trek Bloopers* reel, I suppose."

"I'll watch the table for him if you can get him to do it. I suppose he could autograph a few books before he leaves. And sometime today we'd better let him spend some time in the computer room. The high-tech toys are his greatest joy."

Miles Perry came out of the elevator looking more harassed than ever. His rust-colored hair hung over one eyebrow in a stubborn ringlet, and he was wearing his tie at half-mast. "Here you are!" he called to Dietenbaker. "I'm thinking of enrolling in the federal witness protection program, provided they can grant me a new identity today. I want never to be seen again."

"And let Chip Livingstone run the con?" smiled Dief.

"Very funny," said the director with a sour smile. "I'm serious, Walter. This is fraying my nerves."

Dief nodded sympathetically. "More chaos?"

Miles started with the pre-dawn phone call, and summarized the rest of his hectic morning. "Just now Brian Kramer locked himself out of the wargames room, and he couldn't remember where he'd put the key."

"Did you find it?"

"Finally. After a frantic search. It was in the bag with his Diplomacy pieces. Did you hear that Dr. Zachary canceled?"

"Quasars at eleven? Yes. I was just asking Marion if she thought Dr. Omega would do something instead."

Miles Perry shook his head. "Don't bother. You know Jack Carlton from the hucksters' room? Comic book dealer? He's agreed to try to explain the alternate Earth systems in the Superman series and how they were resolved."

Dief whistled. "In an hour?"

"Well, it's a start. Now, what are you doing on registration?"

"Calm down. Dixie went to breakfast."

"Okay. What else should I worry about?"

"Me," said Dief. "I haven't eaten."

Miles Perry pulled half a Mars bar from his jacket pocket. "With my compliments and best wishes," he said.

At ten o'clock the hotel lobby resembled an evacuation center for Sherwood Forest. A colorful crowd in homespun cloaks and rope-belted tunics milled about, discussing their player characters and speculating about the live role-playing game that was about to begin.

"I don't see why we can't use our weapons in this thing. Realism is what it's all about."

"Do you think Appin Dungannon will show up?"

Diefenbaker listened to the conversations swirling about him, but he was trying to concentrate on formulating his character. He had been assigned the part of an elf-thief, chaotic-good, with the usual agility and night vision. The other elves in the party, three giggly young women in burlap dresses, had decided to name themselves Rowan, Saffron, and Rosemary.

"And who are you going to be?" they asked him.

"Herb," said Diefenbaker.

In the center of the throng the Dungeon Master, in a monk's robe and sandals, waved his scenario and shouted for quiet. "Listen up, people!" roared Jack Larson with a most unmedieval New Jersey accent. "We're going to start now, so shut up while I read you about the quest."

He glared belligerently at the few remaining talkers, and suddenly caught sight of a familiar white-haired personage in the crowd. "Clifford Morgan! Is that you? Don't you ever learn?"

Morgan had joined the party of adventurers attired as usual in his Tratyn Runewind costume. He twirled the edge of his cloak in a bow to the Dungeon Master. "The golden Rune warrior honors you with his presence. May his skill in battle and his Druid wisdom serve you well."

"Oh, let him go," said one of the clerics. "Dungannon won't be around anyway. He's writing, remember?"

Monk Malone in his usual Dominican friar's outfit joined the group, acknowledging a flutter of applause with a modest wave. "I must be a wizard, of course," he told the Dungeon Master.

Jack Larson sighed. "I've already got a wizard."

"My apprentice," said Monk Malone smoothly. "Certainly I shall be the principal wizard in the party."

"Uh huh." Jack Larson glanced at his game plan, trying to decide how long it would be necessary to wait before letting the wererats eat the people who gave him a hard time. Jack Larson's calligraphy button said:

GOD IS DEAD,
AND I WANT HIS JOB.

When the twenty-two participants had seated themselves around the overstuffed chair, the Dungeon Master explained their mission. The human fighters were all apprentice knights in the fourteenth-century court of the king of France.

"But what about me?" asked Mona Walton. "I'm human/fighter but—a woman squire?"

Jack Larson thought fast. "Yes. Because ... because a famous wizard has predicted that a woman warrior will someday save France, and when you asked to be trained, they were afraid to turn you away in case you turned out to be the one."

Mona nodded. "Joan of Arc. Am I?"

"No," said a Scadian. "Wrong century."

"Right. Now one of you human warriors ..." He consulted his notes. "Gawaine ..."

"You pronounce it *Gavin*," said the Scadian.

"Whatever. He's from Scotland. Who's Gawai—Gavin?"

One of the better-looking fourteen-year olds raised his hand. "I am."

"Okay. You're nominal leader of the group. You're the son of a clan chief, and he sent you to France to learn warfare, but you don't want to be a knight. You want to study magic. Okay?"

The boy nodded.

"Now, one day you're in your room studying your Latin when a message arrives for you from your father in Scotland." Larson paused for effect. "Someone has been stealing black horses throughout the Borders. Only black horses."

The adventurers whispered among themselves.

"So you decide that something magic and dangerous is happening. You don't know what. But you decide to go back to Scotland with some of your friends and try to find out."

"We're going to Scotland?" Tratyn Runewind applauded. Sensing their cue, the human fighters got to their feet.

"One more thing," said the Dungeon Master. "At the bottom of the letter is another note."

"What does it say?" asked Gawaine anxiously.

Jack Larson grinned at the group. "Come back when you find it."

Bill Fox, setting up "The Trouble with Tribbles" on the VCR, caught a glimpse of Walter Diefenbaker wandering down the corridor wearing the myopic lost look of Mole in *Wind in the Willows*. "Hey, Dief!" he called. "How's it going?"

Dief sighed. "I am a very stupid Scottish elf named Herb, and I am supposed to warn the adventurers to look out for 'Beans in the Road.' Whatever that means. Most of the others are searching for— not the message; they found that—a ring of Saracens, I think. Although having infidels in Scotland, even near the time of the Crusades, strikes me as being a bit far-fetched. Still, I suppose it means something sensible. The Scadians will probably know."

Bill Fox grinned. "The fantasy people are probably in their rooms thumbing through their folklore texts."

"Herb!—Yoo hoo!—Herb!"

Dief, finally realizing that he was being addressed by the name of his player character, turned to find his fellow elf Saffron waving at him from the elevator.

"Excuse me," he said to Bill Fox. "Delusion calls."

Saffron held the elevator until he arrived. "You'll never guess what I found out!" Her elfin eyes shone with excitement.

"Probably not," Dief admitted.

"The Ring of Saracens! I know what it is."

Dief remembered Bill's remark about the folklore texts. "Which book was it in?"

"None that I know of. I was right here in the elevator trying to figure out the clue . . . You know, muttering to myself, over and over, Saracen . . . Saracen . . . And this short, oldish guy got on at the third floor, and on the way down, he overheard me. He said, 'Why are you blethering about a pub in Glasgow?' "

"That's what it is? A pub in Glasgow?"

"No. Did I mention he talked funny? It turns out he's from Scotland himself."

Dief nodded. "That would be Mr. McRory."

"I guess so. Anyway, I asked him if that pub would have been around in the fourteenth century, but he said no, so I asked him what else the word *Saracen* could mean in Scotland. And he told me!"

"Well?"

"It's a ring of big stones. You know, like Stonehenge. That's what they call them in Scotland. Saracen Stones. Isn't it great that I got it?''

Diefenbaker hesitated. "I guess so, Carolyn. I mean, Saffron. But remember that you're an elf. It's the humans who have to find out what it means."

"That's okay!" said Saffron brightly. "I'm a very unusual elf. Lawful good. I can befriend a human and tip him off. I think I'll tell Gawaine. He's cute."

"Hmm. Where's everybody else?"

"Running all over the hotel, I guess. The Dungeon Master has people going everywhere looking for clues."

Appin Dungannon was pleased with his chapter. It shone on his computer screen like a bad deed in a saccharine world, and as usual he had enjoyed the thrill of finality in rereading that special chapter. He glanced at his watch. Nearly ten-thirty. His editor was due to arrive soon. In time for lunch, he hoped. Louis could always charge it to the publisher's expense account.

Suddenly he remembered that he would be addressing the entire convention at one. Damn! He hoped Louis wasn't hungry. Given a choice between a burger at rush hour and a lunch deferred, he would always choose the latter.

Pressing Home, Home, Up, Appin Dungannon scanned the chapter from the beginning, looking for typos and other lapses of concentration. Thus far he hadn't found any. His work had been pretty good this weekend, all things considered. No one had bothered him all morning. He was pleased that he had frightened the fen so thoroughly that they had left him alone.

Of course, one of them hadn't been frightened. He glanced again at the note he'd found under his door last night. Not frightened at all. But Dungannon was pleased with the overall results of his weekend. His image was intact.

He supposed he ought to get a printout made for Louis, archaic bastard that he was. As a science fiction editor, Louis would believe in six impossible things before breakfast, including a civilization of cloud beings, but you couldn't convince him that a floppy disk was as good as a manuscript. It was a pain to lug a printer around in his travels. Appin Dungannon smiled to himself: not that he ever lugged personally, of course.

He adjusted the paper feed in the printer and flipped on the machine. There was probably something ironic about creating rune sagas on a computer; he wondered what *Beowulf* would have been like, had it been word-processcd. Longer, probably. He reached for a blank notecard and scribbled a memo to himself. That might make an interesting talk: the effects of technology on world perception. It had occurred to him before. Late twentieth-century people saw landscapes as a moving panorama, going by at fifty-five miles per hour. Surely this made their thinking different from the rest of humanity, who had seen landscape as a static view, like a painting. Such differences in perception probably meant that he had failed miserably at capturing the ethos of Celtic Britain, but at least he had the wit to realize it. Unlike the buffoons who thought they could live his works and still cook their dinners in a microwave. There was more to capturing the past than dressing the part. He wondered if such a lecture to a fantasy audience would be a waste of breath.

The printer was noisy, but probably no more than a television tuned to one of those mindless game shows. No one should be trying to sleep at this hour of the morning anyway. Appin Dungannon leaned back in his chair and watched the machine spit out pages of pseudo-Celtic drivel. Maybe in the next one he would have a French character named Louis confined to a leper colony near Glastonbury. Louis the Leper. It had a ring to it. He wondered if his editor would let that one go by. Tratyn Runewind goes to find someone at a leper colony near Glastonbury . . . It was the wrong period, of course. There weren't any lepers in Britain until the time of the Crusades, but he doubted if any of his readers knew that. He turned the idea over in his mind. Yes, it was interesting. One might bring in the healing wells . . . He grabbed for another notecard, and wrote down "Lepers. Glastonbury." What could he use for a working title? Books went better for him if they had names.

Appin Dungannon was still snickering at his new creation, *A Farewell to Arms*, when he heard the knock on the door.

Louis, already? Dungannon glanced at the printer. Judging by the size of the paper stack, it still had a good bit to go. With a sigh, he bent over his notecard, intent upon looking busy, and called out, "Come in! It's open."

The visitor wasn't Louis.

Appin Dungannon looked at the long hair, the medieval costume, the pseudo-Norse medallion, and then at the pistol that was leveled at his chest.

"Young man," he said. "That is an out-of-period weapon."

CHAPTER 10

LOUIS WARREN STUDIED the Rubicon program posted in the hotel lobby while he considered his options. It was now eleven twenty-nine A.M. He could either go up to Appin Dungannon's room now, and be shouted at for wasting the author's valuable time with a social call, or he could wait until a few minutes before Dungannon's scheduled one o'clock lecture, and be accused of slighting his company's top author.

As usual he wondered why he hadn't stayed in teaching, and as usual he told himself that the chairman of the English department was probably much like Appin Dungannon. At least as an editor, he could limit his encounters with the ogre to two or three times a year, instead of having to endure him more or less constantly as a faculty member. Like chest X rays, one had to give the system time to overcome the toxicity before exposing oneself to another dose.

It seemed a shame to end his stay in Washington with a visit to Appin Dungannon, but they did need the new manuscript quickly, since the withdrawal of the Maysfield novel had left a hole in their September list. Of course, Dungannon had refused to send the manuscript by courier: too expensive; too much trouble; he didn't trust the company. Louis Warren sighed. He should never have let Dungannon know that their trips to Washington coincided. Of course Dungannon would insist on personal attention. His ego required any amount of that nonsense. For one uneasy moment, Warren wondered if the author had something even more humiliating planned for their meeting. He pictured Dungannon ordering him to stay for the lecture, and then introducing him to the fannish multitude of would-be authors and instructing him to accept unsolicited manuscripts. The very idea of being deluged with several dozen incoherent Tolkien ripoffs made the editor queasy. Perhaps he should try to find a copy of the *Chronicle of Higher Education* to take back on the plane. It always featured several pages of job listings.

Deciding to get it over with, Louis Warren inquired at the front desk for Dungannon's room number. "He's expecting me," he explained to the hesitant clerk.

"Better you than me." The young man grinned. "Shall I call him and say you're on your way up?"

Warren shook his head. "One interruption is enough." Besides, he thought, advance notice would only give him more time to work on his rage.

Warren hardly noticed the assorted costumed fen who swarmed about him in the hotel. At least once a year the publisher sent him to do workshops at one of the larger cons, where he would explain to an audience of elves and Conans that the world didn't really need another book about six cloaked adventurers in search of a magic sword. And, no, he wasn't interested in the one about the Vietnam vet transported back to the time of the Visigoths, either. A variation of that one came in about once a month. Fantasy fans worked very hard on their literary creations, and seemed to have an infinite capacity for churning out pages—much greater than his capacity for reading them—but they were sadly lacking in originality; probably all that television they'd watched since infancy: formula and imitation. It was a rare young fantasy writer who managed to escape its pall.

When the elevator stopped, Louis Warren edged past two Imperial Storm Troopers, and followed the room numbers to Appin Dungannon's lair. The DO NOT DISTURB signs came as no surprise; he'd half expected barbed wire as well.

"Mr. Dungannon! Are you there? It's Louis Warren." He accompanied this announcement with a discreet and, he hoped, inoffensive tap on the door.

All was silent within.

Naturally Appin Dungannon would not bother to answer the door right away. He probably had a standard chart for how long to keep people waiting: room service five minutes, reporters eight minutes, associate editors fifteen minutes. Fans: twenty to life.

Louis Warren knocked again. "Mr. Dungannon, I'm here to pick up the manuscript." Putting his ear against the door, Louis could hear the faint clack of a printer in operation. Surely Dungannon would not leave the room with the printer going. Or perhaps he would. Warren looked at his watch. Quarter to twelve. It was perfectly possible for Dungannon to have gone to lunch, leaving it up to the editor to collect the manuscript. He supposed he ought to check, since the alternative would be to camp out in the hallway for a couple of hours, wishing pestilence and famine on Appin Dungannon, while passing Trekkies mistook him for an autograph hound.

Louis Warren tried the door handle. It wasn't locked, so he eased his way into the room, wondering whether Dungannon was present, and about to hurl a lamp at his head, or absent, and planning to have him arrested for breaking and entering. Perhaps he ought to leave a note.

The only sound in the room was the clack of the printer. Warren looked at the unmade bed, the row of bottles on the window ledge, the cowboy hat atop the computer monitor, and finally at Appin Dungannon, seated in a chair by the desk.

He looked much as usual: bulging piggy eyes, gargoyle face, unfashionably long hair. . . . The pallor was a change from his usual boozy redness, though, and the stain on his shirt was definitely not Chivas Regal. . . . Louis Warren kept staring at the body, idly wondering if he had two more wishes coming.

Finally the shock wore off a bit, and he stumbled back into the hall, nearly colliding with a tall, black-cloaked vampire. "Excuse me," murmured Louis Warren. "I wonder if you would know anything about death?"

Several minutes later, the still-dazed editor had been taken to Miles Perry and Walter Diefenbaker, who had been on their way to lunch. When he explained who he was and what he'd found, Miles Perry frantically hurried off to notify police and hotel officials, leaving a shaken Dief to cope with Louis Warren, and wondering if he were ever going to get another square meal.

"Poor, poor man!" said Dief, shaking his head. "I'm afraid that I always found him rather . . . unpleasant—probably my fault for not getting to know him better. I expect he was a rather lonely soul really. Still, I'm quite sorry he's passed on."

The editor didn't seem to be listening. Probably shock, Diefenbaker decided. One was never prepared for something like this.

"Can I get you a Coke?" murmured Dief, hoping for an excuse to seek out the vending machines. "I'm sure you must be quite shaken up."

"No, I'll be fine," said Warren vaguely. "It was a shock, that's all. And there's so much to do."

"I'm sure there must be. Had he any family?"

The editor wasn't listening. "Really, a lot of things to do. His book jacket biography will have to be rewritten, and publicity will have to design some new ads for the magazines. 'Appin Dungannon's Last Book,' something like that."

"I see."

"And I'll have to call Harlan Ellison and get him to work on a eulogy for Dungannon."

"Harlan Ellison? But I thought he hated Dungannon's work," said Dief.

Warren didn't respond, but looked over at Diefenbaker, suddenly remembering that he was there. "Is there a phone I could use?"

Walter Diefenbaker sighed. "Perhaps you ought to wait until you've talked to the police."

At one-ten P.M. most of the fen had gathered in the auditorium to hear Appin Dungannon's lecture. His lateness did not surprise them, but the absence of a stammering con official apologizing for the delay was noted as being unusual.

Jay Omega and Marion had joined the group about one-oh-five P.M., after a salad-bar lunch in the dining room, and the stragglers from the morning's role-playing game came in shortly thereafter.

"Has anybody seen Appin Dungannon?"

"He doesn't skip out on scheduled lectures, does he?"

"Nah. He has to keep getting the venom out of his system, or else he'll need dialysis."

Marion recognized the monk's robe in the row in front of her. "You were the Dungeon Master for the game this morning, weren't you? How did it go?"

"Pretty well," Jack Larson replied. "Some of them were a little slow with the clues, but they finally figured out who'd be stealing black horses in fourteenth-century Scotland."

"Who?" asked Jay Omega.

"Thomas the Rhymer," said Marion. "Right? I expect he'd need them for the Sleeping Warriors."

"Very good," said Jack Larson. "It took the group an hour and a half to come up with that. How'd you know?"

Marion smiled. "Ph.D. in folklore."

"Who are the Sleeping Warriors?" asked Jay Omega.

"I'll give you a reading list," Marion replied.

At the sound of sporadic applause they looked up at the stage to see Walter Diefenbaker making his way hesitantly to the microphone. "I just remembered you," he blurted out.

Shaking his head, he began again. "Your master of ceremonies, Miles Perry, has been detained by an emergency, and I've been asked to tell you that—" The police had not yet arrived, and he didn't really know what he was authorized to tell them. Squinting out into the audience, he saw Marion and Jay Omega giving him puzzled looks.

Diefenbaker decided on discretion; explanations could follow. "I came to tell you that our guest speaker, Appin Dungannon, is unable to be with us this afternoon due to a sudden illness—"

"Cirrhosis isn't sudden!" someone called out.

"—and so, instead of Mr. Dungannon, we will have our other guest author, Jay Omega, discuss the contemporary science fiction market with you." He motioned for Jay Omega to take the stage.

"What the hell!" hissed the substitute speaker.

"Go on!" whispered Marion. "They're obviously in a bind, so you might as well help them out. You can do it! You lecture six hours a week."

"On engineering. I've never tried to talk about writing."

"Go on, Jay! It'll be good for the book."

Jay Omega, grinning nervously, joined Dief on stage.

"What's going on?" he muttered under cover of the applause.

Diefenbaker muttered back, "Dungannon has been murdered. Try to keep them here at least till two." He hurried away.

Jay Omega stared open-mouthed at the departing Dief until he remembered that two hundred people were staring at him from the darkened audience. He summoned up a faint smile and tried to collect his thoughts. Dungannon was dead? He couldn't have been much more than fifty. Omega wished he could say something—some expression of regret—but obviously the con people didn't want it made public. He felt a twinge of guilt for having envied Dungannon his celebrity as a writer.

Jay Omega adjusted the microphone stand a few inches upward to accommodate the height difference. "Good afternoon," he said to the audience. "I'm sure I won't be as helpful as Appin Dungannon would have been, but I'll do my best. As you know, I write hard science fiction, so I may not be much help to you aspiring fantasy writers, although I will say that if you plan to write about things like the Sleeping Warriors, a doctorate in folklore wouldn't hurt. Now before I talk about my own work, does anyone have any questions?"

A student in the third row raised his hand. "Do you make more money from your first novel or from teaching engineering?"

Marion sighed. "Now there's a fantasy for you!"

Miles Perry did not think that things boded well for Rubicon. "If You Never Attend Another SF Convention in Your Life: Go to Rubicon. —They'll Guarantee It!" He could imagine the snide com-

ments in 'zines across the country. Meanwhile, he was waiting for
the police officers to finish their work in Dungannon's room. He said
he'd be available for questioning. At least he didn't have to worry
about an alibi: never having had a moment's peace all morning ought
to provide one nonstop.

He found that he was sweating profusely and, alert to appearances,
he took out his handkerchief to mop his brow. A real murder! He
had half hoped that the police would invite him up to the room, so
that he could watch the photographing and the gathering of evidence.
Would they put a chalk outline where the body had been? But upon
reflection he decided that the time to himself might be more valuable
in his present state of agitation. What did one do when the special
guest expired at the con? Canceling the banquet was out of the question. He supposed it ought to be a subdued affair, in memory of the
deceased.

Someone was sure to suggest a chorus of "Ding Dong! The Witch
is Dead!" That had to be quashed at the outset. Decorum would be
the watchword. He hoped the murderer wouldn't turn out to be someone else famous, like Jay Omega. That would be too much notoriety
for any con.

"Mr. Perry? We're ready to ask you a few questions now." Lt.
Thomas Ayhan, with a gray crewcut and a rumpled brown suit, was
easily the most distinguished person at the con. Miles thought he
looked more like a bank vice-president than a policeman, and one
made him as uneasy as the other. Ayhan smiled reassuringly and
pulled out a little blue notebook. "Oh, before we begin, I need to
ask you: was the deceased a Roman Catholic, by any chance?"

Miles Perry stared. "I very much doubt it," he said. "Why?"

"Well, we wondered. There was a priest asking for admittance to
the room, and I thought he might want to administer the last rites."

"Hmm. Long black robe with a rope belt? Skinny guy with a
beard?"

Lt. Ayhan nodded.

"Don't let him in. That's Monk Malone. He's not a priest; he's a
fan."

"One of the members of your convention, then?"

"Yes. But we haven't told anybody that Dungannon is dead, so
how did he know?"

"We're not all that inconspicuous," smiled Ayhan. "I think he
must have seen us come in, and followed to see what was going on."

"If he knows, it'll be all over the hotel soon," said Miles.

*   *   *

Louis Warren had missed his plane, but that was the least of his worries. Sometime during his frantic review of things to be done, it suddenly occurred to him that the manuscript he had come for was lying in a room that was now sealed and guarded by the police department. He rushed to the door of the conference room, but unable to think of anything he could actually do about the situation, he sat down and tried to think up arguments for getting the detectives to return the manuscript. Ought he to call the legal department?

He looked up as Diefenbaker came in, carrying a couple of Cokes. "I got Jay Omega to take over the lecture," he said, puffing a little from the unaccustomed haste. "Have the police spoken to you yet?"

"No. I suppose they'll insist on it, since I found the body, but there's really nothing I can tell them."

"Do you know who would have wanted to kill him?" asked Dief.

"Sure. Get a copy of the *Directory of American Poets and Fiction Writers* and start with A. You could have raffled off chances to kill Appin Dungannon."

Diefenbaker thought about last night's performance at the costume competition. "He didn't seem to mind making enemies," he conceded.

"No. He had quite a gift for it," Warren agreed, sipping his drink.

"I suppose your company will miss a best-selling author, though."

"They might, but I won't," said the editor. "Imagine being able to edit a Tratyn Runewind book without having to wrangle over every semicolon, or justify every deleted adjective. It's going to be wonderful!"

"I suppose a woman could have shot him," said Diefenbaker thoughtfully. "Didn't he have an ex-wife?"

"Yes. Doubleday is bringing out her book this spring: *Beauty and the Beast: A Marriage Made in Munchkinland*. If it's still in galleys, they'll probably want to do a rewrite on her last chapter."

"You don't think she's in town, do you?"

"She lives in California. She'll be easy to find. Check the talk-show circuit. I don't think she did it; no motive, really. The same goes for all the relatives. Alive, they got all the money they needed. But Dungannon stipulated that, upon his death, the estate would go to the Scottish Archaeological Society. Everybody knows that, especially the ex-wife. Still," he mused, "it would make great publicity for the book if she did! I wonder who has the paperback rights?"

*   *   *

Jay Omega had stressed the value of reading to improve one's writing style; he had recommended a computer for ease of corrections; and he had urged them to write what they knew, insisting that in today's world of high technology, a knowledge of science could not be faked.

The audience of would-be writers had countered with questions about publisher's advances, agents' percentages, and movie rights. Jay Omega, whose experience in all of these was limited, advised them to hold such questions until after the rewrite of the first draft.

"Any more questions?" he asked, trying to sound cheerful.

A clean-cut young man in a suit stood up. "I am interested in becoming a writer," he said, with the unctuous charm of a business major. "And I was wondering about this business of setting up an office in your home in which to write. I know it can't double as a guest room, but I was wondering whether you can deduct the entire cost of your computer and office furniture in the first year, or if you have to spread it out over several years. And also, can you begin to deduct depreciation on the equipment in the year of purchase?"

Jay Omega, who doubted that his royalties would ever equal his advance for *Bimbos*, blinked at the questioner. He hadn't expected to see a yellow spotted tie in this crowd. "Well . . ." he said at last, "I think that depends. Not all writers bother with home offices . . ."

"Since most of them couldn't afford the furniture," muttered Marion.

"What have you written?" Jay Omega asked the young man.

"I haven't written anything," came the reply. "I'm sure I could, but I wanted to get all the business aspects straight before I became a professional."

Jay Omega was beginning to understand why Appin Dungannon threw folding chairs. He wondered how to answer someone who thought of writing as just another business, and then he remembered a line that might apply. "Uh . . . well . . . it's like this," he stammered. "Being a professional writer is a lot like being a hooker. You'd better find out if you're any good at it before you start charging for it."

Marion giggled to herself. If he doesn't stop quoting me, I'll charge him for speech-writing, she thought.

The rest of the audience was still snickering appreciatively when Monk Malone mounted the steps to the stage. He was still wearing his black friar's habit, and beneath the dark, matted hair, his solemn face seemed to burn with purpose. Probably wants to start a children's crusade, thought Jay Omega.

"Excuse me, Mr. Omega," he said with ecclesiastical dignity. "I must make an announcement."

"I don't think—"

Monk Malone commandeered the microphone. Raising both hands as if he were offering an invocation, he called out, "I have an announcement of the utmost gravity!"

"How many G's?" yelled a NASA freak.

Monk Malone silenced him with a smoldering stare.

"The Force is with us in the person of its darkest horseman. You may see it as a judgment, or as the caprice of the goddess Weird, but it has come to pass. I must now inform you that Appin Dungannon is no more."

Marion's jaw dropped. For once, she found herself speechless.

Jay Omega clutched the lectern and looked down at his shoes, half in embarrassment, half with genuine regret.

For a stunned second no one moved. Then a voice near the back row blurted out, "Holy shit!" and the audience sprang to life.

"Cut down in the flower of his creativity . . ." Monk Malone was saying.

"What was it? Heart attack?"

"I saw some cops in the lobby!" someone called out. "I figured it was a disturbing-the-peace rap."

"Cops! —Was he murdered?"

Suddenly a clarion voice rang out like a battle cry above the babble. "The hucksters' room! While we still can!"

In the row in front of her, Jack Larson snatched up his cloak and prepared to join the stampede to the door. Marion leaned over and touched his arm. "The hucksters' room?" she echoed. "What does that have to do with Appin Dungannon's being murdered?"

The Dungeon Master smiled at her. "Not a thing," he replied. "But life goes on. And now autographed copies of Appin Dungannon's books are worth triple what they were five minutes ago."

CHAPTER 11

MILES PERRY DIDN'T think that homicide detectives ought to giggle while investigating a murder. Still, he supposed it was better than a granite-faced Joe Friday look that radiated suspicion. Beneath his salt-and-pepper crew cut, Lt. Ayhan reddened with suppressed chuckles. Tears appeared at the corners of his eyes, and he kept taking deep breaths that would almost turn into whoops.

"I'm glad he wasn't stabbed with a broadsword," he managed to say. "I'd hate to have to book an elf!"

"Elves use shortswords," said Miles Perry.

Ayhan continued to chuckle. "Or pixie dust poisoning. That would have been a toughie!"

Miles endeavored to look stern. "We are seriously concerned over Mr. Dungannon's death, both personally and as a reflection on the integrity of our convention," he said stiffly.

Ayhan dabbed at his eyes. "Sorry," he said cheerfully. "After years of winos with their heads bashed in, and a slew of unpremeditated bar brawls, this does make a change. The captain asks me, 'So who do you have for suspects?' and I say, 'Dopey, Bashful, and Doc!' " He shook his head. "This is one for the memoirs."

"I trust the murderer will turn out to be someone sufficiently colorful," said Miles politely.

"No matter," said Ayhan. "We'll get him. People watch too much TV these days. They think if they wipe off the fingerprints and ditch the murder weapon, they're safe. Nah. We got all kinds of fancy lab tests. Did you know that firing a pistol leaves a minute powder residue on your hand? True. All we need are a few likely suspects. Now if this was one of them Mystery Writers of America conventions, I might be worried. Those folks are all hopped up on police procedure, but here? Not to worry. Twelve hours of legwork and a little questioning, and it'll be a wrap."

"It will be all right to go ahead with the con, won't it?" asked Miles with a worried frown. "We have a banquet tonight that can't be canceled, and we couldn't afford to give refunds."

Lt. Ayhan considered it. "I don't see why not," he said. "It'll keep everybody in one place, which will be nice from our point of view. My people will probably be finished with the death scene soon anyhow. The hotel people always want the room back post haste. Shocking, isn't it?''

"I guess so. Will you want to question everybody? They're all in the auditorium now. I could make an announcement.''

Ayhan grimaced and looked at the ceiling. "Everybody?'' he sighed. "All the Merry Men? That would take forever; waste of time. Why don't you tell me what the victim has been up to here? Any quarrels? Anybody have a grudge against him?''

Miles Perry's lips twitched. "And that's going to narrow it down?'' As quickly as he could, he described Appin Dungannon's general outrageousness, from the Yorkie bars to the breakfast croissants, hitting all the tantrums in between.

Lt. Ayhan noted it all very carefully in his little blue book. "So if annoyance is a motive, you could be in the suspect semifinals, right?''

"If you could kill by mental telepathy, I'd probably be guilty, but physically I wouldn't lift a finger toward anybody.''

Ayhan glanced up at Miles Perry's comfortable bulk. Physically he probably lifted as little as possible, the detective was thinking. "So he insulted everybody last night, in a general way? How about this kid he threw chairs at? What's his name? Morgan?''

"Oh, he wasn't angry about that,'' Miles assured him. "Clifford Morgan was thrilled to have drawn so much attention from an Eminent Pro. He'll be famous now.''

"Famous? How? He's going to sue?''

"No. I mean in fandom. People will write up stories in fan magazines describing the incident, and it will become part of fannish history. Some cons may pay Cliff's way now, just to have him on hand to tell the tale.''

Ayhan frowned. "Are there any drugs floating around this thing?''

"Of course not!'' gasped Miles, indignant. "The fen are not into drugs, except maybe the old ones, left over from the Sixties. You don't have to worry about that.''

"I wasn't worried,'' said Ayhan. "I understand drugs. Drug killings are straightforward. All this elf-and-image stuff is a real bear, though. But I've heard of it. My kid, when he was in junior high, got into a D&D group for a while. I think he was a warrior.''

Miles Perry looked interested. "Your son is a fan?''

"Nah. He was. But then he got to tenth grade, and discovered girls and j.v. football. I guess you could say he outgrew it. He's at Wake

Forest now, in pre-law. Now, did Mr. Dungannon attend the con by himself? No wife, girlfriend, agent?''

''He was alone. He is or at least *was* married. He was divorced a few years ago. She is writing a book about her life with him, and we had hoped to have her as a guest at one of our future cons.''

''Hmmm, who did he spend time with while he was here?''

Miles Perry thought about it. ''When he wasn't sort of being available—you know, for autographs and that sort of thing—he was in his room finishing his book. I guess the only people who really saw much of him were at dinner last night.''

''Ah! I'll start with them.'' He flourished his notepad. ''Their names?''

''Uh, Walter Diefenbaker—you've met him. Jay Omega, he's also a guest author. Marion Farley, she's a professor who teaches science fiction, and is also Jay's—what do they say nowadays—'significant other'—''

''S-i-g-n-i-f-i-c-a-n-t O-t-h-e-r,'' wrote Ayhan.

''—and, er, of course,'' clucked Miles guiltily, ''myself.''

''Oh?'' Ayhan raised an eyebrow, and scribbled furiously.

Miles labored to produce an innocent smile.

There was a tap on the door, and Bill Fox appeared. ''Excuse me, folks, but I thought you'd like to know that Monk Malone just announced to the whole auditorium that Dungannon is dead.''

Miles Perry gasped. ''Was there a panic? Are people leaving?''

Bill shook his head. ''They're all in the hucksters' room, cornering the market on signed copies of Dungannon's work. That's free enterprise for you.''

Bill Fox lingered at the door. ''One more thing,'' he said. ''That publisher guy who came to see Dungannon is real anxious to talk to the police. I promised I'd pass the word along.''

Lt. Ayhan shrugged. ''Somebody wants to see me? It'll make a nice change. Okay, I'll talk to him. When you see the college professor, tell him I'd like to talk to him, okay?''

With a wave of his blue notebook, the lieutenant was gone. Miles Perry frowned. Murder was so complicated . . . and incriminating. Apart from which he had forgotten to ask Ayhan what he should say to reporters should any appear. He pulled out a rumpled Rubicon program and began to scribble notes.

Louis Warren was a little embarrassed to have a police detective catch him reading the *Star Trek Officers Manual*, but it had been a tedious wait since Diefenbaker had wandered off to supervise the con activities. Thrusting the telltale volume under a sofa cushion, he sprang up to greet the officer, hand outstretched.

Lt. Ayhan responded with the cordial reserve one usually keeps for used car salesmen and unhousebroken puppies. "Do sit down, Mr. Warren. Would you show me some identification, please?"

The editor fished out his wallet and handed it over to the lieutenant, hoping that he was projecting an aura of candor and a total willingness to help the police.

"New York driver's license. You're a brave one. Health club. Very good. My wife keeps after me to join one of those. She says it's either that, or come to aerobics with her." Ayhan flipped another card, and looked up inquiringly at Warren. "Lt. Colonel in the Time Police?"

Warren reddened. "That's just a joke. The publisher sends me to a lot of cons, and at one of them, these guys were making photo I.D. cards for different things. Vulcan Science Academy Student I.D.; U.N.C.L.E. Personnel Badge. I keep it around for a joke."

"Too bad," said Ayhan with a straight face. "I was hoping you could go back to your squad room and tell me how the case was solved. Oh, well. Let's talk about Appin Dungannon."

"He was murdered, wasn't he?"

"Looks that way. Don't tell the *Enquirer* till the autopsy report comes through, though, okay? Now, what can you tell me about it?"

As he had rehearsed it during his long wait, Louis Warren explained his reason for coming to the con, but with less emphasis on his dread of meeting the author. "The door was ajar when I went in, and the printer was going. He was dead in the chair. I didn't touch him. I didn't touch anything. At least, I don't think I did. Maybe I did. Did I?"

"We'll print you," smiled Ayhan. "And I'll get back to you on that question. So you had just arrived at the hotel at approximately eleven thirty A.M.?"

"Yes. And I didn't see . . . Yes, I did. Going down the hall toward the room, I passed two Imperial Stormtroopers, and when I came out I ran into Dracula."

Lt. Ayhan sighed. "I love this case."

The windows in the Patrick Henry Nook were shrouded in mourning, and the chandelier overhead was on *dim*. It seemed appropriate. At least two of the four people convened to cope with the death of Appin Dungannon were torn between grief and panic. After all, the con must go on, but what ought to be the proper atmosphere? Miles

Perry spread out his grubby Rubicon program on the coffee table in front of Marion, Jay, and Walter Diefenbaker. "The police say it's okay to continue the con—"

Jay Omega stood up. "The Lieutenant seems very bright. I have no doubt he will solve the crime before the weekend is up. Now, if you have no further need of me, I've been meaning to stop by the computer room . . ."

Miles Perry looked stricken. "You're leaving?—Oh, please don't! The rest of the committee is all over the place trying to keep things under control, and I don't want to make all the decisions by myself."

"It would be very kind of you to stay," said Diefenbaker. "If we wouldn't be imposing on you too much."

Jay looked at Marion and shrugged. "I don't mind, if you really think we'd be of any use to you. I don't know anything about cons, though."

"He chaired the Engineering Health and Safety Conference last year, though," Marion offered.

"Splendid!" cried Dief. "I know you'll be ever so sensible and organized."

Jay Omega sighed and sat down. "I'll see what I can do. You say the police have given you permission to continue the conference?"

"What about the hotel people?" asked Marion.

"Yes. I spoke to them first," said Miles. "They're all for business as usual. The less disruption there is involved, the better they can weather the publicity. They don't want the word *murder* spread around too much, by the way."

Diefenbaker nodded. "So we carry on, with certain modifications?"

"Right. I think the banquet ought to be in Appin Dungannon's honor. We could get somebody to do a tribute to him." He looked hopefully at Jay Omega.

" 'I come to bury Caesar, not praise him,' " murmured Marion.

Jay Omega divided his sour look between her and Miles Perry. "Look," he said, "I'm very sorry that Dungannon is dead, but I didn't know the man, and didn't particularly like what I saw. And besides that, I never read any of his books."

"You know who would be the logical person to eulogize him?" said Diefenbaker helpfully. "Harlan Ellison!"

Miles Perry looked at him as if he had lost his mind. "We can't afford Harlan Ellison."

"Oh," said Dief, deflated. Then he said, "What about Clifford

Morgan? The greatest Dungannon fan of all? Who's read everything three times? Who lives it, for God's sake!''

Marion blinked. ''Tratyn Runewind?''

Dief nodded. ''He lives and breathes Dungannon. If he's not too devastated by the series ending to do it, he'd be perfect!''

''But Appin Dungannon hated Clifford Morgan!'' said Jay Omega. ''He threw folding chairs at him!''

Marion nodded. ''It doesn't seem like a very respectful tribute. I'd be afraid he'd haunt us!''

Miles Perry had thought it over. ''Well...'' he said at last. ''I think Dr. Omega would be a more distinguished speaker, but if he won't do it, we'll just have to do the best we can.'' He sighed. ''If you can get Morgan to do it, Walter, I have no objection.''

''I think Morgan will be sincere,'' said Dief. ''I'll impress upon him that it's a solemn occasion. Imitation is supposed to be the sincerest form of flattery, so Cliff should be the most genuine mourner there.—Well, that's settled. What else needs to be changed?''

''Dungannon's last appearance. On Sunday morning he had agreed to act as Dungeon Master for an exhibition game featuring Tratyn Runewind.''

''He was going to let somebody play Tratyn Runewind?'' gasped Marion.

''No. Runewind will be a non-player character controlled by the DM. The participants just get to accompany him on an adventure.'' Miles looked again at Jay Omega.

''I'm already signed up to play,'' said Diefenbaker.

Miles Perry sighed. ''I have to see that the art auction gets set up. I'll have to be in and out.''

Marion turned to Jay Omega. ''It isn't very difficult,'' she said coaxingly. ''I can show you all the basic things. Look at it as a chance to play God.''

Jay Omega glowered at the three pleading faces before him. ''Oh, all right. But don't blame me if I make a mess of it.''

Louis Warren appeared at the door, looking as if he were in pursuit of the Holy Grail. He was followed by Lt. Ayhan, who looked considerably pained.

''Does anyone know anything about computers?'' Louis asked feverishly.

With a straight face, Jay Omega raised his hand.

''He's designed a few,'' said Marion.

''Oh. I need someone to help me with a discus.''

''A disk!'' said Miles, Dief, and Jay Omega in unison.

"Whatever. I've explained to the lieutenant that my company absolutely has to have that manuscript now . . ."

His voice was suddenly shrill.

". . . or we will sue Dungannon's estate for return of the advance." Noticing Ayhan's raised eyebrows, Louis added defensively, "We *do* have a deadline to meet."

"Must be a pretty valuable manuscript," mused Ayhan.

"The manuscript is worth very little without the contract," said Louis wearily, as if explaining the concept of electricity to a child. "The ex-wife, the distant relatives, the mysterious fellow in a jeep in the desert who may have picked him up hitchhiking . . . Lieutenant, they have nothing, nothing to gain. Dungannon left all of his money and rights to the Scottish Archaeological Society. Everybody knows that."

"Now," said Ayhan, "we're getting somewhere." He patiently logged another suspect on his notepad. "And who are they—or it?" he asked, not really expecting a comprehensible reply.

"Scottish history-diggers," said Louis indifferently. "Big on excavation work. Dungannon was very keen on Celtic history. No doubt they'll be pleased to receive this windfall a few years ahead of schedule—"

"Hmmm," said Ayhan, in his best speculative manner.

"—Besides," continued Louis, "Dungannon always said he liked dead people better than live ones."

"He should be ecstatic now, then," Lt. Ayhan remarked.

"So they're going to let you take the manuscript?" asked Marion.

"No way," said Ayhan.

"No," the editor admitted. "Everything in that room is evidence in the case. In case of fingerprints, or whatever."

"Policy," said Ayhan calmly.

"But I've persuaded him to let me make a copy of the disk on which the book is written."

"Correction," said Ayhan. "Under my supervision, you can get a reputable person to make a copy of the disk, provided that you obtain the second disk from a source other than the room containing the deceased."

"So all you want is for somebody to make a backup copy of a floppy disk?" said Jay Omega.

The editor nodded. "Can you do that?"

"I could do that," said Marion.

Lt. Ayhan smiled at her. "It's a handsome offer, ma'am, but we'll let the professor do it, since he has the Ph.D. and all."

Jay Omega smiled wickedly at Dr. Marion Farley. "Yes, Marion, better leave it to me, since I have the Ph.D."

"Later," said Marion between clenched teeth.

"What do you need to do this?" asked Ayhan.

Jay Omega turned to Diefenbaker. "Go to the high-tech room and ask Joel Schumann to bring me a couple of blank disks and the *Diskcopy* program." He turned to Lt. Ayhan. "Dungannon's machine is PC-compatible, isn't it?"

The detective shrugged. "For all I know, it could run on kryptonite."

Dungannon's body had been removed, but several uniformed officers were still in the room examining the deceased's personal effects and taking photographs.

Jay Omega could see no sign of a struggle, and no traces of blood in the bland modern cubicle. Dungannon's suitcase lay open on the chair, and his computer and printer occupied most of the desk space. Omega was relieved to see that it was a Sanyo portable, about 90% IBM compatible. He was afraid that Dungannon might have used some sort of mini-machine that took microdiskettes; they'd have needed a scavenger hunt to round some of those up. He was glad the regular floppies from the high-tech room would work.

"Good afternoon, gentlemen," said Lt. Ayhan to his troops. "Have we solved the case yet?"

One of the officers shook his head. "Give us a few more minutes," he grinned.

"I came back to do my good deed for the day," the lieutenant announced. "These fellows want to make a copy of the disk that Mr. Dungannon's book is on. And I said that under my careful supervision, they may do so. Have you dusted it for prints yet?"

Jay Omega winced at this suggestion.

The uniformed cop favored Ayhan with a pitying smile. "Lucky for them we didn't, Lieutenant. Rafferty tried it on a larceny case a couple of months ago, and it wrecked the disk."

"It wouldn't do the computer any good, either," Jay Omega observed. "Those little grains of powder would scratch both the disk and the reader head."

Ayhan eased himself down on the edge of the bed. "Do any of you whiz kids have any bright ideas?"

"Sure," said his grinning subordinate. "We're going to do just what they want to do. Make a copy, and then dust the original."

"It'll be an exact copy?" asked Ayhan.

"Yes," said Jay Omega. "It'll copy all forty tracks on both sides."

"The fingerprints, too?" asked Ayhan.

Jay Omega took a deep breath, and prepared to launch into a disk lecture.

"He's putting you on," said the uniformed cop. "Here's the disk. Have you got a blank one?"

Jay Omega looked up just as Joel Schumann arrived at the open door. "I brought the disks, Dr. Mega!" he called out.

"Here they are now," said Omega.

The photographer waved Joel through.

Joel and the uniformed cop grinned at the solemnity with which Jay Omega sat down to carry out this simple computer task. He inserted the DOS disk in drive A, and reached for Dungannon's master disk, but Ayhan, holding one corner with a handkerchief, signaled that he would do it himself. Finally the computer was ready to copy: master disk in A; blank disk in B.

"You brought an extra disk?" asked Ayhan.

Joel handed him one.

"Good. Consider this our fee for the favor. Another copy, please."

Two minutes and a series of clicks later, Jay Omega handed the copies to Ayhan and Louis Warren. He pointed to drive A. "You can take it out now," he told the young policeman. "Just make sure nobody tries to put it back in a computer after that."

Louis Warren held his disk gingerly between thumb and forefinger. "How do I get this on paper to give to an editor?" he asked.

Joel Schumann shrugged. "The high-tech room's IBM doesn't have a printer. You can read it on a screen there, though."

"Read it!?" Louis drew back in horror.

"You know, check to make sure it's all there—" said Joel soothingly.

"Oh," said Louis, still dubious. Joel smiled at the editor's expression of distaste and suspicion; he'd often seen that reaction in people over thirty being confronted with new technology. "Come on," he said, leading Louis away. "I'll set it up for you."

Ayhan handed his copy of the disk to the young officer. "Anything else interesting?"

Jay Omega smiled at the note of triumph in the young guy's voice.

"We found this in the wastebasket, sir."

The Lieutenant unrolled the crumpled piece of paper and studied the elegant, black calligraphy of the message:

APPIN DUNGANNON:
  You are a tiny, insufferable primadonna, and a blight on the face of fandom. You are a vain, embittered old hack who ought to give

*up public appearances and spend the time going to charm school . . .
or reading Anne McCaffrey. Either would improve you immeasura-
bly. If you cannot bring some measure of joy and inspiration to the
world you touch, then you ought to die and let the sparrows have
your share of the oxygen.*

After reading it twice, Ayhan glanced at the officer. "Dusted?"
An affirmative nod. The lieutenant passed the paper to Jay Omega.
"What do you think?"

Omega ran his finger over the page, squinted at the calligraphy,
and finally said "Macintosh."

The younger cop nodded. "That's what I thought."

Ayhan whipped out his blue notebook. "Macintosh? Description?
What's his first name?"

Jay Omega shrugged. "Apple?"

"London Font," said the young cop.

"I make it eighteen point."

Ayhan stopped writing. "Somebody's babbling," he announced.
"Have you called in a handwriting expert?"

Jay Omega handed him back the note. "You don't need a handwriting expert," he explained gently. "This is a computer-generated
document. We think it was done on a Macintosh in calligraphy
script."

"So how do we find out who wrote it? Do we know who owns
one of these things?"

"Well," said Jay Omega. "There's a Macintosh with a printer in
the high-tech display room downstairs. My guess is that it was done
there. If so, maybe Joel could tell you who used it."

"The kid that just left?" Ayhan motioned to the young cop. "Go
talk to him, Simmons. Since you speak the language."

"I guess you got your first real clue," said Jay Omega, trying to
be soothing.

"Yeah," growled Ayhan. "And the suspect is a fifty-pound hunk
of plastic named Macintosh. I love this case."

CHAPTER 12

THE RUBICON BANQUET and Costume Ball began promptly at seven in the main ballroom of the hotel, which had been decorated for the occasion with streamers and SF movie posters. The speakers' table was set beneath a vintage *Thief of Bagdad* poster, and sported centerpieces of yellow candles and blue Tribbles, arranged in small clumps around handfuls of grain. The second chair to the left of the podium was conspicuously empty.

At the long banquet tables perpendicular to the main one, an assortment of medieval dignitaries and extraterrestrials sipped grapefruit punch (listed on the menu as Pangalactic Gargleblaster), and exchanged the latest rumors about the murder of Appin Dungannon. Since Lt. Ayhan had spent a long and tedious afternoon interviewing a cross-section of Rubicon participants, many of them had a good idea how the investigation was going, and what matters were likely to interest the police.

"Did you mention the costume contest?"

"Of course! If you didn't, they'd think you were suspicious! But did you tell them how he ruined Douglas's books with a Tolkien signature?"

"I hear Douglas told them he was glad someone had iced Dungannon, when they questioned him."

"Did they ask you about a note?"

"Yeah. And a lot of funny computer questions, too."

"Did somebody steal Dungannon's computer?"

"I heard he threw it at the murderer. Is this punch alcoholic?"

At the elevated speakers' table, above rabble and rumors and to the right of Miles Perry and the empty chair, sat Marion, sandwiched between Jay Omega and Walter Diefenbaker. The other side of the podium was reserved for the guest artist, three Rubicon board members, and the chief mourner: Clifford Morgan, a.k.a. Tratyn Runewind. Of the honored guests only a woman board member and Morgan/Runewind had appeared in costume. Dief wore his Canadian formal attire, a brown turtleneck and tweed blazer with maple-leaf lapel pin; the other men wore suits and ties. Marion had decided to be an elegant Mrs. Peel in green watered silk and pearls, but she kept the Sixties hairstyle as a tribute to her heroine.

"What is that music?" she whispered to Diefenbaker.

"Schubert. 'Death and the Maiden.' We were going to use *Star Wars* soundtrack albums, but Miles thought that this would be more fitting under the circumstances."

"Better than 'Happy Days Are Here Again,' " Marion conceded. "I'm sure somebody suggested that."

Jay Omega sipped his Gargleblaster. "I don't have to say anything formal, do I?" he asked Miles Perry.

"Not a speech," Miles promised. "But I'll introduce you later, and you can stand up."

Jay nodded toward the audience. "Are you going to introduce him, too?"

"Who?"

"Lt. Ayhan. He's sitting at that table on the left."

After an invocation by a board member directed to the Entity Who Engineered the Universe, a visibly moved Miles Perry took the podium. "Tonight is a more solemn occasion than we had meant it to be," he stammered, trying not to stare in Lt. Ayhan's direction. "At this year's Rubicon we wanted to honor one of the giants of fantasy literature—"

Several people in the audience snickered.

"A writer whose stature—"

Miles Perry reddened and pawed at his notes. "Unfortunately, Appin Dungannon is not able to be with us tonight . . ."

"Unfortunately?" called a heckler.

People began to chant "The Monkey's Paw!"

Against his better judgment, Miles glanced at Lt. Ayhan. Blast the man! He was smiling again! "Our program designed to honor Appin Dungannon, creator of the Tratyn Runewind series, has instead become a tribute to his memory. We ask that amid the festivities you keep within you a solemn remembrance of Appin Dungannon . . . a shining star in the annals of fantasy!"

Someone kicked over a folding chair.

Further speeches were not scheduled until after dinner, by which time Miles hoped that the hilarity would have worn itself out. He ate his tepid chicken with a grim expression suggesting that he could hear it pleading for mercy. For once he hoped there weren't any journalists present; the mood of facetiousness thus far exhibited at the banquet would show them in a very bad light if reported in cold newsprint.

Lt. Ayhan had decided that as long as he had to do some questioning at the con, he might as well observe things at the banquet—when all the cracked eggs were in one basket. He was seated now across from a desperately plain young man in a brown polyester leisure suit, and a courting couple who reminded him of Kermit the Frog and Miss Piggy. He had planned to say that he liked a good science fiction novel now and then, if anyone had asked why he was there, but so far no one had taken any notice of him at all. The people he had questioned were seated at other tables. Ayhan decided that he would just listen to the general discussions, and if that proved unhelpful, he might try a few conversational gambits of his own.

"Pass the salt," said the leisure suit, whose name tag identified him as J. Bonnenberger.

Ayhan handed him the salt shaker, but before he could venture a get-acquainted remark, Bonnenberger turned to the "Kermit" kid with the turtleneck and medallion. "So who do you think killed McAfee?"

Ayhan's fork froze in midair. Who was McAfee?

"Terrorists, I guess," shrugged Richard Faber. "My organization doesn't have any plastic explosives. We can't afford them yet."

"I think he was a double agent, anyway, so it's probably none of my business who killed him. Unless he still had the microchip on him, of course. We want that."

Ayhan's hand itched for his blue notebook. He might have to call in the NSA on this one.

"So, if he was a double agent, Bonnenberger, who do you think he was working for?" asked Faber.

"Probably the KGB. And if that was the case, then the hit was only made to *look* like a terrorist attack, to divert suspicion from the real power-brokers." Bonnenberger's last remark was somewhat garbled by the mouthful of lettuce impairing his consonant-formation. Dribbles of salad ran down each side of his mouth like a thousand-island Fu Manchu.

"Okay," nodded Faber, unaffected by his comrade's table manners. "So you think it was the Girl Scouts."

"Definitely," Bonnenberger managed to say.

"Okay. Then it was probably O. O. Wolfe. He'd have access to explosives at Fort Belvoir, and he has a high skill rating in demolitions. The Girl Scouts have nuclear capability now, too. Did you know that?''

"What are you talking about?'' demanded Lt. Ayhan, who felt that he would explode if he didn't ask.

His table partners looked at him with faint surprise at such rude inquisitiveness from a stranger. The fat girl, eager to show off her limited supply of knowledge, explained. "They're in a TSR game called Top Secret. It's sort of like D&D, but it deals with spies and secret organizations. You get characters to control, and your organization assigns you a mission. . . ."

Lt. Ayhan stopped listening, and went back to his chicken. He supposed he ought to see if Miles Perry could help him find one of the con guests who had been mentioned as a vehement critic of Dungannon. Some kid named Chip Livingstone. Truly elusive. Half a dozen people had showed him mimeographed newsletters containing criticisms of Dungannon, all signed *Chip Livingstone*. But he couldn't get a decent make on the guy. White male, early twenties—that was ninety percent of the con. And the guy wasn't on the hotel register, either. Hmmm. Also true of half the people at the con. Everybody seemed to be sleeping on couches, or six to a room. If Ayhan wasn't in Homicide, he could have a field day writing up misdemeanors. But he had put the word out to find Chip Livingstone and sooner or later he would turn up.

So far, though, zilch. Probably afraid to. Half the people Ayhan had talked to had mentioned this guy as an enemy of Dungannon. Maybe that was a bit obvious for a murder suspect, but in Ayhan's opinion, most murderers were obvious. And if the guy was innocent, where was he? Pulling out his notebook, he scribbled a note to Miles Perry, finishing it just as the waiter appeared to refill his iced tea.

"Could you give this to the gentleman sitting next to the speaker's stand?'' he asked the waiter.

Faber and Bonnenberger glowered suspiciously as the white-coated waiter glided away with the note. Suppose the old guy with the crew cut was an agent for the Girl Scouts? You couldn't trust anybody these days.

When Miles Perry unfolded the note from Ayhan, he lost all interest in his second piece of pecan pie. Two minutes from now he was due at the podium again to introduce Clifford Morgan for the memorial speech. He wondered if he ought to make an announcement first. Probably so. Gumming up a murder investigation could probably put you in prison right along with the murderer. With a sigh and the certain knowledge that the Force was not with him, Miles Perry stood up and faced the mob.

"Fellow fen . . ." He looked again at the note. On second thought, why not wait until after the eulogy? He didn't want to upstage Morgan's big moment, and besides, he needed time to figure out what to say. Should he warn anyone? "As you know, our guest speaker tonight was to have been Appin Dungannon, so it is only fitting under the circumstances that we offer instead a tribute to that gifted writer by one of his greatest fans. If imitation is the sincerest form of flattery, then Clifford Morgan's admiration of Dungannon knows no bounds. In the persona of Tratyn Runewind, ladies and gentlemen, I give you Clifford Morgan."

With a swirl of his blue satin cloak (for formal occasions), the white-maned Tratyn Runewind bowed to Miles Perry, and fixed the audience with a solemn stare. "Men say there shall be no more sagas," he intoned in a booming voice suggesting John Wayne's portrayal of Genghis Khan. "But as the pen is mightier than the sword, so is the legend hardier than the scop. Appin Dungannon has died, but Tratyn Runewind is a child of the gods, and he will live forever. . . ."

"This is an odd tribute," whispered Jay to Marion. "What's he getting at?"

"Oh, just the usual bit about the writer gaining immortality through his works. Shakespeare said it much better. These people could really use a copy of *Bartlett's Quotations*. I think it really means that he doesn't want to stop dressing up as Tratyn Runewind."

Jay nodded. "The author's death must have really hit him hard. Sort of a vicarious death. No more Runewind adventures."

"Don't bet on it," said Marion. "*Star Trek* ended twenty years ago, and fans are still writing new adventures for the crew of the *Enterprise*."

Clifford Morgan, with his blond hair bleached bone-white and his aquiline features, sounded less ridiculous talking "Hollywood Beowulf" than one might expect. Unlike most fen, who attended each year's con in a different costume, Morgan was always Tratyn Runewind; indeed, few people would have recognized him in nonmedieval garb. His knowledge of his alter-ego's adventures was encyclopedic, and rumor had it that during cons he was so much in character that he slept on the floor of his hotel room and ate only bread and meat, as vegetables were not part of the Celtic winter diet. Even his normal Pennsylvania accent disappeared during a con, to be replaced by his impression of Celtic speech: a cross between Richard Burton's *Hamlet* and the poetry of Robert Burns. All of this had become so familiar to the fen, and so habitual to Morgan, that it scarcely seemed artificial anymore. Occasionally, back in the "real world," Morgan would push his maintenance cart around the hotel he worked for in Philadelphia, and mutter to himself in "Runewind," causing guests to think he was an immigrant.

He had begun his alternate identity as a skinny and backward twelve-year-old, when he first discovered the *Runewind* books. His identification with the white-maned rune warrior was strengthened in scores of D&D games, in which his fellow players allowed him to *be* Runewind. Now, ten years later, he could almost be said to commute between ancient Britain and twentieth-century America, so much of his life was invested in both places.

In some ways, he looked on Appin Dungannon as a parent: irascible, neglectful, and inadequate, perhaps, but a father-figure, nonetheless. He scanned the biographical notes he had brought with him as an aid to memory, although he scarcely needed them. Dungannon's life was as familiar to him as Runewind's.

After a few more heroics, Clifford Morgan's speech degenerated into a biography of Dungannon, gleaned from funzines and a writers' *Who's Who*. With monotonous precision, he detailed Dungannon's education, early jobs, first publications, and so on through the Runewind books, the lawsuits, the stay at the alcohol treatment center, and the unsuccessful award nominations. The audience grew restive.

"And as a final tribute to Appin Dungannon, we have an unscheduled performance," Morgan announced. Ignoring Miles Perry's look of stricken disbelief, Tratyn Runewind continued. "As you know, the author disliked representations of his hero—"

"As *you* know!" someone yelled out.

"But since the legend has outlived its maker, we will assume that Mr. Dungannon's objections have been laid to rest with him, and so we will present a short drama by the Rubicon players, entitled 'Tratyn Runewind and the Druid Priestess.' "

Miles looked across the table at the other board members and pantomimed the washing of his hands. They shrugged in reply.

In the space between the audience and the speakers' table, Clifford and several other costumed players assembled for a whispered conference. Finally a thirtyish man in Robin Hood garb came to the podium to act as narrator.

Marion recognized him as the weapons vendor from the hucksters' room.

In ringing tones the narrator described the encounter between the

Celtic hero and a Druid priestess, who, judging from her wig and costume, had spent her winters in Egypt. After a ritual dance by the priestess, and some divination by way of a magic goblet filled with water from Annis' Well, a barbarian in leather and fake fur appeared, brandished a sword at the hero, and the inevitable combat scene took place in pantomime.

Jay Omega watched the performance with a thoughtful attentiveness, just as he would watch the lab's oscilloscope to detect an electrical problem.

"He's not planning to have Tratyn Runewind die, too, is he?" he asked.

"Not a chance," Marion retorted. "He'd rather shoot his mother."

After a few minutes' clattering and slashing with the reproduction (but genuine metal) swords, the barbarian gave way to the superior strength of the Rune warrior, and allowed himself to be symbolically skewered as the drama ended. He stayed dead until Runewind and the Priestess had received the initial applause, and then he and the narrator joined them to take their bows.

Miles Perry, realizing that it could have been worse, joined in the applause for the actors, and quickly turned the program over to another board member for the announcement of the scholarship winners, and for the recognition of last night's winners in the writing contest and the costume competition.

Several certificates later, he was back at the podium for the final summation, and last-minute announcements of schedule changes. "The Tratyn Runewind D&D Adventure will take place tomorrow morning as scheduled," he told the crowd. "And the DM will be none other than Rubicon's remaining guest author Jay Omega!" Jay Omega stood up for a millisecond, and Miles Perry continued, "At ten tonight, in the hotel's William Byrd Conference room, there will be a *Star Trek* wedding—this is a real wedding, folks—uniting in marriage Dave Phillips and Pamela Jarrod, as Mr. Spock and Saavik. Guests of Rubicon, particularly those in *Star Trek* costumes, are invited to attend."

Miles Perry looked nervous again. "There is one last announcement I have to make before we declare the banquet officially over. As you know, the police are investigating Appin Dungannon's death, and of course, we are all anxious to help in any way we can."

He saw that he had Lt. Ayhan's undivided attention.

"The Lieutenant in charge of the investigation has made it known to me that in his questioning of people about those with grudges against Appin Dungannon, one name is mentioned again and again.

This person has written savage book reviews of the Runewind series in a number of fanzines, and in personal letters he has indicated an antipathy toward Dungannon personally, and in general he has been the most vocal critic both of the author and his work. And the Lieutenant would like to interview this individual. So . . . I thought . . . rather than mislead anybody anymore . . ."

"My god!" muttered Diefenbaker. "He's going to do it!"

"Do what?" whispered Marion.

"Will the real Chip Livingstone please stand up?"

CHAPTER 13

THANKS TO THE unscheduled murder of Appin Dungannon, Rubicon had earned its place in fannish history long before the banquet degenerated into a shouting match between rival fanzine publishers over the heretofore unexplained identity of the mysterious, fiendish Chip Livingstone, and before one desperately sincere femme fan burst into tears and subsequently severed all contact with the hobby.

Lt. Ayhan, who had simply muttered, "I love this case!" was probably the calmest person present.

The chaos had begun approximately thirty seconds after Miles Perry had asked superfan Chip Livingstone to stand and identify himself. After a moment of ionized silence, Bill Fox pushed back his chair and stood up. So did Diefenbaker. Miles Perry, who was already standing, raised his hand to indicate that he too was "standing." A wargamer from Minnesota and a Texas fanzine publisher also got to their feet.

Miles Perry explained. "Chip Livingstone has been in the hobby for only two years now, and already he has made himself prominent among the fen. He is a prolific letter-writer—of computer-generated letters—and a regular contributor to a number of fanzines. He doesn't take phone calls, but he always answers letters. And from time to time people report having met him or seen him at a con. Usually Dief, or Bill, or I will claim to have seen him at a war-gamers' convention, or in a private visit."

"I broke up with my boyfriend over him!" wailed the femme fan.

Miles Perry hesitated. "Well, he did write good letters. What happened is that the five of us created him, and we took turns writing his articles and answering his mail."

"Hold it!" yelled Richard Faber. "He was in the god-damned costume competition. I saw him!"

"Yeah! Me, too!" mumbled several wargamers.

"That was Bill," Miles Perry told them. "Remember, 'Chip' was dressed as an Imperial Stormtrooper, with full body covering and a mask you couldn't see through. You couldn't tell who it was."

"And remember," said Bill, "his character was called Sanyo the

Stormtrooper, which was a tip-off. More than anything else, Chip
Livingstone is a product of a Sanyo MBC-775, because all five of us
own one. Think about the name! *Chip Living-Stone*.''

"First a Macintosh and now a Sanyo," muttered Ayhan. "I love
this case!''

"Anyway," said Miles Perry, "I thought we'd better explain that
Chip Livingstone's hatred of Dungannon was just a personality trait
that we invented to give him a quirk. All of us are war-gamers, so
we didn't care one way or the other.''

He had to raise his voice to compete with the angry mutterings of
the crowd. Bernard Buchanan kept saying, "But he liked my writing.
He liked my writing.''

"I tell you this now, because the belief in Chip Livingstone was
impeding the police investigation of Dungannon's murder. Now that
you know he doesn't exist, please think harder for anyone you might
know who had a reason to want to kill Appin Dungannon, and please
give the police any help that you can. That's all I have to say. Good
night.''

No one moved. Ayhan looked skeptical. The rumblings grew
louder.

Finally, above the wrangling, Bernard Buchanan's voice rang out,
"Fellow fen! In the video lounge in ten minutes! There will be a
memorial service to honor the memory of our lost friend—Chip Livingstone!''

"All right!" someone yelled. "To the video lounge.''

Scattered applause grew into a standing ovation, and the bereaved
and indignant Bernard Buchanan marched off toward the TV room
with a trail of bewildered mourners in his wake.

Despite the bouquet of plastic flowers on the table at the front, the
William Byrd Conference room looked not much like a chapel, and
nothing at all like the bridge of the *Enterprise*, where the wedding
was supposed to be taking place. The imitation wood paneling and
short green drapes were more conducive to a discussion of tax shel-
ters than to a marriage ceremony.

"In the midst of death we are in life," murmured Jay Omega, who
thought it was time he said something profound.

"Don't you start!" hissed Marion. "You've done quite enough
already. Besides, I was counting on you to remain sane.''

"How can I be sane? I think we've fallen down the rabbit hole!''
He nodded toward the lectern at the front of the William Byrd conference room, where an embarrassed-looking gentleman in the red

dress uniform of a Star Fleet officer stood holding a white leather Bible. Ushers who were evidently members of the *Enterprise* engineering crew were escorting fellow shipmates and other costumed guests to the folding chairs on either side of the red-carpeted aisle.

"Romulan or Vulcan?" the ushers asked each guest.

Marion, who had been poised to say "friends of the bride," had responded to the question with an open-mouthed stare, and Jay Omega answered, "Klingon!" which got them seats in the back row of the Romulan side.

"Do you suppose their parents are here?" asked Marion.

"Why not?" asked Jay Omega. "*Your* mother once remarked that if you'd get married again, she'd be so grateful she'd come to the ceremony, even if she had to sky dive out of the Concorde."

"She didn't say anything of the kind!"

"Well, she probably *thinks* it."

Marion made a face. "Going to make an honest woman of me, then?"

"You mean stick one of those worms in your ear, like in *The Wrath of Khan*, so you'd tell the truth?"

Marion told him to stick it in his ear, and further discussion was precluded by the sound of "Amazing Grace" played on a bagpipe. The audience turned to stare at Donnie McRory, stuffed into a homemade kilt two sizes too small, marching slowly up the aisle holding— but not playing—the bagpipe.

"Pipe her up, Scotty!" someone called out.

The music, which when one listened carefully, was actually several bagpipes, plus a few drums (the entire Strathclyde Police Pipe Band, to be exact), was coming from a cassette tape recorder on a chair by the window. Donnie McRory, who owned neither kilt nor bagpipe, was authentically Scottish, as *Star Trek*'s James Doohan was not, but as a stereotype he was remarkably disappointing. Only his Glasgow accent tallied with American expectations of the "typical" Scot.

"How do I get meself into these situations?" McRory was asking himself as he marched down the aisle. "Is it the American beer, or what?"

Having given the matter some thought, McRory decided that he got into these situations because there wasn't much else to do when you're by yourself on a tour, and also because people kept *asking* outrageous things of him. Being a reserved Briton, McRory was psychologically unprepared for the American audacity of imposing on people. He was usually so taken aback at the pushiness of their requests that he found himself complying rather than compound the embarrassment by refusing.

As the tape recorder launched into "Scotland the Brave," the bridegroom, in his blue science officer's uniform, came and stood by the lectern, accompanied by a heavyset, blond "Chekov." He gave the four-fingered Vulcan peace sign to the audience, and smiled.

"What do you think of getting married in costume?" asked Jay Omega.

Marion shrugged. "What do you call spending eight hundred dollars for a white satin gown you'll only wear once? —Was that question academic, by the way?"

"Absolutely," Jay assured her.

They turned around to watch as bridesmaids representing Nurse Chappell and Lt. Rand inched up the aisle in their black boots and the sexist Sixties costumes that passed for the "women's wear" of the twenty-third century. In their hands they carried small black gadgets decorated with white satin ribbons and baby's breath.

"Isn't that sweet?" said Marion. "They're carrying Tri-Corders."

Jay Omega leaned over for a closer look. "Tri-Corders, hell!" he muttered. "Those things are stud-finders."

"Ooh! Where can you buy one?"

"No, Trashmind! I mean a device for locating wooden beams inside the walls. Carpenters use them."

"Oh. Too bad, because it sounded—"

"Shh! Here comes the bride!"

In deference to her well-padded thighs, Pamela Jarrod wore a knee-length modification of Saavik's mini-skirted uniform, and very high boots. Her dark brown hair, augmented by a fake chignon, was swept up in accordance with regulation Star Fleet dress codes, revealing a very convincing pair of pointed ears. She carried a metal sculpture bouquet of aluminum flowers.

The reverend "Captain Kirk" extracted a typed notecard from his Bible, and summoned up a wan smile. "Dearly beloved," he said to the assembled company, "we are here to launch a life voyage of this *Enterprise* couple, David and Pamela, whose lifetime mission is to seek out strange new worlds—"

Jay Omega clutched Marion's hand, looking as if he were going to choke.

"What is it?" she whispered anxiously.

He managed to hiss back, "Is the groom going to go where no man has gone before?"

For the rest of the wedding, they had to pretend they were crying.

*   *   *

Donnie McRory was relieved to discover that the blue Romulan ale served at the wedding reception was in fact draft Moosehead with food coloring. The general good will of the festivities had mellowed him to the point of actually volunteering to play for the reception, but the happy Trekkies explained that he would only be needed to appear in the wedding photographs, and that they would be quite happy with their tape-recorded soundtracks from the *Star Trek* movies.

He decided that he would make a really late night of it, and then call Margaret in Glasgow just about the time she'd be getting up. She wouldn't believe a word of it, of course, but the newlyweds had promised to send him prints of the pictures. Nice lot these sky-fi people were, he thought. Odd how interested they were in Scotland. Just before the wedding, a funny old gent with a gray crew-cut had come up to him in the hall, asking if he were a member of the Scottish Archaeological Society. Fancy that. Not wanting to disappoint a culture-minded Yank, Donnie had claimed a deep personal interest in the organization. After all, he had sent them a donation of two pounds when the Lewis chessmen went on exhibit in Edinburgh, and he'd been on their mailing list ever since. The old gent seemed excited no end by Donnie's knowledge of the Scottish archaeologists; took notes about everything in a little blue book; said he'd like to drop by in the morning and talk about it.

Donnie McRory sipped his beer, wondering why Mr. Ayhan had asked so many questions about the archaeologists' fund-raising efforts. He shrugged. Probably just another potty American. They were always on about something.

Marion didn't know whether it was the bilious blue color of the "Romulan ale" or the almost palpable reek of body odor emanating from the guest in the brown leisure suit, but she was ready to call it a night. She looked around at the clumps of Trekkies and Middle Earthlings nibbling Kroger-Deli carrot cake and cheese puffs, and decided that it was all unutterably sad. She supposed that the bride and groom would go home to a one-bedroom apartment filled with tatty paperbacks, stacks of back issues of *F & SF*, and furniture from their parents' garages. The bride had happily confided that she had just graduated with a degree in history, and that she had already landed a job at Burger King which would see them through the groom's two more years as a computer science major. Marion hoped that one of the elves around the beer tap could grant wishes: this couple was going to need a gross of them.

"Are you ready to go yet?" she asked Jay Omega. "Don't forget that you have to figure out how to run a dungeon between now and tomorrow morning."

He nodded. "I guess so. The first thing I need to know is where this game is supposed to take place. Nobody mentioned that."

"You're going to feel right at home," grinned Marion. "It's scheduled for the high-tech room. I think the hotel needed a couple of the other conference rooms for other groups, and since you won't have more than fifteen people there shouldn't be any problem . . ."

"Computer room?" Jay evinced enthusiasm. "I think I'll drop down and check things out. I didn't see that editor around tonight, did you? I wonder how he's getting along with the disk . . ."

"Who cares? Joel's helping him anyway, isn't he?"

"That's right," said Jay distractedly. "Joel . . . I think I'll just see how they're doing. Do you want to come?"

Marion shook her head. "I'll be up in the room, studying the scenario they gave you. Don't be too long!" She kissed him on the cheek. "You know how jealous I am of computers."

"I know. I think it's a glitch in your programming."

By now it was nearly midnight, and most of the con participants had dispersed to private parties in the guests' rooms. Lt. Ayhan had called it a night shortly after eleven, deciding to wait for the ballistics report and the results of other inquiries before continuing his investigation in the morning. In the video lounge Bonnenberger and two other Top Secret players were planning a surprise attack on that dreaded terrorist organization, The Omaha Rotary Club, while on the television screen *Superman II* played to an audience of empty couches. Somewhere on the sixth floor, Richard Faber lay on his back, panting, and reflecting on the fact that he was no longer eligible to capture unicorns; that he had lost all hope of performing miracles as Lancelot once could; and that he was now Unfit for Minotaur Consumption. Virginity did have its mystic qualities, but he thought, as he reached for Brenda Lindenfeld, experience was handier on a day-to-day basis.

Jay Omega reached the door of the high-tech exhibit room before it occurred to him that it was nearly midnight on a Saturday, and that any con personnel in their right minds would keep the place locked. He was sure that the equipment was all on loan from various electronics firms.

He had been wondering how to go about finding Joel Schumann, and whether he should even bother, when he noticed a line of light under the closed door of the room. Trying the door knob, he found it was unlocked after all.

Joel Schumann was asleep all right, but not in his room. He was curled up in a swivel chair using his windbreaker for a pillow, while at the computer table Louis Warren peered into the TV monitor, flicking up another screenful of green letters.

Jay Omega tiptoed up to Warren's chair. "Is that Appin Dungannon's book you're reading?" he whispered.

"Yes," the editor whispered back. "I just wanted to make sure that the manuscript's all there, and in some kind of publishable form, because when I get back to New York, my bosses will ask me that as soon as I walk in. I'll be finished soon. I didn't know how to turn this stuff off, so Joel very kindly volunteered to stay."

Jay Omega looked around the room. There was an empty table and a collection of folding chairs in readiness for the morning's D&D game. He noticed the Macintosh in its usual place beside its printer. "Did the police check out that computer?"

"The one the note was written on? Yes. Joel made them be pretty careful with the fingerprint powder, so I don't think they damaged the machine. There weren't any prints, though. I overheard one of them telling Ayhan."

"Did Joel remember who had used it?"

"About half the convention, I think. Apparently this room is very popular with wargamers. Some of them were very annoyed tonight because I wouldn't give up the IBM-PC." Louis Warren yawned. "These machines aren't too bad, I guess. I'm just afraid I'll push the wrong button and make everything disappear."

"That's not likely," smiled Jay Omega, who had had the same conversation with Marion. "Just don't agree to anything that says *delete.*"

The editor still looked worried. "Do you suppose there's another disk containing part of the manuscript? Is this disk full?"

With a few taps, Jay Omega summoned up the directory. "No, it's fine," he said. "There's still about twenty percent of the disk space left. Why?"

"Well . . . unless Appin Dungannon changed his methods, there's something missing."

"The book doesn't make sense?"

"No. It's all here. Once we correct the typos and his variations in name spellings, it'll be ready to go, but I was expecting to find something that isn't on this disk.''

"What's missing?"

Louis Warren explained. ''. . . And on every one of the eighteen Runewind books that I've edited, it has always been there. It's sort of a trademark. His own form of protest, I guess. We never let it get into the publicity releases, of course, because it wouldn't look good for the series. But I don't think he'd quit doing it, no matter how rushed he was.''

Jay Omega studied the disk's directory. "It could have been erased," he conceded.

"I guess we'll never know, then." The editor shrugged.

"Oh, sure we will. Unless the guy really knew his stuff, we can probably get it back. Excuse me while I wake up Joel."

While Joel Schumann sipped his Dr. Pepper, yawned, and tried to boot up his brain, Jay Omega explained the situation to Louis Warren. "You see, when you erase a file on a disk, you don't really erase it right then. You just render that file unable to be found by the directory. So if you—''

Louis Warren smiled and nodded and smiled some more. It was gibberish; it was technical; it was Sanskrit. In the back of his mind he wondered if the publisher would switch him over to something more restful, like Gothic romances. SF was making his head hurt.

Joel Schumann yawned again and stretched. "You mean you just want to take a look at a file that somebody erased, but the disk is okay?''

"It's the one you put in the computer for me," Louis Warren told him.

"Oh, that one. Because if it had Coke spilled on it, or a staple through it, or you'd stepped on it, there's a place out on the West Coast that'll read it for you anyhow. They charge two hundred bucks, though, and it takes a while.''

"No, this is just a regular disk," said Jay Omega. "If you've got your Norton disk, it shouldn't take us very long.''

Louis Warren thought that they might as well draw pentagrams on the floor and rattle chicken bones, while they were at it. None of it made much sense to him, and he was too tired to devote many brain cells to it, anyway.

Joel Schumann rooted around in a file box full of disks, pulled out the one he wanted, and shooed Louis away from the computer. "Won't take long," he remarked cheerfully.

Louis sank into the swivel chair and closed his eyes. "If you find anything, let me know.'' His mind settled into a happy reverie involving Jackie Collins, *Vogue*, and a word processor with keys that said CHOP and PUREE. Every now and then he could hear remarks from the sorcerer's apprentices across the room. Things like, ''. . . file may be displaced by a later entry . . .'' and ''eight two-sector clusters . . .''

Several best sellers later, he heard the talking grow louder. ''Okay, the right arrow takes you from sector one to sector two, and F8 finds the next pair in sequence.''

''It'll be choppy, but it's coming.''

Someone shook his arm. ''Wake up, Mr. Warren. We've got something on the screen for you to look at.''

The editor ambled back to the computer desk and peered at the gaggle of words in mid-screen, surrounded by various bits of technical hieroglyphics.

> *The ruddy Norse blonde, who was built like a human draft horse, winced a bit as Tratyn Runewind came toward her. He had only had two baths in his life: one the day he was born and one the day after he got drunk in the cow byre, but that was not the . . .''*

''Hmm. Sector two is garbled. Try another pair,'' said Jay Omega. Joel hit another key, and soon a new scrap of text materialized on the display monitor.

> *Tratyn Runewind strained at the ropes which bound him to the stakes in the floor of the mead hall.*
>
> *When he had agreed to let Ole Redbeard's men tie him down spreadeagled on his stomach, he had naturally expected a romantic evening to follow, but the playful nibble at his left buttock was not foreplay from a burly oarsman, but an enterprising rat who liked his meat fresh. Runewind felt little cold noses at his ears and toes . . .*

Joel Schumann sank back in his chair. ''What is this stuff? I've read the Tratyn Runewind books, and they're definitely not like this!''

''Is this what you're looking for?'' asked Jay Omega.

Louis Warren nodded. ''Yes, it's fairly mild compared to some of the alternate last chapters I've seen.''

Jay shook his head. ''I don't get it.''

''Appin Dungannon hated Tratyn Runewind?'' asked Joel.

''Bingo!'' said Louis. ''But he had to keep writing the novels, because they were so popular. So to vent his frustration he would write two last chapters to every one of his books.

"You should have seen some of the others," grunted the editor. "Tratyn Runewind having a bout with dysentery during a battle, and getting stabbed by a twelve-year-old boy; Runewind being castrated by a Druid priestess who greatly resembled Mrs. Dungannon. I never knew what to expect. He'd send it in along with the manuscript, just before the last chapter, and I'd always take it out before I sent it to press. But that's one piece of Dungannon trivia that nobody knew; people might get upset to know how much he hated the series."

Joel Schumann nodded. "The fantasy people would freak if they read this, all right."

Jay Omega gave a start. He looked at Joel and then back at the screen. "When do you suppose this was written?"

"Judging from the times on the existing directory entries, I'd say sometime Friday night. The real last chapter was written Saturday morning. Why?"

"Oh, nothing . . ." He stared at the green letters on the monitor, lost in thought. It seemed to make sense. He wondered if that was an ominous sign that he had been around the fen too long.

He was still gazing at the monitor. He had an idea. "Let's see how much more of this there is," he said to Joel.

At one-thirty in the morning, Marion was sprawled across the bed in a pile of maps and D&D manuals, fast asleep. Jay Omega smiled down at her, thinking that she looked like a vulnerable little girl when she slept. She wouldn't thank him for that observation! Despite the fact that she was a complete rabbit about math and at the mercy of almost any mechanical device, she liked to think that there were no intellectual differences between them. She seemed to think that his inability to quote Auden and the fact that Thomas Hardy put him to sleep evened the score. She didn't seem to realize that the intelligence he admired in her had nothing to do with literature. He liked the fact that she really listened when he explained something technical, and that she kept asking questions until his explanations made sense to her; he admired her versatility—they had lunch almost every day and never ran out of things to talk about, without resorting to shop talk or campus gossip; and he was a little afraid of her perceptiveness: she knew things about him that he'd never dream of telling her.

He wondered if she would guess what he was up to now. He wasn't quite sure himself, or at least he didn't really want to discuss it. It was just the glimmering of an idea, and he felt it would be better kept to himself—just in case he was wrong. How hard could it be to run a Dungeon? Maybe he could manage without her. Jay Omega picked up the game scenario and studied it for a few minutes, but he decided that it was too important for him to bluff his way through it.

"Wake up," he said, gently shaking the bed. "You have to teach me how to run a Dungeon, and I have a few variations to put in."

Marion groaned. "Sorry. Your fairy godmother is on down time. Unless you want to do an R-rated version of *Sleeping Beauty*, in which case you have a chance of waking me up."

He shook the bed again. "Wake up, Mrs. Peel! The game's afoot!"

CHAPTER 14

MILES PERRY WAS reflecting on how correct Einstein had been about time being relative. This con, for example, had managed to last for about twenty years within the space of one weekend. He found himself actually looking forward to the real world, in which he could manage the grocery produce section with relatively little turmoil, without having to worry about hotel damage fees, elves who lost their room keys, and famous dead people.

He had spent a weary hour the night before with Lt. Ayhan, who had questioned the entire "Chip Livingstone Consortium" right after the banquet. They had all been fingerprinted, and all had assured him that they had no access to guns, but the Lieutenant had pointed out that since his other suspects were computers and fictional characters, they were his best bet.

When Ayhan had appeared in the hotel lobby early this morning, Miles had braced himself for another round, but the Lieutenant was there, he said, responding to a phone call from Dr. Marion Farley. Miles Perry sat down and started to search the newspaper for a write-up on Dungannon.

"You through with the book section, yet?" asked Diefenbaker, sinking down in the chair beside him.

Miles Perry handed it over without a word.

"Thanks," said Dief. "I think I'm setting a new world record for lack of sleep. And I thought grad school was bad!"

"Who cornered you this time? You didn't go to the Chip Livingstone Memorial Service, did you?"

"No," said Dief. "I'd have felt like a murderer. They didn't invite me anyway. But I hear that Bernard Buchanan is trying to figure out which one of us praised his writing."

Miles grunted. "The one with the most sadistic sense of humor."

"I thought it was you!" said Dief.

"I thought it was you!" echoed Miles innocently. "So, where were you till all hours?"

"In a Far Brandonian council meeting. I can't figure out why Rich-

ard Faber wasn't there. He's been moaning about armies on his southern border all weekend.''

"I think he has something else on his southern border at the moment," said Miles.

Dief grinned. "I've been waiting for Lt. Ayhan to start looking for
C.D. Novibazaar. People certainly talk enough about him."

"Ah, yes, your player character in the game. Yes, that's all Ayhan
needs, another imaginary suspect." He folded the paper and stood
up. "Good morning, Dr. Omega!"

Jay Omega managed a groan that resembled the syllables of "good
morning." He looked as if he had forgotten to shave. "I usually get
more rest than this," he mumbled.

Miles Perry looked anxious. "You'll be ready for the D&D game
at ten, won't you?"

Jay Omega nodded. "Yes. That's what I came to talk to you about.
Is Lt. Ayhan here yet?"

"He's around somewhere, asking questions. Why?"

"Just ask him to look me up, will you? I'll be in the high-tech
room."

He wandered off in the direction of the dining room, and Miles
Perry went back to his newspaper. When he had any energy to spare,
he would wonder what that exchange had been about.

The prospect of a celebrity Dungeon Master had lured a cross-
section of con participants to the high-tech room for the exhibition
D&D adventure. The computers and tech equipment had been shoved
to the back to make room for the circle of participants, and onlookers
were crammed into available space. A few lucky ones had latched
onto wooden chairs. Of the twelve chosen to demonstrate their skill
for the audience, only one had dropped out after the substitution of
Omega for Dungannon as DM. Miss Megan (Beef) Wellington had
withdrawn from the game, deciding that an acquaintance with the
author of (shudder) *Bimbos of the Death Sun* would do nothing to
help her chances of publishing her fantasy novel, the 560-page
Chronicles of Karamecia. Three others had either overslept or left
the con early, leaving eight remaining adventurers to play the game.

Most of the players had come in some sort of costume. Richard
Faber had borrowed a cloak from his beloved Brenda in honor of the
occasion. She had come to cheer him on from the spectators' gallery.
Diefenbaker, who was a born experimenter given very few chances
outside Fandom, had borrowed a feathered elf cap from Saffron; and
Clifford Morgan was in full Tratyn Runewind regalia, complete with

cape and broadsword. Bill Fox had on a tunic and shortsword, and
the jock from the costume competition was back in his Conan costume. Bernard Buchanan wore a T-shirt stretched to the bursting
point, and a button that said: KISS ME, I'M ELVISH.

"Should I wear some kind of get-up?" Jay had asked Marion.

"The cap and gown you always wear to graduation comes to
mind," said Marion dryly. "No, seriously, I don't think it's necessary. The DM is basically God, and God wears anything He wants.
—He looks particularly nice in jeans and a sweatshirt," she added,
smiling.

A few minutes before ten, Marion, back in her Mrs. Peel jumpsuit,
appeared carrying a stack of weapons charts and other data necessary
for conducting the adventure. "God could use a computer for this,"
grumbled the Dungeon Master.

"Don't panic," said Marion. "As long as you're plausible no one
will complain. If they do, turn them into a pillar of salt."

Jay Omega glanced again at the scenario, and out at the rows of
spectators, seated on the floor between computer displays. Lt. Ayhan
was not among them. He glanced at his watch: ten o'clock. Let the
games begin.

"You realize," he said to Clifford Morgan, "that you can't play
Tratyn Runewind. He's an NPC. You'll be assigned somebody else."

Morgan nodded impatiently. His white hair was held in place by
a leather thong tied around his head, and he wore a rope belt around
his tunic of homespun wool. As he eased himself to the floor in front
of the Dungeon Master, he took care not to sit on his blue velvet
tunic, which had been brushed spotless, and was not the sort of gar-
ment one usually wore to loll about on a tile floor. While the other
players looked like partyers anticipating a good time, Morgan managed a look of intense dedication, suggesting a soldier awaiting battle
orders.

"Okay," said Jay Omega. "Everybody, listen up!" He turned back
to Marion. "I don't have to say forsooth or anything, do I?"

"No!" whispered Marion. "But try not to talk like Bear Bryant,
either."

"Who is she?" asked one of the younger elves.

"I'm the Oracle of Delphi," Marion replied. "He consults me on
close calls."

"But the DM is omnipotent," said the elf.

"Don't hassle an oracle, kid. You could end up as souvlaki."

Lt. Ayhan appeared in the doorway. "Somebody here wanted to
see me?"

Jay Omega motioned for him to come over. "I asked you to sit in on this, because I think something interesting may develop."

Ayhan looked pained. "Even if it were my day off, I don't think I could find the time for *this*."

"Trust me. It's important."

"I don't play kids' games, and I definitely don't sit on floors."

Marion patted the desktop beside her. "You can come and sit beside me. I'll even explain the game to you."

Ayhan consulted his watch. "I'll consider this a coffee break." He hoisted himself up on the desk beside Marion.

"I'll have to whisper, so that we don't disturb the game, Lieutenant. What do you want to know?"

Ayhan studied the scene in front of him. "I see a bunch of kids sitting around on the floor wearing funny outfits and playing with dice. What's to know?"

"Plenty. It's a role-playing game. All the action is imaginary."

"Where's the board?"

"There isn't one. Jay has a script of the adventure, but it all takes place in the imagination."

Ayhan sighed. "Then what am I supposed to watch?"

Marion smiled. "Get into the spirit of it, lieutenant. If Jay does a good job of describing things, it can come to seem very real after a while."

"So who's Dr. Omega supposed to be?"

"He's called the Dungeon Master. He's like the Stage Manager in *Our Town*."

"Thanks for the clarification," said Ayhan, stifling a yawn.

Marion sighed. "How can I put it? He tells them where they are and what they see, and they tell him what their reactions are. For example, he could say: 'You see a stone with a gold statue sitting on it.' And then the players talk it over, and decide whether to leave the statue alone, in case it's a trap, or to risk taking it."

"Okay. Suppose they decide to pick it up."

"Then they relay that information to the Dungeon Master. And he tells them what happens next, like: you have just triggered an earthquake, or an alarm goes off, or whatever."

"What are the dice for?"

"There's a whole bunch. Four-sided, six-sided, eight-sided, ten-sided, twelve-sided, twenty-sided . . . even one-hundred-sided nowadays, or you can just throw two d10s, which we in the know call a *percentile*. Had enough?" she asked, noticing Ayhan's mystified expression. "Relax. All you need to know is that a throw of the dice—

whichever dice—determines the outcome of something that depends on chance. If a rope breaks and you fall, how badly did you get hurt? In real life, it will depend on whether you fell on your head or not, whether you hit a rock or soft ground, and all the other variables. In the game, the dice take care of all of life's possibilities.''

Lt. Ayhan digested this information. ''So you sit on the floor and imagine an adventure, and you throw dice. —Does this sound boring to you?''

''Yes,'' smiled Marion. ''Unless you are playing with very creative people, it can be stupefying. Young male players tend to invent adventures that are all combat, and those are especially monotonous. This one should be better than that.''

''Why?''

''Because I helped to write it.''

''And why am I here?'' asked Ayhan.

''Command performance,'' Marion replied. ''The Dungeon Master insisted.'' She had wondered about that herself, though.

The adventurers were looking up at Jay Omega with eager faces. Several of them had produced pads and pencils so that they could make notes about the things he described for future reference. It was a good idea to draw a map, too, so that when the adventure was over, the party could find its way back.

Jay Omega consulted his notes. ''Okay, the adventure begins. — No, that's not right.'' He read the pencil notes in the margin. ''We have to do something else first.'' What did ''gen. char.'' and ''leg'' mean? His learning capacities did not function well at two A.M., which is when Marion had explained it all, and he had scribbled reminders to himself.

He tried not to look at the row of earnest players in front of him. He was rattled enough. In the audience, somebody giggled. ''Gen. char''—''Generate characters!'' he cried, just as the silence was becoming ominous. ''First, you have to generate your characters, and then I'm going to distribute legends to some of you.'' Legend cards were sort of house rules; Omega held up the handprinted note cards which bore extra information about the adventure and which would augment the more usual procedures. ''After that, I will explain the adventure.''

Marion didn't wait for Ayhan to ask. ''Generating characters. Each member of the expedition will have certain skills like strength, dexterity, intelligence, and so on. They're rolling the dice to see what their attributes are. Think of it as a gene pool.''

''Suppose you get lousy marks in everything?''

"Then you start over. Better than life, huh? —And your dice scores determine who you are. If you are high in intelligence, but low in strength, you might be an elf, for example. Someone high in dexterity might choose to become a thief."

Ayhan frowned. "Thief, huh? There wouldn't be any murderers in this game, would there?"

Marion hesitated. "That's a rather philosophical question, lieutenant. All the adventurers are soldiers of fortune, and as such, they might be forced to kill in self-defense, or in order to complete their mission, or—"

"Okay! Okay!" Ayhan made the football time-out signal. "It's bad enough I have to watch this without getting commercials in metaphysics."

More than twenty minutes later, the eight players had been transformed into elf fighters, clerics, human warriors, thieves, and the other usual components of a fantasy *A-Team*. They had used imaginary gold to buy imaginary weapons, and each knew his strength and other abilities, because they had been determined by a roll of the dice.

"This is, of course, a Celtic adventure," Jay Omega told the party. "Your leader is Tratyn Runewind himself."

Scattered applause came from the audience.

"Your mission, should you decide to accept it—" Jay saw Marion frown and shake her head. Get serious, he told himself, this has to be believable. He tried again:

"The adventure is to ... er ...*'* He glanced at the notes on the first page of his plot outline. "Oh, yes! You have to fight a group of Norsemen who have taken over Scotland's sacred island of Iona. That's where the Scottish kings are buried, and there's a monastery there."

"It ought to be dynamite for magic," Bill Fox remarked.

"Okay ... You're standing on a rocky beach on the west coast of the Scottish mainland ..."

Marion leaned over and whispered to the Lieutenant. "You probably understand this already, but he has given them their assignment, and he has just told them where they are. Now they decide how to proceed."

The commandeering of a boat to take the adventurers to Iona was relatively uneventful. In his role as omnipotent game-controller, Jay Omega gave them a little rough weather to contend with on the crossing, but nothing to really worry about.

"Now," said Marion. "Try to picture all of them on a little Scottish fishing boat, crossing the choppy sea."

Jay Omega was also trying to picture the scene. "Let's see . . ." he stammered, unnerved by the eight pairs of eyes waiting for his instructions. "It's a very gray day . . . sort of spitting rain, windy. The boat is lurching in the waves. . . ."

Marion leaned over and touched Jay's shoulder. "Now!" she hissed.

"Tratyn Runewind is seasick," Jay Omega added, trying to sound casual. "He's puking over the side."

Bernard Buchanan looked puzzled. "Tratyn Runewind is *seasick*, but—"

He shrugged. Talking back to a DM could be hazardous to your health.

Jay Omega glanced at his notes for "Arrival at Iona." Marion had augmented the original adventure with a few touches of her own, for which her doctorate in folklore had proved very helpful. She sat on the Macintosh table behind the Dungeon Master's chair, trying to convey no emotion at all in her expression. Oracles, she felt, should be objective. Lt. Ayhan, looking less confused, was equally impassive. While the descriptions were being given, he had waved a dollar bill at a boy in the audience and had pantomimed drinking. The kid nodded his comprehension and took off with the money.

"As the boat comes in to the shallows of the island— I don't know how far out—" Jay turned to Marion. "Would they have to worry about rocks near the beach?"

Marion scribbled a note and handed it to him. It said: "Don't be so hesitant! In this game, the truth is whatever you say it is! Be positive!"

Jay Omega folded the note and slid it into his pocket. Mustering up his most commanding expression, the one he used for discussing grades with undergrads, he said, "As the boat nears shore, you see a beautiful black horse wading in the surf."

"The sleeping warriors!" muttered Diefenbaker, remembering yesterday's adventure. Today he was a middle-aged cleric whose specialty was magic. "Thomas the Rhymer collects black horses to give to King Arthur and his army. That horse should be magic. Catch it!"

The elf with the highest dexterity rating said to Jay Omega: "I leap over the side of the boat and I try to grab the horse's mane." He rolled the dice to determine whether probability was on his side. "Did I make it?"

Jay Omega almost said, "How should I know whether you made

it or not?'' but then he realized that it was up to him to decide things like that, and because he had the notes about the adventure, he knew something about the horse that the players did not. ''Yes,'' he nodded. ''You have the horse's mane, but you can't let go. It starts to swim out to sea. It is now level with the boat.''

''Okay,'' Ayhan whispered to Marion. ''That kid jumped off the boat to try to catch a horse. Now how did Dr. Omega know that he can't let go, and that the horse will swim out to sea?''

Marion looked exasperated. ''Because! I told you! The Dungeon Master is like God. He can make anything happen if he wants to. In this case, he has the script, which tells him that the horse is really a demon.'' She grinned. ''I came up with that.''

Sensing the danger to their comrade, the adventurers whispered among themselves on how to effect a rescue. No one offered to dive in after him.

''I consult my magic book,'' said Diefenbaker quickly, holding up an imaginary volume. ''Do I find Thomas the Rhymer?''

''No,'' said Jay Omega. ''Because . . . because . . .''

''You're six hundred years too early,'' said Marion. ''Thomas the Rhymer is twelfth century.''

''So I look under Water Horses,'' said Diefenbaker, pretending to flip pages.

''They're using imaginary books?'' said Ayhan.

''Sort of. Diefenbaker is a cleric, which means he is also a scholar, so there's a chance that he'll be able to find some information that will help with the problem. He pretends to consult the book, and if Jay feels like letting him have the answer, he will pretend to let him find it in the book.''

''This sounds like the way city hall operates,'' grinned Ayhan. His Coke arrived just then, and he took it with a smile of thanks, and waved away the change.

Jay Omega decided to give Diefenbaker a break. ''Your magic book says 'See Kelpie.' ''

''Kelpie!'' Mona, the female warrior, who read nothing but folklore, clutched at Diefenbaker's arm. ''They're demons. They play around in the water's edge until somebody gets on their backs, and then they drown them!''

Marion nodded approvingly, pleased at finding another folklore enthusiast present.

''I am running to the side of the boat with my flask of holy water!'' cried Diefenbaker. ''I throw the holy water on the kelpie.'' He rolled the dice.

Jay Omega picked a chart at random and pretended to study it. Real Dungeon Masters actually used charts to determine probability, but Marion had said that he might as well fake it, because otherwise things would get too complicated. "Okay," he said confidently, as if the chart had settled things, "the kelpie had started to dive into deep water, but you caught him on the rump with your holy water, and he disappears. Now who's going to rescue the waterlogged elf?"

"Can't I swim?" asked the elf.

"You're unconscious."

"What about Tratyn Runewind?" asked Clifford Morgan. "He swims, and he's stronger than all of us put together."

"Which one is he?" asked Ayhan.

"Runewind? None of them. He's what is called a non-player character. It's up to Jay to tell them what he does and says. They just imagine his presence."

"How can you have an imaginary player?" Ayhan demanded.

Marion shrugged. "They're in an imaginary boat, aren't they?"

Jay Omega tossed dice of his own. "Ah, yes. Tratyn Runewind. He tries to get to the side, but the boat lurches in the waves, and he falls and hits his head against the anchor." He braced himself for a storm of argument from the players, but there was only a stunned silence. Good, thought Jay Omega, maybe this will actually work.

Little gasps came from the adventurers as they realized that their leader had been injured so early in the game. "Roll for damage," somebody said gravely.

"I get it!" whispered Ayhan, sipping his drink. "They're checking probability to see how bad he was hurt."

"Lieutenant, you're catching on," smiled Marion.

"Sixteen," said Bill Fox.

Jay Omega glanced at Marion. "He'll be out for four hours game-time, and he's down ten hit points," he told them. Too many damage points could have fatal results—but this one, while serious, was not life-threatening.

"Am I drowning?" wailed the elf, who was still flailing in the sea near the boat.

The party looked worried. Maybe this wasn't going to be such a Monty Haul dungeon after all.

Donnie McRory tossed his clothes into his suitcase, wondering if he ought to call the British Embassy just to let them know he'd been questioned in a murder case. Probably not, he decided. The police hadn't even asked him to postpone his next booking, just to leave a

list of the places he'd be staying for the rest of the tour. Still, it had
been an annoying interview.

"I suppose I'll have to call Scotland Yard to verify this information," Lt. Ayhan had warned the suspect.

"Bloody hell!" moaned Donnie McRory. "Don't you Yanks know
anything? New Scotland Yard—*New* Scotland Yard, mind you—only
deals with crimes in London."

"Sorry," grinned Ayhan. "My investigations are more likely to
involve the Salvation Army flophouse than Interpol, so I'm not up
on these things."

"Yes, well, when you figure out who to call, by all means check
me out. I assure you that I am no more than a name on the Scottish
Archaeological Society's mailing list. And I've done my share of
charity benefits in my time, but shooting a bloke in the States just to
get a donation for a lot of moldy castles is not my idea of philan-
thropy."

"Just the same," said Ayhan, not entirely convinced, "we must
stay in touch."

Donnie McRory sighed and shook his head. It was just as well that
he was leaving this loony bin, before things got even more cocked
up. He wondered if his agent would consider a murder charge good
publicity. Probably not. The punkers would thrive on it, but as a
folksinger he attracted the more sedate crowd himself. Aging Sixties
types who didn't want to let go of Back to the Earth. Anyway, the
whole thing was too bloody stupid. Why would anyone shoot a fantasy writer? Probably one of the Martians had gone off his head. He
shouldn't be easy to spot in that crowd, then. "I wish you luck in
your investigation, Mr. Ayhan," he had told the policeman at the end
of the interview. "I think you should be looking for a crazy person,
and it'll be like trying to find a tree in a forest."

Ayhan had only smiled. "I've got my computers working on it."

Watching the D&D game from the sidelines, Brenda Lindenfeld
smiled to herself, basking in a feeling of exhilaration that she usually
got only from two scoops of Swiss chocolate almond ice cream. It
was an unlikely reaction to occur from staring at Richard Faber—
certainly no one had previously gotten much pleasure from contemplating him, but Brenda felt that he was the answer to prayer. He
was still as unattractive as ever, a dismal bed partner, and gratingly
boring, but she had learned that he was majoring in computer engineering. Brenda saw the words spelled out in a string of little credit
cards across her mind. Finding a computer-anything major was like

winning the state lottery—and the odds were better. These microchip nerds were paid indecent amounts of money. Brenda wasn't sure just what it was they did for all this money, but then she didn't care, either. If you could manage to marry one, you were home free. No more parents to nag you about school; no more hassles to support yourself on a minimum wage job; no more worries about how to pay your long-distance phone bill. Brenda didn't think she ought to take a chance on letting this one get away. She'd better get pregnant.

During a lull in the action, Richard Faber looked over to the side-lines at his beloved, watching from among the spectators. He gave her a little wave, thinking how lucky he was to have found such a soul mate; and Brenda, thinking of a big-screen TV and the complete collection of *Star Trek* videos, smiled back.

Since Jay Omega was handling things so well on his own, Marion was taking an Oracle break, leaving Lt. Ayhan in charge of miracles. She had slipped out to the Coke machine in the hall where Joel Schumann was feeding a succession of nickels into the money slot. "Getting rid of my small change," he explained. "I think there's a hole in these jeans. How's the Professor doing?"

"Surprisingly well for a novice," said Marion. "He's very adaptable."

"Yeah, he's a nice guy," Joel conceded. "Even students like him. Are you two engaged or something?"

"Or something," Marion agreed. "We'll let you know in two years."

Joel looked puzzled. "Two years?"

"Right. That's when we both come up for tenure. If we both get it, then everything's fine, and if we both get turned down, that's okay, too. But if only one of us gets it . . ."

She might as well have been speaking Bantu to a puzzled Joel. "Yeah, well, I gotta get back to this program I'm running on the IBM in there," said Joel. "I hope it works out for you two."

Marion smiled. "That's why I keep writing journal articles."

In the high-tech room the mood among the adventurers was tense. Everyone was down at least two hit points, meaning that their chances of survival had diminished greatly, and the only thing anyone had gained thus far on the expedition was an ivory chessman they found on the beach at Iona. An hour and a half had passed, hitting them with a succession of insect swarms, rock falls, rainstorms, and other unheroic inconveniences. Diefenbaker found something else quite un-

usual, according to his legend card, his healing spells did not work
on the elf's sprained ankle, and the woman warrior was more upset
by maggots in the food supply than she had been by the rock fall.

"Things are looking pretty bad for the group," whispered Ayhan
to Marion. "Imaginary maggots and all."

"Yes, Jay is giving them a run of bad luck," Marion agreed. "Sort
of like Job in the Bible, isn't it?"

At a quarter to twelve some of the spectators began to wander
away. Brenda Lindenfeld was signaling frantically to Richard Faber.

"Can we break for lunch?" Faber asked the Dungeon Master.

"No," said Jay Omega. "We play straight through. Until you win
or die."

A few more people got up and left.

"Is it okay if I go to lunch now?" asked Lt. Ayhan, tapping the
Dungeon Master on the shoulder.

"No," said Jay Omega without turning around. "You stay, too.
I'll explain later."

Lt. Ayhan groaned. "Now what?"

Marion grinned at him. "How about an imaginary sandwich?"

Jay Omega ignored the looks of discomfort on the faces of the
adventurers. Those who skipped breakfast for economy reasons were
experiencing very real misery. The Dungeon Master consulted his
game plan, and announced: "You are walking through a meadow on
the way to the Iona monastery, and up on the hill, you see a stream
of water."

"Do we see anyone there?" asked Bill Fox. "Weapons ready,
everyone."

"No," said Jay Omega. "You don't see anything except a couple
of rowan trees, rocks, and the creek."

"I say we keep walking," said Faber to the other adventurers.

Jay Omega paused for effect. "Tratyn Runewind claims to have
seen something."

The adventurers looked alert, waiting for the Dungeon Master to
produce a clue as to the next situation.

"We ask him what he sees," said Diefenbaker.

Jay Omega relayed the information from the nonplayer character
Runewind, whose actions and utterances could only be conveyed
through the Dungeon Master. "He says it looks like a woman washing clothes in the stream. She is dressed in green, and she is weeping.
The clothes leave trails of red in the water."

"Oh, blast!" whispered the woman warrior, recognizing the description from her folklore text. "The Bean-Nighe! Has she seen us yet?"

"Wait a minute!" said Clifford Morgan. "What's a Ben-Nee-Yah?"

"They're supposed to be the ghosts of women who have died in childbirth," the folklore fiend explained. "They are always seen washing the blood-stained clothes of *those about to die* . . ."

"Why did Tratyn Runewind see her, when we didn't?" Morgan demanded.

Mona shrugged. "Maybe he's . . ." Her voice trailed away when she saw the look on Morgan's face.

Jay Omega pretended not to hear. "You see a stone tower on a hill in front of you. It seems to be in ruins."

Bonnenberger peeked through the door of the high-tech room, and saw the D&D game in progress. He had decided that watching a few minutes of D&D might be preferable to seeing *The Wrath of Khan* for the seventh time. Besides, someone might have a sandwich that was going to waste.

"Pardon," he said to a scowling Brenda Lindenfeld, who was trying to edge her way past him. "Lunch break soon?"

"Apparently not," she snapped. "Apparently he's going to keep them in there until they drop!" Brenda's cash reserves of two dollars and twelve cents would not cover the lunch in a Chinese restaurant promised her by the unavoidably detained Richard Faber. Brenda wished he would die so that he could buy her lunch.

Bonnenberger blinked and shrugged. "Candy machine."

Brenda Lindenfeld looked at him with a loathing undisguised. *"Bon appétit!"*

The adventurers had taken a few minutes to discuss the implications of a stone tower on the horizon. Some of them felt that it might be a fort full of enemy soldiers, but others suggested that the monks might have used it as a hiding place for items that might prove useful to the expedition. Magic swords, perhaps. Jay Omega sat silently through their deliberations, offering no divine inspiration to help them out.

Finally Thrumpin the Elf decided to continue the action. "I approach the tower by myself. Do I see anything?"

"You see a partially open wooden door with weeds growing around it," said Jay Omega. "Tratyn Runewind offers to go with you."

"Hmm. That might be helpful in case of ambush. Okay, I accept his offer to go with me," said the Elf. "We walk up the hill toward the ruins, and I push the door open."

Jay Omega could have invented an ambush, or a booby-trap, but he didn't. "Nothing happens."

"I use my elf vision to look around in the darkness."

Written on the Dungeon Master's plan for the adventure was a list of all the things contained in the tower. Jay Omega noted that the Elf was in Room One, and he informed him of the contents listed for that room. "You see a door in the far wall, and a wooden chest beside it. Above the inside door is a branch of oak leaves that has been dipped in gold. The chest is an old one with a carving of mistletoe decorating the lid."

"Hey, look what I have on my legend card!" cried Bernard Buchanan, who had been injured in a pit trap near the beach, and wasn't good for much anymore. "My card says 'Treasure by the Golden Bough.' A bough is a tree branch, isn't it?"

They looked around for the folklore expert, but she had gone to the bathroom. Knowing that she could help them out of his well-planned trap, Jay Omega decided to force them into a hasty decision. "You hear a sound from outside."

The Elf thought fast. "I'm only six on strength," he said. "I tell Tratyn Runewind to open the door and look for the treasure."

"Okay," said Jay Omega. "Tratyn Runewind opens the door . . ."

"What's going on?" asked the returning woman warrior, stopping to peel a bit of toilet paper off her shoe. "What have you done?"

Bernard Buchanan told her about the golden bough legend. "So Thrumpin the Elf sent Tratyn Runewind through the door under the gold oak leaves."

Despite her status as Oracle, Marion was grinning.

"You dummies!" yelled Mona. "The golden bough is *mistletoe*. Haven't you read Frazier? Don't you know anything?"

The chastened adventurers looked back at the Dungeon Master for a verdict. With a solemn stare, Jay Omega sprang his trap. "Opening the inner door has weakened the structure of the ruin. Rocks begin to fall."

Thrumpin gulped. "I dive after Tratyn Runewind."

"A boulder hits you as you approach the doorway. Roll for falling damages."

Ashen-faced, the Elf threw the six-sided dice a grand total of twenty times. Fellow adventurers gasped as the numbers mounted up. "Sixty-three," he said hoarsely.

"I'm sorry," Jay Omega said, forgetting his omnipotence. "You have died."

"Doesn't he get a saving throw?" asked Richard Faber.

"No."

Clifford Morgan turned as white as his hair. "What happened to Tratyn Runewind?" he whispered, plucking at the edge of his cloak.

Jay Omega met Morgan's wide-eyed stare with a look of detached interest. He almost told him the answer to his question but then he remembered to picture the scene. In order to know what happened to Tratyn Runewind, Morgan's character would have to have been present in the tower, so the Dungeon Master was not obliged to tell him. Omega deliberately prolonged the suspense a bit by pretending to consider the matter. At last he said to Morgan, "You are down the hill with the rest of the party. Are you going to go up to the tower and find out?"

"I'm dead," said the Elf wonderingly. "Should I go to lunch or what?"

"Okay, I think we ought to discuss this. It could be an ambush," said Bill Fox, ignoring the deceased Elf.

"If it was just a rock fall, it ought to be over by now," Richard Faber pointed out. "We haven't hit any signs of the enemy yet."

"The rocks killed Thrumpin, though," said Bernard Buchanan. "And what about the treasure? It should be in the chest, right?"

The Dungeon Master consulted his watch. "You have wasted three minutes," he informed them. "In a medical emergency that's a long time."

"We have to rescue Tratyn Runewind," cried Clifford Morgan. *"Now!"*

"I don't think we ought to rush into it," grumbled the Conan-jock.

"I think it's a trap," said the woman warrior.

"Four minutes," said Jay Omega ominously.

"I'm running up the hill," yelled Clifford Morgan. "I have my sword out . . ."

"Is anyone going with him?" asked Jay Omega.

"I'm staying here under the tree," said the Conan player nervously.

"Yeah," said Mona the warrior. "Me, too."

The others, with varying degrees of enthusiasm, said that they would follow Morgan up the hill.

"All right," said the Dungeon Master. "You are walking up the hill. When you are within one hundred yards of the castle, you hear screams."

"Runewind?" asked Diefenbaker.

"No. From down the hill. The tree you were resting under was a shapechanger. It has grabbed the other two members of your party."

"We go back and rescue them," sighed Bernard Buchanan. "Don't we?"

Bill Fox looked at Diefenbaker and shrugged.

"Inside the ruin, you think you hear a faint cry for help."

"I go on up the hill," said Clifford Morgan.

"Me, too," said Richard Faber.

Diefenbaker sighed. "What *kind* of a shapechanger is it?"

CHAPTER 15

By TWELVE-THIRTY MOST of the spectators had drifted off in search of lunch. Lt. Ayhan was grumbling about missing lunch and having his time wasted, and Marion had promised to go for a hamburger to pacify him. Joel Schumann was still tinkering with a program on the PC, but he seemed to be paying more attention to the D&D game than he was to his own project.

The players—what was left of them—were suffering from combat fatigue. The shapechanger had managed to kill both Mona the woman warrior, and the Conan-jock, and Diefenbaker had been so badly hurt in the rescue attempt that he was down to one hit point, and his healing spells were used up.

A party of Norsemen had attacked the adventurers on the road to the monastery, killing Richard Faber with an arrow through the throat in the ambush, and mortally wounding Bill Fox in sword combat.

"Whew!" said Bill, when his fate had been pronounced. "The tension was getting to me!" He helped Richard Faber to his feet. "Wanna go to lunch?"

Faber looked guilty. "Maybe. I think I have to find somebody first. Do you like Chinese?"

The three remaining players looked at each other. Clifford Morgan was down to three hit points, which meant that any serious injury would kill him, and he had a slight concussion incurred when he pulled Tratyn Runewind out of the ruined fort. Bernard Buchanan's character was still limping, and still useless; as was Diefenbaker, who as a cleric could not use edged weapons, and his spells were gone. Their chances against the enemy looked bleak.

Jay Omega glanced wearily around the nearly empty room. "Tratyn Runewind says that only a fool would attempt such a mission with two wounded warriors and a cleric. He suggests that you plan your escape."

Clifford Morgan was pale and tired-looking, but his eyes flashed angrily at the suggestion. "Tratyn Runewind is more than mortal," he said. "He never retreats."

Marion stood up. "The Oracle is going out for hamburgers," she announced. "Would God like one?"

"No," said Jay Omega, who was as caught up in the game as the players.

Clifford Morgan was conferring with the remnants of his troops. "If we rely on the element of surprise, I think we may still have a chance," he told Bernard Buchanan. "We sneak into the monastery and pick off the Norsemen one at a time."

The Dungeon Master said, "You approach the monastery. It is surrounded by a white wall. There are Norse guards at the only gate. They do not see you."

"We duck behind some rocks," said Morgan. "We can go over the wall."

"I can't," said Bernard Buchanan. "I can hardly walk."

"My dexterity is practically nil," said Diefenbaker, "but if you insist, I'll give it a try."

Several more minutes passed while they described sneaking up to the wall, throwing the rope and grappling hook over the top, and while they debated on who should go first. Bernard Buchanan was to stand at the bottom to steady the rope.

"I'll go first," said Dief. "If any Norsemen come along the wall, you can defend the rope, and I couldn't. I do wish clerics could use weapons." He sighed. "All right, here goes. I start to climb the rope."

In real life, Walter Diefenbaker could no more climb a vertical rope hand over hand then he could spin straw into gold, but in D&D all things are possible, and one does not feel wounds and exertion except in one's ego.

Jay Omega rolled a die. "You get about halfway up the rope. One of the Norse scout parties spots you. They let fly with an arrow."

Diefenbaker slumped over. "That's it, isn't it?"

Jay Omega shrugged. "I'll roll and see."

The dice indicated that for someone with his limited stamina and hit points, it was definitely over. Diefenbaker got up rather stiffly. "I'll just sit over here and watch," he said, ambling over to an empty chair near the Macintosh.

"Too bad, kid," said Ayhan as he went past. "You gave it a good try."

"Thanks," whispered Diefenbaker, wiping his forehead with a handkerchief. "I'm afraid I wasn't any use, but you're right, I did try."

"The Norse scouting party is coming at you," said Jay Omega to Morgan and Buchanan.

"We run," said Clifford Morgan grimly. "We look for a place that will give us better odds in combat."

"I can't run!" wailed Bernard Buchanan. "My leg never healed!"

The Dungeon Master regarded Morgan with interest. "What do you do, Warrior?"

After a moment's hesitation, Morgan said, "Leave him. The mission takes precedence. Runewind and I run for . . . Is there a forest?"

"No. There's a cemetery, though. It has a lot of tall Celtic crosses."

Morgan nodded. "Good cover."

"What happens to me?" moaned Bernard Buchanan.

Jay Omega picked up the twenty-sided dice. "Hope for less than twenty," he advised.

Bernard Buchanan blew on the dice and sent them skittering across the floor. "Eighteen!" he said triumphantly.

"Oh, very good!" said the Dungeon Master. "That entitles you to something quick and painless. . . . They cut your throat with a dagger, and you die instantly."

Buchanan's expression suggested that this was not the sort of happy ending he had in mind. Dumping his character sheet and his legend paper into the nearest wastebasket, he headed toward the door. "This was not fun!" he announced to the room in general.

Lt. Ayhan looked thoughtfully at Jay Omega. Omega's face was pale and strained, and his body was tense. He seemed as deep into the fantasy as the kids were. Ayhan had been planning to walk out soon; he'd shot the whole morning here watching the game, and he still didn't know why. Just lately though, he'd felt a change in the atmosphere of the room, like a storm building up. Although all the other spectators had left, something told him to stay. Anyway, he had a hamburger coming. He could always stay and call it a lunch break. At the rate the players were dying, it couldn't be much longer now. He settled back and tried to picture Morgan and Runewind running from a horde of Vikings.

Jay Omega nodded to Clifford Morgan. "Over to you, sport."

Morgan licked his lips. "We're hiding behind crosses in the Celtic cemetery. It must be late by now. What time is it?"

"On Iona? Past nine in the evening."

"Good. Twilight. That means—"

"Not in Scotland. Sunset in the summertime is past eleven at night.

Northern latitudes, you know. They can see you fine. There's eight of them, all carrying swords, none wounded.''

"Runewind still has his talisman of charisma, doesn't he?'' asked Morgan, frowning.

"Yeah, but it won't work on the Norsemen. They don't speak his language.''

"Okay. He pulls his magic sword . . .''

"Three Norsemen rush the cross he's hiding behind. You can roll combat for him.''

Morgan threw the dice.

"Fifty-one. It doesn't look good,'' said Jay Omega.

"He's magic,'' Morgan insisted. "He's got *mega*-hit points.''

Tratyn Runewind, nearly invincible and nearly immortal, had never been in so much trouble before. Morgan was shaken, but still a believer. The Dungeon Master looked at the player's hands, trembling as they scooped up the dice. It was time.

Jay Omega said carefully, "Tratyn Runewind takes a good look at one of his opponents. The guy is carrying a very familiar-looking sword. It has carvings all the way down the blade.''

Morgan gasped. "That sounds like Runewind's sword.''

"It looks like Runewind's sword, too. It is the twin of his weapon, forged at the same time. This one is black, and it's called *Runeslayer*.''

"We haven't heard about this before,'' Morgan protested.

"It was on a legend card,'' Omega lied. "But the person who had it is already dead.''

"Tratyn Runewind attacks the Norsemen,'' whispered Morgan. He was beginning to sweat.

Jay Omega pointed to the percentile dice. "He got hurt the first time he tried that.''

"He tries again!'' shouted Morgan.

"Roll again, and see what happened.'' The more agitated Morgan got, the calmer the Dungeon Master became. His voice took on a tone of soothing indifference, of inevitability, as fatalistic as the Norsemen themselves.

Clifford Morgan looked at the dice as if they were cyanide capsules. His white hair was matted against his forehead with sweat, and he had kicked off his leather buskins, so that he was barefoot. As he crumpled the edge of his cloak in his fingers, Morgan kept trying to think of some amulet of protection he might have overlooked, or some bit of legend which would provide the key to Runewind's deliverance. There was none. None! Ten years of D&D games, and twenty-six Runewind books offered him no alternative to the choice before him: pick up the dice and throw.

His hands shook as he picked up the red plastic dice. He felt the Dungeon Master's stare, and wondered if it concealed amusement at his anguish. Clifford Morgan closed his eyes, and his lips moved, as he let the dice fall gently to the floor. The numbers blazing up at him were an eight and a one. Eighty-one. High damage, even for an immortal.

"That's no normal eighty-one," Jay Omega pointed out. "That's from a weapon that is the twin of his. Runewind's blade snaps from the counter blow."

"*What?*" screamed Morgan. "That blade was forged in the world fires by Gefion herself!"

"So was Runeslayer. And its owner is fighting at full strength— no loss of hit points. Tratyn Runewind goes down."

Morgan was breathing as hard as if he were living the adventure. "I run to cover him."

"You're too late," whispered the Dungeon Master. "The Norseman raises the hilt of Runeslayer level with his eyes and pushes it straight down into Tratyn Runewind's chest. You hear the crunch of steel against bone, and one thin wail of pain and fear. The Norseman straddles the body and grinds the sword in until it touches the dirt beneath. Blood comes out of Tratyn Runewind's mouth, and he dies."

"He doesn't die!" cried Clifford Morgan. "He's the hero of the saga. He *doesn't* die!"

"The Norseman kicks the body. Like a dog."

Morgan sprang to his feet and drew his own authentic reproduction broadsword from its velvet scabbard. "He doesn't die!" he screamed again.

Lt. Ayhan was suddenly alert. He reached for the pistol in his shoulder holster. "Calm down, kid," he ordered.

"Take it easy, Cliff!" said Diefenbaker quietly, from the sidelines. "It's only a game."

"No, it isn't," said Jay Omega, getting up off the desk and backing away. "It's for real, and for keeps. Tratyn Runewind is really and truly forever dead."

"*No!*" wailed Morgan, thrusting his sword at the Dungeon Master. "You're lying!"

"I'm the DM," said Jay Omega, backing toward Joel Schumann's desk. "I say he's dead."

Morgan swung the sword again, coming closer this time.

Lt. Ayhan drew his pistol. "This has gone far enough."

Morgan turned toward the sound of Ayhan's voice, but he didn't seem to understand the words. He swatted impatiently at the noise, as if it were a fly buzzing in his ear. "Leave me alone!"

"That's enough of that," said Ayhan. "Omega, I want everybody out of here."

"I'm staying," said Jay Omega. "Keep out of this, and let me talk to him."

Morgan, his sword point wobbling, looked from one to the other of them. Finally his gaze settled on Jay Omega, the murderer of his idol. He leaned forward, steadying the sword. Lt. Ayhan started for him.

Morgan's reflexes were good. He detected the movement out of the corner of his eye, and brought the blade of the broadsword down against the lieutenant's outstretched arm. It wasn't a sharp blade, but eight pounds of tempered steel impacting at full force is still a formidable weapon.

Ayhan felt the bone snap. The gun sprang from his fingers, clattering across the floor in Morgan's direction. He waved the sword menacingly to keep them back, while he bent and picked up the gun.

"He said it was an out-of-period weapon," giggled Morgan, examining the gun. "Not meant for a Rune Warrior." He fired once at Ayhan, shot the rest of the clip into the ceiling, and threw the gun into a corner.

The shoulder of Ayhan's gray suit leaked red, and he slumped to the floor. Diefenbaker, who had been sitting on a vacant desk watching the game, dived for the floor as soon as the shooting began. After a few frozen seconds in which he felt the gunshots echoing through his head, he calmed down enough to look around. Joel was gone, having managed to escape the room during the shooting. Ayhan was injured and Morgan seemed to have turned his attention to Jay Omega; at least his back was to Diefenbaker. He had thrown the gun away. Diefenbaker looked at it, across the room, ruefully. Maybe, he reflected, he might be able to hit Morgan over the head with something.

Alas, this was not a D&D game. In real life, Diefenbaker's strength was minimal and his dexterity was nil. If he tried any heroics, he would only make a mess of it. Still, he felt he ought to do something besides cower under the desk. He looked over at Ayhan, unconscious on the floor. Dief thought he could creep over to Ayhan without attracting Morgan's attention. Then he might try to help the injured man or make a run to the door for help.

"Runewind" seemed unaware of Ayhan and Dief. It was as if he were alone with Jay Omega. "You must die by the sword," he said, advancing on the Dungeon Master. "It is fitting."

Jay Omega dodged behind Joel's desk. Picking up the Amdek 722 computer monitor from the IBM, Jay Omega kept repeating, "He's really dead, Morgan. "I'm an author and I know. If you're an author, you can make someone really dead."

He held the computer monitor, still plugged in like an umbilical cord, in front of him for a shield. "Really dead, Morgan."

"I saved him!" screamed Morgan. Tears were coursing down his face, and he lunged again at his tormenter. "He was going to die before, but I saved him!"

At that moment Marion appeared in the doorway with a McDonald's bag for the lieutenant. She saw Omega, still holding the computer monitor, dodging a sobbing youth who was flailing with a broadsword. For a stunned moment, she thought that this was part of the D&D game. It looked no more real than any of the other antics that took place at a con, but then she saw Diefenbaker kneeling over an unconscious Ayhan and trying to staunch his wound with a reddening handkerchief. "Dear God!" she murmured, dropping the bag. "JAY!"

Jay Omega did not glance in her direction. He kept watching Morgan and talking in a slow, steady voice. "Yeah, you've saved Tratyn Runewind once, Morgan, didn't you? He died on Dungannon's computer disk, and you erased it, didn't you?"

"Yes!" Morgan kept circling with the quivering sword, waiting.

"And then you saved him again when you shot Dungannon, so that he couldn't rewrite that chapter, didn't you?" The computer monitor was getting heavier in his hands. He had barely managed to evade Morgan's last thrust; if the kid hadn't been crying so hard, he'd have had him.

"Well, Morgan, you saved him twice. But three times is the charm. Your spells have run out. I've killed him for time and eternity."

Clifford Morgan packed all of his rage into one mighty thrust of the broadsword, aiming with all his strength for the Amdek monitor, dead center, intending to ram all the way through its plastic case and into the entrails behind it, just as the Norseman had gutted his beloved Runewind.

Jay Omega's muscles froze as he felt the sword splinter the screen of the monitor, but he realized that the simultaneous scream was not his own. Through the flash and the smoke, the acrid smell, and the far-off scream that was definitely Marion, Omega heard one last dwindling cry from Clifford Morgan. He dropped the monitor, and Clifford Morgan, his hands still welded to the hilt of his broadsword, went down with it. The blade, still buried inside the monitor, flashed with little arcs of electricity.

Jay Omega kicked the plug out of the wall. "Somebody get some help," he said quietly.

Still in the doorway, Marion stood watching the scene, unable to break the spell of the shock, until she felt someone touch her arm. She jumped, trampling the lunch bag, and almost crying out, before she recognized a young police officer. His young face looked uncharacteristically grim. She saw the gun in his right hand.

"You won't need that," she murmured.

"Just what's going on in here, ma'am?" he demanded. "Where's the lieutenant?"

Marion felt tears on her cheeks. "You know *Hamlet*?" she asked him. " 'The play's the thing, wherein I'll catch the conscience of the king.' He played it by the book."

Bonnenberger, still maintaining squatter's rights to the video lounge, tried to concentrate on his paperback, despite the loud talking and general distraction from the group on the couches. That Mrs. Peel person couldn't seem to stop crying, and the guest author kept having to stop talking and hug her. Bonnenberger couldn't be bothered to find out why.

Miles Perry, looking somewhat less haggard, had put on a coat and tie in anticipation of television reporters with minicams.

Diefenbaker appeared in the doorway, looking solemn. "I just spoke with the rescue squad people. Lieutenant Ayhan is already conscious, and roaring about people trying to be TV heroes. He seems to have a broken forearm and a flesh wound, but he says he'll be out of the hospital by six, and none of the medics argued with him." He sighed. "I'm so glad. I felt quite inadequate with my little handkerchief. You know, at one point, I actually whispered one of my cleric's healing spells over him—in desperation!"

Marion smiled up at him through tears. "It couldn't have hurt."

"What about Morgan?" asked Jay Omega quietly.

Diefenbaker hung his head. "Oh, dear. I'd hoped you'd have heard already . . . I . . ." He took a deep breath, and plunged on. "They couldn't revive him. Too many volts."

Marion began to dab her tears. Then, as if she suddenly remembered something, she looked stern. "You might have told me, Jay," she said.

"I wasn't sure myself. I thought he'd killed Dungannon, but I couldn't figure out where he got the gun," said Jay Omega. "He obviously tried not to use one with me."

"It was Dungannon's," said Diefenbaker. "Lt. Ayhan's assistant said that ballistics phoned to tell him that it was a Smith & Wesson Model 1917, and when he asked the editor about it, Mr. Warren said that Dungannon always carried it around with him. It went with the cowboy hat."

"That makes sense. I figured Morgan had broken into Dungannon's room just after the costume competition fiasco, while we were still in the ballroom. He must have wanted to see the new book. How did he get in? Credit card in the lock?"

"Swiped the maid's keys." It was Simmons, the young cop. "He must have been hovering around the hotel somewhere. Morgan works for a hotel maintenance firm back in Philadelphia. He'd know his way around. As far as we can make it, he let himself in—"

"So," said Miles, catching on, "he erased the disk and swiped the gun?"

"Yeah. They found it in the tank of the toilet in his bathroom. It was a great place to hide it. I expect he saw it done in a movie once."

The Godfather, thought Bonnenberger, still half listening.

"I'm sorry he's dead," said Jay Omega. "I just wanted to rattle him enough to make him confess. I guess I got kind of—"

Diefenbaker cast a stricken look at Jay Omega, terrified that he might actually break down. "You were very fortunate to have escaped," Dief said hurriedly. "I'm thankful it was no worse than it was."

Marion reached for Jay's hand, but then drew back in a snit. "You might have been killed, you know. He could just as easily have shot you. I might have been sorrier for you then! Why didn't you trust me with your little secret? I wrote the damned Dungeon for you!"

Jay sighed. "I wasn't sure it would work. I shouldn't even have let you stay in the room. I didn't realize it was going to be so dangerous!"

Marion glared at him. "Thank *you*, Conan-the-Barbarian! Dangerous for me. One fantasy game and you suddenly start seeing yourself as the lord of the loincloth, and think you have to protect *me*?"

Jay looked sheepish. "Sorry, Marion. The old stereotypes do die hard. Look—can we get out of here? I don't want to talk anymore."

She sighed. "Oh, and you don't need me hassling you about it anymore either, right? Well, I'm sorry."

"No," he said, "I just said I don't want to *talk* anymore. I'm going up to the room now."

She hesitated. "Do you want to be alone?"

He held out his hand. "We still have a couple of hours before check-out . . ."

As they left the room, still holding hands, Jay Omega turned to Dief and Miles Perry. "We'll catch you before we leave."

When they were gone, Diefenbaker leaned back on the couch and sighed. "Well, Miles, I'm sorry you had so much chaos to contend with at Rubicon."

Miles had been thinking resignedly about returning to the produce section at the Food Lion, but Dief's remark brought on the glimmer of a smile. "Yes, but it will certainly give people something to talk about all year, won't it?"

"No doubt about that, Miles," said Dief cheerily. "Even fen who weren't here will have to claim they were."

"Of course . . ." said Miles with exuberance, "we do have our work cut out for us next year. This will be a hard act to follow."

Diefenbaker blinked. "Oh, yes. Next year! I suppose we ought to start planning it now, shouldn't we?"

"Yes. We'll need some ideas to show the committee before they leave today and . . ."

Dief began to scribble notes and names on the back of his program. He paused with what he hoped was appropriate solemnity. "Too bad we won't have Clifford Morgan around," he said. "I'm sorry to lose such a colorful personality."

"I'm sorry Cliff didn't live to stand trial," Miles answered. "Can't you just imagine a courtroom full of ordinary people when 'Tratyn Runewind' stood up and pleaded self-defense?"

Diefenbaker nodded. "The mundane world wouldn't understand."

"I'm also glad the case got solved before Lt. Ayhan got around to asking me who wrote that threatening letter to Appin Dungannon," Miles added.

"Did you?" gasped Diefenbaker.

"Sure, but I didn't kill him," Miles hastened to append.

"No, of course, Miles. That goes without saying," Dief protested.

"I was planning to let Chip Livingstone take the credit for it in his next fanzine article. —Imagine my surprise when Dungannon ends up dead, and Chip Livingstone is a suspect."

"Well, at least Lt. Ayhan solved the case," said Diefenbaker. "And I think in police circles, a wound in the line of duty is something of a badge of honor, is it not?"

Miles Perry smiled. "Ayhan may get more out of this case than congratulations from his captain. Earlier today he was down in the lobby talking to Louis Warren about the possibility of publishing his memoirs. I think he was planning to call this investigation *The Case of the Killer Elves*."

Joseph Bonnenberger shook his head. These people weren't talking about the plot of a science fiction novel at all. They weren't even discussing their player characters in a role-playing game like Top Secret. Apparently they were talking about real life. Real life bored him. Bonnenberger stopped listening, and went back to his book.

ZOMBIES
OF THE
GENE POOL

To Michael Dobson,
the State of Franklin Science Fiction Society,
and Francis Towner Laney

With thanks to Don Johnson, for the
use of *Watauga Drawdown*.

Even death will not release you.

An expression of the
Los Angeles Science
Fiction Society, ca. 1949

CHAPTER 1

JAY OMEGA DECIDED to wait until the shouting stopped before he knocked. Against his better judgment he had left the happy anarchy of the Electrical Engineering building and ventured into the English department to see if Marion wanted to go to dinner, but the sounds coming from her office indicated that Dr. Marion Farley was otherwise engaged. The typed index card on the door announced that she had office hours from 4 to 5 P.M., so Jay assumed that she was in conference with a student. He had put his ear to her office door to see if she was nearly finished and had heard the following exchange.

"This is a world literature class, not a science fiction class!"

"But—"

"And I can't believe that you actually wrote a paper comparing Joseph Conrad to Robert Silverberg!"

"But, Dr. Farley, when I read *Heart of Darkness,* I recognized *Downward to the Earth* almost exac—"

"And you accused Joseph Conrad of plagiarism!"

Jay Omega sighed and walked away. Marion was going to be a while. He wondered how late their dinner date was likely to be. Jay Omega and Marion Farley had little in common besides the fact that they were both carbon-based life forms, but despite the differences in temperament, interests, and income, they had been a couple for two years now. The relationship began when Jay ventured into the English department with the manuscript of his first book, and Marion asked if he had a note from his adviser. He still looked young for a Ph.D., and his jeans from the tenth grade did still fit, though Marion had made him throw them away. He supposed he had changed for the better since then. Marion had once seen his high school yearbook photo and said, "You looked like a mosquito." Now he had contact lenses instead of Coke-bottle glasses, and his brown hair was cut in a longer, more flattering style. They had both blossomed after ado-

lescence. Marion had endured high school as a fat and friendless
intellectual; now she was a slender, dark-haired Ph.D. who ran in the
local marathons and sparred with the women's fencing team. It was
no coincidence that the poster above her desk featured *The Avengers'*
Emma Peel, Marion's role model in adolescence.

Jay looked down at his khaki work pants and plaid shirt. He still
didn't dress like the dapper young professors in English, but Marion
had given up on him in that department. He didn't wear power ties,
but he kept her decrepit car running, which more than made up for
it. Jay and Marion were in a romantic holding pattern, waiting to see
if they would both get tenure so that neither would have to leave the
university and start over elsewhere.

Jay ventured back to the office door. She was still at it. He sighed.
If things dragged on for too long, he could always go in search of a
snack machine, but since most of the English professors seemed to
be on a health and fitness kick, he wasn't even sure that they *had* a
snack machine, and if they did, it might offer such arcane items as
wheat germ and carob candy bars. Long ago he decided that the
English department was about as alien as anything Robert Silverberg
could come up with. Even after several years' association with one
of their assistant professors, he didn't understand their tribal customs.
Or their bulletin boards. Every now and then he would come in and
read the notices while he was waiting for Marion, just to see if any
literary culture had worn off on him. Apparently, it hadn't.

WARREN WRITES BETTER THAN ANNE.

Now what did *that* mean? Jay Omega turned to a pink-haired young
woman in overalls who was pinning a Literary Lions notice over the
campus newspaper clipping announcing that Professor Byron Snipes
had just been published in the avant-garde (which Marion said was pronounced "mimeographed") literary magazine, *The Maggots Digest.*

Jay knew about the Literary Lions. They were a group of English
instructors and other town writers who gave readings every Sunday
afternoon in the New Age Café. Marion had dragged him there once
when her office mate Toni Richardson was reading from her stream-
of-consciousness novel about a Labrador retriever who thought it was
Virginia Woolf. Every time the dog had to go into the water to retrieve a duck, there would be pages and pages of inner dialogue over
whether or not it would get back out. Jay didn't understand it at all,
but everyone else had told Toni that it was very experimental and
definitely not accessible. (Marion said that "experimental" meant
writing in the present tense, and "not accessible" meant that they
didn't understand it either.)

Jay Omega's opinion was not solicited. He was the only nationally published author in town, but since he had written a science fiction novel called *Bimbos of the Death Sun,* he was not invited to read with the mineral water and tofu crowd at the New Age Café. Not even for their four-dollar beans and rice fund raisers in support of El Salvador. (Or was it *against* support in El Salvador?) Anyway, Jay didn't remember any Literary Lions called Warren or Anne. So what was that about?

"Excuse me," he said, pointing to the hand-lettered graffiti. "Could you tell me what that means?"

The pink lady glanced at the sign. "Warren Writes Better Than Anne." She nodded, with a frosty smile. "Beatty, of course. Only they spell it differently." Seeing that he still looked blank, she explained kindly, "Warren Beatty is Shirley MacLaine's little brother."

Before he could explain that it was Anne he had never heard of, she had walked away with her sheaf of notices, and another student was tugging at his sleeve. "Dr. Mega, I'm glad I ran into you!"

The tall red-headed guy with a Starfleet patch on his jacket looked familiar. What was that kid's name? Second row, first seat in engineering fundamentals. Jay managed a feeble grin, hoping he wasn't about to be asked for a reference.

The young man set his books on top of the covered trash can and chattered on, happily unaware of his anonymity. "When I was home on spring break, I tried to buy a copy of your book for my high school physics teacher, but our local bookstore said it wasn't on their order list."

Dr. James Owens Mega—aka science fiction author Jay Omega— heaved a mighty sigh of resignation. "Did you look under G?"

"No. Is that a new one? I wanted your first book—*Bimbos of the Death Sun.*"

"I know. It's listed under G. For *Galactic Wonders #2: Bimbos of the Death Sun.* The first part is the series title. Alien Books lists all their titles that way. The first one in the series is *Galactic Wonders #1: Betrayal at Byzantium* by Susan Shwartz." She's not happy about it either, he finished silently.

Several months earlier, when they found out about this nationwide blunder, Marion had remarked, "This is the only book in history that requires a password in order to purchase it!"

The student was looking at him as if he were crazy. "Under G," he repeated carefully. "Uhh—I've taken some marketing courses, Dr. Mega, and I have to tell you, that doesn't sound like a good idea."

Jay Omega nodded sadly. "So my royalty statements would indicate."

It seemed to Jay Omega that he had the worst of both worlds—another reason that the English department made him uneasy. The way he figured it, an author could either go for respect in the literary world—critical reviews in prestigious journals, scholarly articles on one's works, small print runs at respected university presses—or he could write popular fiction and receive fan mail and big bucks. The lurid bikini-clad girl on the cover of Jay Omega's paperback original left no doubt in the English department as to which category *his* work fell into. They assumed that he was making a fortune, and that it was easy money.

Every time Marion talked him into attending a faculty party, one of her colleagues would sidle up to him, margarita in hand, and say, "You know, maybe during spring break I'll dash off a science fiction novel. I could use the extra cash."

Apparently they didn't intend to be insulting. They all thought that he was rich and lazy. Jay suspected that if he admitted to them how hard he worked and how little he made, they would simply replace their envy with contempt, so he left well enough alone.

The professorial misconception was that genre writing was easy and high-paying, and that anyone with scholarly training could do it in a matter of hours. Occasionally one of them tried. Jay Omega had been forced to read some of these dashed-off manuscripts, and he found them to be plodding exercises in obscurity. They sounded like dissertations. Finding excuses not to give out the name of his agent or his editor was beginning to require more creativity than his latest book. He was losing patience. Sooner or later one of them was going to sneer at him once too often, and he was going to say, "Look—if you really want a surefire scheme for cash from trash, forget genre fiction. Just write a long convoluted novel in the present tense with no quotation marks and sell it to a university press. Get your friends to write reviews of it in the *MLA Journal,* get tenure on your literary reputation, and then sit back for the rest of your life collecting a fat salary and teaching two classes a week."

Marion would kill him.

He decided that he'd better stop loitering in the halls of the English department, before one of them accosted him with a new plot summary. Perhaps he could write Marion a note asking her to meet him at his office.

"Ah, Dr. Mega! I've been meaning to speak to you."

Too late!

Jay Omega looked up, hoping that he wasn't about to be presented with another manuscript. To his relief he saw Erik Giles, empty-handed, beckoning from the door of his office. Professor Giles taught nineteenth- and early twentieth-century British literature, and as far as Jay knew, he wrote only for scholarly publications.

"I take it that Marion is busy," Giles was saying. "Why don't you come in for a cup of coffee, and you can keep an eye on her door." He raised one eyebrow. "Or at least monitor the noise level."

With a grin of considerable relief, Jay Omega hurried into Professor Giles' shabby, book-strewn office. Compared to the engineering offices, it was a Victorian parlor. (Marion once said that *his* office looked like the inside of a pinball machine.) He removed a stack of papers from the Goodwill armchair and sat down. Despite the clutter, it was a comfortable room, well suited to Giles himself. It had the same air of *old, but still serviceable,* and its genial mix of well-worn books and prints of English landscapes suggested an old-fashioned gentility indicative of an aging scholar. This, of course, was a carefully cultivated pose on the part of Erik Giles, and it served him very well. His Dickensian office, his rimless glasses, and his baggy cardigan sweaters tallied with everyone's expectations of a kindly but dull middle-aged professor of English, few people bothered to look beneath the facade.

Marion had found out the secret quite by accident, on her way to her science fiction class to lecture on the history of the genre. Four minutes late as usual, she had scurried around the corner, balancing a chin-high stack of paperbacks, and crashed into Professor Giles, who was just leaving his lit class on Kipling. The collision sent the books flying. Ever the gentleman, Erik Giles had stooped to help his colleague gather up her belongings.

"So frightfully clumsy of me," he murmured, although it had clearly been her fault.

Marion claimed all of the blame for the mishap and tottered on to her classroom. She hadn't given the incident another thought until midway through her lecture when she was discussing the writers of the early fifties. "... And one of the most visionary and lyrical of the new generation of S-F writers wrote as C. A. Stormcock, which, as I'm sure you've guessed, was a pseudonym. His major work was *The Golden Gain....*" She began to rummage through the stack of books in search of her copy. She found that she had acquired an edition of Kipling's poems during her collision with Professor Giles. Idly, she opened the volume at a place marked with a paperclip, half intending to save herself further embarrassment by pretending that this was the volume she sought. She looked down at a well-marked passage of "The Mine Sweepers," intrigued by a phrase in the poem.

She looked up to find thirty pairs of eyes staring at her expectantly. She resumed her search for the real book. "This landmark work, totally ignored when it was first published . . . it's here somewhere . . . illustrates the theory that . . . no, that's not it."

It wasn't there.

In the end, Marion bluffed her way through that part of her talk, dispensing with the reading of the death scene of Selig in chapter nine, but for the rest of the lecture, Dr. Farley was on automatic pilot. As she recited the particulars of genre history, her mind was analyzing the problem of the missing volume. She had taken it off the bookshelf in her office, and she remembered placing it in the stack. . . .

"It is only in recent years that S-F scholars have taken any notice of Stormcock. His paperback originals were virtually ignored by the critics of the time. C. A. Stormcock was, as I said, a pen name. Many writers—especially in science fiction—used pseudonyms in those days."

"Like Jay Omega," said an engineering major.

Marion reddened, almost losing her train of thought. "Oh, yes. Our own Dr. James Owens Mega, of the electrical engineering department, writes as Jay Omega, which is a physics term—"

"Frequency times the square root of negative one," said the engineer.

Marion scowled. "I knew that."

"So what was Stormcock's real name?" someone called out.

"There are several theories. One is that he did not exist, and that Curtis Phillips and the notorious Pat Malone actually wrote his works in collaboration. Others think that—"

"Is this going to be on the test?" asked a serious-faced little blonde.

Marion sighed. "No," she said. "Because, after all, we really don't know who he was."

But suddenly she did.

When the chimes sounded the hour, Marion got out of the room faster than the football players. She ran down the hall and into Professor Giles' turn-of-the-century lair without bothering to knock. "Why did you take my copy of *The Golden Gain?*" she demanded.

He looked up from a stack of term papers, genial but apparently puzzled. "Did I?" he said mildly. "It must have got mixed with my own papers."

Marion almost wavered, but then she remembered. "You weren't carrying any papers when I ran into you."

He sighed. "Oh dear. Well, I'm afraid it isn't a very good book. Reverse alchemy, in fact—turning gold into lead. Must you include it?"

Marion looked stern. "May I have my copy back, please?"

With a sheepish smile, Professor Giles reached under the stack of term papers and brought out the tattered paperback.

Marion made no move to retrieve it. "May I have it autographed, please?"

He blinked in confusion. "I beg your pardon?"

Marion sat down on the arm of the easy chair. "Look," she said, holding up the volume of Kipling. "You're a Kipling scholar. God knows why, but you are. And on the frontispiece of this book, someone has written 'Stormy.' And I think I know where the name C. A. Stormcock came from. Listen to this." She turned to the page on which "The Mine Sweepers" was printed and read aloud: " 'Mines reported in the fairway,/Warn all traffic and detain./'Sent up *Unity, Claribel, Assyrian, Stormcock* and *Golden Gain.*' "

Marion snapped the book shut with an air of triumph. "I can't imagine why no one picked up on that before."

"The Stormcock and *Golden Gain* connection?" said Giles. "Science fiction people wouldn't catch that. They don't do much out-of-field reading. Why, the great Irish fan Walt Willis had a column once called 'The Harp That Once or Twice,' and for years fans asked each other where the title came from."

Marion allowed herself to be diverted from her prey. "It's vaguely familiar. *The harp that once through Tara's halls . . .*"

"Exactly. Thomas Moore. An Irish poet. And *no one* got it!" Professor Giles smiled sadly. "Of course, this isn't literary scholarship, because neither Willis nor Stormcock matters. It's a form of Trivial Pursuit. All the same, it was well noted on your part. But it does not give you the identity of the author."

"Oh, no?" said Marion sweetly. "How about this? The main character is Selig Stone. Selig is Giles spelled backwards, and that comment you just made about 'reverse alchemy' is the punchline from the review of the novel in a fifties fanzine called *Grue*. Now don't try to tell me all that is a coincidence, or you'll find yourself in *Locus* so fast it'll make your head spin!"

He groaned. "Oh, please! Not that!"

"We thought you were dead," said Marion. "We weren't even sure you *existed*. Why all the secrecy?"

Erik Giles smiled sadly. "I grew up."

Just like a Daugherty project, except that it will actually happen . . .

—FRANCIS TOWNER LANEY
*An expression of anticipation
in Fifth Fandom*

CHAPTER 2

"I'M VERY GLAD you're here, Jay," Erik Giles was saying. "Actually, I need your help."

Jay Omega immediately looked around for a broken radio or a new-looking computer. That's what people usually meant when they said they needed his help, but he saw no evidence of electronic disasters in the English professor's office.

"Your help *and* Marion's, actually," the professor amended.

Then it definitely wasn't auto repair. Jay waited for enlightenment.

"There's a journey I need to make, and I'd like the two of you to go with me. You may have heard about my heart attack last year." He smiled at Jay's expression of concern, but signaled him not to interrupt. "No, I'm fine. I've lost a few pounds since last spring, and my blood pressure has improved somewhat. I'm not going to keel over on you. Anyway, I've received an interesting invitation, and because of my health and for other reasons, I don't particularly want to go alone. Actually, I don't want to go at *all*, but I believe I should, and I thought it was something that the two of you might be interested in."

Jay sighed. "Where *is* Worldcon this year?"

Professor Giles smiled. "It isn't that. And it isn't the MLA, either, which is just Worldcon hosted by Chaucer scholars." He looked intently at Jay Omega. "You *do* know who I am?"

Jay understood at once that Erik Giles was referring to his literary past as C. A. Stormcock, and since he seemed to expect an affirmative response, Jay decided to admit that he did. "Marion mentioned it to me a while back," he said.

"Yes, I thought so. Restraint is not one of Marion's virtues." Giles grinned at his colleague's unease. "And what was your reaction?"

"To the fact that you passed up fame? Well, I suppose I thought that it was a little strange. I mean, so many people seem to want to be famous writers, and science fiction is such a cult anyway, that it seemed odd for anybody who got mixed up in it in the first place to just walk away from an achievement like yours."

Professor Giles smiled sadly. "In a kingdom of the blind, the one-eyed man is king. When Marion found out who I was, she asked me the same thing, and I told her *I grew up*. It wasn't much of an explanation, but it was true. As time went on, I began to be less enchanted with my accomplishments. To give you one small example— I learned that almost any reasonably clever person can make puns. The truly intelligent person refrains from doing so."

Jay couldn't for the life of him make puns, but he decided not to argue the point. He was still wondering about the mysterious invitation, but Erik Giles had launched into a one-sided discussion of philosophy—probably a holdover from his days in science fiction.

"I am one of those unfortunate people who cannot appreciate a compliment unless I respect the person giving it," he said, with the air of someone who has given the subject much thought. "A great many people liked my book—but what else had they read? I felt hampered by their opinions and their expectations. There are a good many six-book critics in the genre."

"Six-book—?"

"People who have read six books and think that it entitles them to be critics. The sort of person who doesn't recognize a pastiche of *Lysistrata* because he's unfamiliar with the original."

Jay nodded. He had heard Marion say much the same thing, although at greater length and with considerably more venom.

"Anyhow, I got tired of being Gulliver. What I really wanted to do was to explore my potential as a writer."

"And what are you writing now?" asked Jay uneasily, thinking of the New Age Café readings. He wondered if Erik Giles was churning out slices of monotony in the present tense.

"I'm not. I discovered I couldn't do literary fiction. I'd got out of the habit of being tedious. So I said the hell with it, and now I teach undergraduate courses and do a bit of scholarly research to keep the department happy. How about you? Burned out yet?"

Jay was saved from having to reply by the appearance of Marion, who still glittered from her recent bout of intellectual combat. Her dark hair was tucked behind her ears, and her reading glasses were balanced precariously on the top of her head. Clearly she was still in office mode. "Somebody told me they'd seen you come in here," she said, scowling.

"Good afternoon," said Jay tentatively, in case she hadn't got all the rage out of her system.

Erik Giles was chuckling. "Finished your conference?"

"It is a fortunate thing that electric pencil sharpeners are too small to accommodate the heads of sophomores," Marion growled. "Well, at least I set him straight on his chronology."

"We heard," said Jay.

Marion sighed. "I know that tone of voice. You sound like someone making small talk with a hand grenade. I'm fine, really!" She managed a smile. "What have you two been up to?"

"Erik was just telling me that he wants us to go somewhere with him."

"Oh?" Marion looked interested. "And where is that?"

"To dinner," said Professor Giles quickly. "This is going to be a long story, and I feel that I owe you both a steak just for listening to it."

Marion sighed. "I wish more authors felt that way."

The Wolfe Creek Inn was an eighteenth-century farmhouse that had been converted into an elegant restaurant. When the pasture lands adjoining the university were sold off one by one for apartment complexes and gas stations, most of the large old houses were torn down as detriments to the land value, or perhaps because they clashed with the current ambience of neon and asphalt. The Wolfe family farmstead was salvaged by a resourceful couple of Peace Corps veterans, who had not managed to make much of a dent on the problems in Bolivia during their years there, but who had learned carpentry themselves, a skill infinitely more useful than their majors in political science. They figured the Wolfe house would be easier to tackle than the Bolivian rural economy, so they bought the eighteenth-century house with its graceful wraparound porches, its oak floors buried under fifties linoleum, its huge stone fireplaces, its field mouse population, and its dry rot. The house was priced at only fifty-one thousand dollars, a price roughly equal to the cost of restoring it. With loans from their long-suffering parents, the Peace Corps veterans rewired, refinished, and rehabilitated every square inch of the old mansion and turned the result into a cozy, antique-filled restaurant much favored by faculty members and visiting parents. The meals were priced at roughly the average monthly income in Bolivia. Undergrads eager to impress their dates confined their visits to Friday and Saturday nights, particularly during football season, but tonight—a Tuesday in late May—the place was nearly empty.

Giles-Party-of-Three, as the waitress called them, was tucked into a pine-paneled alcove decorated with Bob Timberlake prints in rough wood frames. They were trying to read the hand-lettered menus by the light of the candle in a red jar, which doubled as a centerpiece on the oilskin tablecloth.

"This looks like a séance," said Marion, watching their shadows flicker against the pine wall.

"It is," said Erik Giles. "I'm about to raise a number of ghosts."

He waited until the waitress had taken their order and had gone to fetch the drinks before he began. "You want to know where it is that I have to go, but in order to explain that I'll have to backtrack." He began to trace patterns on the tablecloth with his knife. "Do you know much about science fiction fandom?"

"I read science fiction," said Jay. "Does that count?"

"No," said Marion. "Erik means the organized subculture that grew up around the genre. It began in New York in the thirties when the people who had been writing to the letters columns of the pulp science fiction magazines began writing to each other instead. Then clubs sprang up, and people began to publish amateur fanzines, reviewing books and arguing about topics of science or technology. By the fifties, it had become an end in itself."

Professor Giles smiled. "By then, there were people who scarcely bothered to read the genre, because they were so busy with the social aspects of fandom."

"I missed all that," said Jay. "I was into crystal radio sets as a kid, and after that computers. So you two were fans?"

Marion blushed. "If you grow up as a social misfit in a small town, it can be a very attractive option. I was smart when girls were supposed to be bubblebrains, and I wasn't very pretty in high school, which is a real burden for the teenage ego. Fandom is good about accepting people for being kind and clever, without caring about age, sex, race, or appearance."

Erik Giles looked thoughtful. "Why was I in fandom? I wanted to be a writer, I guess, and these people encouraged me. It's easy to get 'published' in fanzines. Of course, later I realized—" He shook his head sadly. "Well, it doesn't matter. I was explaining the reunion, wasn't I? Have you ever heard of the Lanthanides?"

"Sure," said Jay, reaching for a bread stick. "The lanthanide series is a group of fourteen elements on the periodic chart, consisting of lanthanum, cerium, samarium—"

"Hush! We're discussing literature, not chemistry!" said Marion.

"I think that Erik is referring to a group of writers back in the Golden Age of Science Fiction."

Erik smiled. "I'd put the Golden Age a little farther back than that group of chowderheads. The early forties, maybe. Whereas, the Lanthanides began publishing in—"

"1957?" asked Jay Omega.

"About then," Giles agreed.

Marion stared at him. "How did you know, Jay? You never read that stuff!"

Erik Giles laughed. " 'What do they know of literature who only literature know?' " he said, misquoting his beloved Kipling. "Jay guessed correctly the date of the Lanthanides' fiction debut because he was right about the origin of the term. The group's name was chosen from a chemistry book, and the lanthanide series begins with element number 57, which is the year the members thought they'd all be published authors." He sighed. "It took a bit longer than that, of course, even for the luckiest members, and some of them never even got published."

"Pretty good name for a science fiction group, though," said Jay with a glint of mischief in his eyes. "The lanthanides are the rare-earth series of elements."

The older man nodded. "Yes, that was the real reason we chose it. We thought rare earth described our visions rather well. And, of course, the name itself— Lanthanides—is from the Greek *lanthanein,* meaning to be concealed, which is perfect for a secret society of adolescent crackpots."

"Now, wait a minute, Erik. Those writers were—" Marion gasped. *"We?"*

He smiled modestly. "Yes, I was a member of the Lanthanides. Of course, back in 1954 we were just a bunch of redneck beatniks in Wall Hollow, Tennessee."

"Tennessee?" echoed Marion. "Wasn't Brendan Surn one of the Lanthanides? I thought he was from Pittsburgh."

"He was. And Curtis was from Baltimore, Mistral was a Brooklynite, and Peter Deddingfield and I grew up in Richmond. But the year that the group was formed, most of us were in our early twenties, and our job prospects were middling. It was 1954. We didn't want to become the men in the gray flannel suits, and nothing else was paying too well. Anyway, we weren't ready to settle down.

"Dale Dugger and George Woodard were just back from Korea and Fort Dix, New Jersey, respectively. A couple of us were just out of college—with or without degrees—and a few were tired of the jobs they did have. We all knew each other the way science fiction fans do—through correspondence and a mimeographed fanzine—and we decided to get together. Nobody had anything better to do.''

Marion frowned. ''This is not an era I've done much reading about. It's the beginning of Sixth Fandom according to S-F fannish history. I'm familiar with Walt Willis and the *Wheels of IF* . . . Lee Hoffman and *Quandry*. . . . Wasn't there a fanzine associated with the group?''

''*Alluvial*. George Woodard still publishes it. Or at least something called that. Of course, none of the rest of us have contributed to it in years.''

''I never knew Stormcock was a member of the Lanthanides.''

Erik Giles smiled modestly. ''I wrote *The Golden Gain* while I was there.'' His fingers trembled a bit on the hilt of the table knife, and he suddenly looked old.

''So you formed a commune?'' Jay prompted.

''Slanshack!'' murmured Marion, correcting him.

''Back then, with Joseph McCarthy's witch hunters hiding under every bed, I don't think we would have called it a commune, but by your generation's standards I guess it was. We called it the Fan Farm. Actually, Dale Dugger's daddy had died while Dale was overseas, leaving him a hardscrabble farm in the east Tennessee hills, and we decided that life didn't get any cheaper than that, so we all packed our belongings and typewriters, and descended on Dugger's farm. We planned to live on beans and hot dogs while we each wrote the science fiction equivalent of the Great American Novel, and then we figured we'd all drive away in Cadillacs and live on steaks for the rest of our lives.'' He smiled, remembering their youthful naïveté.

The waitress appeared just then, balancing three plate-sized skillets on a tray. ''I have two prime ribs and a broiled-flounder-no-butter.''

''The fish is mine,'' said Erik Giles. ''Doctor's orders.''

Marion attended to her dinner for a few minutes, but her thoughtful expression indicated that she was more interested in the conversation than the food. ''So you actually lived with Surn and Deddingfield in—what did you say the name of the place was?''

''Wall Hollow, Tennessee. That's where the post office was, anyhow. Dugger's Farm was seven miles up a hollow. It was beautiful country. Green-forested mountains that looked like haze against the sky.''

''*The Green Hills of Earth*,'' murmured Marion.

''No,'' said Giles, catching the reference. ''He wasn't there. I didn't meet him until the late sixties.''

''Well, your crowd didn't do too badly,'' said Marion, thinking it over. "Maybe you didn't leave the farm in Cadillacs, but you certainly produced some giants in the field of science fiction."

"Peter Deddingfield," nodded Jay. "Even *I've* heard of him. I loved the *Time Traveler Trilogy.*"

"He writes in a very *literary* style," said Marion, offering her highest praise. "Critics have compared him to Herman Melville."

"Well, I like him anyway," said Jay.

Marion frowned. "And Brendan Surn is the greatest theorist in the genre. I think he's required reading in NASA. I always think that he looks like a snow lion with that white mane of hair and his white beard. Who else was in the group?"

"That you would have heard of? Pat Malone, of course."

"He's a *legend*. What was he really like?"

"You mustn't rely on my judgment," said Erik Giles. "I didn't know at the time which of my friends to be impressed by."

Jay Omega, who had no memory for authors' names and was thus at a dead loss at Trivial Pursuit, was trying to place Pat Malone. "Should I have heard of him?"

"Yes!" said Marion. "He wrote *River of Neptune,* which wasn't a classic or anything, but it was a very promising work for a young writer, but then Pat Malone did another book that will be remembered forever in fandom—*The Last Fandango*. It wasn't officially published—just mimeographed and distributed by FAPA, the Fantasy Amateur Press Association—but it was so caustic and critical of certain fans that it became an underground classic. He revealed their sexual preferences, their lapses in hygiene, and their petty machinations in fan politics. I hear that it was really hot stuff in its day."

Erik Giles nodded. "It was an unpleasant duty that Pat positively reveled in doing. The glee in his tone is at times unmistakable."

"I imagine that publication cost him a few friends," said Jay. "I have friends in engineering who dream of doing that on a faculty level, but they dare not."

"I would strongly discourage it," said Marion, with a repressive glare suggesting that she suspected *which* engineer harbored such a fantasy. "Because a professor who did that would have to live with the consequences, while Pat Malone did not. He simply dropped out of sight. Apparently he became very embittered with science fiction because of his disillusionment with all his old associates and he gafiated."

Jay stared. "I beg your pardon?" He was picturing Japanese rituals of disembowelment.

Marion blushed at having been caught speaking *fanslang*. "GAFIA.

It's an acronym for getting away from it all. It means dropping out of the world of science fiction.''

"And lived happily ever after?''

"Apparently not. My source materials say that he died in mysterious circumstances. The word is that he was found dead on a mountaintop in Mississippi.''

"There *are* no mountaintops in Mississippi,'' Jay pointed out.

Erik Giles laughed. "A grasp of material facts has never been a strong point in fandom. That was the story that went around the grapevine back then, and I never heard otherwise.''

"Those are all the Lanthanides I know about,'' said Marion. "I confess I've never heard of Dale Dugger or George What was his name?''

"Woodard. He's still around. He never published much of anything, but he lives in Libertytown, Maryland, now; and, as I told you, he puts out a fanzine called *Alluvial*. That and his incessant correspondence seem to take most of his energy. Aside from that, he teaches algebra.''

"And Dale Dugger?''

A spasm of pain crossed Erik Giles' face. "He died some years ago. He became an alcoholic, and finally at the end, a street person. I heard about it later. Wish there was something I could have done.''

"There aren't many of you left then,'' said Marion, doing a mental tally.

"No. There's Surn, but he's quite feeble now, I hear. And Woodard. Angela Arbroath. Jim and Barbara Conyers, and Ruben Mistral.''

"Mistral,'' murmured Jay. "That name sounds familiar. He's a screenwriter, isn't he?''

"Yes. When I knew him his name was Reuben J. Bundschaft. We called him Bunzie. He's probably got more money than Surn and Deddingfield by now, with all those movie deals. Still, I hear he's coming to this little show.''

"What show is that?''

Erik Giles sighed. "The Lanthanides are having a reunion.''

Noticing the lack of enthusiasm in his announcement, Marion said gently, "Don't you want to go?''

"There's more to it than that. I have to tell you *why* there's a reunion, and why we didn't have it in 1984 like we'd planned.''

"Why didn't you?''

"Because Wall Hollow, Tennessee is at the bottom of a lake.''

* * *

It was late. After cheesecake and several cups of coffee, the three professors had finally called it a night and said their good-byes on the porch of the Wolfe Creek Inn. Jay was driving Marion home. She leaned back in the passenger seat of Jay's temporarily functional MG, clutching her headscarf against the wind that whipped through a crack between the canvas roof and the windscreen. "I was just thinking about Erik Giles and his extraordinary reunion," she called above the roar of the wind and the 1600 engine.

"Quite a story!" Jay agreed.

"After he told us about it, I remembered hearing bits of it before. The underwater slanshack. It's a legend in science fiction circles, of course. But before my time," she added hastily.

"I can see why it's a legend," said Jay. "It's the Atlantis of fandom."

"And they held their own substitute convention! Wouldn't that be a wonderful story to write for a volume of fan history?" mused Marion, whose brain was never quite out of gear.

"Surely someone has already written that tale," said Jay.

"Knowing the Lanthanides, they probably fictionalized it. I'll bet that if we read all of Deddingfield, all of Surn, all of Mistral, and so on, *somewhere* we'd find the story of the unfinished journey and the time capsule. Writers always cannibalize their own lives for fiction."

"Oh, so you recognized yourself as the green lizard woman in *Bimbos*?"

Marion made a face at him and went back to contemplating the moon. "I can just see them in 1954, can't you? A bunch of post-adolescents with plenty of idealism and ambition, but no money or common sense. And because the Twelfth Worldcon is being held in San Francisco, six of them decide to pile into a disintegrating Studebaker and off they go!"

Jay Omega shrugged. "Why not? Gas was about eighteen cents a gallon then."

"But they were still broke. How much cash did he say they took with them? Twenty-five bucks? For a cross-country trip!"

"I guess it wasn't much money even for that era, because Giles said that when the car broke down in Seymour, Indiana, they couldn't afford to get it fixed. Apparently mechanics were expensive even then."

"Thank goodness it was only a radiator leak, so that they were able to limp back to the farm. I can't imagine Brendan Surn having to hitchhike."

"They must have been pretty game, though," said Jay. "If I had been unable to make a trip I'd had my heart set on, I don't think I'd have taken it as well as they did.''

"No, you'd sulk for days. But, then, why should they have cared about missing that convention? As far as future generations are concerned, the great literary minds of the era were all in Wall Hollow, Tennessee, that weekend. Except for Friday night when they went to Elizabethton to see the movie. Wherever *they* were, there was science fiction." Marion sighed. "That's the con I would like to have attended: all the great minds of the genre in an old farmhouse miles from anywhere, swapping story ideas.''

"It should be easy to arrange. Erik Giles told us what they did that weekend. So we rent a copy of *War of the Worlds,* buy a couple of cases of beer—"

"It wouldn't be the same. I'd like to know what Peter Deddingfield said to Pat Malone about the movie. I'd like to have heard them talk about their work!"

"Well, at least you may have a chance to see what they were writing at the time. If they can find the pickle jar," said Jay. "To me that is the most amazing part of all. An anthology of unpublished works by the greatest minds in science fiction, and it has yet to be recovered. It must be worth a fortune.''

"I expect so. When Giles said that all the Lanthanides were coming back to this reunion, I realized that there must be quite a lot of money in it somewhere. Sentiment seldom guarantees perfect attendance, but money usually does.''

"I don't know, Marion. Maybe—and this is farfetched—this reunion could be helpful to my career as an S-F writer, but you don't stand to gain anything by going, and it isn't just out of kindness to Erik Giles that you're going either. You wouldn't miss it.''

Marion sighed. "But I, my dear, am a recovering fan.''

Erik Giles studied his reflection in the bathroom mirror. There was a colorless look to his lined face, as if he were gradually fading to black and white. Even his eyes were gray. He glanced at the assortment of pills on the rim of the basin and wondered if he ought to go back to his doctor for a new prescription. How many formulas are there to stave off death? Can you switch from one nostrum to another and stay one jump ahead of it?

Not forever.

His mouth looked thin and sunken, and the muscles in his neck stood out like cords. Worse than any monster in Curtis Phillips' horror stories, he thought. This specter of death was much more invincible than the puny demons of *Weird Tales*. No magic words or pentagrams would drive it away. He must live with that mirrored reminder of his own mortality for whatever time he had left. He didn't think it would be long. The doctor tended to address him in patient, gentle tones that were more terrifying than any rudeness.

Was that why he wanted to see them all again? A moment's consideration told him that he did not particularly want to renew the acquaintance with his old companions, but at least the immediacy of his fate would ensure that the encounter would be mercifully brief. And he was curious after all these years to see how they had turned out. And what they looked like now. How much youth can you buy with Hollywood money? Perhaps they would still be fit and youthful looking. After all, he was just past sixty. He should have quit smoking years ago. The heart condition had devastated his health. Was he the only one who was old? Then he remembered that some of the Lanthanides hadn't even made it to sixty. Giles supposed that he could consider himself lucky that cancer or heart disease hadn't carried him off sooner. But he didn't feel fortunate. Not compared to the boys of summer out there in the Land of the Lotus Eaters. He suddenly realized that he was picturing them as men in their early twenties. Except for Brendan Surn. His white-maned features had become so famous that everybody pictured him as he looked in that one godlike publicity shot, clutching his malacca cane and staring out with what seemed to be infinite wisdom and pity.

Funny . . . In his mind, the others had not aged at all. He always imagined them as they had been thirty-five years before. He had to admit that most of them hadn't looked young even then. Dugger was pudgy and bespectacled; Phillips' hairline was beginning to recede; and Woodard had looked middle-aged since puberty. The Lanthanides had never been prize physical specimens, but he supposed that their interest in science fiction may have stemmed in part from that. Shunned by their classmates for being "eggheads," they retreated into a world of books and pulp magazines. They found their peers in the magazines' letters columns, and formed friendships by mail.

He could see them now, owlish young men in jeans and white T-shirts, loading up that old '47 Studebaker with cans of pork and beans and moon pies. It was a hot morning in mid-August, and the sky blazed blue and cloudless above the encircling mountains of Wall Hollow. The house was a weathered one-story structure nestled in a grove of oaks, in an acre of scrub grass and lilac bushes fenced in from the surrounding pasture land. No other human habitation was visible from the farm; it might have been an outpost on a genesis planet.

The car was parked in the patch of red dust by the front porch, and the six departing members of the group were standing on the porch bickering about what to take along. George Woodard wanted to take two boxes of books to be autographed and a carton full of copies of *Alluvial* to give away to prospective contributors. Dugger insisted on packing food instead. While the debate raged on, Jim Conyers opened the Studebaker's trunk and began to hoist boxes into it, without a word to the quarrelers. Conyers wasn't even going on the expedition—he had opted to stay behind with Curtis Phillips to feed the three cows and fourteen chickens—but he was the only member of the group who could do anything without analyzing it for two hours beforehand. What ever happened to Jim?

Bunzie was going to drive. The pilgrimage to the San Francisco science fiction convention had been his idea to begin with. Even then—years before he became the celebrated screenwriter Ruben Mistral—Bunzie had been fascinated by California.

The others were less enthusiastic.

"San Francisco?" said George Woodard with his customary worried frown. "Isn't that where they had the earthquake fifty years ago?"

"I don't care if they're having regular afternoon tidal waves!" yelled Bunzie. "They're hosting the Worldcon! Everybody in the world will be there! Slan Francisco!"

Since this was the tenth time Bunzie had made that particular joke, no one bothered to laugh. Finally Woodard called out, "Fans are slans!" but it was more out of politeness than conviction. The phrase would be chanted often in the days to come. Slan: a type of superior being described in the 1940 novel by A. E. Van Vogt. The Lanthanides had almost believed it in those days. They thought that they were the superbeings who had evolved one step beyond the mundanes of the planet. They would be the titans of the next century (and maybe the one after that; they all agreed that aging ought to be curable).

Erik Giles sighed wearily, remembering the mole-faced Dugger, the pedantic pettiness of Woodard, and the '54 version of himself: a bantam intellectual full of youthful arrogance. Slans, indeed. Because they understood the in-jokes in the magazines; because they knew who had written which pulp novella; because they were clever—too clever to really work hard at anything (low threshold of boredom) but endlessly capable of memorizing the facts that interested them. (What year did Asimov first publish? Who was the cover artist for the

December 1947 issue of *Astounding*?) Might as well call a ghetto kid a genius because he knew the batting averages of every one of the Dodgers. So the Slan/Fans wrote to each other, and argued with each other, and created endless feuds by gossiping about absent friends, secure in the knowledge of their slandom, and all the while, the world trickled right on past them. Now Giles could look back and see that *they* didn't break the sound barrier; *they* didn't walk on the moon; *they* didn't invent the transistor. The mundanes did that . . . while *they* were busy arguing over the ethical considerations of time travel, or writing exhaustive accounts of the last science fiction convention they attended.

It wasn't fair, though, to filter the memory of that summer through the glare of his later understanding. They had been so innocently pleased with themselves back then, and so sure that merit was the only determinant of success. They might as well have believed in fairy godmothers.

He smiled ruefully. They had certainly believed that Dugger's dilapidated green Studebaker, the Tin Lizard, would make it across country. Fortunately it had died in Indiana instead of stranding them in the desert farther west.

It had been a glorious beginning, though. They set off from Wall Hollow for a three-hundred-mile straight shot to Nashville before heading north on Highway 31, which went through Kentucky on its way to Indianapolis. They had got a late start because most of them were night people anyway, so the first day's drive only got them as far as south Kentucky, just past Bowling Green. They spent the first night camping near Mammoth Cave, swapping stories about John Carter, Edgar Rice Burroughs' Virginia gentleman who was chased into a cave by Apaches and ended up on Mars. As they sat around their campfire, Dale Dugger told them a true story about the Kentucky caver Floyd Collins, who was trapped in the Mammoth cave system twenty years back and died of exposure while rescuers bickered about the best way to rescue him. "Who does that remind you of?" said Pat Malone.

The others ignored his comment, preferring to discuss the existence of deros, and debating whether they ought to go looking for them in Mammoth Cave.

"What are deros?" George Woodard wanted to know. He had got so caught up in his fan correspondence and in *Alluvial* that he had very little time anymore for reading science fiction.

"Didn't you read that stuff in *Amazing*?" asked Surn. "About ten years ago, Richard Shaver published a short story called 'I Remember

Lemuria.' Shaver claimed that a race of insane beings lived beneath the surface of the earth.''

"Deros," said Bunzie. ''That's short for disentegrant energy robot. Someone whose mind has been destroyed by the Dis rays given off by the sun. Wouldn't that make a great movie?''

"It would," Surn agreed. ''But Shaver claimed that it was all true.''

Bunzie shrugged. "Curtis believes it, too. He told me so.''

The conversation had ended there.

The next morning the Stalwart Six, as they called themselves, climbed back into the car and headed north toward the Indiana border. The direct route from east Tennessee to California would not have led through Indiana, but Surn, the navigator, decided that since it was August and since Dugger's car was decrepit, they had better avoid the southern desert country. Besides, like most fans they had a nationwide network of friends and practically no cash, so the logical route would be the one that led from one fan hostel to another. Another bonus of the expedition was the chance to see famous fan landmarks along the way. Before they reached the second night's stopover with an unsuspecting fan host in Bloomington (showers optional, but highly encouraged), they wanted to drive through New Castle, Indiana, which was famous for being home to one of fandom's famous eccentrics, Claude Degler. Degler had formed a newsletter staffed by a whole society of fellow enthusiasts, who, upon investigation, proved not to exist. People still talked about Degler and his grape jelly—his only form of sustenance when traveling. He mixed it with water, an economy that provoked sneers even among the impoverished denizens of fandom. Degler didn't live in New Castle anymore, but that didn't matter. The traveling Lanthanides wouldn't have wanted to stay with him anyway. They just wanted to look at where he lived, and maybe ask a few townspeople for anecdotes about Degler so that they could report their findings to the rest of fandom at the convention.

Bunzie drove at whatever speed he felt like, and Brendan Surn played navigator, while Dale Dugger read the Burma-Shave signs aloud and made comments on the landscape in general. He kept trying to convince the others that there was more than one kind of cow, but was hooted into silence. In the back seat, Erik was crammed between Woodard and Pat Malone, who were keeping a running travel diary of their great adventure for publication in the next issue of *Alluvial*.

They sang "Shrimp Boats" for hours on end, trying various harmonies, and they took turns reading aloud from Poul Anderson's latest book, *Brainwave,* amid Dugger's bitter complaints that Ballantine Books had the nerve to charge thirty-five cents for it instead of the usual quarter.

The trip ended in a puff of smoke outside Seymour, Indiana. The Stalwart Six stood at a safe distance from the Tin Lizard's radiator, watching their dreams of Worldcon evaporate in clouds of steam.

"Well," said Woodard at last. "It could have been worse. At least we didn't hit a train."

"Can we fix it?" asked Bunzie, close to tears. He clutched his Esso road map as if it were a talisman.

"Can't afford a new radiator," Dale Dugger told him. "That would cost at least twenty bucks. We can stop every half hour or so and fill this one up as it leaks. That will get us home. But the Lizard would never make it across the prairie like that. It's too far between water holes."

"We have to turn back," Brendan Surn announced, and nobody argued. With a last look westward, they climbed back in the car, and for a full half hour no one's voice dispelled the gloom.

The ailing Tin Lizard headed for home, with her six Gunga Dins running for water at every streambed. By the time they reached Nashville, their spirits had revived, and Giles and Surn had immortalized the journey in a parody of Kipling's poem:

> *You may talk o' Blog and Bheer*
> *When your fellow fen are near,*
> *But Tin Lizard doesn't give a damn for boozing;*
> *Studebaker's bastard daughter*
> *Runs on Indiana water,*
> *And about six quarts an hour she was losing.*

It went on from there, with dwindling coherence and many forced rhymes, for some fourteen verses. Long before the composition was complete, Malone had retreated into the pages of *Brainwave,* and he kept ordering the revelers to shut up so that he could read.

They reached home just after nine, trailing ribbons of steam in the lingering twilight of a summer evening. The dark mountains closed behind them, walling out California and all the rest of the inaccessible world. Fireflies flashed like tiny meteors among the clumps of tiger lilies, and from the cow pond, the rhythmic chirrup of frogs welcomed the travelers home.

"How ya gonna keep 'em down on the farm?" said Bunzie. As

he climbed out of the Tin Lizard, he kicked a tire in disgust. "So much for the goddamned Worldcon."

"What do we do now?" asked George Woodard.

Pat Malone, who was helping to unload the trunk, looked thoughtfully at the box of supplies he was holding. "We've got the makings for a hell of a party."

"We could have our own convention," said Bunzie. "We have everything but the Worldcon guest of honor. John W. Campbell Jr.—hell, I'll be him!"

"We have no femmefans," Pat Malone pointed out. "Jazzy is at the con, and Earlene has to work Saturdays."

"We can call Angela Arbroath. She couldn't make it to 'Frisco, but I'll bet she could drive up from Mississippi. Maybe she could bring a girlfriend."

"We still have most of our travel money," said Brendan Surn. He was tall and lean in those days, with a hawklike face that seldom smiled. He was smiling now. "Twenty-two dollars will buy a hell of a lot of beer."

Dale Dugger took a running leap at the pasture fence and disappeared into the darkness.

"Where are you going?" Woodard called after him.

"To get some more water for Tin Lizard's radiator!" Dugger yelled back. "The closest beer joint is eight miles up the road!"

Professor Erik Giles closed his bedroom window, shutting out the night air and the sound of chirruping frogs. He didn't want to think about the Lanthanides anymore. The years in Wall Hollow had been enjoyable but useless blocks of time out of his life. Not long after the Worldcon expedition, they had gone their separate ways. Shortly after the dissolution of the group, the Tennessee Valley Authority had condemned the entire valley, paying its residents nominal value for their land. Then, in order to keep the Watauga River from flooding farther downstream, the TVA built a dam, creating a vast artificial lake in the sprawling valley. He had never been back to see it. There had been a letter from Dugger at the time it happened, but he had waited too long to answer it, and his reply came back marked "No forwarding address." Dugger was gone by then, drinking up his settlement money in the honky-tonks of Nashville, giving up fandom for different and more dangerous obsessions. Giles wondered if the government's seizure of the Dugger land had caused Dale's downward slide into alcoholism and poverty. It was too late now for Dale Dugger, but for the rest of them, there was a chance to get together again and to recapture at least some of the past. In his last letter, Dugger had written: "I didn't dig up the time capsule. I got no future to take it to."

*For three months gravity feeds the main sluice pulled
nightly at the dam. The reservoir drains. Each afternoon
he stops on the bluff to watch the valley fill with air,
light wrapping the fine branches of trees rising from the
surface full-grown but leafless, though no wind has blown
for thirty-seven years.*

—DON JOHNSON
Watauga Drawdown

CHAPTER 3

THEY MIGHT AS well be exhuming a corpse.

Jim Conyers stood on at the edge of the grass line—the spot where he usually fished—and stared at the dead landscape stretching out below. Where once the opaque green water of Breedlove Lake lapped at the hillside, there was now red mud, a no man's land of bare trees and asphalt roads leading back into the mire. This patch of grass used to be the edge of the lake, but now if Conyers wanted to he could walk farther down, into the valley of . . . *the shadow of death* . . . Wall Hollow, into the remnants of the drowned village. He could revisit the farm and the other places he remembered from long ago. If he would just go down, he could go back.

He stood as still as the black trees that had appeared from beneath the receding waters of the man-made lake. Conyers could imagine the body of a drowned swimmer caught by the hair in the skeletal branches of those trees, like some modern Absalom condemned for his trespasses. He did not want to go back.

In early May, the Tennessee Valley Authority had decided that after nearly four decades under water the foundation of the Gene C. Breedlove Dam needed inspection, and the only way to examine the structure and to effect any necessary repairs would be to create a drawdown. They were going to drain the lake.

A drawdown was a slow process, a matter of opening the sluices to let the lake water bleed into the Watauga River, so that gradually, over a period of three months, the green shroud would diminish, exposing the valley for the first time in thirty-five years. There wasn't going to be any big ceremony, though, to mark the event. Even peo-

ple who never got over losing their homes in Wall Hollow didn't feel
called upon to celebrate its temporary resurrection. Everyone seemed
to feel a little embarrassed at the prospect of having to look at the
decayed remains and then having to say good-bye again. The drawdown was not a permanent reprieve, merely an incident in a bureau-
cratic summer. For approximately three weeks the valley would have
a horizon of sun and sky instead of mud clouds in a sheet of green
water. And then the floodgates would close again, and the water
would come stealing back.

All summer long the people came quietly, in groups of twos or
threes, to stare at the ebbing lake, straining for a glimpse of the ruins.
Jim Conyers always went alone. A couple of afternoons a week he
would leave Barbara to mind the shop, and he would drive the fifteen
miles or so from Elizabethton to his fishing spot to watch the progress
of the drawdown. It shamed him to come, though. He felt like a man
at a peepshow, or, worse, like a spectator at the scene of an accident.

In one more week, the drawdown would be complete, and what
was left of Wall Hollow would be visible to all comers. Perhaps by
then he would be so busy with the reunion that he would not mind
about the lake anymore. He tried to imagine meeting the guys again,
but no clear image would form in his mind. He was somebody else
now, and that somebody didn't have much in common with the Hollywood types like Mistral, or with Woodard, who had just turned
eighteen for the forty-fifth time.

Jim Conyers reckoned that he had never been one of them, really.
He was just Dugger's buddy from home. He and Dale had gone to
high school together, and they were probably kin somewhere on their
mothers' sides of the family, if you went to the trouble to trace all
the Millers and the Byrds in that end of the county. They had never
bothered. Everybody in east Tennessee had a passel of cousins;
friends were even more special. He and Dale had pooled their dimes
to send away for copies of *Astounding Stories* and the other magazines that were the staples of adolescent reading back then. They'd
swapped tattered Zane Grey novels for dog-eared copies of H. Rider
Haggard, and they'd sat side by side in the dark watching Flash
Gordon battle the moon men. But Dale had been the one who took
everything a step further.

When the army sent them their separate ways, their approaches to
the hobby began to change. While Jim went on reading Damon
Knight and Jack Finney in blissful solitude, Dale began to answer
the "Pen Friends" ads in the science fiction magazines, and he became involved in all the fan publications. All this was detailed in

Dale's carefully typed letters to him, but Jim, who was stationed in Korea, was too caught up in events there to notice when Dale's hobby turned into a way of life. When they got home to Wall Hollow, fandom didn't particularly interest Jim, but he was glad to see Dale again, and it seemed as good a pastime as anything else in east Tennessee, so he put up with it.

Maybe it would have been different if he had moved away. As it was, he enrolled in Milligan College on the GI bill, and took a job at the Esso station in Wall Hollow to cover his other expenses. In order to save money on rent, Jim moved in with Dugger and the collection of fan friends he had accumulated on the Fan Farm. The new guys were intelligent—certainly more interesting to converse with than anyone down at the gas station—and although he found them a bit silly at times, they were good people who shared his interests. He was the only practical one of the bunch, though. Take the great expedition to San Francisco, for example. The Lanthanides had talked about going to Worldcon for months. They had written to their entire network of pen friends announcing the journey, but not one of them had saved a penny toward expenses for the trip. In the end, they had borrowed five dollars from him—his gas station paycheck—so that they could go.

He remembered the bustle of activity as they prepared to leave . . . *on that bright and cloudless morning.* That phrase from the old hymn had fit both the morning and the mood of the Lanthanides on the day of their departure. "When the Roll Is Called Up Yonder I'll Be There." Dugger had been singing it all morning, but he was probably referring to the Golden Gate of San Francisco rather than to the Pearly Gates of Heaven. They reminded him of pilgrims headed for Mecca in their mixture of ecstasy and zeal.

But for all their enthusiasm, they were very inefficient pilgrims. They announced that they were going to leave at seven, but it was well past ten before they even got around to loading the car. In the end, Jim had to load it for them, because they had no more idea of utilizing space than a bluejay. Then, when he'd offered to check over the car for them, Bunzie had protested that they were in a hurry, and off they went, promising him postcards and autographed paperbacks upon their return.

He smiled at the memory of their return the next night. He and Curtis had been sitting on the dark front porch, smoking Camels and watching the lightning bugs flash in the fields, when they heard the sound of an engine and a discordant version of "Shrimp Boats" carried on the wind from the direction of the highway. A few minutes later, a gleam of headlights along the gravel drive signaled the return of the Lanthanides. He had expected them to be despondent or enraged over the ruin of their plans, but they were all in good spirits, already bubbling with an alternate scheme. He would always remember the courage and good humor they had showed in the face of disaster.

Without a word of regret for their ill-fated journey, the Lanthanides had plunged into their preparations for their own convention. Erik, who fancied himself a ladies' man, got on the phone and persuaded femmefan Angela Arbroath to borrow her mother's car for the weekend and drive up to join the festivities; Dugger had gone off to spend their travel money for beer and party snacks; and Surn, as usual the serious one, had proposed that they commemorate the event with a time capsule.

"A time capsule?" snorted Deddingfield. "In Wall Hollow, Tennessee?"

"Sure," said Woodard, eager to ingratiate himself with Surn. "When the Russians bomb Washington, the Smoky Mountains will protect us from the clouds of radiation. It's one of the logical places for civilization to be reestablished."

If Dugger had been there, he would have pointed out that the prime target of nuclear attack, Oak Ridge, lay just to the west of them. Jim said nothing; bickering was his least favorite of the Lanthanides' attributes. Besides, since they were stranded on the farm with a crippled car, there seemed no point in debating where to place a time capsule. It seemed to him to be a fine and solemn gesture. Leave logic out of it.

The others spent an hour discussing the properties that a time capsule should have, with Dugger, who had returned by this time with "refreshments," arguing that what they really needed was a deactivated torpedo. That being pronounced generally unavailable, they were about to agree on using an old carpetbag that had belonged to Dugger's grandmother. At that point, Jim decided that it was time to put logic back into the discussion.

"You need something waterproof," he said. "There's a lot of groundwater here in the valley, especially in the spring. What if we got another flood like the one they had in 1903?"

Surn agreed with him. "We need something airtight and waterproof. Preferably something that won't rust, too. Remember that a lot of what we're putting into the time capsule is paper. You want your short story to be readable in 1984, don't you?"

The others nodded. "How about a milk can?" asked Dugger.

The suggestion was thoroughly discussed but finally vetoed on the grounds that milk cans might be susceptible to rust. By then they had reached the two-hour mark in the discussion, always a danger point in Lanthanide planning sessions, as it was the time at which things either dissolved into a shouting match or were postponed indefinitely for lack of sustained interest. To keep the previous two hours from having been a total waste, Jim Conyers spoke up. "How about a pickle jar?"

"Too small," said Deddingfield. "It wouldn't even hold *one* story."

"Not the pickle jar in the refrigerator," Jim explained patiently. "I mean one of those ten-gallon jobs that they keep on the counter at McInturf's store. It's made of glass so it won't rust, and it's watertight, and it's big enough to hold just about anything you'd care to save."

"We don't have a ten-gallon pickle jar, though," said Woodard.

"True, but I was in McInturf's this morning, and there were only five or six pickles left in the jar. I say we buy whatever ones are left and offer Xenia McInturf a dime for the jar. All in favor?"

The motion carried, after Bunzie added a rider that the pickle jar expedition be extended to include a trip to Elizabethton to see *War of the Worlds* at the Bonnie Kate Theatre. After that, another two-hour discussion began over what was to be put into the time capsule, but Jim went to bed and left them wrangling. Knowing the Lanthanides, he was sure that they wouldn't actually get around to burying the time capsule for a couple of weeks, and that whatever went in would depend upon their moods on the day of the burial. He had been right on both counts.

For another ten days they had worked on their short stories for the time capsule, and Bunzie had written to John W. Campbell Jr., asking him for "a letter to the future" to be included. When the reply came a few days later, it was placed unopened in the pickle jar along with the *War of the Worlds* poster that Pat Malone had swiped from the theatre in Elizabethton and the rest of the Lanthanides' treasures.

The burial ceremony took place at sunset one Tuesday evening. The Lanthanides had marched up the hill behind the house to a spot chosen by Jim and Dale Dugger, and pronounced by them "easy to locate again." It was midway between the stone fence and an old sycamore tree that grew about ten feet south of the fence line. After the first ceremonial spadeful of earth had been dug by each of the Lanthanides, accompanied by speeches in varying degrees of pomposity, Jim and Dale took turns digging the three-foot hole. After that, the pickle jar/time capsule was wrapped in a burlap feed sack and buried, while the group sang "Off We Go into the Wild Blue

Yonder," referring not to the Air Force but to the future of space travel. Jim Conyers' last memory of them all together was on that September day, standing in the shade of the sycamore before a tiny mound of freshly turned clay, gazing skyward and singing.

That had been the last perfect day, and when he felt twinges of nostalgia it was always that scene that he pictured. He wasn't really sorry when it ended, though, as it had a few months after that September day. Pat Malone had taken off a short time later, after what was reported to be a huge fight with Surn. Jim wasn't there at the time; he had been spending more and more time with Barbara since the fall term began. After that breach in the Lanthanides' solidarity, more factions began to form, so that there was nearly always a feud going with somebody at the Fan Farm. Jim took to studying late at the library with Barbara. He had already begun to be tired of the slanshack by early 1955, when Stormy got that teaching job in Virginia, and Bunzie finally took off for California. Jim had just become officially engaged to Barbara, which meant that he had less time to spend at Dugger's. Finally he found a roommate at Milligan and moved on campus to be closer to his bride-to-be. By March they were all gone except Dugger. When the TVA announced that it was constructing a man-made lake in the Wall Hollow valley, there was no one left to care except Dugger, who couldn't afford to hire a lawyer to fight it. Not that it would have done any good. Poor people never did seem to stand much of a chance against the government, as far as Jim could see.

He remembered Dugger's last day on the farm. The TVA had spent most of the spring months preparing its new lake bed. It had hauled farmhouses away to higher ground, lumbered the oaks and poplar trees from the yards of the former residents, and relocated some—but not all—of the family cemeteries. The day the floodgates closed, Jim had driven out to Dugger's farm, partly out of curiosity and partly on a hunch that Dugger would be there alone and in need of a friend.

He had found Dugger sitting on the rocks that had once been the foundation of his farmhouse. The house was long gone, and the empty cellar looked like a bomb site. Together they looked out at the bulldozed desolation, and Dale had said, "Kind of puts you in mind of Korea, don't it, Jim?"

They walked on past the house site then, into what had been the backyard, and they sat for a long time on the stone fence, talking about the rest of the guys, and about books—about anything except the water that was spilling over the banks of the Watauga and coursing into the valley. Conyers thought of asking about the time capsule then, but he decided that it would have been rude, a denial that there would even be a future. So he tried to keep Dugger's spirits up by talking about his forthcoming wedding. Dugger must come, of course. He didn't remember what plans, if any, Dugger had been making for his own future. He wasn't going to live in the new Wall Hollow. A lot of the old residents chose not to.

When the sun was low in the sky, they could see the shine of water from the old cow pasture, and in order to get Dugger out of there Conyers offered to buy him a fifty-cent dinner at the college cafeteria. Absently, Dugger agreed. His eyes kept straying back to the valley, as if he were trying to take a picture of it in his mind.

They got out by going straight up the wooded hill past the stone fence and coming out on the paved roadway that skirted the mountainside. Jim had parked his motorcycle there, knowing that vehicles weren't allowed down in the valley anymore. With Dugger riding astraddle behind him, he gunned the bike and took off for town, too fast for Dugger to look back.

It was on this same road that Jim Conyers was standing now, looking down into muddy water that receded day by day. He was twice a grandfather now, and Dale Dugger had been dead for thirty years. He couldn't get over the feeling that somewhere down in that lake bed was his youth, waiting for him to come back and dredge it up. Conyers smiled at this bit of fancy, wondering if the other Lanthanides felt that way or if the reunion was a colorful way to make a buck. Impossible to tell. They had long been strangers to him. He wasn't sure he wanted to get reacquainted with these successful old men who had once been his friends, but he supposed that he would have to try. Barbara was very excited about the prospect of the reunion, and about meeting famous people from Hollywood. It was only a few days, after all.

He kept looking at the lake, trying to get his bearings. Was this the spot where the farm had been, or the cliff overlooking the town? Near the bottom of the slope a skeletal tree had risen out of the depths. Was it the Dugger sycamore? The blackened trunk might have been any species of tree, and the other landmarks were still submerged. He would have to wait. Soon the lake would diminish even more. Then perhaps he would be able to distinguish the ruins of Dugger's house and the road that had led to McInturf's store. Perhaps when the drawdown was complete, they could locate the time capsule which now seemed so valuable. But that was not what brought him week after week to the fading shore. Jim Conyers knew that whatever he was looking for in the dead waters of Breedlove Lake, it was not that.

Fans are always at their best in letters, and I took them at their self-stated value.

—FRANCIS TOWNER LANEY
"Ah, Sweet Idiocy"

CHAPTER 4

FORTY YEARS AGO, when the Lanthanides were reading comic books instead of selling serial rights to them, there was a comic series called "The Little King," featuring a diminutive cone-shaped monarch with a red robe and a perpetual scowl of ill-humor. People of a certain age invariably remembered that cartoon character when they encountered the less regal but equally peevish George Woodard.

The resemblance at the moment was great. Wearing a tatty red bathrobe over his clothes to combat the chill of the basement, the stout and shortsighted George Woodard paced the damp concrete floor, back and forth between the clothes drier and the mimeograph machine, in search of literary inspiration.

The next issue of George Woodard's fanzine *Alluvial* was due out in a week, and he had to begin the page layouts tonight. There were many articles to be typed up, and many estimates of column inches to be calculated to make sure that everything fit in the correct number of pages, which is to say: the most that could be mailed for a single first-class postage stamp. George believed in getting his money's worth from the post offal (or *post orifice* or *post awful*—the puns varied per issue), but since his three dozen subscribers were of mostly straitened means, he could not expect them to pony up more money for a bigger *ish*.

He knew that some of the younger "publishers"—indeed, most of them—used word processors these days, and some even had software packages like *Pagemaker* which could produce very professional-looking 'zines, but George would not be converted by the lure of technological ease. The mimeograph machine was within his ability to operate, and it was paid for. The prospect of a complex and expensive computer strained both his self-esteem and the uneasy peace within the family on the subject of his hobby.

It was late. His wife had long since gone to bed, advising him to do the same since he had "school" tomorrow. It was the same phrase and tone of voice she had employed when the children were young. She said "school" as if he were a pupil rather than a professional educator. Indeed, there was much in Earlene's manner toward him lately that suggested she had abandoned the role of wife for the more authoritative one of mother. The mousy little girl of the fifties was now tart and forthright, bossing him about with contempt masked as concern. Her attitude implied that it was he who forced this change in her behavior. *What but a mother can one be to someone who refuses to grow up?* But all of this had taken place without the utterance of one cross word, without one syllable of reproof from her. Gradually, the shy waif had given way to the Valkyrie, and one of the chief illusions lost in the process had been her image of George.

He sighed. Women were too mired down in the here and now to really be idealists, he told himself. They were always ready to turn practical at the first phone call from a creditor, or when the baby got sick, or when someone they knew saw them using food stamps. No devotion to causes. He had long ago stopped asking her to help him address issues of *Alluvial*.

He yawned. He should go to bed, of course. Those hellions in Algebra I would require every ounce of patience and stamina in him tomorrow, but his self-imposed deadline for *Alluvial* forced him to keep working. After all, this was a special issue, containing actual *news:* the announcement of the Lanthanides' reunion in Tennessee. He picked up the article, which he had composed on stencil, and read through it again.

LANTHANIDES REUNITE
TO RETRIEVE TIME CAPSULE

Has it really been thirty-six solar years since we left the Fan Farm?

Indubitably it has. The Lanthanides, as an organization, is but a golden memory in the minds of those of us who were a part of it, but its effect on SF springs eternal. From this group of devoted fans, living in idyllic squalor in Wall Hollow, Tennessee, came many of the names in the genre's (illusory, because we can't afford to build one) Hall of Fame: Angela Arbroath, Dale Dugger the original co-editor of *Alluvial*, and of course your faithful correspondent: myself.

The group spawned a few dirty old pros, too: Surn, Deddingfield, Phillips, Mistral. (Just kidding, guys!) In the last ish of *Alluvial*, I recounted our adventures on the Great 1954 Tennfan Expedition to Slan Francisco, and how it came to grief in the Indiana outback due to an excess of hot air. (Always a problem with the some of the Lanthanides, most notably P. Malone.) Your humble chronicler went on to recount how he managed to at least partially repair the auto (much to the admiration of Surn, who only knew theoretical rocket mechanics), so that the Stalwart Six were able to make it back to the Fan Farm. He then suggested that they use their remaining funds to have a Con of their own.

It was during that weekend that the Lanthanides Time Capsule was planned, and subsequently buried. In the last ish (back issues of *Alluvial* available for $1/postage), I told how we came to bury that amazing cache (after much bheer had been consumed) which included a short story by each member of the group. Since we had no copy machines and nobody typed on stencils, all these stories are unpublished! No one has ever seen them! (A pity. Curtis Phillips said that Yours Truly's story was the best he'd ever read.) For a list of the rest of the contents of the Time Capsule, see page 4.)

In the last issue's article, we lamented the fact that no one ever would see those unpublished yarns of ours. As all Trufandom knows, in the mid-Fifties, after the Lanthanides had gone their separate ways, the TVA turned the whole valley into a lake, and the famous Wall Hollow Fan Farm was hundreds of feet under water. For the past thirty-five years the *time capsule* has been at the bottom of the Gene C. Breedlove Lake. (Known to fandom as the Gene Pool.) (Gene C. Breedlove was some mundane Tennessee politician. *Not* important.)

Be that as it may (and I'm not sure that it was), after I printed this tale in the last *Alluvial*, I had a letter from a Tennfan, who enclosed a newspaper clipping from the *Bristol Herald-Courier*, saying that THEY'RE GOING TO DRAIN THE LAKE. The dam needs repairing (no noun omitted here, folks), so the TVA is going to drain the Gene Pool, and after a few phone calls from Ye Editor, it was all settled. It turns out that Jim Conyers and his lovely femmefan Barbara (would you believe she's a grandmother now?) still live in the area, and they were receptive to the idea of a reunion. Jim's going to make the lodging arrangements for this micro-mini con. Many of the Lanthanides are going back to Tennessee to attempt the recovery of the Lanthanides' Time Capsule. Surn! Mistral! Angela Arbroath! And Moi. What a reunion! Fan history in the making. And a new chapter in the annals of Science Fiction. Yours truly will be on the scene, and the next ish will carry a full report!

#30

TO THE FUTURE WITH LOVE:
The Contents of the Lanthanides' Time Capsule*

(*To the best of my recollection and that
of Jim Conyers)

- One WAR OF THE WORLDS poster, wheedled from the manager
  of the Bonnie Kate Theatre in Elizabethton.
- Deddingfield's treasured copy of the August 1928 issue of AMAZ-
  ING, signed by E. E. "Doc" Smith and Philip Francis Nowlan.
- One jar of grape jelly (in case Claude Degler should survive the
  Nuclear Holocaust).
- One typewritten manuscript of a short story or novella from each
  member of the Lanthanides.
- John W. Campbell's Letter to the Twenty-First Century.
- Curtis Phillips' copy of THE OUTSIDERS by Lovecraft, annotated
  by Lovecraft expert Francis Towner Laney.
- Letters from various people now famous, or infamous for being
  nonexistent (e.g.—Sgt. Joan Carr).
- Copies of all the issues of *Alluvial* up to that time.
- Copies of ASTOUNDING and WEIRD TALES, including a dummy
  issue of the last, never published issue of WEIRD TALES, contain-
  ing a story by Peter Deddingfield.
- Some Ray Bradbury fanzines.
- A picture of a dog (To confuse the Aliens).
- One propeller-beanie.
- Other stuff that we have forgotten over the years.

EDITOR'S NOTE: All you Trufan collectors out there know that this
stuff is worth a lot of money in today's market, but of course the
greatest treasure of all is the manuscript collection of the Lanthanides
themselves. (Little did we know!) (But we had a hunch!)—Anyway, I
foresee all kinds of excitement over this resurrection of the Holy
Grail of Fandom. Look for news about a forthcoming anthology in
future issues of ALLUVIAL! (Sure LOCUS will report it, but WE'LL
KNOW FIRST.)

#30

George read the articles, inserted a few open parentheses, and pronounced them up to his usual standard, despite his fatigue. He thought
he'd better make himself a pot of coffee before he tackled the article
on the future of NATO. He would have to pull an all-nighter to finish
the issue. It would be better to get it in the mail to his subscribers
before Earlene read it and found out he was going to raid their Christ-

mas club account to fund a trip to Wall Hollow, Tennessee. At least the phone bill wasn't too bad this month. Woodard didn't have telephone numbers for most of the Lanthanides, even if he could have afforded to call them. He did manage to reach Ruben Mistral, and Bunzie had put one of his secretaries to work arranging the rest. George clutched the lapels of his bathrobe, trying to keep out the basement chill. It was good to know that somebody still treasured the old days, even if he had become rich and famous. Ye Editor resolved not to use the term "Dirty Old Pro" quite so often in the next few issues.

Brendan Surn, the legendary lion of science fiction, no longer lived on earth. For some time now, his mind had been elsewhere; it returned from time to time for increasingly shorter intervals, but the ties between the author and his life and work were nearly severed. Soon he would be gone for good.

Surn sat in his monogrammed deck chair, staring out at the placid sea. He wore a cowled beach robe of natural fibers and leather sandals, and his white mane of hair reflected the sunlight in a halo around his serene face. He looked like a monk in holy contemplation. Even the architecture of the house fitted the conceit: its exposed-beam cathedral ceiling formed a nave above Surn's head, and the setting sun turned the window to stained glass. With his classic features and that expression of sorrowful contemplation, he could have posed for a portrait of a medieval saint. He might have been Thomas à Becket, saying his last mass at Canterbury.

Lorien Williams wondered what Brendan Surn did think about these days. He spent most of his waking hours gazing out at the ocean, saying little and writing nothing. She liked to think that he still lived in the dreaming spires of Antaeus, the world featured in his greatest works, but he never mentioned his books to her. She hoped that he had not forgotten them. The sound of the ringing telephone a few moments before had pierced the silent house, but it had not reached his still point. He sat as calmly as ever, studying the endless motions of the green waves.

Lorien stood with her finger poised on the hold bar of the phone, wondering what she ought to do about the call. There wasn't anyone to ask. When she had first arrived on her fan pilgrimage to Dry Salvages, Surn's futuristic aerie on a cliff in Carmel, she had been afraid that no one would let her in to meet the great man. His reputation for solitude was legendary, and few people dared to test it. But Lorien had read all of Surn's works, and she felt that she had to express her admiration for him in person. She hoped for an autograph; maybe even a picture of herself standing beside him.

Surn himself had answered her knock, shambling to the door in his robe and slippers and admitting her without question. A few moments' conversation, and the litter of spoiled food and unopened mail told Lorien what she had stumbled into. Her grandmother had been much the same in the last years of her life. Lorien didn't remember being affected much by that, but Brendan Surn was her idol, and she could see that he needed her. So she cleaned up the mess and fixed him a hot meal, and then she decided to stay until someone else turned up. Surely he had a housekeeper?

As the weeks passed, Lorien became used to her new surroundings. Her fast-food job in Clarkston, Washington was not something she had wanted in the first place, but it supported her science fiction activities and placated her parents. She wrote to them and said that she'd found a better job in Carmel, which, in a way, was true. She noted that Surn had good days and bad days. Sometimes he was almost normal. He could still carry on a conversation, write checks, and decide what he wanted to eat, but he seemed very much like a little boy. The depth of adult emotions was missing, and he compensated for it by becoming more pleasant, and by agreeing with almost anything she suggested. Lorien thought it was lucky that it had been she who found him, rather than some gold-digging blonde or some unscrupulous business person. She wondered if Surn ought to see a doctor, but when she suggested it, he would become agitated, making her afraid that he might tell her to leave. That would be bad for both of them. It would mean that she would have to go back to a dead-end job somewhere, and he would be thrown to the mundanes. He might even end up in an institution. It was better this way; at least, until he was much farther gone.

At first she was afraid that someone would turn up and tell her to go away. Now she thought she would view eviction as a rescue; but that possibility grew more remote with each passing day. Months passed and no one came, so gradually she began to belong here. She learned the routine at Dry Salvages, and she picked up the skills to take over the business side of Surn's life. The editors and other business people who telephoned for Surn accepted her without question. If anything, they seemed relieved to have someone capable and courteous to talk to, and no one seemed to care who she was or why she was there. Least of all Brendan Surn.

She identified herself now as Surn's assistant. Perhaps some of them thought she was his daughter. She looked quite young, with her sexless body and her dark hair worn flower-child long. She had sad brown eyes in a dreaming face, and no one would ever mistake her for a bimbo, the human furniture for the rich man's beach house. She was not that. Surn seemed to take her presence for granted, but sex did not appear to be one of his physical needs anymore. Even when she bathed him, he gave no sign of arousal. He had never even asked her name.

She looked again at the telephone, wondering what she should say. Most of the decisions were easy: *Yes, you can reprint that,* or *please add a jar of coffee to the grocery order.* But this was different. Would Surn want to go to Tennessee to see his old friends? Could he handle it?

It wasn't a decision that Lorien Williams wanted to make. She thought she'd better try to make him understand about the call. She knelt down beside his deck chair and touched his arm to rouse him from his reverie. "Brendan?" she said softly. At first she had called him Mr. Surn, but it seemed silly to be so formal with someone who could not even fry an egg. Now she thought of him as two people. There was Mr. Surn the great writer, and Brendan, the sweet, child-like man who needed her so much.

He blinked once or twice, as if he had been asleep. "Yes, Lori?"

"There's a man on the telephone who says to tell you that his name is Bunzie." A note of awe crept into her voice. "It's really Ruben Mistral, from the movies."

Surn nodded. "I know Bunzie," he said softly.

"He's calling about the Lanthanides." Lorien had read the biography of Surn, so she knew about his early years on the Fan Farm. "They're having a reunion back in Wall Hollow, and he wants to know if you would like to go. It's in Tennessee," she added, in case he had forgotten.

"Yes," said Surn in his mild, dreaming voice. "I know Bunzie. I'd like to see him again. Will Erik be there?"

"I don't know," said Lorien. She had not asked for details. "I can find out more about it now. I just wanted to see if you were interested in going."

"And Pat. Will he be there? Pat Malone?"

"I don't think so, Brendan," she said, patting his arm. Pat Malone had been dead for a long time. Everybody knew that.

On one side of Ruben Mistral's weekly engagement calendar there was an astronomer's photo of the Horseshoe Nebula, a billion pin-points of light making a haze in the blackness of space. Under the picture, Mistral had written: "This scene represents the number of meetings I attend per year!"

"Damn it!" he thought. "It's almost true." The many components of his film and publishing empire required considerable maintenance. He could delegate the day-to-day chores, but he supervised his underlings closely. After all, it was *his* money and *his* reputation on the line. The next few weeks of his datebook looked like a timetable for the Normandy invasion; nearly every damned hour was filled. When did they expect him to write? They didn't, of course. These days he had rewrite men and assistant screenwriters and a host of other flunkies to see that his barest idea was transformed into a two-hour movie. But Bunzie missed the old days, and the seat-of-the-pants style of production: the days when he was "Bunzie" instead of "Ruben Mistral." Being a Hollywood mogul had seemed like a wonderful dream in those far-off days; too bad reality never lived up to one's expectations.

Bunzie, clad in a red designer sweatsuit and matching Reeboks, was pedaling away on the exercise bike in the corner of his office. He hated it, but it kept his doctor happy. He was supposed to be able to think "creative thoughts" while he exercised, but his brain wouldn't stay in gear. Instead of considering his current project, he looked appraisingly at his chrome and glass office, decorated with posters from his hit movies. He had probably spent more to furnish that office than poor old Woodard had spent for his house in Maryland. So, he told himself, life wasn't perfect, but he shouldn't kvetch. He was successful. The money was certainly okay; he still had his hair and his teeth; and his health was good thanks to the diet and exercise, every minute of which he hated. But, he thought, at his age, who had any fun anyhow? Better he should be rich and fit and miserable than poor and fat and miserable.

He looked up at the large framed photograph above his desk, as he usually did when the word "poor" entered his head. Most people thought that the picture of the blue mountain lake, nestled among green hills was a soothing landscape, a device to relax him like the crystals on his desk, but for Ruben Mistral the lake picture was a memorial to the days when he *could* relax. It was the only picture he had of Wall Hollow, Tennessee. It had been taken years after the guys left the Fan Farm, but he knew that somewhere under that expanse of green water lay his youth.

Bunzie forced himself to keep pedaling the damned exercise bike. That was the story of his life, wasn't it? Keep pedaling. Maybe everybody else was willing to give up, willing to take no for an answer, and willing to settle for less, but not Ruben Mistral. Mistral would have the best for himself, and he would demand the best from himself and from everyone he worked with.

After all these years, Bunzie still felt schizophrenic about his two identities. In the Wall Hollow days, he had dreamed of becoming Ruben Mistral—rich and famous—and several decades later, that person certainly did exist in all the imagined glory of Bunzie's day-dreams. But inside that tanned and calorie-controlled body, the old Bunzie still existed, too. Science fiction legend Ruben Mistral bought two-thousand-dollar suits; Bunzie the fan from Brooklyn saved paper clips from the business letters he received. Mistral had discreet affairs with starlets whose year of birth coincided with his age; Bunzie secretly preferred Alma Louise, his wife of thirty years. Mistral was a tiger shark who could smell blood in a business deal a mile away; Bunzie missed his old pals from Dugger's farm.

Most of the time, Bunzie felt that he was a flunky who worked for Ruben Mistral; the great man never did the actual scutwork of writing, or editing scripts. That was Bunzie. Mistral was the glad-hander in Beverly Hills; the maven of the talk shows; the one with a thousand associates, contacts, and employees, but no friends. Bunzie had once had friends. Mistral had his business cronies and, now that the movie versions of his books had made him a celebrity, he had "people," those who were paid to like him, and paid to keep anyone else from ever getting close to him. Mistral was cold company for a nice guy like Bunzie. He was necessary though; Bunzie had to admit that. The cold and brilliant Ruben Mistral made merciless deals, paid all the bills, and he enabled Bunzie and Alma to live in a beautiful house in Topanga Canyon. He even tossed a few scraps to worthy charities from time to time. Not a bad guy by the local lights. He made so much money that he could *afford* to endow a hospital ward. What could goodhearted Bunzie have done without the ruthless Mistral ambition: give quarters to panhandlers? Bunzie knew that if there ever came a time when irreconcilable differences forced one of them to depart from the body for good, it would be Bunzie, not Mistral, who would have to go.

Still, in the brief periods of solitude when Mistral's presence was not required, Bunzie thought back on the old days with nostalgia and regret. If you were a true pal, he told himself, you'd have taken your buddies with you to the Promised Land.

"But I tried," said Bunzie to himself—or rather, to Ruben Mistral, who was sneering as usual. "Didn't I try to get Woodard to go to that Worldcon in the sixties and meet some people? Editors buy stuff from people they know, I told him. But he couldn't take the time off work, he said. And didn't I tell Stormy everything he needed to know about promotion, so that he could make a name for himself with his book? But, oh no, he wanted to be a college professor, and college professors are above that sort of merchandising.'' On the exercise bike, Bunzie kept pedaling. He *had* tried to help the old gang; not that some of them needed it. Surn was a legend, and Deddingfield had been the richest required-reading author he knew. As for the others, he figured that there were some people who could not even have greatness thrust upon them. But he had tried. And sometimes, when Mistral was too busy to sneer at what a bunch of woolly-headed losers they were, Bunzie missed them.

He remembered the pizza. Years ago, when he had just moved out to California to pursue his dream of a screenwriting career, he was living on beans and buying old scripts at the Goodwill, trying to teach himself how to write one, but his letters to the gang scattered up and down the East Coast were always cheerful, full of hope. Bunzie agreed with Churchill that one should be an optimist; there wasn't much point in being anything else. Still, some glimpse of his dire straits must have shown through in the letters, because in the mail one day Bunzie found a check for fifteen dollars and a note saying: ''You sound really down. Go buy yourself a pizza.'' And it was from Dale Dugger! Fifteen dollars must have been hard to spare for Dale back then, but he'd sent it anyhow, not even making it a loan. Just a gift from a pal. Bunzie never forgot that, and even these days, when Alma paid fifteen dollars for a cake of soap, Bunzie was still touched by the memory of that gesture. They had been his *friends,* not like this new bunch with their little axes to grind, their deals to make.

That was why Bunzie, ignoring the protests of Ruben Mistral, had agreed to organize the Lanthanides' reunion. George Woodard had called him about it, bubbling over with enthusiasm, but short of money as usual, and completely hopeless when it came to organization. If George handled it, it would end up being a three-man get-together in a cheap motel, and nothing would come of the book. Bunzie saw the potential, and he was pleased at George's eager display of gratitude when he volunteered to take over. Sometimes it helped to be famous. ''Leave it to me,'' he had told George. Poor old humbug, thought Bunzie with a sigh; this reunion will be the thrill of a lifetime for George. Who could I bring along as a treat for him? Nimoy? Bob Silverberg? But he dismissed the idea of bringing other celebrities. That would mean that Ruben Mistral would have to come, too, and he'd insist on bringing some bimbo starlet to impress his pals. Bunzie didn't want that to happen. He wanted this weekend trip to yesteryear to belong just to him. But he wanted it well organized, and he wanted its potential mined to the fullest.

Wall Hollow, Tennessee?, one of his "people" had sneered. Is that anywhere near Hooterville?

But for once Bunzie had overruled the snobbery of Ruben Mistral and his minions. This time he wasn't going to take no for an answer. Dale Dugger had been dead for thirty years, but still there was a debt there that Bunzie wanted to pay. And a debt of friendship to poor old hopeless George Woodard, and to Conyers and Erik, and to the memory of that silly ass Pat Malone, who might have made it if he'd lived.

So Ruben Mistral would call in favors from a few influential people in the media, and he'd start the publicity ball rolling about the proposed anthology in the time capsule. He couldn't even remember what he'd written for it anymore. But he did remember doing one, handwritten with a cartridge pen in peacock-blue ink. Maybe he could revise it a little before publication. There are limits to the charm of nostalgia. He'd get a couple of his editor friends and his New York agent, and some movie people to film the event, and he'd fly the whole caboodle of them first class to the Tri-Cities Airport outside Blountville, Tennessee.

Then what? God only knew what accommodations there'd be. He had people working on it, though. They would charter the nearest acceptable motel. Maybe two motels. No point in having the press and the editors underfoot all the time. They were all a bunch of kids, anyway.

The thing was a natural from a publicity standpoint. A sunken city, a buried time capsule full of priceless manuscripts, a reunion of the giants—hell, the thing could be a movie in itself. (The Mistral part of his mind delegated somebody to work on that.) With all the hype he could arrange (Steve King to write the introduction to the anthology, maybe?), the collection of stories in that time capsule could be worth a pot of money. They could easily get a million at a literary auction. Not that Ruben Mistral needed the money—Bunzie hastily told himself that he was doing it for old times' sake—but the prospect of a big literary kill would make things more interesting. Why shouldn't they capitalize on it? And he'd split it with the gang. *They* certainly needed the cash. Say, ten percent for each of them, the rest to him . . .

The wall phone by the exercise bike buzzed once, and, still pedaling rhythmically, he picked it up. "Ruben Mistral here," said a cold, smooth voice.

And he was.

Real Soon Now—When the MSFS/DSFL was going to have: a convention, a decent fanzine, an active membership, a properly run meeting, and many other fine things that didn't quite happen.

—Fancyclopedia II

CHAPTER 5

"I AM LOOKING," said Marion Farley. "It isn't on the map, I tell you!"

It was a blazing day in late July, and the reunion journey to Tennessee had begun. Jay Omega was driving his *other* car (the gray Oldsmobile he used for trips and for times that his MG was in the shop; i.e. the car he used), and Marion had been assigned to the front passenger seat on the condition that she act as navigator and that she use her reading glasses when consulting the map. She was dressed for the expedition in khaki shorts, an Earth Day T-shirt, and several layers of sun block. Jay had suggested that the outfit needed chukka boots and a riding crop to really complete the look, but Marion was not amused.

Erik Giles, in a white suit and straw hat, looking like a clean shaven version of Mark Twain, was settled into the backseat, reading the current issue of *Atlantic.*

"I thought they saved Wall Hollow," said Marion, running her finger over the area south of Johnson City. "I mean, I thought that a new town bearing that name still existed. Didn't the TVA move the church and several of the town buildings to higher ground? I thought that some of the residents moved there."

"They did," said Jay Omega. "I asked Wulff in civil engineering about it. Dams are his specialty. According to him, the present village of Wall Hollow is one street, with half a dozen buildings, one general store, and a scattering of houses. It's smaller than it was in the old days before the lake. Rand-McNally didn't think it worth mentioning."

Erik Giles leaned forward and peered between the seats for a closer look at the map of Tennessee. "Never mind," he said. "I know how to get there. See if you can find Hampton on the map."

With her nose almost touching the map, Marion finally announced, "Hampton. Got it. Highway 321. It doesn't look very large, either."

"I don't suppose it is. It wasn't much more than a crossroads in the early fifties. Back when we lived on the farm, the little diner and service station there kept a black bear in a cage as a tourist attraction. Tourists used to buy bottles of chocolate soda to feed it, and the bear would hold the bottle in its forepaws and chug it down in one gulp."

Marion looked stern. "If that is an example of the good old days, I'm thankful to have missed them."

"Look at the map again," said Jay Omega, hoping to forestall another of Marion's lectures. "We're not going to Wall Hollow, are we? I thought the reunion was being held somewhere nearby."

Marion consulted the reunion brochure, a three-paneled flier on baronial ivory paper. It had been printed in considerable style by MistralWorld, Inc. and mailed to everyone connected with the science fiction genre. On the front was a blue computer-designed graphic of Atlantis sinking beneath the waves, and above it in gold-foil avant garde script were the words: Return of the Lanthanides. The first panel gave a brief history of the Lanthanides and the fate of Dugger's farm, probably taken from a reference work on science fiction, since several of the less important members were omitted altogether (Woodard, Giles, Conyers). The center panel gave a schedule of events, culminating with the Saturday trek to the newly drained Fan Farm to recover the time capsule (proceedings to be filmed by the television program *A Current Affair*). The literary auction would take place on Sunday morning, followed by a press conference with the surviving Lanthanides and their newly acquired publisher, the high bidder of the auction. The last panel, authorship credited to George Woodard of *Alluvial,* listed the contents of the time capsule and a brief description of the mini-con weekend that led to its creation. One of the two back panels provided a map of the Gene C. Breedlove Lake area of east Tennessee, with instructions on how to get there by air or car, and the last panel said "MistralWorld Productions" in the customary and instantly recognizable flourish.

"There is a map on the back of the folder," Marion announced. "According to this, we are staying at a state park motel on the shores of Breedlove Lake."

Jay Omega snickered. "Not the Breedlove Inn?"

"Alas, no," grinned Marion. "It's called the Mountaineer Lodge. It's beside the dam, on the western side of the lake, a few miles from the present Wall Hollow."

"The best local motel by a dam site," chuckled Erik Giles.

Marion turned to stare at him. "I thought you didn't make puns anymore."

He sighed. "It's the reunion. God knows what I shall be saying and doing after a few hours of their collective presence. Singing 'Shrimp Boats,' I expect. I hope we don't shock the editors."

Marion consulted the brochure. "Not much chance of that. I believe they will be lodging at the Holiday Inn in Johnson City so as not to cramp your style."

"I suppose Bunzie will have them bused in for the auction."

"You wouldn't shock the editors, anyway," said Jay Omega. "Writers are supposed to be eccentric. Besides, they're filming this reunion, aren't they? If you all clown around, the media will love it. It will be good for the auction."

"They're having a literary auction in Wall Hollow, Tennessee?" said Marion. "That doesn't sound like publishing as *we* know it, Jay, because your editor wouldn't cross the street . . ."

"I know," said Jay, "but this is a publicity deal. Remember that the whole thing is going to be filmed for national television, and Mistral is connected with the movies. Even New York is impressed by the presence of movie people."

"It's Bunzie's doing, I am certain," said Erik Giles. "He had an instinctive grasp of publicity. He faxed press releases to *Publishers Weekly* and to all the major newspapers, announcing the reunion. A couple of reporters are actually being sent down to cover it. To me it all sounds like a scheme to get an outrageous sum for the anthology. I confess that I am not averse to such a plan."

"It will probably work, too," said Marion after a moment's consideration. "People don't buy books unless they've heard of them. All of this star-studded publicity could turn this into a best-seller."

"That would be a pleasant surprise after all these years."

"Aren't you worried about what the English department will say when they find out who you really are?" asked Jay Omega.

Erik Giles looked startled. "What do you mean?"

"C. A. Stormcock."

The professor smiled. "I imagine that the department will forgive that youthful indiscretion if I promise not to lapse again."

"Don't you think you might like to write science fiction again?"

He shook his head. "Definitely not. To quote Mr. Woody Allen, I plan to take the money and run."

"Well, the auction should provide you with plenty of that," said Jay Omega.

"Do you think Alien Books will be there to bid?" asked Giles.

"No," said Jay, reddening a little at the mention of his neglectful publishers. "They only do paperbacks. I don't think they could afford a deal of this magnitude."

"They're probably all in summer school, anyhow," giggled Marion, who contended that Alien Books filled its editorial vacancies by calling the Runaway Hotline.

"Well, it should be a very profitable venture for you, Erik," said Jay. "Imagine getting thousands of dollars for a short story thirty-five years later. What was your story about, anyhow?"

Erik Giles smiled ruefully. "I've been trying to remember. I believe that all our stories were very much in the style we later became known for. Surn did a story on colonialism set on a distant planet; my old friend—er—Pete—Deddingfield, I mean, wrote a poetic alien encounter thing that reminded me of *Moby Dick*. Or maybe *I* wrote that one. We lived in each other's pockets in those days, and some of us dabbled in each other's styles. Well, if Pete wrote that one, then I think I wrote one about a man dying of radiation poisoning."

Marion shuddered. "In 1954?"

"Oh, yes. The Fan Farm library had a paperback copy of *Hiroshima* by John Hersey, and I remember being very struck by his account of the aftermath of the bombing."

"It will be an interesting story to read in today's world," Jay remarked.

Giles blushed. "I hope I got my details right. We didn't do much research in our Fan Farm days. Too far from a library."

"Do you remember anyone else's story?"

"Dugger wrote a high-tech yarn from the point of view of an alien PFC. He was drawing on his army experiences. I remember laughing a lot when he read it. Dugger had a keen sense of irony." He paused for a moment, remembering his friend. "Let's see, who have I forgotten? Woodard. I can't remember Woodard's story. I never could. Not even five minutes after I'd read one of them. And, of course, poor old Curtis wrote about demons."

Marion nodded. "Curtis Phillips. I don't suppose any of you realized back then?"

"No, of course not. We thought he was a fine storyteller with a gifted imagination and a genius for description. We had no idea."

"Such a pity," sighed Marion. "He was a gifted writer."

"I'm not following this," said Jay Omega. "What didn't they realize? What was a pity?"

"About Curtis Phillips," said Marion. "The great fantasy author who wrote *Demon in My View*. He was considered the successor to Lovecraft, and he wrote a whole series of novels and stories relating his characters' lives and even world events to the intercessions of demons.''

"I haven't read any of Phillips' books, but I've heard of him. He's supposed to have been a brilliant fantasy writer. What is so tragic about him?''

"He was writing nonfiction," said Marion softly.

The four-lane highway that led from southwest Virginia into east Tennessee was built to run through the flattest and widest of the valleys so that it missed most of the beautiful mountain scenery of the Blue Ridge, but it was the fastest and most efficient route. On this trip, no one bothered to look at the scenery. When the three professors ran out of conversation, Jay Omega turned the car radio to the local National Public Radio station and lost himself in a program of classical music, while Erik Giles dozed in the backseat.

Marion soon lost interest in the novel she had brought along. The bulletin board was right about Warren, she thought. Deprived of other distractions, she thought about the weekend ahead, and the phrase *there but for the grace of God go I* came to mind and would not be dispelled.

The prospect of attending a reunion of old fans of science fiction reminded Marion of the days when she had been a member of fandom herself, and her memories were not altogether pleasant ones. I wonder why Erik asked us to come along with him, she thought. They had never asked him to explain the invitation, which, after all, could be considered an honor, but after the initial excitement wore off, Marion found herself questioning her colleague's motives. Erik Giles had hinted that he was worried about his health and that he did not want to travel alone, but he seemed completely recovered from his heart attack of the year before, and she wondered if that was the real reason for his asking them or just a convenient excuse. Of course, meeting the famous Lanthanides, and all the agents and movie people who attended them, might be good for Jay's career, but she doubted if he had the drive to pursue it. Although Jay Omega was a nationally published novelist, he was essentially a hobby writer, quite content to be an electrical engineer. He had no reason—financial or otherwise—to put forth the time and effort to become a successful full-time writer. He was happy in engineering, and in that profession he was considerably better paid than most writers. If Jay had wanted to try for a serious career as a novelist, Marion would have helped him, but she knew better than to push him. You couldn't change people.

She had learned that finally, after ten years and half that many relationships.

That was one thing fandom had taught her. Within its ranks she had met many talented people who could have made a fortune illustrating comic books, designing dresses, developing computer games . . . but. She sighed, remembering the frustration she had felt in her relationships with her fan friends. After years of stymied friendships and bitter romances, she had learned that you cannot give people ambition as if it were a virus. It is not. It is a genetic trait, and either it is waiting deep inside you to evolve, or else it is entirely absent, and it cannot be imparted to someone full of talent but lacking the drive to succeed. Nothing that anyone can do—not praise, or scolding, or work on one's behalf—can make them try.

Marion had watched her brilliant acquaintances fritter away talent that she would have killed for. The comic book creators answered endless pages of correspondence on their computers, ignoring their own deadlines, while their artistic creations died of neglect. Another gifted friend scrapped her dream of becoming a costume designer in favor of a new boyfriend who wanted to go and live in the wilds of Oregon. The computer whiz *went home one night and put a bullet through his head.*

Edward Arlington Robinson, thought Marion, mentally acknowledging the quote. When life became painful she always turned to literature. That was how she had become an English professor; it had been the ultimate escape from a marriage that she later compared to two years in an opium den. Only Jeremy hadn't done drugs; he had done dragons. To a sober outsider the addictions had seemed similar and equally incomprehensible.

Marion had met Jeremy when they were undergrads. He had been a computer science major, and she was a smart girl with enough personal problems to keep the psych department busy for years. She was overweight; she had no idea how to manage her thick, curly hair; and she came from a cold and repressive family. Batting a thousand, thought Marion in retrospect. Hello, Middle Earth! She had possessed all the qualities necessary for psychological emigration: she had been rejected by the world, and she was perceptive enough to know it. So she left. She still went to her classes—well, most of the time—and her parents received dutiful letters that discussed the weather and asked after the cats, but Marion was gone. She had found the *real people,* and joined their ranks.

The real people. Another literary reference. She wondered if Frederic Brown had ever realized the enormous impression his short story made on young egos. It was a simple fantasy story, probably suggested by the coincidence that began the tale: you are humming a song, and suddenly that very song comes on the car radio. The story's hero discovers that most of the people in the world are not real, they are like walk-on players in a film. Just there to set the stage, to create an illusion of reality. But a few people are *real,* the characters for whom the drama exists. Those people think and feel and care about things; everyone else is an automaton who ceases to function as soon as a real person leaves the scene. The reason the song came on the car radio was that the driver humming the tune was *a real* person, and he was able to will things to happen.

It was an excellent fantasy story; Fredric Brown was one of the best. But to the troubled adolescent Marion that story was not just an entertaining tale, it was a serious philosophy that explained her feelings of alienation.

When Marion read that story, she knew at once that she was one of *them.* She knew that she could think and feel, that she was more alive somehow than most of the bubblebrains in her dorm. So *that* was it. They weren't real. She didn't exactly believe that they were robots, or hallucinations, but on some deeper spiritual level she felt that she possessed something that *they* lacked. In medieval times, she might have termed it a soul.

Armed with her new understanding of the world, Marion neglected her classes and her correspondence in favor of the search for more *real* people. Every now and then she would find one—someone with whom she got along especially well from the moment they met—and she'd catch herself thinking, Ah. He's *real,* too.

Jeremy had been the realest of the real. They had shared the same ecological politics, the same yearning for things medieval, and the same bewilderment over contemporary society. For two years they had a wonderful relationship, exasperating their parents and their respective university departments, before Marion grew tired of the game and of Jeremy's endless defiant failures. "I couldn't take midterms," he would explain earnestly. "Because I had to go to Maryland for a meeting of the Shire that week. After all, I am a baron." Such priorities had seemed logical when they were dating, but when Marion was a student wife, working low-wage jobs to pay his tuition, the logic in his actions escaped her entirely. She began to feel like the sober guest at a beer blast. Finally, deciding to bet her money on her own abilities instead of his, Marion enrolled in graduate school, moved out, and never looked back.

Still, she wasn't sure she had ever got the old philosophy out of her system. She had consciously renounced it a few years later when she discovered that most of her *real* friends bickered endlessly and accomplished very little. Later she came to the uneasy realization that her concept of *real* and *unreal* people was very similar to the chauvinistic male's idea of women, the bigot's perception of other races, and, most troubling of all, similar to the way in which serial killers view their victims: *they're not real, but I am. They don't matter, but I do.* That was when the philosophy of exclusion had begun to frighten her.

Now, of course, she told herself that everyone had a soul and feelings, and that *mundanes* were very worthwhile people, but some times the old attitude came back anyhow. Just last week, Marion had been in line at the Chinese restaurant's lunch buffet, and the pixy-faced young woman in front of her had taken forever, staring at the rice and bean curd as if she couldn't remember what they were. Marion had caught herself thinking, Well, *she's* not real! The realization that she had thought that about someone even for an instant was an unsettling feeling. It gave her kinship with people she would rather not think of at all, and it made her wonder where such arrogance might have led. Did any of the Lanthanides share this view of reality? Now that she thought of it, it was just the opposite of Curtis Phillips' problem: Marion thought that most people weren't real and didn't matter; Curtis Phillips had fervently believed that demons were, and did.

"So tell me about Curtis Phillips," said Jay Omega, as if on cue. (Marion could never decide if Jay was *real* or not, but he was utterly unlike Jeremy, and that was enough.)

"Poor Curt," said Erik Giles, who had suddenly awakened. "He had such talent."

"When someone mentions Curtis Phillips, I always think of Richard Dadd," said Marion. She glanced at Jay to see if he recognized the name. It was obvious that he did not. Dadd was one of the things Marion had learned about in her "Middle Earth" period. "Richard Dadd was a mid-nineteenth-century English artist who became famous for his wonderfully complex paintings of fairy life. His paintings—surrealistic in style and much ahead of their time—were much admired, right up until the night that the artist cut his father's throat."

"Another practitioner of nonfiction?" asked Jay.

"Apparently so. He seemed to be having delusions about demons, and hearing voices ordering him to kill, so perhaps he was painting what he saw. He was tried and found insane, and they put him in

Broadmoor, where he spent the remainder of his life painting increasingly bizarre landscapes peopled by demons.'' In lecture mode, Marion prattled happily on. ''The asylum kept his paintings, and many of them are still on display there. They're worth a fortune.''

''It sounds very like poor Curtis,'' Erik Giles agreed. ''He didn't kill anyone, of course, but after the early success of his horror novels, his behavior became more and more erratic, and I believe there were a few episodes of violence with various editors.''

''What sort of episodes?'' asked Jay, possibly in search of inspiration.

''I believe he mailed a dead opossum to one of them. And he threatened another one with a razor. He confounded the local police a few times by confessing to murders.''

''Murders?''

''Yes. President Kennedy, Janis Joplin, and, I believe, Joan of Arc. I'm told that every police department has cranks whose hobby is confessing. He once wrote to me saying that he had killed George Woodard and Pat Malone, but since Pat had been dead for a couple of years and I had a letter from George that same day, I dismissed it as wishful thinking.''

''It sounds as if he needed psychiatric treatment,'' said Jay.

''He got it. That was when it was decided that he had to be institutionalized. I am told that he continued to write his fantasy stories even while he was in Butner, and in fact two of his short story collections were written there. In the end, of course, his personality became too fragmented for the discipline of composition, and he degenerated into—well, I didn't go and visit him in those final years. I did go once in the mid-sixties, and he seemed lucid enough then.''

''Did he seem well enough to be released?'' asked Marion.

''Oh, no. He asked about Brendan and Peter, and I told him what they were doing, and then he told me about his demons and what *they* were doing. I never went back.''

''Do you suppose the asylum owns the copyright to Curtis Phillips' later work?'' asked Marion. ''You know, the way Broadmoor owns the Dadd collection?''

''I don't know. I doubt it, though. Curtis was so well known before he was committed that I would have expected his family to take legal steps to administer his estate.''

''It will be interesting to see if anyone turns up to represent his interests at the auction.''

''Bunzie will know about all that. His people contacted us, because we all had to agree to let Bunzie's agent represent us in the book deal. He thought negotiations would be much simpler if we had only one representative working for the entire group.''

"He has put a lot of work into this reunion," said Marion, taking another look at the brochure.

Erik Giles grinned. "He hates to see other people screw up. Besides, he can delegate most of the arrangements to his staff."

"I suppose he can," said Marion, but she made a mental note to observe Bunzie carefully. She tended to distrust altruistic people.

Jay Omega slowed the car. "Look! A 'Welcome to Tennessee' sign. Shall we go in search of the Mountaineer Lodge, stop for dinner, or go and look at the lake?''

Marion shivered. "I don't think I want to look at the lake just yet."

"Nor do I," said Erik Giles.

*In the town's open grave he lies under star spillage, bone
cold and sore, thinking his way home.*

—DON JOHNSON
Watauga Drawdown

CHAPTER 6

THE MOUNTAINEER LODGE had been designed to be picturesque. In the
early eighties an architect for the Tennessee State Park Service had
designed a rustic-looking hotel of timber-framed oak and glass, intended to make out-of-state visitors think of Davy Crockett and to
satisfy environmentalists that the new building harmonized with its
pastoral surroundings. The Mountaineer Lodge was an imposing fret-
work of rafters, joists, beams, and purlins slotted together with hand-
tooled joints: a modern version of the pioneer cabin, expanded to
accommodate fifty guests in neo-rustic splendor, i.e. with central
heating and air conditioning, multilevel decks encircling the building,
and floor-to-ceiling vistas of the Gene C. Breedlove Lake. Nestled
into a hillside of oaks and mountain laurel, the lodge was known for
its simple elegance and for its breathtaking views of the lake.

At present, one of these attributes was missing.

Gone was the shining green lake that had formerly stretched out
from beneath the lodge's decks to meet the green hills on the far side
of the valley. In its place was a mud hole two miles wide, dotted
with rubble and dead trees. In the center of this moonscape, the Watauga River coursed along in its accustomed banks, carrying the lake
water on downstream in daily increments.

Erik Giles stood at the glass wall of the hotel lobby and stared out
at the desolation. His suitcase sat forgotten beneath the ledge of the
check-in booth.

"Do you think we ought to go and talk to him?" whispered Marion
to Jay, who was filling out a reservation card.

"I don't know," said Jay. " 'What company are you with?' Should
I put the university?"

"No. This isn't an academic conference." Marion looked at Giles'
unmoving figure in the fading light. "It's a wake." Without waiting
for Jay's reply, she hurried to Giles' side, touching him lightly on
the arm. "Are you all right?"

He turned to look at her. "Yes, of course. I was just a bit surprised by the look of it. I'm trying to get my bearings, but this bears no resemblance to the valley I remember, so I've no idea where we are in relation to the farm. Still it's fascinating to see what engineers can do in such a short time. I wonder what they did with all the water."

"I expect Jay would know," said Marion, still trying to gauge Giles' mood. She pointed to the dead landscape of rocks and red mud. "You don't find this depressing?"

Giles seemed puzzled by her concern. "Why? They're going to put it back, aren't they? It isn't as if it were strip mining. Three weeks from now this will be a lovely lake again." He started back toward the registration desk. "Well, that's enough sightseeing for now. I suppose I'd better go and check in. Are any of the others here yet?"

"I didn't ask. Of course, the reunion actually begins tomorrow, but you could ask if anyone else has arrived early. Someone may have left you a message. Jay and I thought that we would wait to see if any of your old friends had turned up, and then we'll go to dinner. Unless you need us to stay around. Or you're welcome to join us if you like."

He smiled at her. "Let me see what my options are."

"Good idea," said Marion. "While you check in, I think I'll help Jay take the bags up to our room. We'll meet you here in the lobby in ten minutes."

She found Jay Omega hauling suitcases out of the trunk of the Oldsmobile and loading them onto a rolling cart that he had borrowed from the hotel lobby.

"That was organized of you," said Marion approvingly. "I came out to volunteer my services as a bearer, but I see that you don't need my help after all."

"I'm an engineer," Jay reminded her. "We are trained to be efficient and organized. That's what we do."

"And English professors are trained to be sensitive, but I don't see much of that in Erik."

Jay Omega finished loading the luggage cart and began to maneuver it toward the glass doors of the lobby. "What do you mean? How is Erik being insensitive?"

She shrugged. "I thought that he would be more upset by the destruction of the valley he used to live in, but he seemed to think it was exciting. As far as he was concerned, the whole process was an engineering conjuring trick." She looked suspiciously at the self-confessed engineer. "I suppose *you* agree with him?"

Jay stopped the cart in mid-lobby to take a long look out the window. "It's probably a very nice lake. I grant you that the site looks hellish at the moment, but that's what lakes look like underneath. The question is, was this lake necessary, and I don't know the answer to that. I'm not a civil engineer."

The elevator opened, and they hurried to get the cart inside before the doors closed. Marion was silent until they arrived on the second floor. "Perhaps I'm being overly sensitive," she remarked. "But I think that if this valley had once been my home, I would be upset at seeing it so desolate."

"Well, Marion, he's had thirty years to get used to the idea."

She shuddered. "I don't think that would be long enough for me."

"Here's our room, 208." Jay fumbled for the key. "Are we meeting Erik back downstairs?"

"Yes. I told him ten minutes."

The key clicked in the lock, and he pushed open the door, signaling for Marion to enter first. She glanced at the quilted twin beds, the framed silkscreen prints of mountain scenes, and the little round table placed under a swag lamp. "It looks okay," she conceded. "Nouveau rustic motel."

At the far end of the room the floor-length curtains were drawn to keep out the evening sun. Marion pushed back the curtains and called out to Jay Omega, "Oh, goody! A view of the lake."

When they returned to the lobby ten minutes later, Erik Giles was sitting on one of the earth-tone sofas, leafing through a travel brochure on Ruby Falls. "In my day the big attraction was Rock City," he remarked. "Half the barns in the region had 'See Rock City' printed on the roof in white letters. I never did, though. Wonder if it's still in business."

Marion frowned. "I think that's down near Chattanooga. This part of east Tennessee seems fairly devoid of tourist traps."

Giles grinned. "Don't tell Bunzie. He might try to turn this into a permanent exhibit."

"Is he here yet?" asked Marion, trying not to sound starstruck.

"No. He must be on his way, though. There was an invitation to a cocktail party for the Lanthanides in the Franklin Suite at nine tonight, so apparently we're all getting together to socialize before the media gets here to cramp our style." He looked up at Jay Omega. "Speaking of the Lanthanides, I'm afraid that I must ask a favor of you. There was another message here, too. It was addressed to 'Whichever of the Lanthanides Arrives First.' "

"Interesting," said Jay Omega. "A door prize?"

"Alas, no. It's from George Woodard. He's stranded at the State Welcome Center with car trouble. He wants us to go and get him."

The invisible woman was enjoying her plane ride. At least she was registering ironic amusement at the fact that no one seemed to notice her or cared to speak with her. She was not enjoying the trip in the sense that she was actually *happy*; she did not particularly care for plane rides. But it was pleasant to be going on an unexpected vacation, and at the moment it was entertaining to contemplate the lengths to which this invisibility might extend. Could she get up and dance naked in the aisles? Could she sing at the top of her lungs? No, but she could certainly observe her fellow passengers without fear of return scrutiny. She was the closest thing there is to nonexistent: an overweight, middle-aged woman.

Perhaps, thought Angela Arbroath, such women were like General MacArthur's old soldiers: they didn't die, they just faded away. Angela, who had never been a beauty in the first place, had been fading away for twenty years now, and she thought she must have achieved the ultimate in nonentity. Now when she walked down the street, people pushed past her with their eyes staring straight ahead as if she were merely a pocket of dead air.

A different sort of woman might have been offended at this universal slighting of her humanity, but Angela Arbroath, who considered herself quite charming and not particularly human, thought it was a wonderful cover. It was like having a secret identity. Let people ignore me, she would tell herself; that way they will never know what they missed. It was odd that people assumed that quiet, unglamorous people were also meek and unintelligent. She was neither, but she didn't see any point in letting the whole world in on the secret. Her friends knew what a special person she was, and that was enough.

Thirty years ago she might have minded being universally overlooked. But back then she still cared what strangers thought of her; she still had feelings to be hurt. Now she had adjusted very nicely to a world of her own making, which centered around her century-old cottage in Clemmons, Mississippi, and her garden of medieval medicinal herbs. And of course, her mailbox. Angela had assembled a carefully chosen family of cats, entertaining correspondents, fantasy and medieval history books, and a few eccentric old friends, and that was her world. *The Soul selects her own Society—Then—shuts the Door.* She had that line from Emily Dickinson done in calligraphy and framed. It rested on the mantel above the stone fireplace. On winter evenings Angela would sit on her red velvet settee beside the fireplace, with cats curled up all about her, and she would answer letters to people without really wishing they were there.

She leaned back in her seat and smiled with contentment at her lot in life. Pat Malone would have been proud of her—insofar as he would have given a damn, she amended hastily. Poor old Pat. He was the only one of the Lanthanides that she would really like to see, and he was dead. A pity—she wondered what he would have thought of the mature and mellow Angela, the one who would rather bake zucchini bread than argue.

"About damn time," she pictured him saying. "Arguing is a waste of time. You cannot convert a fan; you can only enrage him."

But Pat might have minded that she had let herself go a bit. There was no getting past it: men were shallow. Even clever and unconventional ones like Pat Malone would probably prefer the sloe-eyed gamine of yesteryear to her present grandmotherly self, but even that didn't trouble her much. She still wore her hair long and straight, because it was the least troublesome thing to do with it, and her wardrobe ran to comfortable shifts, oversized jackets, and flat shoes, because fashion did not concern her either. For festive occasions she had homemade and hand-embroidered dresses in a medieval style, because it pleased her to wear them. Angela had come to terms with who she was, and had there been a psychiatrist in Clemmons, Mississippi, he would have pronounced her well adjusted.

Angela was still in high school when she began writing to the Lanthanides. One of them had written a comment in one of the fanzines she subscribed to, and he mentioned the Fan Farm. Their Tennessee address had reassured her somehow that these were *nice* boys. You never knew with the ones from New York or Minneapolis. Her mother had drummed it into her head that Yankees couldn't be trusted, that they weren't the right sort of people. After all, look what they did to Vicksburg. By the time she discovered the northern origins of most of the Lanthanides, they were solidly entrenched as her friends and confidantes, and she had become a fan publisher with her very own 'zine, reaching out to Yankees and other alien beings from coast to coast. She used the church's mimeograph machine, paying for her ink and paper supplies with money she earned on a paper route. The response was astonishing. For the first time in her life, Angela found herself *popular*.

She hadn't intended to be a self-published magazine editor. At first she merely wanted to correspond with the people she met through other people's 'zines, but a few samples of these grainy, amateurish efforts convinced her that she could produce a better one, and she quickly realized that it was much simpler to produce one magazine than it was to try to write twenty-five personal letters.

So *Archangel* had been born. Either by luck or uncommon good sense (she refused to remember which), Angela had written to Brendan Surn and Pat Malone and a couple of the fan-elite of the day, asking them to contribute articles to her first edition. And because most of them would have given an article to anyone who asked them nicely, they responded by sending her amusing and informative columns that she dutifully typed in on her father's old Underwood typewriter. When the issue was complete, she sent it to a few of the People Who Mattered in fandom, and suddenly she was a celebrity. People clamored for subscriptions to *Archangel,* and overnight she had a hundred new friends.

She would be the first to admit that *Archangel* was not the legendary fanzine that *Alluvial* was. It was generally acknowledged that *Alluvial*'s chief editor, Pat Malone, was brilliant, but because Angela had a less abrasive personality and was able to get along with almost everyone in fandom, she could get a wide variety of interesting articles from almost everyone. By the time some of these fans went on to become famous pros, Angela was one of the most respected and influential amateur publishers.

She smiled again, remembering the heady feeling of acceptance in those early days. It was like being cheerleader, prom queen, and secretary of the class all rolled into one. And the letters were so *interesting.* They read the books that she read, and they seemed absorbed in worthwhile subjects, like space travel and future societies. Whereas her other correspondent, her dreary cousin Betty in Texas, only talked about her boyfriends and what she wore on dates. This was definitely an improvement.

Looking back, Angela knew that most of those people were not her friends at all. They sent her lectures on their own pet obsessions with a word or two of personalization, or they sent mimeographed letters to who-knows-how-many correspondents. Convoy duty was not her idea of a relationship, but it took her a good many years to realize that. The letters that were personal were mostly from unattached young men, who viewed her as a rare prize, because in the fifties women in the hobby were few and far between. She had indulged in a few long-distance romances with some of the more eloquent souls, but the spark never survived an actual meeting.

Over the years, though, Angela had become more perceptive, and more selective about her friends, and she had found some good ones and had managed to keep most of them for several decades now. She no longer published *Archangel,* though. As the years went by, she found that fans were getting younger and younger, and she no longer had much interest in communicating with the new bunch. She went to an occasional science fiction convention, upon prearrangement that friends she wanted to see would be there, but they paid little heed to the scheduled events, preferring to hold their own reunion. And every so often, someone would work up a privately published tribute to fandom, and she would be asked to include an article about *Archangel,* which she always did, reasoning that it was a debt she owed to the hobby in return for its earlier kindnesses to her.

Aside from that, she answered a few of the correspondents she chose to keep with *real* letters, and a score of less intimate acquaintances with a modest letterzine, really a round-robin letter in which she answered everyone in one letter and then sent copies to all of them. This lesser publishing effort she called *Seraph,* a pun both on *Archangel* and on the serif fonts she preferred in her IBM Selectric typewriter. Aside from these pastimes, Angela worked the night shift at the lab at the county hospital so that she could afford postage and cat food.

She had been surprised to hear from—she smiled at the conceit—MistralWorld, Inc. about the Lanthanides' reunion. The former residents of the Tennessee Fan Farm did not number among the friends she kept. She didn't suppose they had noticed, though. She still got eight-page letters from George Woodard about three times a year, but at least six of the pages were photocopied essays with no personalization whatsoever on them. They usually discussed the Woodard daughters, favorable comments received about *Alluvial,* and a bit of name-dropping: "... Had a nice note from my Maryland neighbor A. C. Crispin (*Yesterday's Son*) ..." Occasionally George would dredge up a math puzzle, like Gauss' theorem of consecutive numbers, to amuse his readers, and once he had begun a mock-serious campaign to introduce another integer between two and three. He called it umpty, and encouraged his correspondents henceforth to count *one, two, umpty, three.* ... Then between the numbers twelve and thirteen, one would insert the related digit *umpteen.* She wondered how many people got George's manufactured letter. Dozens, probably. Whenever she got one, she would skim the biographical monotony looking for the bits pertaining to herself (few, but close together, so that the page could be inserted into the pre-existing sermon). Then she would write back a cordial but inconsequential reply, similar to the tone of her letters to Cousin Betty, and George appar-

ently never noticed that there was no real communication or sentiment between them at all. When Angela's mother died of a stroke,
her letter to George went off as perfunctorily as ever, but with no
mention of the family circumstances. She couldn't bear to receive a
one-sentence-personalization condolence.

As for the others, she had lost touch with Bunzie and Surn, half
afraid that if she did write to them, she would receive a reply from
some secretary treating her as another piece of fan mail. Occasionally
they would appear at a science fiction convention, but she never
looked them up. There was always too much else to do in a short
weekend. She and Barbara Conyers exchanged Christmas cards, but
she hadn't heard from Stormy or the others in years, and the fandom
grapevine reported several of them dead.

She thought about the Substitute Con party, and the long drive she
had made to get there, using most of her birthday money for gas! It
would be strange to see all those idealistic boys again as old men. In
retrospect, a lifetime was not very long. And what strange bread upon
the waters to have her 1954 gas money expenditure repaid with a
plane ticket from Ruben Mistral (Inc.). She wanted to cry just thinking about the distance between then and now, and about how short
life is, and how easy it is to lose the thread between people.

"Excuse me, ma'am, are you all right?"

Angela looked up into the concerned eyes of a male flight atten-
dant. He was about to hand a diet Coke to her seatmate, and apparently he had noticed her tear-stained cheeks. *Apparently he had
noticed.*

Angela Arbroath summoned a gentle smile. "Why, I'm right as
rain," she told him.

"It's no trouble at all," said Jay Omega for the fifth time. "It isn't
far to the State Welcome Center. We passed it on 81 on our way
in."

Erik Giles reddened and heaved a weary sigh. "How like George
Woodard to have car trouble! Do you remember that character in
'L'il Abner' who always had a black cloud over his head? That's
Woodard exactly. We used to call him Disaster Lad. I think Pat
Malone once wrote a Superman parody using Woodard as Disaster
Lad."

"Cars are tricky things," said Jay Omega, to whom they weren't.
"Marion once made me drive all the way to Roanoke to get her
because her car wouldn't start. Turned out she hadn't put gas in it.
Marion believes in mind over Mazda."

Erik Giles grunted in what may have been amusement. "Well, I hope this is the last of George's bad luck for the weekend."

As they rounded a bend, an open space between the oaks afforded them a glimpse of the dry lake bed. "It's a strange sight, isn't it?" Jay remarked.

Erik Giles shrugged. "Only because the hills around it are so green. Out west it wouldn't look strange at all."

"I haven't seen any sign of the town yet. I suppose everyone will visit that tomorrow when the reunion actually begins."

"I doubt if there will be much to see after all these years. In fact, I wonder how Bunzie can be so sure he'll be able to locate the time capsule."

"You must have had landmarks when you buried it."

"A fence and an old tree. Do you suppose they'll still be there?"

"I don't know. Traces of them may remain. Once you locate the town, you should be able to get your bearings and pinpoint specific landmarks."

"Perhaps so. I was just thinking how foolish we would all feel if we brought everyone here and then ended up finding nothing."

"Well, I hope you won't be disappointed." Jay hesitated at broaching the touchy subject of money. "You weren't counting on the anthology sales to finance your retirement were you?"

Erik Giles stared. "Retire? You talk as if I were *old*. I shall be at the university for another dozen years. In fact, I have a hunch that Graham may be leaving to take a job at Carolina, which will put me in line for department head." He rubbed his hands together, smiling. "You see what I do to their deconstruction program then! I intend to enjoy myself hugely."

Jay, who still remembered the headache that resulted from his last discussion of deconstruction, hastened to change the subject. "I'm glad to hear that things are going so well," he said. "So you aren't considering returning to science fiction?"

"C. A. Stormcock is dead," said the professor solemnly.

They drove on in silence for the thirty miles that it took to reach the Welcome Center and Rest Area. Jay Omega enjoyed driving, and the rolling hills of east Tennessee provided the ideal setting for an evening's excursion. The winding road had been designed to accommodate the mountains. It clung to the hillside, a narrow path scarcely disturbing the rich vegetation that crept back on either side.

Jay didn't mind playing the Mechanical Samaritan, but he rather wished that it had been Surn or Mistral who had needed his help instead of Woodard, because he was sure that he'd be tongue-tied around writers of their stature, and an informal meeting over a disabled car would have done much to ease the tension for him. Still, he knew that he could count on Marion to be charming and chatty, and that was fine. He was glad to come along for a pleasant evening in the country if Erik wanted company, but apart from that, he had no agenda.

He was sorry when the two-lane blacktop ended at an overpass directing them onto the four-lane interstate. The rest of the drive was a less pleasant ramble, dodging trucks and staying out of the way of cars with Ohio license plates doing eighty. The shadows had deepened to a gray twilight when they finally reached the Welcome Center. Jay eased the Oldsmobile into the parking lot and began looking for the stranded George Woodard.

"Over there, I'll bet," said Erik Giles. "The old AMC Concord with Maryland tags."

Jay pulled into the space beside the white Concord and waved a friendly greeting to the distressed little man who was pacing the sidewalk in front of it. He was wearing tan walking shorts and a *Star Trek* T-shirt that held his physique up to ridicule. When he saw them, he hurried to the car and poked his head in the driver's window.

"Have you come for me?" he asked breathlessly. His glasses had slid down to the end of his nose, and his face was still sweaty from panic or the summer's heat. The air-conditioned Welcome Center stopped welcoming people to Tennessee promptly at 5 P.M.

Erik Giles summoned a brief smile as he climbed out of the car. "Hello, George!" he drawled. "Traveling by yourself?"

Woodard winced at the mention of a sore subject. "Earlene had things to do at home," he said. "So I came by myself. Almost made it, too. Drove down from Maryland in eight and a half hours, and then the bloody contraption quits on me in the Welcome Center." He smiled. "I fancy there's an article to be written in *that* irony."

Erik nodded. "It isn't a leaky radiator this time, is it, George?"

Woodard intoned solemnly, " 'You may talk of Blog and Bheer when your fellow fen are near . . . ' "

Jay Omega glanced at his watch. "Excuse me," he said. "Could you tell me what's wrong with the car?"

Woodard shook his head. "Henry Ford was a magician as far as I'm concerned."

"I mean, what did it do? What were its symptoms?" Jay persisted.

"It did nothing, and those were its symptoms." Woodard began to pace again. "I pulled into the rest area to—" He giggled. "—to jettison some recycled Pepsi, and when I came out of the men's room, the car wouldn't start again.''

Jay looked thoughtful. "Could be a vapor lock. Did it make a noise?''

Woodard shrugged. "I think it laughed at me, but I can't swear to it.'' He turned away to speak to Erik Giles. "Are you still Stormy these days?''

"I prefer to be called Erik Giles,'' said the professor.

Jay Omega interrupted again. "I mean, did it crank when you turned the key, or did it click or what?''

George thought. "I think it clicked. I tried it umpteen times.'' He did not seem interested in the diagnosis, because he immediately resumed his previous conversation.

The volunteer mechanic waited patiently for a lull in the monologue. Finally George glanced at him again, and Jay said, "I hate to trouble you, but could you undo the hood latch for me?''

At this point, Erik Giles made a belated introduction, and George, upon learning that his mechanic was a science fiction author, became noticeably more cordial. He remarked that he had heard of *Bimbos of the Death Sun,* but had been unable to find a copy, and he offered to review Jay's next book in a forthcoming issue of *Alluvial.*

"The hood latch?'' said Jay.

"We're in Tennessee now, Mr. Surn.''

The plane ride had been uneventful, for which Lorien Williams was thankful. They had sat side by side in first-class seats, and throughout the flight Brendan Surn had stared out the window at the changing landscapes beneath them. Just east of the Mississippi, when cumulus clouds obscured his view, Surn went to sleep, awakening only when the green crests of the Smoky Mountains swelled beneath them, twenty thousand cloudless feet below.

This was one of Surn's good days. He had talked briefly, and he seemed to understand the purpose of the journey. Lorien hoped that things would go well over the weekend. She didn't want Mr. Surn to be hurt or embarrassed by the experience. She hoped that it would please him to see his old friends again.

"Sit here in this nice plastic chair, and I'll go and see about the bags.'' Lorien's face assumed an expression of sternness. "You won't wander off, will you?''

Smiling, he shook his head. "Not in Tennessee,'' he said carefully.

"All right, then. I'll be back as soon as I can.'' She hoped that she had brought enough money for the trip. They had Surn's Visa and American Express cards, and two hundred dollars in cash for cab fares and tips. That ought to do it. It had to, because Surn couldn't remember the automatic teller code to get cash with his credit card, and she didn't want to draw too much attention to them by asking for help.

"I have to be crazy to think I can pull this off," thought Lorien. "But what an opportunity—for both of us!" She had purchased a new wardrobe for the reunion, reasoning that people would be more likely to accept her as Surn's assistant if she were *not* wearing jeans and sandals. Since Lorien had never met an employee of anyone famous, she wasn't sure what sort of attire was required, but she decided that if she copied the style of the woman vice-president at Mr. Surn's bank, she ought to succeed in looking both respectable and businesslike. She had even had her hair done for the occasion. Catching sight of herself in a restaurant mirror, Lorien touched her newly styled tresses and frowned. "I look just like Marilyn Quayle," she muttered to herself.

Brendan Surn was a good deal more casually dressed, because as a famous Californian he was not even expected to own a tie. Lorien had studied the pictures on the book jackets of Surn's novels, and she had packed a "representative selection" of similar attire, adding his silver NASA jacket, a gift from the astronauts, in case it was chilly in Tennessee.

So far things seemed to be going well. Perhaps the Piracetam was working. Someone at the health food store had mentioned that the drug was used in Europe for Alzheimer's patients and people with memory problems, so Lorien ordered some. It wouldn't hurt to try, she reasoned. She wasn't sure if there had been any improvement. Sometimes he seemed fine and sometimes not, but she kept up the dosage in hopes that long-term effects would be more noticeable. If he didn't get any worse, that would be enough.

Brendan had done a couple of short telephone interviews concerning the reunion, and he had sounded fine. Lorien thought it odd that a man who couldn't remember how to turn on the stove could talk knowledgeably about literature, but she supposed that the things that would stay with him longest were the things that he cared about, not necessarily the simplest things he knew. She hoped that this meant he would remember the old days at the Fan Farm. If not, she could cover for him by staying close and changing the subject if things got awkward. There was only one problem Lorien Williams had not worked out: What happens if someone offers Brendan Surn big money to write another book? And what if he agrees to do it?

Managing Surn's business affairs and his laundry were one thing, but Lorien was not at all sure that she was up to writing a best-seller.

While George Woodard talked about his teaching job and the next issue of *Alluvial,* speculated on the content of the next *Star Trek* movie (and whether there would be one), and lamented his health, Jay Omega probed under the Concord's hood for signs of trouble. The possibilities were legion. Woodard's engine looked like he had just followed an Exxon tanker through a mud hole. Disaster Lad indeed, thought Jay Omega, but immediately he felt ashamed of himself for this harsh judgment. Surely, he told himself, if George Woodard could have afforded the maintenance on this car, he could also have afforded to trade it in for a newer model. A few moments of study told him what the trouble was.

"It's your battery cables," he announced, fingering the wires barnacled with white corrosion at the terminals.

Behind him the conversation continued unabated. In Woodard's eagerness to discuss old times, he had apparently forgotten his car, his mechanical difficulties, and his new acquaintance. Not that it mattered. Fixing the car would take three minutes and required no assistance from the owner. Jay went back to his own car to get the wet rag and wire brush he would need to clean the battery terminals.

As he went past them, George Woodard called out, "Found the trouble, have you? I hope it's not expensive."

"I can fix it for nothing," said Jay Omega.

Bunzie hated people who accepted telephone calls on airplanes, which was unfortunate, because it was a practice that Ruben Mistral indulged in quite a bit. At the moment he was conferring with his office to reschedule meetings and to see who had left messages in reply to *his* messages. While he had his secretary on the line, he asked how the final arrangements for the reunion had gone. The response was reassuring. The chartered plane had taken off from LaGuardia at six, and the two hotels had declared themselves ready for the reunion and the editorial contingent.

Bunzie wondered what the reunion would be like, aside from all the hype. Did he really have anything in common with those guys anymore? It had been so long since he had talked about anything besides business that he wasn't sure he could carry on an ordinary conversation. And what if the guys were worse than boring—what if they didn't like him? Suppose they resented him for *going Hollywood*? Bunzie figured he had enough enemies throwing negative ions at him without inviting rejection from old friends. For one stifling moment he felt like faking an excuse not to attend and going home. But the plane full of book people had already left New York, and it was unthinkable that the auction should go on without him. The gang stood to make some nice money off this stunt, and it had been *his* doing. How could he think they'd dislike him?

Besides, he thought, these guys were his friends when he was broke and nobody. They had liked him then. There was even more reason to like him now. It was going to be all right.

Bunzie leaned back in his seat, watching the clouds roll by. Now maybe he could sit back and enjoy his friends and let the business take care of itself. He told Ruben Mistral to take the weekend off, and went back to reading the in-flight magazine.

. . . One family returns
every year on Memorial Day to row out
and sink a wreath on what they think
is the ancestral burial plot. But one
of the older boys admits that he thinks
an aging uncle confused the spot with his
favorite fishing hole and they have
for years been honoring a living channel cat.

—DON JOHNSON
"The Mayor of Butler"

CHAPTER 7

"I WONDER HOW it's going," said Marion for the third time.

"The reunion? Fine," said Jay Omega, spearing another forkful of barbecue. "Are you going to eat that last hush puppy, because if not—"

After the rescue of George Woodard from the Welcome Center parking lot, Jay had returned to the Mountaineer Lodge, leaving Erik Giles to go off to his private reunion party while he and Marion drove off in search of a decent restaurant. He wasn't entirely convinced that they had found one, but Marion insisted that it would be wonderful, and as far as the food was concerned, she was right. He wasn't too sure about the ambience.

The Lakecrest Café, as the place was called, sat on a mound of clay too small to be termed a hill, with its back to the narrow shore of Breedlove Lake. Marion had declared that the restaurant's name was either a reassurance for customers or a neon prayer that the lake's crest should go no higher than the bottom of the slope even during the spring runoffs. She conceded that it might also be a message to hydroelectric-happy Tennessee bureaucrats: the lake stops here.

The wooden building was at least thirty years old, and sported a rusting thermometer advertising Coca-Cola, fading posters from last year's fair, and a gravel parking lot full of pickup trucks, which, according to Marion, guaranteed the best food around. Jay muttered something about cholera, but she shushed him, and they went in.

Once inside, Jay's apprehensions began to subside. The green tile floor was well scrubbed, and the pine booths were free of graffiti. Fresh wildflowers sat on red gingham tablecloths, and the jukebox was playing quiet country songs at a reasonable volume.

As they slid into the corner booth, Marion laughed at his evident relief. "What did you expect?" she asked.

Jay pantomimed the strumming of a banjo and hummed a few bars of *Dueling Banjos,* the theme from *Deliverance.*

"Honestly, Jay! What if someone sees you? Anyway, I thought you were a little more sophisticated than that. Wait until I tell Jean and Betty in Appalachian Studies that I found another *Deliverance* sucker."

Jay pretended to be studying the menu, but Marion saw him blush.

She went on. "Everybody has seen that movie, and from the way they've reacted to it, you'd think it was a documentary, but it wasn't. It was an allegory. The author, James Dickey, is a poet. Talking to someone from Appalachia about *Deliverance* is like talking about *Moby-Dick* to a member of Greenpeace. In both cases, you're confusing symbolism with reality." Marion waved her hand to indicate the rest of the café. "Do you see anybody in here who looks like one of those caricatures in *Deliverance*?"

Jay swallowed the last bit of hush puppy. "Well, there's a guy coming toward us. . . ." He nodded toward a large bearded man in jeans and a Charlie Daniels T-shirt. He looked like a cross between a linebacker and a bear.

Marion turned to look at him and her lips twitched but she said nothing.

"Don't worry, Marion!" whispered Jay. "I'll handle this."

"Howdy," said the man, easing into the booth beside Marion. "Did you all come for the show?"

"No," said Marion. "Is there one?"

"Well, most Thursday nights a few of us get together to do a little pickin'. Have a few beers." He eyed Jay Omega, who was noticeably paler. "Not too awful many knife fights, though," he added.

"We don't want any trouble," said Jay carefully.

Marion looked solemn. "What's a barbarian like you doing in a nice place like this?"

Jay's jaw dropped. "Marion!" he hissed.

She continued her scolding as if he had not spoken. "I mean, we come all the way from southwest Virginia, hoping for a little decent barbecue or some down-home cooking, and what do we find trashing up the place? A goddamned Joyce scholar!" She threw a hush puppy at him.

The bearded man grinned. "Shoot, Marion! What'd you wanna give the game away for? I really had your friend going there, and you know I just love *Deliverance* suckers!"

"Very funny, Tobe. What if somebody believed in that hillbilly act of yours? You could be perpetuating a stereotype, you know."

The big man sighed. "I reckon I could come in here in a Savile Row suit and a rep tie, and some people would still think the mountains were full of savages."

Jay Omega continued to look puzzled. "Is this the floor show?" he asked.

They laughed at his dismay. "Jay, may I present Tobias J. Crawford of the English department at East Tennessee State University."

"And one of the best clawhammer banjo players in these parts," Dr. Crawford added without a trace of modesty. "A bunch of us old boys from around here get together Thursday nights to play at the Lakecrest. Straight bluegrass. No ballad singing, dulcimer playing, academic storytelling, or Scottish country dancing allowed. Nobody in the group answers to 'Doc,' and the lawyer who plays bass has to tell people he's a truck driver."

Jay blinked. "You're another English professor?"

"That's right," nodded Crawford. "The woods are full of 'em in tourist season. Mostly they're backpacking on the Appalachian Trail, but a few of them are running around with tape recorders trying to pick up an authentic mountain folk song." He grinned. "I once gave a fellow from Carmel, California, a bluegrass rendition of 'Because I Could Not Stop for Death,' and told him it was a Child ballad that my great-great-great-grandpappy had brought over from England. He's probably tried to publish it in a journal somewhere by now."

Marion nodded. " 'Because I Could Not Stop for Death.' Very good. And I suppose you sang it to the tune of 'The Yellow Rose of Texas'?"

"Oh, sure. You can sing quite a few of Emily Dickinson's poems to the tune of 'The Yellow Rose of Texas.' "

To Jay Omega's further dismay, the two English scholars proceeded to demonstrate this literary discovery, amid giggles and spoons tapped on beer mugs for percussion. When the tribute to Emily Dickinson was finished, Marion wiped her eyes and attempted to speak. "You should see Tobe at an MLA conference!" she said between gasps. "But it was mean of him to scare you like that. Tobe, this is James Owens Mega, an electrical engineer who writes science fiction."

Crawford stuck out his hand. "Sorry to startle you," he said, "but when I saw you mime that banjo imitation, I knew you were discussing *Deliverance,* so I figured I'd come on over. We get pretty tired of that hillbilly crap.''

Jay smiled. ''I know what you mean. I have stereotypes of my own to contend with.''

''Jay is the author of *Bimbos of the Death Sun,*'' Marion explained.

Tobe Crawford nodded. ''That would take some effort to live down, I expect. Science fiction? Are you connected with that reunion going on in Wall Hollow?''

''Yes. Do you know Erik Giles from my department? It turns out that he was C. A. Stormcock, the author of *The Golden Gain,* who was one of the Lanthanides back in the fifties. He was invited back for the reunion, and because his health is not good we came with him.''

Dr. Crawford looked interested. ''Has the reunion started yet? There's been a ton of publicity about it. Newspapers, local television. I even saw an article that said *A Current Affair* was coming in to film it.''

''I believe that's true,'' said Marion. ''Did you see the interview with Mistral in *People* magazine?''

Tobe Crawford shook his head. ''I get my news from the *National Inquirer,*'' he said solemnly.

Marion made a face at him. ''That's right! Make English professors look bad too, while you're at it! Anyway, I wouldn't expect a Joyce scholar to understand a complex field like science fiction, but these writers are very important in their genre, so all this publicity is to be expected.''

''I hear that all sorts of movie types will be there. Have you seen any of those guys yet?''

''The Lanthanides are here, but all the business people arrive tomorrow.'' Marion gave Tobe Crawford a stern look. ''I hope you're not thinking of taking your mountain man act on the road. Anyhow, I haven't seen any gullible city slickers. Tonight the writers are having a private party, so we haven't even met them yet.''

''I've met them, but it was a long time ago,'' said Tobe.

''At a science fiction convention?''

''No. I remember when that bunch lived at Dugger's farm. I was just a kid then, so I didn't know any of them very well, but people used to think they were strange. I worked Saturdays in my uncle Bob McInturf's store, stocking shelves and sweeping up, and they used to come in every now and then to buy groceries. I figure that time capsule they buried was the pickle jar I gave them.''

"Did they tell you what it was for?"

"Not that I recall. We didn't pay much attention to them, on account of them being so odd and keeping to themselves like they did. We knew Dugger's people, of course, and Jim Conyers is a good old boy—for a lawyer—but back then, people kept shy of them. I remember they set off some fireworks one time that damn near started a forest fire. Folks around here were about ready to run them off."

"I think they've mellowed since then," said Jay Omega.

"I didn't realize that you came from this part of east Tennessee, Tobe," said Marion. "So people here didn't know that the Lanthanides buried a time capsule?"

"Nobody would have cared. Those guys weren't famous back when I was a kid, so no one was particularly interested in what went on out there, as long as they didn't burn down the mountain." He grinned wolfishly. "A time capsule, huh? Too bad James Joyce didn't bury one of those."

Marion gave him an acid smile. "He'd probably have dumped a box of Scrabble tiles into the canister and let it go at that."

Jay had begun to be afraid that the evening was going to degenerate into an English professors' version of sniper warfare. In his desperation to think of a new topic for discussion, he said, "You're the first local person we've met so far. What do you think of the drawdown?"

Tobias Crawford looked sad. "People hated that lake when they put it in. One old fellow compared the TVA's taking of our valley to the expulsion of the Cherokees on the Trail of Tears. When they announced the drawdown, I thought we'd all be thankful to see that lake gone, even for a couple of weeks, but now I don't know. It sure has dredged up a lot of memories."

"I wonder how it's going at the reunion," said Marion again. "Imagine—all the titans of science fiction in one little village!"

"Well, if they're as great as you say they are, I reckon they picked the right place to get together," said Tobe Crawford.

"What do you mean?"

"Wall Hollow. Haven't you heard how it got its name?"

Marion shook her head.

"Okay, I'll give you a hint. The present name of the town is a local corruption of the original. The town was settled in the early eighteenth century by German immigrants. Try saying it out loud. Wall Hollow."

"Wall Hollow," Marion repeated thoughtfully. "German . . ."

"Valhalla," said Jay Omega. "The home of the immortals."

* * *

Erik Giles had been reluctant to go to the reunion. For a long time he sat in his room, debating over whether or not to wear casual clothes instead of his white suit, whether or not to wear a tie, whether or not to improvise a name tag to spare himself embarrassment. And what if the others had changed so much that he failed to recognize them? Would that be a social blunder? In the end, hunger and boredom drove him out of his solitary bedroom, sporting a hand-lettered name tag drawn on a page of the nightstand note pad. He had folded it over his shirt pocket and secured it in place with the clip of his ballpoint pen. "Erik Giles, Ph.D.," the sign said, and in smaller letters beneath it he had written "Stormy." Fortified by that social insurance, the professor followed the arrows to the Laurel Room and steeled himself for the encounters to come.

It was a quiet party in a small banquet room. A photo mural of the lake in autumn adorned one wall, and the addition of chintz loveseats and potted plants instead of tables converted the space from banquet hall to salon. Soft canned music flowed from hidden speakers as an unobtrusive waitress glided about the room, retrieving empty glasses and offering hors d'oeuvres.

Thankful to go unnoticed, Erik Giles stood in the doorway studying the guests. The most familiar face was that of George Woodard, hunched over a little plate of appetizers, with a cup of punch balanced precariously on the arm of the sofa. He had changed from his *Star Trek* T-shirt to a brown turtleneck and polyester pants, and his black hair, grown long on one side and combed across the top of his head, shone like the surface of a bowling ball. Standing near George was a plump, pleasant-looking woman with braided hair and a medieval gown of green and gold. She was talking to a florid fellow in a wrinkled beige jacket and an open shirt. Giles caught a glimpse of the gold medallion around the man's neck and correctly deduced that this must be the host of the party, "Bunzie" Mistral. The young man hovering at Bunzie's elbow was either a relative of someone in the group or, more probably, one of the Mistral minions, on hand to see that things went smoothly.

Turning his attention to the far end of the room, Giles found Brendan Surn—by now a household face—standing beside the lake mural with a secretarial young woman in a navy blazer and skirt. Surely not a wife, thought Erik Giles. She doesn't look expensive enough to be the great man's consort. Perhaps she was another one of the staff. The two of them were talking quietly with a lean, distinguished-looking man who was quite well preserved for sixty, but more con-

servatively dressed than Surn or Mistral. Definitely not a movie
person. Erik Giles tried to remember who else was coming. It took
him another few minutes to remember Dugger's quiet boyhood friend
Jim . . . O'Connor? Conrad. Ah, he had it now. Conyers. Jim Conyers. And the plump woman in white linen at his side must be the
fiancée of long ago—Barbara. He had met her a couple of times,
years ago, but he could remember nothing about her. There probably
wasn't much to remember.

Giles took a deep breath. This wasn't going to be so difficult, he
told himself. He had a pretty good idea who everyone was already,
and if any gaffes were made, there was no one important around to
observe it. Things were going to go well, he thought, if only he could
manage to be kind about his old acquaintances' follies, and if he
weren't too overbearing about his own scholarly importance. He
straightened his name tag, squared his shoulders, and strode pur-
posefully into the room.

Ever the genial host, Bunzie hurried to greet him, enfolding him
in a bear hug, which Giles supposed to be the Hollywood equivalent
of a cordial nod. He noticed that as Bunzie pulled out of the embrace,
he sneaked a look at the name tag. "Stormy! Stormy! Stormy!" he
intoned. "Great to see you again, kid!" Turning to the assembled
guests, Bunzie announced, "Look, folks! It's Dr. Erik Giles—complete with name tag! And how about you, Stormy? Recognize the old
gang?"

"I think so, yes," said Giles, edging away from his host. "How
have you been, er—Reuben?" He pronounced it with the accent on
the first syllable, the way Bunzie had said it in the old days, before
he became the fashionable "Ruben," accent on the second syllable,
Mistral.

"It's still Bunzie," grinned Mistral. "Especially to family. And
we're family, aren't we? Boy, when I think of those wonderful times
we had back on the farm."

"It would have been nice to have central heating," said Giles.

"Well, Dugger could afford it now, couldn't he? After we sell this
anthology for a bundle . . ."

"Poor Dugger. I wish he were alive to see this. He could have
bought another farm somewhere. And wouldn't Curtis Phillips love
to see his name coupled with Lovecraft's in scholarly articles?" Erik
Giles looked around the room. "This is a reminder of what we've
lost, isn't it? Curtis, Deddingfield, Dale Dugger? Intimations of our
own mortality."

"You forgot Pat Malone," said Bunzie.

Giles shrugged. "I don't miss Pat. He was a cynical pain in the ass."

Bunzie's smile was all-forgiving. "Poor old Pat. Such an idealist! He was trying to be sophisticated, that's all. But he was a great mind, and in his own way, he thought the world of us."

"Well, perhaps." Erik Giles didn't want to beatify a departed nuisance, but it would have been rude to disagree. He shook Bunzie's hand. "Good to see you again."

He made his way toward Brendan Surn, the farthest point in the room from the effusive Bunzie and the limpet Woodard.

As he approached them, Brendan Surn turned his attention from the Conyers couple, his face lighting up in a warm smile. "Hello, Peter!" he called out. "They told me you weren't coming."

The little mudhen secretary looked stricken. "Mr. Surn!" she gasped. "This is Erik Giles. You remember. Mr. Mistral was telling us that he's a college professor now."

Brendan Surn looked blank for a moment, but then he put out his hand and smiled again. "Erik Giles. Of course. In that white suit of yours, my next guess might have been Mark Twain."

They all laughed merrily to cover the awkward moment. Then the secretary offered her hand to Giles. "I'm Lorien Williams, Dr. Giles. I'm Mr. Surn's assistant."

"Lorien?" echoed Giles.

She blushed. "I was born in the sixties, when my parents were heavily into Tolkien. And before you ask, no, I don't have a brother named Gandalf. Anyway, it's an honor to meet you. And you know Mr. and Mrs. Conyers, of course. We were just talking about the movie version of *Starwind Rising.*"

"Er—yes," said Giles, trying to remember a movie he had seen once ten years ago. "Too bad they had to leave out so many of the subplots, but I suppose a nine-hundred-page book presents many problems for screenwriters."

"So you live over in Virginia now?" said Barbara Conyers, who was the family conversationalist.

"Yes. I teach at the university. I don't get over this way very often."

"Jim and I still live in Elizabethton. Jim is semiretired now from his law practice, and we have a little nursery of trees and bedding plants. I've always loved working with flowers. And our daughter Carol lives over in Johnson City. Her husband is at the university, and they have two little ones, Andrew, who is four, and Amy Allison, two-and-a-half."

Giles turned to Lorien Williams. "Is this your first trip to east Tennessee?"

She nodded. "First trip east of Idaho. There are a lot of trees here. In California I get homesick for trees sometimes."

"You should see the country when the lake is full," said Barbara. "Especially in June when the mountain laurel is in bloom. It's about the prettiest place on earth then."

"I find it interesting to see the valley exposed again after all these years." Giles nodded toward the mural of Breedlove Lake.

"I know," said Barbara earnestly. "It's strange, isn't it? Like digging up an old grave. I swear Jim's been having nightmares about the whole thing. He wakes up sometimes of a night in a cold sweat. He talks about water running down the walls."

Conyers frowned. "Probably indigestion," he grunted.

Barbara chattered on. "Still, I guess it's a good thing they did decide to drain the lake, because otherwise, you all would never have been able to recover your stories, would you?"

Lorien Williams nodded excitedly. "Isn't it wonderful about the time capsule? After all these years, new stories from Peter Dedding-field and Curtis Phillips! I've read everything they ever wrote."

Jim Conyers looked solemn. "I don't care much for myself. Barb and I are happy as we are, but maybe after all these years Dugger will finally get something published. Wish he could have been around to enjoy it."

Barbara sighed. "He would have been so proud of all his friends. They've all become so famous." Giles' frown reminded her that this was too sweeping an accolade. "And even the ones who aren't celebrities are doing *real* well," she amended. A glance in George Woodard's direction suggested that she knew better, but was going to leave it at that anyhow.

A new voice chimed in. "I wonder what Pat Malone would have thought of all this hoopla."

Giles turned to see the woman in medieval dress smiling up at him. There were lines around her eyes and at the corners of her mouth, but she had an appealing air of youthfulness about her.

"Angela Arbroath, Stormy," she said, offering him a much be-ringed hand. "I published *Archangel*. Remember?"

"Yes, of course," said Giles hastily, giving her an awkward peck on the cheek. "*Archangel*. Quite a nice little magazine, as I recall."

Angela blushed. "Well, it wasn't a patch on *Alluvial*, of course, but Pat Malone was a much better editor than I was. And of course, he could offer articles by Surn and Deddingfield. You wouldn't believe how much *Alluvial* sells for today.''

Giles gave her a mirthless smile. "One dollar per issue, I believe."

"Oh. Of course. George still publishes something called that, doesn't he?" She paused for a moment, trying to think of something kind to say about that. Finally she blurted out, "Well, you certainly are looking well, Erik!"

"And you haven't changed a bit," he assured her. "And of course you were here the weekend we decided to put that time capsule together. You even sent us back a story, didn't you?"

"That I did," grinned Angela. "And if Bunzie is the magician he thinks he is, it'll keep me in my old age."

"Do you remember what you wrote?" asked Barbara Conyers.

"Not really. Something with a woman protagonist, I think, to annoy the guys. In most of *their* early works the women were like cheeseburgers—they were either trophies or dessert."

Erik Giles laughed. "Remind me to introduce you to Marion Farley," he said. "I believe you two are soul mates."

It was nearly ten o'clock. The supply of hors d'oeuvres had dwindled to a few selections that nobody wanted, and the champagne had been abandoned in favor of decaffeinated coffee, but the talking was louder and more animated than before, and frequently punctuated with laughter. As the reunion rekindled their memories of each other, the Lanthanides had pulled the couches close together, and they all sat around in a circle, arguing about subjects they hadn't cared about in decades.

None of these subjects concerned science fiction, science, or literature in general. In the years since the dissolution of the Fan Farm, they had resolved all their uncertainties about those subjects to their own satisfaction, and they were past the need to discuss such matters. What still rankled was the personal issues.

"I didn't know that was moonshine you kept in that mason jar in the bathroom. And anyway, it took the paint off my brush, didn't it?" After all these years, Woodard was still stung by Bunzie's old grievance. "Besides," he added petulantly, "I probably saved your life by using it up. Drinking that stuff can make you go blind. It gives you lead poisoning, I believe."

Giles laughed. "Speaking of that sort of lead poisoning, remember that issue of *Alluvial* that Curtis and Pat Malone put out when they were stinking drunk? 'An Interview with Cthulu.' And they filched a couple of love poems that Deddingfield wrote to Earlene Riley and put those in. I thought the post office was going to send the feds in after us when that issue went through the mails. Remember the verse about 'Your succulent nipples spark fusion in my teeming loins . . .' Ugh! And Deddingfield wasn't even embarrassed. He swore he wrote it from memory!'' Hearing a silence instead of indulgent laughter, Giles looked up to see shamefaced smiles on the faces of the others. George Woodard had turned scarlet, and seemed intent upon a petit-four.

Finally Conyers said quietly, ''Well, Peter always was an old lying hound, wasn't he?''

Erik remembered that George Woodard referred to his wife as Ear-lene. A glance at Woodard's red face told him that it was the same girl. Girl! She must be sixty now. They had met her at an East Coast S-F convention. He wondered if she still attended them.

To break the silence, Angela said, ''Do you remember how much Dale hated Erik's jazz records! Pat told me that Dale wrote a story once contending that jazz was the sound of alien invaders fine-tuning their spaceships' engines.''

Erik Giles looked puzzled. ''I can't remember having any special fondness for jazz. Well, perhaps I did. I fancied myself a bohemian in those days.''

''I remember you used to argue incessantly about whose turn it was to do the dishes,'' said Brendan Surn.

''We were always arguing incessantly about something,'' said Bunzie. ''That's what adolescent intellectuals do. Bicker. Protest. Whine. Censure. But we laughed a lot, too.''

''Dissent is the sign of an active and inquisitive mind,'' said George Woodard, for whom bickering had remained a way of life. ''In *Alluvial* I welcome disagreement from freethinking individuals, exercising their First Amendment rights. Speaking of *Alluvial,* I'm planning to write this up in a forthcoming issue, and I'd welcome some guest columns. How about you, Angela?''

Angela looked away. ''I'm not sure I have the time, George. I'll see. Okay?''

''I guess we ought to talk about the reason we're all here,'' said Bunzie, drawing a well-scribbled index card out of his hip pocket. ''The business part of this reunion starts tomorrow. I thought we'd begin with an introductory meeting here at our hotel. Jim, I think you agreed to give the media people some background on Wall Hollow and the construction of the lake?''

''Yes. I did some research, and I can answer anything that isn't an engineering question. History, facts and figures, local legends, and so on.''

"Good! Colorful anecdotes will make good copy for feature stories. I leave it to you.'' Bunzie consulted his notes. "After the introduction here, we will make our way down the hill, where several small motorboats will be waiting to take us to Dugger's farm. Expect to pose for pictures during this process. We have boots for all of you.''

Tentatively, Lorien Williams raised her hand. "Excuse me, but how can boats get around out there if there is nothing left but mud?''

Bunzie's smile was intended to make her feel at ease. "Good question, Lori!'' he beamed. "You know, the best thing we could have used would have been those hovercraft things they use in the swamps of the Everglades. What do they call them? Whatever. Anyway—'' He shrugged. "Try to find those swamp boats in east Tennessee. Try to find a *bagel*. But rowboats they got. So we rented a couple, complete with outboard motors and navigators. The boats will stay in the original channel.''

Jim Conyers felt the need to translate. "When they drain the lake, Miss Williams, the water doesn't go away entirely. The Watauga River simply returns to its original banks and flows through the valley just as it did before the lake was formed. We will travel on the river.''

"But once we get to the farm, we slog it out on foot,'' said Bunzie, wagging a playful finger. "So don't forget your boots!''

Taking the silence that followed for assent, Bunzie resumed his lecture. "Now, as to the time capsule itself. That's the real reason for our being here, and we don't want to disappoint all those editors who have come in search of treasure, do we? Does anybody remember any landmarks that might still be standing, to help us in locating it?''

Jim Conyers was tired. Ten o'clock was usually his bedtime, since he got up at five. But Barbara seemed to be enjoying herself, so he stayed. All the talk was making him sleepy, though. It seemed to him that all the Lanthanides ever did was talk aimlessly and wait around for something to happen. He had forgotten that feeling of waiting; he'd always had it at Dugger's farm. Everybody seemed to be killing time, *waiting* for something, and while they waited they talked, but nobody ever seemed to know what they were waiting for, and nobody ever tried to make anything happen. And, as far as he could tell, nothing much ever did happen at the Fan Farm. Except a lot of feuds between one another over trivialities. They could sulk for three days over a magazine cover that one liked and the other didn't. Finally, everybody just got tired of sniping at everybody else, and one by one, they left.

Now, thirty-five years later, here they were again, the dearest of old friends, remembering Wall Hollow as if it had been a paradise of sweet accord. The feuds were forgotten. He wondered if dredging up the past would bring the old enmities to the surface again. Perhaps not. If their lives did not touch at any point, what could there be left to quarrel over?

He studied the aging Lanthanides. Bunzie still seemed amiable and enthusiastic, but the lines about his mouth and an occasional sharp look at his assistant suggested that he could also be a demanding tyrant. And Giles had come to the reunion, but he seemed embarrassed to be reminded of his youthful foray into fandom. Jim didn't know what to make of Surn. He seemed like the patriarch of the reunion, but his detachment could mean anything. Angela Arbroath seemed happy, and Jim figured that was good enough. He expected less from women, and he knew it, but he told himself that his generation couldn't change the way it saw the world, and it saw women as lesser beings. He hadn't expected much of Angela, and he had not been disappointed.

Only Woodard had not changed. He had grown older without growing up, still living for his fanzine and his pen pals as if there were no other goals in life to aspire to. At least the others who had stayed in science fiction had gone on to bigger accomplishments: novels, films, and in Surn's case a Medal of Freedom from the President. But for George it was still 1954. Jim sighed at the waste. By rights, Woodard ought to be allowed to live an extra fifty years, so he'd have time to *do* something if he ever emerged from his cocoon.

"Have you seen the lake?" Lorien Williams was asking Bunzie.

"Not *lately*!" said Bunzie, laughing loudest at his own joke.

"It looks like a giant hog wallow right now," said Angela. "That mud must be knee deep out there. How are you all going to get around in it?"

"Small boats in the wettest parts," Bunzie told her. "And after that, wading boots. I brought a case of them, all sizes."

"A lot of people are upset about this drawdown," said Barbara, leaning forward confidentially to impart the local point of view. "You know, they didn't move all the graves when the TVA made the lake back in the fifties, and some people are afraid that there'll be bodies floating in the mud when the water recedes."

Angela Arbroath gasped. "Where is Dugger buried?"

"Somewhere else. The lake was already here by that time," Jim told her.

"I've heard that some pilots in private planes have flown over the valley and reported seeing bodies floating in the channel," Barbara insisted.

"Catfish," said her husband. "Those channel cats can get up to six feet long."

Barbara Conyers tossed her head. "Well, I just hope y'all don't stumble across any unearthed corpses when you go out hunting your time capsule."

"I hope not too," said Bunzie. "The film crews couldn't use that sort of footage for promotion."

"Speaking of skeletons in the valley," said a new voice, "I should think we had quite enough of our own."

The Lanthanides looked up to see three newcomers standing in the doorway: a dark-haired woman and a young man who looked startled by their companion's outburst, and the speaker himself. He was a gaunt man in late middle age, and his somber outfit—a black jacket over black shirt and trousers—emphasized the pallor of his skin. He leaned on the door frame and studied the group with a smile that might have been derisive or challenging. It was anything but friendly.

Bunzie decided to ignore the impertinence. Frowning at the intruders, he waved them away. "I'm sorry!" he called out. "This is a private party. The Lanthanides will not be giving interviews until tomorrow."

The younger couple turned to leave, but the man in black still stood in the doorway, enjoying the disturbance he had created.

Erik Giles stood up. "They aren't reporters, Reuben. At least, two of them aren't. These are my friends Jay Omega, the writer, and Marion Farley, from my department. They came with me. I'm afraid I don't know the other gentleman."

Jay Omega looked apologetic. "We met him in the lobby as we were coming in," he explained. "He was looking for the reunion. He said that you would know him."

The Lanthanides looked questioningly at each other. No one spoke. Bunzie nodded to his assistant, signaling him to be ready to handle an awkward situation. "I don't think any of us knows the gentleman," he said dismissively. "So if you will excuse us—" The man in the doorway smiled. "It'll come to you, Fugghead."

"My God!" whispered George Woodard, peering at the stranger. "It's Pat Malone!"

Pseuicide—The fannish term for faking someone's death.
Since most of fandom is conducted by mail, hoaxes are
relatively easy to perpetrate.

CHAPTER 8

"WHAT WAS THAT all about?" whispered Marion when the door to the reception closed behind them.

Jay Omega shrugged. "I guess they knew him. What shall we do now? Call it a night?"

Marion glanced at her watch. "Not until I find out what's going on. Why don't we go out to the lobby and get some coffee? That way, we can waylay Erik when the party breaks up, and try to find out what's going on."

Her companion stifled a yawn. "All right. If you insist, but I don't see—"

"Shh!" Marion gestured toward the closed door of the banquet room. "Someone may come out unexpectedly. It would be a considerable blow to my self-esteem, not to mention my professional standing, if someone came out and caught us loitering in the hall like a couple of groupies. Let's talk about it over coffee."

Several minutes later, Marion had commandeered the coffee shop booth with the best view of the lobby, and she was hunched over a steaming mug of black coffee with the furtive air of an unindicted co-conspirator. Jay Omega, whose attention had been captured by a piece of Dutch apple pie, was doing his best to humor her.

"I'm sure they didn't mean to be rude," he said. "They seemed quite upset."

"It's all very strange," she murmured, stirring furiously. She kept casting sidelong glances at the hallway to the banquet room as if she were expecting a stampede, but all was quiet.

"He's another one of the Lanthanides, isn't he?" said Jay. "When we met him in the lobby, and he said that he was Pat Malone, I assumed that he was an editor or a film person, and that he was joking, but Woodard seemed to recognize him."

Marion scowled. "Woodard called him Pat Malone, which is ridiculous. Pat Malone has been dead since 1958. Everybody in fandom knows that. I know that and I wasn't even in fandom in 1958. I was in diapers!''

This was something of an exaggeration, but Jay wisely did not correct her arithmetic.

"I admit that it *sounded* like Woodard said 'Pat Malone,' but it's impossible. Pat Malone is dead. All the books say so.''

Jay smiled. "That would explain the shocked looks on the faces of the rest of them.''

"It certainly would," snickered Marion. "Pat Malone! I wonder how he found out about the reunion?''

"Ouija board?'' suggested Jay Omega, trying to keep a straight face.

Marion, who had gone back to trying to figure things out, acknowledged his wit with the briefest of smiles. "Very clever. Actually, his knowing about the reunion is probably the least part of the mystery. Thanks to the dramatic effect of the drained lake, and to Ruben Mistral's excellent publicists, this reunion has been covered in everything from computer bulletin boards to the *National Inquirer.* You'd *have* to be dead not to know about it.''

"I wonder if Elvis will show up," Jay mused. "He's from Tennessee, too, isn't he?''

"Don't be silly," said Marion. "Elvis Presley is dead.''

"That doesn't seem to have stopped Pat Malone," he pointed out. "Can you explain that?''

Marion nodded. "I think so. Mark Twain said it best: *All reports of my death have been greatly exaggerated.* Actually, in fandom such misinformation isn't even uncommon. Fans chiefly correspond by letter and by hearsay, so it's very easy for someone to start an unsubstantiated rumor, which soon gets repeated as fact farther along the grapevine.''

"Somebody said he was dead, and nobody checked?''

"Hardly anybody ever checks *anything* in fandom. Remember all the garbage that came out in fanzines after *Bimbos of the Death Sun* first came out? People thought 'Jay Omega' was a pseudonym for half of SFWA.''

"I told you not to read the amateur commentary on my book," said Jay, downing the last of his milk. "It only upsets you. Even *good* reviews upset you.''

"I couldn't believe how shallow most of those reviewers were," said Marion, momentarily distracted. Then, noticing her companion's amused smile, she decided to jettison the tirade. "Well, never mind about literary criticism! The subject at the moment ought to be history. Apparently we have just witnessed the debunking of a death hoax of thirty years' standing.''

"Hoax?" Jay looked bewildered. "So you're saying that somebody deliberately made an announcement that Pat Malone was dead, and everybody just believed it and let it go at that?''

"Something like that. Given the mentality of fandom, death hoaxes are inevitable occurrences. Some people do it as a practical joke; some declare themselves dead in order to get rid of people who otherwise will not go away; and some people do it in order to annoy the person they report as dead. Back in the fifties, fans were taking up a collection to bring the brilliant Irish fan Walt Willis to Chicon II in Chicago, and a neofan named Peter Graham sent out postcards announcing Willis' demise.''

"Why?"

"Apparently because Peter Graham felt like it, and because his parents had given him a postcard mimeo and he wanted to use it. He knew that it would cause a sensation because Willis was so popular. Most people realized that the postcard was a hoax at the time, because he had misspelled 'diphtheria,' and because it seemed strange that an Irishman's death announcement should be postmarked San Francisco.''

"I suppose Walt Willis was pretty upset about it.''

"I hear he wasn't. People said that when he got to the U.S., he charmed everyone by answering his telephone, 'Peter Graham speaking.' '' Marion smiled at the memory of one of fandom's finest hours.

"But, of course, you don't approve," said Jay solemnly.

Marion looked stern. "Death hoaxes are cruel and pointless. I wonder who started this one?''

"I wonder why Pat Malone didn't bother to set anyone straight?''

"That may be what he is doing right now." Marion sighed. "I wish Erik Giles would come out. That is one conversation I'd give anything to hear.''

"You may get your chance tomorrow," Jay told her. "Someone is going to have to explain his presence to the media people. Still, thirty years is a long time to wait to correct a mistake like that, don't you think?''

"I don't know. From what I hear about the personality of Pat Malone, he may have staged the hoax himself. And I know why everyone was so quick to believe in it.''

"Why?"

Marion sighed. "Wishful thinking. Before Pat Malone died, he created a stink in fandom that lasted for decades. A lot of people will be dismayed to hear that he's back.''

Alluvial—Volume 7, Number 4
June 16, 1958

***Special Issue of ALLUVIAL
dedicated to Pat Malone***

IN MEMORIAM PAT MALONE
By George Woodard, Editor

One of the most powerful, if strident, voices in fandom has been stilled by no less a censor than the Grim Reaper himself, who swept down with his black wings in the night, and carried off Patrick B. Malone, on June 8 in Biloxi, Mississippi.

Word has reached me here in Maryland that Pat Malone has died, and, since this information has not been generally released and since it concerns a fellow Lanthanide, I consider it my somber duty to relay that which I know concerning his passing to the late, great Pat's many associates in the realm of science fiction fandom. According to Jack L. Bexler (editor of JACKAL'S MEAT), he (Jack) received a letter from his (Pat's) widow, Ethel Lucille Malone, who resides in Cupertino, CA. (She did not write to me, one of Pat's oldest friends in fandom, but that is another matter.) Why he died in Mississippi is not clear to this writer. Bexler relates that Pat Malone had been sick for a number of years with a tuberculosis-related illness of some kind, and that he finally died of it this month, in great pain. His body was donated to the Washington Medical School, by his own instructions.

Pat will be remembered by his myriad correspondents as one of the founders of ALLUVIAL, one of the leading fanzines of this decade, but he is even better known as an incisive critic of the social order, the Jonathan Swift of fandom, the stinging gadfly of all he surveyed. He is the author of one SF novel, *River of Neptune*, which is unfortunately out of print, but somewhere in the Library of Congress, his name will be listed for all time.

Who among us has not felt the barbed tongue of Patrick B. Malone? Of course, he will also be remembered for his perceptive analyses of the works of Jules Verne, and for his detailing the fulfillment of Verne's scientific prophecies (e.g. the submarine), but it is his fan-related writings which will make his name ring down through the ages. His opus *THE LAST FANDANGO* (privately mimeographed) is a classic of social commentary, and it revolutionized the heretofore timid accounts of fan politics and convention activities.

He left the editorship of ALLUVIAL in 1955, when he left the Fan Farm, and I have carried on. I like to think that Somewhere, he will keep reading, and will say, "Well done, Woodard!"

He is gone, and those of us who were his friends will miss his crisp forthrightness. His enemies have lost a chance to change his opinion of them. And we shall not see his like again.

GEORGE WOODARD, ED.

GOOD-BYE AND GOOD RIDDANCE, PM!
A Guest Column By Jack L. Bexler

Providence, Rhode Island
June 1958

I write to bury Pat Malone, not to praise him. Speaking no ill of the dead smacks of hypocrisy and I'll have none of it, so I will at least do Pat the courtesy of being as forthright as he was, and not pretend that death has improved him. (Though I thought it might.)

I never met Pat Malone face to face, but I have certainly felt his typewritten wrath in various altercations that ran between *ALLUVIAL* and *JACKAL'S MEAT*. One such return salvo was sent back to me unopened in mid-June by Ethel Malone from Cupertino, California, enclosed in a letter saying that her husband Pat was dead, and so, ironically enough, it was his chief enemy who was given the task of announcing his death to his friends. (If he had any.) I only regret that, unlike MacDuff, I cannot also bring them his head.

Others will have to eulogize Pat Malone, the man. I knew him as a typeface with one half the "S" missing. It summed him up very well. The half-essed Pat Malone. He came from a dull, but respectable background, and perhaps being something of the alienated intellectual, the perpetual rebel, made him decide to leave the little college town of his birth, and begin his odyssey—to make a fandom of hell, and a hell of fandom.

He found others of his kind through the S-F magazines of the 'Forties, and later drifted onto the Fan Farm in Wall Hollow, Tennessee, where a mimeograph machine salvaged from a redneck's junkyard launched his career as a fan publisher. *ALLUVIAL* was born, and its regularity and reasonably good quality (he had a lot of other people's talent to draw from, and he used it well) quickly made him a celebrity in the genre. Not that Pat cared much about that. He contended that it didn't pay anything, and that the people singing his praises were "nobodies," so Pat tried to make the leap to pro-dom.

He managed to write one novel, *River of Neptune*, which sounded to me like a rewrite of some of Jules Vernes' ideas (most notably "The First Men in the Moon"), but I am not a literary critic. I just know what I like, and in my opinion Harlan Ellison has a better chance to be famous than Pat Malone does.

That one "real" book did not make a happy man of Pat Malone. He didn't become famous with his little paperback yarn. He didn't become the darling of the literati. And he still didn't have any friends. The fact that there is only ONE book by Pat Malone further suggests that it was a fluke, rather than an indication of any real literary talent.

He gained much more notoriety from *THE LAST FANDANGO*, because people are invariably drawn to sleaze, however mendacious it is.

Pat Malone was a failure. He failed at life. He failed at fandom, his retreat from life. And he failed at being a writer, his retreat from fandom. His well-publicized and unprovoked attacks on well-meaning associates in the hobby testifies to his basic instability and to his own misery, which he attempted to alleviate by inflicting it on others.

I do not mourn his passing, and upon contemplating his life and his death, I do not think they let him in to heaven. If they did, I don't suppose he likes it much.

JACKAL BEXLER

GOOD NIGHT, SWEET PRINCE
In Remembrance of Pat Malone
by Angela Arbroath

(Jack L. Bexler writes that Pat Malone has died in Mississippi. And

I write this partly in sorrow for the loss of an old friend, and partly to let you know that I have no further details to give you on his actual passing. I did not know that Pat Malone was in Mississippi, and I believe that he was down near the Gulf, whereas I live up near Memphis, TN. Please don't send me any more letters asking for details. I don't know anything about Pat's death! What follows is a tribute to his life.—A.A.)

It has been several years since I saw Pat Malone, so perhaps the person who has died is not, in the emotional sense, the man that I knew, but, for the annals of fandom, wherein lies his best hope to be remembered, it falls to my lot to eulogize Pat Malone.

On a personal level, I can only say that I liked him as a friend and respected his talent, and then I must try to explain him to his many adversaries, because Pat Malone was truly a stormy petrel, whom few people appreciated and virtually no one understood.

Pat Malone was an idealist who valued intellectual qualities above material possessions, and he very much wanted to be a part of a special group of dedicated and intelligent people. If he could have come to terms with God, he would have become a Jesuit, I think. As it was, he opted for a group of people who wrote with spirit and enthusiasm, made strong friendships (bickering aside), and who built an environment in which intelligence and verbal skill rather than race, social aptitude, sex, or family background determined one's position. Aldous Huxley aside, let us hope that this is the Brave New World. It is certainly the world in which Pat Malone wanted to live.

When his newfound paragons fell short of these utopian expectations, he took them to task for it. He hated the pettiness of some fans, and he was contemptuous of "Big Name Fans," who sought to become celebrities in what Pat considered a solemn intellectual order. He was forthright in his criticisms, and he made people angry. So long as what he said was true, Pat didn't care how people felt about its being said.

But he wanted to love us. I think that the civilization described in his novel *River of Neptune* is an idealization of fandom: the Marilaks are us as he would have liked us to be.

There is not much to say about my personal relationship with the young Pat Malone of the Wall Hollow fan farm. We wrote for a long while and drew mind-close, and later we came together as physical beings, and it was a very special time. I would have liked for us to have grown old together. I'd like to think of us 42 years from now, parking our air-car on a hilltop in Kenya and watching the Millennium come up like thunder, while we reminisced about sixth fandom, and all the wondrous things our old friends had done and been, but such a future was not to be.

Three years ago Pat Malone went out of our lives, and now he has even left our planet. I wish that I could have said good-bye to him before he went, so that I could have tried to tell him that even a stormy petrel is a wondrous creature to his friends.

ANGELA ARBROATH

In the Lanthanides' private party, no one was singing "Auld Lang Syne," and their expressions of shock and dismay left no doubt as to which way they would vote on the question of *should auld acquaintance be forgot?*

Only Angela Arbroath had summoned a tentative smile for the man in black. His expression suggested that he was receiving just the reception that he had expected, and was quietly enjoying it. While the others conferred in a buzzing undertone, he helped himself to straight Scotch and examined the hors d'oeuvres tray without favor.

"Is it really you, Pat?" ventured Angela, coming close to peer at him.

The stranger looked up from his perusal of the label on the bottle of Scotch. After a moment's study of the blushing middle-aged woman, he countered, "Am I to assume that somewhere in there is the former Angela Arbroath?"

She refused to be offended. "I do believe it *is* you, Pat Malone!" she cried. "I don't know of another soul who could be so offensive and ill tempered on such short notice and little provocation. You just want to see what I'll say! Well, here goes. You don't look so hot yourself, Patrick. I don't think I'd have known you." She gave him a hug. "Now where the hell have you been since 1958?"

He smiled, nodding to the others who had clustered around to hear his answer. He addressed them all. "Fandom may be a microcosm, children, but the rest of the world out there is reasonably large. I got lost in it. I found better things to do."

Ruben Mistral was scowling. Before anyone else could speak, he stepped between the stranger and the rest of the guests, as if he were protecting them from an assassin. "Just a minute, folks!" he announced in his crowd-control voice. "Before anybody says anything else to this individual, I think we should consider the possibility that this is a publicity-seeking impostor. This is a media event, you know."

The dark man smiled down at him. "Ah, Bunzie, don't tell me you've finally learned to look before you leap! If you had been able to do that in 1954, maybe Jim here would have checked the car radiator before we left for Worldcon, and we wouldn't have been left high and dry in Seymour, Indiana.''

Bunzie reddened. ''Well, who made us late in the first place, Malone? *You* said you were going to set the damned alarm clock for six-thirty. And when did we wake up?''

Jim Conyers eased his way to Bunzie's side. ''If in fact this is Pat Malone,'' he reminded his host.

With raised eyebrows and a cold smile, Pat Malone was scanning the group. ''Conyers,'' he nodded. ''Always the sensible one. Let me guess. You're an attorney now?''

''More or less retired. But still cautious.'' Conyers seemed pleased to have been pegged so well.

Pat Malone studied the others. ''Brendan, of course. My old sparring partner. And—''

''Erik Giles,'' said the professor quickly. ''Good to see you again, Pat.''

The gaze moved on. ''And—unless someone brought his father to this little get-together—this must be Georgie Woodard.''

Woodard managed a feeble grin. ''I still publish *Alluvial,* Pat.''

''No, George. You put out a silly bit of drivel purporting to be *Alluvial.* That 'zine, I assure you, is deader than I am.'' Malone reached for the bottle of Scotch and took it with him to the loveseat. ''Are you all going to stay in shock much longer? This one-sided chat is getting a bit tiresome.''

''We thought you were dead, Pat,'' said Angela. ''We wrote tributes to you. How could you put us through all that grief when all the time you were alive, probably off somewhere laughing at us!''

''You were grieved?'' He sounded surprised. ''Well, *some* of you weren't. I wonder if it's too late to sue Jackal Bexler for libel?''

''Yes,'' said Jim Conyers.

''I thought so.'' He gave a little mock bow. ''But thank you for your professional opinion, counselor. Anyhow, I rather thought that after *The Last Fandango* came out, I was more feared than esteemed. In fact, I'll bet some people have been looking over their shoulders ever since they heard the news of my untimely death, hoping that it wasn't a hoax.''

''But why did you do it?'' asked Lorien Williams.

Brendan Surn, who had been listening with uncharacteristic attentiveness, patted her hand. ''I expect that Malone considered an obituary the most dramatic form of resignation from fandom. Didn't you, Pat? And with a death announcement, you not only got to rid yourself of old associates, you also got to hear exactly what they thought of you. I've often thought that Peter—''

"Peter Deddingfield is really dead, Brendan,'' said Erik Giles sharply. "He was killed by a drunk driver nine years ago. Besides, he was never the adolescent hoaxer that Malone has proven to be.''

Pat Malone's dark eyes blazed. "Was I such an artful dodger, gentlemen? Or were you simply a bunch of rumormongers who couldn't be bothered to check your facts?''

Ruben Mistral felt that things were getting out of hand. Signaling for silence, he resumed his role as spokesman for the group. "Okay, Pat. We'll skip the whys and the wherefores. You're not dead. How did you find out about this reunion?''

"You do yourself an injustice, Bunzie. The publicity that your people have put out has ensured that everyone on the planet had a chance to hear about this event. As one of the Lanthanides, I considered myself invited.''

Bunzie nodded impatiently. "No question about that. You had a story in the jar, too. But listen, the rest of us have agreed to certain business details. Percentages, representation by one agent, rights offered for sale. I hope you're not planning to come in as a maverick and queer the deal!''

Pat Malone's eyes widened in feigned innocence. "Now I ask you, Erik, would I queer the deal?''

Erik Giles blushed and turned away.

"I did wonder, though, about the wisdom of digging up old sins.''

"What do you mean by that?'' Ruben Mistral demanded.

"Oh, you know, Bunzie, little things that were no big deal in the early fifties, but might be now. Now that some of us are Eminent Pros.'' His tone was mocking.

"Such as?''

"Remember that phrase that a certain member of the Lanthanides paid me a six-pack for? On one occasion, I happened to remark that when I was a child, I had always been puzzled by the phrase 'for the time being.' I took it literally. I thought there really was someone called the Time Being, and that people did things for him.''

"That's the basis of Peter Deddingfield's *Time Traveler Trilogy!*'' cried Lorien Williams. "You mean it was *your* idea?''

"Worth a lot more than a six-pack now, don't you think?'' asked Pat Malone. "What's it in now, its twenty-seventh printing? And then there's that story that Dale Dugger and Brendan Surn collaborated on. It read a lot better when you won the Hugo for it in '65, Brendan, but the original idea was Dale's, wasn't it? And remember how grossed out we all used to be because George Woodard—''

"That's enough, Pat!'' Erik Giles shouted above the others' murmuring. His face was red now, and his eyes bulged from their sockets. "You could be asking for a hell of a libel suit.''

Pat Malone smiled. "Public figures? Truth is a defense? Right, Jim boy?''

Conyers, the attorney, shrugged and glanced uneasily at the others. "I wouldn't venture to give you an opinion. But I don't see what you'd gain by embarrassing a bunch of your oldest friends.''

"Gain?'' Malone surveyed the scowling group and seemed pleased with the effect of his announcement. "Didn't *The Last Fandango* teach you anything? I'm an idealist, folks. And you fat cats have sold out. You all think you're the Founding Fathers of the Genre. Look at old Thomas Jefferson Surn over there in his NASA jacket. I think it's time somebody reminded you of what a bunch of half-assed adolescents you used to be, and how little difference there really is between who made it and who didn't. A lot of luck, maybe, and—'' he looked directly at Bunzie ''—more than a little ruthlessness.''

"So you came back to screw us, did you, Pat?'' asked Erik Giles.

His tormentor surveyed the room again. "Speaking of matters procreational, I see that Earlene Riley and Jazzy Holt aren't here. I'll bet no one has even *mentioned* their names.''

George Woodard attempted to muster his dignity. "My wife was unable to attend.''

Malone whistled. "Oh, Georgie, Georgie, you didn't.'' He turned to Bunzie. "Which one of 'em?''

Bunzie reddened. "Earlene.''

"Ah. *Succulent nipples.*'' His grin broadened as he watched the others' discomfort. "Well, George, I hope you're man enough for the job. Where is Jazzy Holt? Lounging under a lamppost in Biloxi? *Hello, sailor.* No, I suppose not. After all, she's sixty, too, isn't she? Funny how people in our memories don't age.''

Lorien Williams had recognized the name. She leaned over toward Conyers and whispered, "Does he mean Jasmine Holt, the famous S-F critic?''

Pat Malone overheard the question. "She was a critic, all right. She once told me that my dick looked like a tadpole sleeping on two apricots. Another *expert* opinion,'' he said, grinning at Jim Conyers. "Where is the randy bitch? Not still collecting virgins at S-F cons, surely?''

"She lives in London now,'' said Bunzie. "Although she wasn't one of the Lanthanides, I did invite her to attend the reunion, because of her—er—connections with the group, but she declined, telling me to use my own discretion about the disposal of the shares of Curtis Phillips and Peter Deddingfield. She doesn't need the money. Of course, there would have been some legal question about her entitlement anyway.''

"She was married to both of them," Lorien Williams explained. She was pleased to finally be in the know on a bit of Lanthanides gossip.

"Separately?" smirked Pat Malone. "Or did you all take *Stranger in a Strange Land* as a directive from God?''

"I think that's enough, Pat," said Brendan Surn quietly. "There is nothing to be gained by rumormongering, as you put it a few minutes ago."

Bunzie looked relieved that order had been restored. "That's right, Malone. I asked you before, are you going to abide by the business arrangement already established?''

"Certainly, count me in. I'm sure you drove a shrewd bargain, Bundschaft." He ambled toward the door. "I may have another little project to pitch to the editors, though. Strictly on my own. Good night, all." Without waiting for anyone's reply, he was gone.

Bunzie stared dejectedly at the closed door through which Pat Malone had just left. "What the hell do we do now?''

Why have you come here
to this place you say
you never liked, where
mockingbirds read your mind . . .

—DON JOHNSON
"The House in the Woods"
from *Watauga Drawdown*

CHAPTER 9

THE REUNION WAS only seven hours away, but no one was sleepy. The full moon shone on the newly resurrected Watauga River, which coursed again in its original channel, a ribbon of light in the muddy wasteland of the valley. In the long grass on the hillsides above the shoreline, crickets chirped in a ceaseless drone. It was a peaceful night in the mountains, but no one forgot that when the sun rose to reveal the barren lake bed, the dead would be back among them. Indeed, one of them had returned already.

After Pat Malone's invasion of the Lanthanides' reunion, no one wanted to talk anymore about old times. Within a space of ten minutes, everyone at the reception in the Laurel Room had pleaded fatigue or the lateness of the hour, and had retired to their own rooms to ponder the evening's events.

Jim Conyers had been unmoved by the encounter, and he felt a thickening in his senses that he knew was a craving for sleep, but Barbara, who was outraged, wanted to discuss it.

She sat on the foot of the bed, staring at herself in the mirror as she did her customary one hundred strokes a night with her hairbrush. Her shoulder-length curls—still a rich shade of chestnut (now obtained from a bottle)—shone in the lamplight, and her face seemed as unlined as a young girl's.

"That certainly was a performance tonight!" she remarked, brushing vigorously.

"Bravado," said Jim, stifling a yawn. "The Lanthanides loved to make scenes. They used to remind me of a bunch of Shetland pony stallions: terribly fierce and sincere, but so insignificant as to be comical."

"Well, it was a revelation to me," said Barbara, checking out his expression in the mirror. "I never knew that all those sexual high jinks were going on up at Dale's place."

Conyers shrugged. "They weren't, really. Jazzy Holt was somebody the others met at a science fiction convention. She never even visited the farm. They—er—got together at conventions, and spent the rest of the time writing soulful letters to her. She married Curtis after he left Wall Hollow, in '56, I think, and they divorced pretty soon after, about the time of his nervous breakdown."

Barbara sniffed. "Curtis Phillips was always crazy, if you ask me. Not that the rest of them were much of a contrast. Anyhow, it's a good thing for you I didn't know about such goings-on in 1954, Jim Conyers, or I'd have thought twice about marrying you." Another thought occurred to her. "What about Earlene Riley and Angela Arbroath? You can't say they didn't visit!"

"Angie was a high school kid, and built like a pipe cleaner back then. Not exactly a femme fatale. Most of us treated her like a kid sister. And Earlene was a pudding-faced girl who used sex to build her self-esteem."

Barbara stared. "Jim! Do you mean she thought she was worth something because that pack of drips wanted to sleep with her? Lo-ord God! They would have slept with an Angus heifer if they could have caught one!"

Jim's smile was rueful. "Well, *I* wouldn't have!" he told her. "I had the prettiest girl in east Tennessee as my one and only."

She put down the brush and came to hug him. As he enfolded her in his arms and lay back on the bed, he thought how good his life had been, and for the thousandth time he was glad he had never told Barbara about that one little incident with Earlene Riley. He wondered if Pat Malone remembered it.

Several rooms farther down the hall, Ruben Mistral was pacing, while his preppy minion, still wearing a coat and tie, sat at the writing table by the window, notebook at the ready, in case there were instructions to be carried out. "He's not dead!" said Bunzie for the umpteenth time. "The son of a bitch isn't dead!"

The minion, a recent USC film school graduate named Geoff, ventured an opinion. "Excuse me, sir? Are you *sure* he's really Pat Malone? We never asked to see his driver's license."

Bunzie snarled. "Of course it's him! He may not look the same, but there's nothing wrong with that steel trap he calls a mind. His

memory is perfect! Why couldn't he have gone ga-ga instead of poor
old Brendan? Did you notice how out of it Surn was?''

"Not especially, sir. I had never met him before. He did seem less
forthright than Mr. Malone.''

"So did Attila the Hun. I should have known Pat's death was too
good to be true! At that party tonight he remembered enough damaging tidbits to keep the *Enquirer* presses rolling for a month! If he
tries to get chatty in front of the reporters, so help me I'll kill him!''

"Would you like me to see that he is barred from the activities
tomorrow?'' said Geoff, whose job was to anticipate such assign-
ments.

It was tempting, and Bunzie hesitated, thinking of the serenity of
a reunion without the Lanthanides' stormy petrel, but as appealing
as the suggestion was, it was too risky. "He'd call a press conference
the minute our backs were turned,'' he sighed. "He'd use the hotel
fax machine to blitz the media. By the time we schlepped back to
the hotel with the time capsule, he'd probably be booked on Oprah,
Geraldo, *and* Donahue! I think we're going to have to take him with
us—so that we can keep an eye on him.''

Geoff, whose threshold of modesty was considerably lower than
his boss's, doodled a question mark on his note pad. "Has he really
got all that much to tell? It was a long time ago, after all. Sounds
like boyish pranks to me.''

"That's a point,'' murmured Bunzie. "Maybe you're right. After
all, we live in a world where Supreme Court nominees smoke pot,
and elected officials get caught screwing around. Compared to that,
we're small potatoes.''

Geoff thought of adding, "And since you're not as famous as all
that, who'd care,'' but he thought better of it. Instead he said, "It's
not as if there were any terrible secrets within the group.''

Bunzie was silent for almost a full minute before he replied. "No,
I suppose not. But you can never tell what will strike the public fancy
in the silly season! Remember when a moose fell in love with a cow
and made *Newsweek*? All the same, I want you to stay with him
tomorrow. Keep him away from the reporters! And the editors, too!
Don't let him get off by himself with anyone.''

"Sure. No problem.'' Geoff was careful not to react to this pro-
nouncement. Privately, though, he was thinking, Holy shit! I wonder
what those guys were up to back then!

"It went fine tonight. Just fine,'' said Lorien Williams for the third
time. "You were great! Have you taken your medication yet?''

Brendan Surn, who was wearing his homespun monk's robe, was sitting on the edge of his bed, apparently unmoved by the evening's events. He had smiled his vague smile as Lorien helped him change clothes, and he watched the end of a television movie while she got into her pajamas. In response to Lorien's question about his pills, he looked about him for clues that he had taken it, a glass of water, the bottle of pills, but there was no physical evidence to jog his memory. He shook his head, giving her that helpless little smile that meant he didn't know.

Lorien rummaged about in her suitcase. "No, of course you haven't!" she announced. "I hadn't even unpacked them yet. Here, open the bottle while I get you some water."

Surn worked diligently on the childproof cap. From the bathroom, Lorien called out to him over the sound of running water, "Did you enjoy the evening?"

He thought about her question until she returned. "Yes, it was quite nice," he said, accepting the glass from her.

"It was interesting to meet them all," said Lorien, sitting down on the edge of the bed to continue the chat. "I wish I could have met Curtis Phillips and Peter Deddingfield, though."

Brendan Surn frowned. "Weren't they there?"

"No, Brendan," said Lorien gently. "They are dead. It was Pat Malone who came back. And I don't own anything of his that I could get autographed."

He gave her a vague smile. "Pat Malone forgot that he was dead."

Lorien, who was never sure whether or not Surn was joking, thought it best to overlook that remark. "Well, you are going to have a long day tomorrow, Brendan!" she said briskly. "There will be a lot of reporters and a lot of unfamiliar situations. Let's go through it all again, shall we? And then I think you should get some sleep."

"I'm not tired," said Surn. "Is there some work that I should be doing?"

His assistant stifled a yawn. "Do you want to finish your monthly letter to that fanzine you contribute to?" She went over to a small suitcase and extracted a sheaf of papers and a mimeographed journal bound in yellow construction paper. "I've made the notes here about the topics you wanted to comment on to each participant."

Although *Phosgene* was a science fiction fanzine, or more specifically a letterzine, its subjects ranged far afield of the genre. Any given issue might contain essays from various contributors on the subject of Central European politics, solar energy, abortion, or tropical fish diseases. Subscribers would write letters about whatever they cared to discuss, and in the next issue everyone else would comment, usually briefly, on each of the opinions expressed. The fact that almost no one had the slightest pretension to expertise on any of these topics did not deter them from pontificating. Indeed, one might suppose that anyone who had any proficiency in the subject would not be there in the first place, because he could find a better forum for his ideas, i.e., a place where they might actually have some influence. As it was, the *soi-disant* philosophers of fandom preached at each other while the world went by. Offering sermons from the mount of his celebrity to the subscribers of *Phosgene* was one of Brendan Surn's few vanities.

Lorien Williams consulted her notes. "Let's see . . . We have Lois Hutton talking about women in combat, and you wanted to say . . ."

Surn waved his hand. "Tell her that NASA experiments proved that middle-aged women would make the best astronauts. Surely they could be equally effective as soldiers." He giggled. "Besides, who'd miss them?"

Lorien wrote everything down except for that last comment. She felt that Surn was a prisoner of his generation, but that he should be protected from the scorn of his more enlightened younger acquaintances. "The next writer is Gareth Whitney from Culpeper, Virginia."

"Yes. I like him. Tell him that I agree with him that even if A. P. Hill had not been shot, he would not have survived the Civil War, for reasons of health, and that while I cannot agree that he was the equal of Stonewall Jackson, I do think that as a brigade commander, he was exceptional."

Lorien scribbled down this reply. "Ready for the next one? They're arguing about Harlan again."

Surn smiled. "Oh, Harlan. Leave them to it. They're having such a good time, and he can take care of himself. I won't comment. What else?"

"Worldcon."

"San Francisco," sighed Surn. "Snog in the fog!"

Lorien looked away. "It's in Orlando this year, actually," she said in a tone of studied casualness.

"It doesn't seem very long ago," mused Brendan Surn, staring out into the dark void of the Watauga valley. "The San Francisco Worldcon. And living here. But they all look so old. Did I write a story about that once? About a man who comes out of a daydream to find that he has aged fifty years in two minutes?"

Lorien patted his hand. "That was Fredric Brown, Brendan. In

Nightmares and Geezenstacks.'' Sometimes she felt that remembering titles and authors was all the help she could give him, but he seemed pleased at this shared memory.

"So it was," he said with a sudden smile. "I *remember* it!"

Erik Giles looked down at his third cup of coffee. "I really shouldn't be doing this," he remarked. "Either I'll pace all night or I'll have to sleep in the bathtub."

Angela Arbroath patted his hand. "Go on, Stormy! Have a caffeine orgy. After the shock we've had tonight, we ought to be drinking something a lot stronger than coffee."

On the other side of the table, Jay and Marion glanced at each other, wondering if this could be considered an opening for the introduction of a touchy subject. Shortly after the reunion party disbanded, Erik had come wandering out into the lobby, still chatting with Angela Arbroath, and Marion had hurried out of the coffee shop to snare them with the promise of coffee. So far, introductions and pleasantries had dominated the conversation, but now the hour grew late, and the other tables in the coffee shop had emptied one by one until they were alone. Now seemed like a good time to discuss the dramatic events of the evening's reception.

"I imagine it gave you quite a shock," said Jay Omega, "and it's partly our fault, for which I apologize. We ran into the fellow just as we were coming back from dinner. He was coming through the front doors with his suitcase at the same time we were entering, so naturally I helped him with the doors."

Marion smirked. "Virtue is its own punishment."

"Then when he asked me where the Lanthanides reunion was being held, we couldn't very well plead ignorant. I told him that outsiders were not permitted to attend, but he just smiled and said that he was invited."

"And, of course, I asked who he was," said Marion, taking up the tale. "Jay wouldn't have challenged him, but I'm much more assertive. Imagine my surprise when he said he was Pat Malone. It was on the tip of my tongue to say, 'But you're dead'; however, even I can't manage to be that abrupt."

Jay smiled. "You underestimate yourself." To Giles and Angela Arbroath he explained, "In order to convey the impression that he was expected at the party, the fellow said, 'I expect the Lanthanides have been looking high and low for me,' and Marion muttered, 'I thought those were the places to look.' "

"We figured it out, of course," said Marion. "We came in here for coffee and talked it over. It was a death hoax, wasn't it?"

"Apparently so," said Erik Giles dryly. "Even if I believed in resurrection of the body, I don't think the deity would waste it on Pat Malone."

"It was inconsiderate of him," said Angela Arbroath. "Just the sort of silly prank that fifties fans went in for, not caring about the feelings of those who were taken in by it."

"I suppose he came back to get in on the money and the notoriety?" asked Jay.

"I hope so," said Erik. "It would be much more like him to come back in order to upset things, don't you think, Angela?"

She considered it. "Not out of sheer mischief," she said at last. "But I will grant you that Pat was an idealist, and if he thought any of you were selling out, or capitalizing on your old days at Dugger's farm, then he might very well feel self-righteous about putting a stop to things."

"But he's over sixty now, too!" Erik protested. "Surely he could use a bit of cash as badly as the rest of us!"

Angela stared at him. "How odd!" she cried. "I've only just realized that we don't know a single thing about the resurrected Pat Malone! We were all so much in shock that no one thought to ask him what he has been doing all these years. We treated him as if he really were a ghost."

"Even if he did come to spoil things, how much trouble could he cause?" asked Marion. "You all are a bunch of *writers*. How many guilty secrets could you have?" She laughed at her own joke.

Everyone else looked thoughtful.

George Woodard had brushed his teeth, put on his striped pajamas, and cried a few tears of sheer frustration. Now he was ticking off a list of his most sympathetic friends, trying to decide if there was someone he could safely call to discuss the current crisis, but he could think of no one who wouldn't be delighted at the irony and embarrassment of it. George realized that he could crank up the science fiction rumor mill with one phone call, but in doing so, he would not receive one word of consolation or consideration for his plight. It wasn't worth it. Let everybody find out from someone else. He couldn't be bothered.

Earlene was not the first person he thought of to call, but her name did come up in his ruminations. He decided against it. She would probably force a full account of the evening's confrontation from him, and somehow she would contrive to blame George for the fact that it happened at all. Serves you right for going, she would say. No, Earlene would not be pleased that Pat Malone remembered her so clearly. George wasn't pleased, either, of course, but he consoled himself by thinking that it certainly wasn't true.

It had been true thirty-five years ago, but the "hot little number" that Malone recalled had cooled off to glacial proportions several decades back. Now she gave every appearance of being able to fall into a deep sleep as soon as her head hit the pillow. George puzzled over this apparent contradiction in the essence of reality. How could something which was technically true be so utterly false? The polite fiction maintained by everyone else—that Earlene was a dull little housewife—was certainly more accurate, but it ignored a good portion of her life. It was as if Earlene were two people: he had married one, but was forced to live with the other.

For a brief moment, George caught himself wondering if the old Earlene would have continued to exist had she married Pat Malone, but that thought was too damaging to his ego for him to dwell on it for long. He rummaged in his suitcase for the emergency Baby Ruth he had hidden in a sock, and began to quell his anxieties in his customary manner.

In the Holiday Inn in Johnson City, the editors and reporters had taken over the cocktail lounge. They were glad for a chance to get together, although such meetings were far from rare. They just didn't happen in New York. All of the occupants of the lounge worked in Manhattan within a half mile of each other, but in order to socialize, they had to attend conferences in various cities, or turn up as fellow lecturers at a writers' workshop somewhere. If this were a Thursday night in New York, a third of them would be doing their laundry; the other two-thirds would still be at the office.

The fact that Johnson City was a relatively small town did not unduly depress them, because (1) while many of them had fled to New York from small towns, they were well able to tolerate small doses of rural Americana; and (2) the publishing business *is* a small town.

Although the editors were ostensibly camped in Tennessee to engage in a bidding war, their camaraderie was unaffected by the potential rivalry. They were veterans of many such campaigns, and it was, after all, someone else's money that they were playing with. Except for the possibility of added prestige for a literary coup, which might result in money or perks, the Lanthanides Anthology Auction might as well be a Monopoly tournament. Their attitude toward the other group of professionals present—the various media representatives who had turned up for the occasion—was cordial, but more reserved. They didn't want to seem overly interested in the glitz business, and until one of them owned the current project, they had nothing quotable to say anyhow. Besides, editors secretly fear that journalists have the Great American Novel stashed in typing-paper boxes in their closets, and that given proximity to a book editor, they will try to market it. The editors' dread of becoming a literary hostage—trapped in a corner, listening to an endless plot summary—kept them packed into a tight little herd for protection. They imagined the reporters circling them like lions, seeking to pounce upon the weakest member of the herd.

The journalists in turn kept to their own corner of the lounge, swapping war stories about covering the vice-president, discussing software, and exchanging interesting fax numbers (Billy Joel's, for example). They were equally wary of the editors, who, after all, might want to get their names in the paper or might be seized with a guilt-ridden urge to wave to the folks on TV. Among themselves they also swapped horror stories about the most obnoxious "civilians" who had tried to impose on them lately.

At the beginning of the evening the two factions had staked out opposite sides of the room, holding court around their own tables, with occasional furtive glances toward the other enclave, but as the evening wore on, and sobriety wore out, some of the braver souls began to exchange pleasantries across professional lines, and by midnight, the room had become one large mob of *pros,* driving less determined tourists to their rooms to contemplate *The Best of Carson.*

Sarah Ashley, agent for Ruben Mistral and architect of the Lanthanides package, had hosted a prime-rib dinner for the group earlier in the evening, but she had wisely refrained from discussing business except to say that she for one felt privileged to be present at the making of a science fiction legend. After dinner, she had thanked everyone again for coming to the party and had gone up to her room, leaving the pack to speculate on the next day's events.

They had managed to avoid the subject for a good two hours, but finally weariness with the usual topics prevailed, and an Australian with one of the tabloids called out, "What do you make of this bit of grave robbing that's going on tomorrow?"

"The Dante Gabriel Rossetti syndrome," said Lily Warren, an editor who got her start in publishing with a university press.

"What has baseball got to do with it?" asked the *USA Today* reporter.

Lily winced. "Rossetti was a nineteenth-century English poet. When his wife died, he buried some of his unpublished work with her, and then about a year later he . . . went back and dug them up again."

"Geez," said *USA Today.* "Is anybody buried with the time capsule?"

The tabloid reporter had pulled out his pocket notebook and was already composing his lead.

"I wonder if Sarah Ashley would consider splitting up the package," mused Enzio O'Malley, one of the New York editors.

Lily Warren shook her head. "She'd be crazy to agree to that. Think of the publicity value in the time-capsule anthology story! Every book club in the country will grab it, for starters. Then there's the other sub rights. Films, foreign—"

O'Malley sighed. "I know, but I was thinking in terms of actual literary merit." He ignored the snickering of his colleagues. "You see, we own Brendan Surn's back list, and he really is one of the great writers of the genre." More snickering. "I was thinking that it might be nice to acquire just his story—for a lot less money, of course—and put it in a new anthology of his short fiction."

"No way," said Lily. "The package is too valuable as a whole. Besides—" She hesitated.

"Exactly," said O'Malley. "Selling that piece would gut the whole collection, because Surn's story might be the only thing in there that isn't crap."

"Oh, come on!" another editor protested. "Surely, Curtis Phillips—"

"Curtis Phillips was a fruitcake, and you can never tell whether he was being brilliant or deranged on this particular writing binge. Suppose he just raves for twenty pages? And most of the other contributing authors were one-book wonders, whose early work may turn out to be worthless." Enzio O'Malley downed the last of his beer. "Sarah's asking us to take a hell of a gamble here. I'd buy anything of Surn's in a minute, but the whole package? I don't know."

"Suppose it *isn't* any good?" asked another editor.

Lily Warren chuckled. "Goodness has nothing to do with it. The very act of paying serious money for this collection in an auction will make it famous, and the publicity generated by this reunion is priceless. Half the country will know about this collection months before the pub date. By the time the publisher runs major ads, books the old geezers on the morning talk shows, and intimidates the sales force with a six-figure print run, every rube in America will have heard of it, and thousands of them will buy it for the novelty value alone. Didn't *The Satanic Verses* sell big, despite the fact that no one actually read it? Oh, this time-capsule gimmick will sell, all right. Sarah Ashley is no fool when it comes to marketing.''

O'Malley stared mournfully into his empty beer mug. ''The critics will savage it, and the S-F crowd, which is notoriously poor, will wait for the paperback, and you'll have to eat fifty thousand hard-cover copies of a shit-awful book,'' he said mournfully.

The other editors fell silent. Enzio O'Malley's pessimistic, and probably accurate, assessment of the package had brought an unpleasant note of reality to the revels. For a moment they were forced to contemplate whether they actually ought to be trying to publish *good* books, instead of shilling for hyped books. But the feelings of gloom were brief, and almost instantly succeeded by a universally held conviction that Enzio O'Malley's negative comments were designed to throw them off the scent. Obviously, he had been issued firm orders by his publishing masters to acquire the time-capsule anthology at any cost. Silently they began to wonder what kind of money or treachery it would take to beat him out of it.

Jay Omega couldn't sleep. The party in the coffee shop had broken up an hour ago, and now the hotel was dark and quiet. He lay on the side of his bed, unable to relax, listening for night sounds and replaying the day's events in his head. Marion, unused to Lakecrest beer and long hours, was sleeping peacefully, but Jay was still wide awake. He thought he might have been able to fall asleep if he could have lain in bed and read a hard-science fiction novel, full of technical monotony, but the light would have disturbed Marion. He told himself that he needed to sleep because of the eventful day that would begin in just a few hours, but that only made him more alert. The more he pursued oblivion, the more restless he became. Finally, giving in to his own anxieties, he slipped on his jeans and sweatshirt and crept from the room. Perhaps a walk in the cool night air would calm his thoughts and allow him to sleep.

He crossed the deserted lobby and left the building, with the glass door swinging noiselessly behind him. The moon shone above the ridge of oak trees, and the air was crisp and cool, but the parking lot smelled of oil and burnt rubber. It was not a place he wanted to linger. Jay hurried away from it and found the path through the rhododendrons that led down to the edge of the lake. Now the steep moss-strewn trail ended in a gully of dry red clay, ringed like redwoods from the lapping waters of the receding Watauga.

Jay stood alone in the darkness, thinking that it was quiet, because like most country people he didn't register the ceaseless whine of crickets as noise. He looked up at the full moon, a small silver disk hanging above the distant hills, and saw it only as a dry lake bed suspended in the black sky. It illuminated the few clouds hovering near it, but there was no reflecting shine from the dark emptiness of Breedlove Lake, no response from the dead land.

Jay felt a disquieting urge to walk forward into the dark basin of the lake without caring where it would take him or whether he came back at all. Such moodiness was rare for James Owens Mega. Usually, he dealt logically with problems that he could solve, and he wasted little time fretting over the rest, but the Lanthanides troubled him. They seemed to him to be various projections of his own future: Erik, the sedentary academic who had given up writing; Mistral, the Hollywood mogul who had turned his hobby into an empire, and was universally accused of selling out; or George Woodard, who had allowed his alternate universe to consume his life, and lived in poverty and failure as a result. He supposed that Brendan Surn was the most enviable of the company, but he, too, presented a grim specter of a writer's future: obviously suffering from some mental impairment, he lived alone and friendless, except for his various business caretakers and the young nurse/companion who looked after him. Jay could see himself in any of those existences, and he did not like what he saw. Do writers live happily ever after, he wondered.

He was still pondering that waking nightmare when he heard footsteps on the path above him, coupled with the sound of rhododendron branches being brushed aside. The crickets fell silent. At last the figure stepped out from the shadows of the trees, and Jay could see the dark, emaciated figure of Pat Malone wending his way carefully over the rocks and coming toward him.

"You couldn't sleep, either," he called out softly to Malone.

The older man shrugged. "No. You're the young engineer, aren't you? I thought there would be a lot of sleepless people tonight, but I wasn't expecting one of them to be *you*."

Jay Omega sat down on the concrete ramp that had been a boat dock. Now it lay two hundred yards up from the shallows of the receding lake. "My sleeplessness wasn't on your account," he told Malone. "I was contemplating my own mortality, I guess."

"You could always come back from the dead," came the reply from the shadows. "I did."

"It's odd that you should turn up. I was just wondering what you had been doing for the last thirty years," said Jay. He explained his feelings about the other Lanthanides, and his own unwillingness to become like any of them in succeeding decades. "I had hoped that your life turned out happier than theirs," he concluded, straining in the darkness for a glimpse at Pat Malone's expression.

The responding voice was grim. "Was I any better off than they were? Not in the sense you mean, perhaps. I had to be somebody else, that's all. Tonight feels like a kind of resurrection for me. I'm not sure that I care for it, but I had to come."

"The others didn't seem pleased to see you," Jay remarked. "I wondered about that."

Malone laughed. "You *wondered*? Didn't you ever read my little mimeographed masterpiece called *The Last Fandango*? I drummed myself out of the hobby once and for all in that, and along the way I made some very unpleasant but true observations about certain prominent jerks in fandom. The more perceptive of the Lanthanides might assume that I was here to do more of the same."

"Are you?"

"I wouldn't be Pat Malone if I didn't. I am legend."

Jay was puzzled. "We were talking about you tonight," he said. "We all wondered what you have been doing for the last thirty years. You never said."

"Yes, I did. I told you that I had become somebody else. Come to think of it, they all did that, didn't they? But I'm not sure I like the people they turned into. Mistral who is somebody with a capital S. And your professor friend, who is trying to live down his years in fandom. But even the silliest of them—Woodard—came to terms with the real world when it came down to raising kids and making a living, but he trades on his youthful associations to impress neofans. George Woodard: a big-name fan! Some idealists, huh?"

"All except Curtis Phillips," said Jay Omega.

"Yes, I guess that's what happens to people who don't conform. They get locked up. But Curtis was more free than any of them, I think. He got to keep on being himself."

"And you didn't?"

"I could have. But I didn't want to end up like Curtis, so I traded my freedom for—" He seemed to think about it. "For respectability. A different kind of freedom."

Jay thought he understood. "I know. I faced that as a teenager. You have to conform to make money, and in our society, having money is the only way to keep yourself really free. So I became an electrical engineer instead of a journalism major, and now I can afford to do some writing, because—"

Pat Malone began to walk away. "I must go," he called back as he disappeared up the path into the darkness. "You weren't at all who I expected. Go to bed."

"Who ever you—" Jay's words echoed in the hollow stillness. Malone was gone. Go to bed, mused Jay. I suppose my elders have spoken. As he headed back toward the lodge, he was surprised to find himself yawning. "Tomorrow," he said aloud, "I will wonder if I dreamed this."

CHAPTER 10

AT TEN O'CLOCK in the morning—the late hour being a concession to
the long commute from Johnson City—the Lanthanides reunion officially began, with a coffee-and-doughnuts briefing in the Mountaineer Lodge conference room. A gaggle of sleepy editors and
journalists was herded in to the meeting, where a smiling and surprisingly unjet-lagged Ruben Mistral greeted them personally and
steered them toward a sympathetic waitress, who was dispensing the
coffee.

Two dozen metal folding chairs had been set up facing a varnished
pine lectern, and in the front row sat George Woodard, looking like
a mud slide in his khaki safari outfit. He had a lap full of doughnuts,
and a cup of milky coffee wedged precariously between his knees.
Iridescent flakes of doughnut glaze clung to the corners of his mouth,
and his black hair, lank and oily, lay in a collapsed wave across his
forehead. He looked more subdued than usual, daunted perhaps by
lack of sleep, the presence of reporters, and the aura of show biz
emanating from the ringmasters of the show. He had been hoping for
a better breakfast, at the reunion's expense, but failing that and with
the prospect of lunch uncertain, he had stocked up on greasy, sugar-
encrusted doughnuts as his only sustenance. They did not sit well on
his already upset stomach.

Geoff, minion of Ruben Mistral, seemed to be hosting the briefing,
and he had chosen to reflect this authority by masquerading as Indiana Jones. He sported a battered fedora, khaki vest and pants, and

even a stubble of beard over his weak chin, as a tacit reminder of the rigors of the day's expedition. He had omitted the Indiana Jones trademark bullwhip and pistol as a concession to the solemnity of the occasion.

Beside him, cordial to the milling crowd of editors, journalists, and well-wishers, but not courting them, was Ruben Mistral, resplendent in a button-down linen Basile shirt, yellow pleated trousers, and alligator loafers, the latter being evocative of the valley's current swampy condition but hardly appropriate for traversing it. He was drinking his coffee out of a Royal Doulton porcelain cup in the teal and gold Carlyle pattern. He searched the crowd for the missing Lanthanides, and spotted Erik Giles and Angela Arbroath talking to their two professor friends. Conyers and his wife were chatting with a young woman in jeans and a Villager shirt, probably a local reporter. Where were the others? A glance at his Rolex told him that it was time to start the briefing.

For an instant, Mistral considered sending George Woodard in search of the stragglers—he was certainly expendable—but this was a task that required efficiency and speed, both of which were well out of Woodard's range of abilities. Geoff was doing the technical part of the spiel, so he couldn't be spared. He looked around for another minion and finally decided to draft one.

A moment later, a jovial Bunzie-like Ruben Mistral appeared at Giles' elbow. "Good morning, kids!" he beamed. "We'll be ready to get underway in just a moment, but not everybody is here yet." He hesitated for effect, and then brightened as if inspiration had just visited. "I wonder if I could ask a favor. It would certainly speed things up if someone would go after our missing comrades. That is, Brendan Surn and—" a faint expression of distaste punctuated his request "—and, of course, Pat Malone. What a guy! We resurrect the time capsule, and Pat comes back from the dead. Would you mind locating them and bringing them to our little briefing?" He turned his cold smile briefly on Jay Omega, and then, reconsidering, he directed his gaze at the person he considered to be of lowest rank in the foursome. "How about it, dolling?" he said, placing a fatherly hand on Marion's shoulder.

Dr. Marion Farley, who had flunked people for less, managed an expressionless "I'd be happy to" and left the room.

"That's good," said Mistral, glancing at his watch again. "Look at the time! I think I'd better start anyway. The first part is just background. They won't miss much." He hurried back to the lectern to call the meeting to order.

"Ladies and gentlemen. And editors . . ." He waited for the polite laughter before continuing. "I want to welcome all of you to Wall Hollow, Tennessee. The year is 1954. Geez, I wish it was. Gas was eighteen cents a gallon back then. Anyhow, before I introduce my fellow Lanthanides, I'm going to turn Sarah Ashley loose on you to talk about money and percentages, and all that stuff we writers just don't understand." The groan in the audience was presumably from Mistral's editor, who knew better. "Then I'm going to turn the program over to my associate, Geoffrey L. Duke, who will fill you reporters in on the engineering details of this endeavor. After that, we hit the boats!"

Even when she was seething, Marion was efficient. First she checked the restaurant to see if the absentees were finishing up a leisurely breakfast. They weren't. Then, after obtaining the missing Lanthanides' room numbers from an intimidated young receptionist, Marion attempted to commandeer the desk phone, but before she could pick it up, it rang. In the interests of time Marion decided to take the more direct approach of going after them personally. Since both Surn's and Malone's rooms were on the second floor, she decided that taking the elevator up one flight would be faster than waiting for the desk clerk's phone.

She was a bit annoyed at missing the introductory remarks from Mistral, but she was pleased at having kept her temper. Marion was fond of saying that women Ph.D.s do not have to strive for humility: it hunts them down on a regular basis.

Since Brendan Surn's room number put him closest to the elevator, Marion tried him first. She tapped lightly on the great man's door, wondering if she would now be mistaken for a chambermaid. "Mr. Surn! The Lanthanides reunion is about to start!"

After several moments the door opened and Lorien Williams peered out with a worried frown. "Is it nine o'clock already?"

Marion was relieved to see that she was dressed, as was Brendan Surn, who had also come over to the door. They both wore blue sweatsuits and new white running shoes. Marion refused to allow herself even to think any snide remarks about Brendan Surn. He looked tired. "It's a little past nine now," Marion told them. "Would you like me to show you the way? They're serving coffee and doughnuts there if you haven't had breakfast yet."

"That will be all right," said Surn, reaching for the door.

"I'll get the room key," murmured Lorien.

"There's one other missing person," said Marion. "Pat Malone. You haven't seen him, have you?"

"Pat Malone is dead," said Brendan Surn in his gentle way, as if reminding her of an obscure current event.

Lorien Williams hurried over and took him by the arm. "No, Brendan," she said. "It's Peter Deddingfield you're thinking of that's dead. And Curtis Phillips. We saw Mr. Malone last night, remember?"

Marion took a deep breath. "I'll just go and find Pat Malone, then. Someone at the desk will show you to the conference room." She turned and fled down the hall, and her cheeks were wet.

Geoffrey Duke had taken his place at the lectern in the conference room and was giving background information to the press. Behind him were two enlarged black-and-white photos, labeled "Wall Hollow 1954" and "Wall Hollow Today." They were taken from the same spot on a mountainside overlooking the valley. The first picture looked like a calendar illustration of a New England town. It showed a small village of white houses and a steepled country church nestled among the oak trees in a green valley. It conjured up images of Norman Rockwell paintings and old Frank Capra movies.

The second photograph was hardly recognizable as the same spot. The two main roads of the village were still visible, outlining the dimensions of the town, but only a few of the stone buildings remained standing, surrounded by craters marking the sites of the houses, and the blackened skeletons of oak trees. The scene, a study in mud and desolation, evoked comparisons with disaster photos: bomb sites, and towns laid waste by hurricanes. People would study the first picture of Wall Hollow, glance at the second, and then look away at nothing for a few moments before they went back to what they were doing.

Geoffrey Duke consulted his notes on the technical aspects of the drawdown, and called the conference to order. After a few words of welcome, he plunged into his well of statistics. "Breedlove Lake has a water surface area of sixty-six thousand acres, extending sixteen miles upstream," he said to the furiously scribbling reporters. "The dam, which is three hundred and eighteen feet high, is thirteen hundred feet thick at the base and produces fifty thousand kilowatts of power with its two generators."

"How did they construct the dam?" asked the *Times* reporter.

"They selected a deep, narrow mountain gorge and filled it with three million cubic yards of dirt and rock. The dam's core is one million four hundred eighty-four thousand and seven hundred cubic yards of compacted clay, surrounded on either side by two million cubic yards of rock.''

"Where'd they get all that rock?''

Geoff was ready for that question. "Three quarries near the construction site. They loosen the rock with coyote tunnel blasts using Nitramon.''

"Using *what*?''

"It's a brand name for ammonium nitrate. Dupont. Digging and loading the blast tunnels took weeks.''

"What about the people in the valley?'' asked Sarah Ashley. "Did they just get kicked off their land?''

"No. The TVA bought the town for thirty-five thousand dollars.''

Murmurs of disbelief came from the crowd. "What if people didn't want to sell?''

Geoff shrugged. "That was too bad, I guess.''

"How many people were relocated?'' asked another journalist, who was trying to calculate how much each family received.

Geoff consulted his notes. "More than a hundred early on in the project. Seven hundred and sixty-three at the closing of the dam. Eighty-five percent relocated in the east Tennessee counties of Carter and Johnson. Five percent left the state. Including, of course, most of the Lanthanides.''

Bunzie whistled a few bars of "California, Here I Come'' and waved for Geoff to continue.

"The drawdown, which began six weeks ago for the purpose of repairing the dam, was effected by opening the sluice gates—''

Jay Omega was sitting in a front row seat beside Erik Giles. "I wonder what's keeping Marion,'' he murmured.

"I don't know. She may be dawdling on purpose to miss this technical spiel,'' Giles suggested. "I'm surprised that Malone isn't here, though.''

"I doubt if he'll miss the boat,'' said Jay Omega. "He seemed very keen on the reunion.''

Erik Giles grunted. "Are you familiar with the fairy tale *Sleeping Beauty*?'' he asked.

"Sort of,'' said Jay. "Why?''

"Pat Malone reminds me of the bad fairy at the christening.''

In the second-floor hallway of the Mountaineer Lodge, Marion knocked again. "Mr. Malone!'' she said, more loudly this time. "Are you awake? The reunion sent me to get you!'' She put her ear to the door, straining to catch the sound of the shower or the television. All was silent. Marion began to become concerned. After all, she told herself, they are rather elderly. As she straightened up, trying to decide what to do next, she caught sight of the maid, pushing her cleaning cart around the corner by the elevator.

"I hope I'm not about to make an idiot of myself," Marion muttered, hurrying to intercept her.

A few moments and several explanations later, the chambermaid, muttering, "I'm not real sure we ought to do this," used her passkey to unlock the door of Pat Malone's room. As the door swung open, Marion called out, "Mr. Malone! Are you all right?"

An instant later they could see that he wasn't. The smell of vomit and voided bowels reached them and made them draw back, even before Marion saw the stiffening form of the room's occupant, sprawled across the sill of the bathroom. "You call," she said, nudging the maid out of shock, "I'll see if there's anything to be done for him."

While the maid was spluttering into the telephone, attempting to make the front desk understand the situation, Marion knelt beside the body of the recently resurrected Pat Malone. His eyes stared up at her, sightless, with the same glare that had so daunted the Lanthanides at last night's reception. Steeling herself for the sensation of touching dead flesh, Marion reached for his wrist, confirming the absence of a pulse. This time, she thought to herself, there could be no doubt of the death of Pat Malone. This time he wasn't coming back.

Bunzie was in the midst of telling his highly romanticized version of the burying of the time capsule to a captive audience. Each time he mentioned one of his fellow Lanthanides, he prefaced the name with superlatives: the late, great Dale Dugger, the macabre genius Curtis Phillips, and the literary legend Brendan Surn. The more perceptive of the journalists might have noticed that Ruben Mistral did not really discuss any of the stories actually put into the time capsule by himself and his comrades, but perhaps they did not notice this omission, since Mistral was a charming and well-polished speaker. He seemed to be winding down the litany of reminiscences when a balding man in a dark suit appeared at the door and motioned for Mistral's attention.

The ever alert Geoff Duke hurried to the back of the room to confer with the hotel employee. "What is it?" he hissed, grasping the man's elbow and propelling him out of earshot. "We're in the middle of our presentation here."

The hotel clerk was a study in unruffled dignity. "We thought you ought to be notified, sir. One of your party has passed away."

"Oh, shit!" murmured Geoff, caught off guard by the news. "I was afraid one of those old geezers might croak from the excitement. . . ." His voice trailed off when he caught the disapproving glint in the listener's eye. "I mean, what a shock. I can't believe it. What a complete tragedy. Which one of them?" His mind was furiously manipulating publicity options concerning the untimely demise of the literary legend Brendan Surn. Perhaps a cremation and hasty burial in the mire of the ruined farm in place of the time capsule? Visions of *Newsweek* photos danced in his head. He wondered if he could safely paraphrase the Gettysburg Address in the eulogy: *But in a larger sense, we cannot dedicate, we cannot consecrate, we cannot hallow this ground.* His hustler's reverie was cut short by the hotel manager's reply.

"The guest was registered as a Mr. Pat Malone," he said carefully. "I believe there was some trouble over his unexpected arrival last night?"

Geoff cringed. Obviously, the waiters had been gossiping. "His attendance had not been anticipated," he agreed. "Of course, his old friends were delighted to see him."

This bit of social whitewashing cut no ice with the Mountaineer Lodge. "It was our duty to notify the sheriff as well as the medical authorities," he said solemnly. "I came to notify you so that you could break the news to the folks in your conference."

Geoff's pallor and expression suggested that he might welcome the medical authorities himself. "We won't have to call off the boat trip, will we?"

The hotel manager relented. "Probably not," he said. "I expect that it will take them all day to figure out what he died of, and to get all the medical details attended to. If everyone will agree to be available for questioning tomorrow, then I see no reason why you shouldn't go ahead with your plans today. After all, the old gentleman may have simply succumbed to a heart attack."

Pat Malone didn't get heart attacks, thought Geoff Duke grimly, he gave them.

Marion didn't know why she had agreed to stay with the body until the authorities arrived. Perhaps it was a tacit acknowledgment that fandom was a family—or at least a tribe—and she felt a sense of loyalty to another of her kind, both of them self-imposed exiles from the clan. Or perhaps it was a lingering respect for one of the legends of science fiction. She wished that she had been given another chance to talk with fandom's stormy petrel, but stranger though he was to her, she could not leave him lying on the cold floor of a rented room with no one to pay him last respects.

Marion sat on the edge of the double bed, trying to look anywhere but at the shrunken form in the doorway of the bathroom. Irrationally, she felt that it would be an invasion of Pat Malone's privacy to stare at him in his final humiliation, sprawled in vomit on the cold tile floor. But she knew that the body should not be moved, and that no cleaning up could be done because there might have to be an investigation into the death. She also knew that it would be a mistake to touch any of the deceased's possessions in the hotel room, but when boredom and anxiety made her restless she decided that there would be no harm in looking. And if she felt it necessary to pick something up, she could use a tissue to avoid leaving fingerprints. Thus fortified with the tools and rationalization for her actions, Marion began to examine the deceased man's possessions. Above all, she wanted to know where Pat Malone had been between deaths.

His suitcase sat on top of the low chest of drawers, with its lid propped open against the wall. It was a cheap vinyl bag of medium size, without an identification tag on its handle. Inside it were a couple of shirts and changes of underwear and a worn collection of paperbacks: *The Golden Gain,* Brendan Surn's latest paperback reprints, and an issue of *Fantasy and Science Fiction* containing Peter Deddingfield's first (and worst) published short story. These books were bound with a thick rubber band, enclosing a note that read "Get Autographed." Lying loose in the suitcase were a book club edition of Deddingfield's *Time Traveler Trilogy* and a copy of Pat Malone's only published novel, *River of Neptune.* On impulse, Marion picked it up with her tissue-shielded hand, wondering if the author had made any notations in his personal copy, but when she flipped through the pages of the yellowed paperback, she found that the pages were unmarked. On impulse she turned to the title page and found an inscription in faded red ink: "To Curtis Phillips, A Slan for All Seasons, from Patrick B. Malone." She looked through the other books, but found no writing of any kind, except a rubber-stamped notation in the front of the Brendan Surn novel: "USED—$1."

"Why would he have Curtis' copy of his own book?" Marion wondered aloud.

She patted the clothing in the suitcase to see if there was anything else concealed inside it. Nothing was hidden in the clothes, but a bulge in a side pouch of the luggage revealed a bottle of prescription medicine. "Elavil," the label said, and the pharmacist listed was located in Willow Spring, North Carolina. Most interesting of all was the name of the patient, neatly typed on the prescription label: Richard W. Spivey.

"Now who the hell is that?" asked Marion, peering at the corpse as if she expected an answer.

While Sarah Ashley was explaining literary auctions to the reporters, Ruben Mistral went out into the hall to confer with his minion. The arrival of the hotel manager had not gone unnoticed by Mistral, even though he gave no sign of it as he rambled on in his reminiscences. The expressions and body language of Geoff and the hotel man had told him that something was amiss, and he had seized the first opportunity to leave center stage and find out what was going on.

"Pat Malone is dead," said Geoff, in tones suggesting that his chief concern was the possibility of being shouted at for the inconvenience of it.

Ruben Mistral opened his mouth and then closed it again, wondering just exactly what it was he felt, and, more importantly, what he *ought* to be feeling. He couldn't even say that he was shocked, because he hadn't really got used to the idea of Pat Malone being alive in the first place. As far as any of them were concerned, Pat Malone had been dead for thirty years. It was no good resurrecting him for an hour, then killing him off again and expecting anyone to be shocked about it. It was a relief that he wouldn't be around to make trouble, of course. Pat had always had a genius for making trouble.

An instant later he realized that by dying, Pat Malone had caused the maximum amount of trouble imaginable. The tabloid reporters would start grinding out ghost and murder stories, forgetting the time capsule, and even the other papers would dutifully report it, and overshadow the reunion story, because death is more interesting than anything else.

"Don't worry," said Geoff, misinterpreting his stricken look. "It was a heart attack. I don't believe he suffered."

"Too bad," growled Mistral.

"And the hotel manager said that we could go ahead with the day's activities as planned. He has called the sheriff and the medical people, but he thought you might want to make the announcement to the reunion group."

Ruben Mistral reached an instant decision. "Why?" he said. "It had nothing to do with us."

"I'm sorry?" said Geoff, expressing not regret but total confusion.

"We all thought Pat Malone was dead, right? So we didn't mention him in the press releases or the brochures. The press never knew about him at all. So why bring him up now? It will only distract them from the real story. I'll tell the others privately in a few minutes, and instruct them not to discuss it with anyone." Somewhere deep in his consciousness, Bunzie was deploring the unfortunate necessity of having to behave this way, but after all, he told himself, the Lanthanides who are still alive could use the money.

"Are the boats here yet?" he asked.

Geoff glanced at his watch. "They should be. Shall I go and check?"

Mistral nodded. "I'll start herding the group down toward the lake, before any of them can spot an ambulance or a cop. Once we get them out in the boats, everything will be—" He broke off suddenly as a sandy-haired young man in jeans emerged from the conference room. "Not leaving, are you?" he asked heartily.

"No," said Jay Omega. "I just wondered where Marion was. Excuse me."

While Sarah Ashley explained terms like "bidding floor" to the more conscientious journalists, the Lanthanides were chatting together, waiting to be summoned for the boat trip. Brendan Surn and Lorien, who had arrived late, helped themselves to coffee and doughnuts and then joined the group in the front row. Jim and Barbara Conyers came up to join them, exchanging pleasantries with Angela Arbroath and passing around pictures of the grandchildren.

"I think he was hoping they'd have pointed ears," joked Barbara. "The three-year-old can already say the whole thing: *Space, the final frontier...*"

Erik Giles consulted his watch. "It's nearly ten. I wonder what happened to Marion. She's going to miss the boat if she isn't careful."

"She came and got us about twenty minutes ago," said Lorien Williams. "Isn't she back yet?"

"She'll turn up," said George Woodard, who was bored by the troubles of others. "Do you think they'll provide us with Dramamine for the boat ride?"

Angela Arbroath smiled. "I don't think there will be much turbulence in shallow water, George. But you might want to stop drinking coffee. There's no place to pee in an open boat."

"Where is Pat Malone?" asked Barbara Conyers.

"Maybe he overslept," said Woodard. "He was always completely irresponsible. I, for one, won't miss him."

"I will," said Angela. "I forgot to ask if he's still married."

Brendan Surn smiled and patted her arm. "Wouldn't you rather have Pete Deddingfield?" he asked playfully.

"I'm sure she would," said Lorien hastily. "What a guy!" She didn't want to have to explain again who was dead and who wasn't to Brendan Surn.

Ruben Mistral emerged from the crowd of reporters just then, looking grave. "Before we head down to the boats, I need a word with you," he said, pitching his voice to a discreet undertone.

"What's wrong?" gasped Angela, taking a mental tally of who was present.

Mistral looked faintly disapproving, as if he were anticipating hysterics. "Just a little bad news," he murmured. "But the important thing is that we must not discuss this with any of the media people present."

"Who died?" asked Jim Conyers.

Mistral winced at the plain speaking. "It's Pat Malone, I'm afraid. He wasn't looking too well last night. Heart attack, I imagine. It's something we have to face when we get to be our age. But you know how reporters are. We wouldn't want to distract them from the real story, would we?" He looked sharply at George Woodard, traditionally the weak link in the chain. "After all, if we make a fuss, it could diminish the importance and the monetary value of our time capsule. Not to mention the possibility of our being detained by the police for questioning."

The Lanthanides looked at each other nervously. Finally Jim Conyers said, "I don't see any harm in keeping quiet about this for the time being. It isn't obstructing justice to refrain from mentioning a death to a bunch of reporters and book editors."

"Exactly!" nodded Mistral, visibly relieved.

"None of their business," said George Woodard.

Angela Arbroath was pale, and her eyes were red-rimmed. "I suppose you know best," she murmured. "But it *was* natural causes?"

"Sure," said Mistral. "What else could it be?"

*　　*　　*

"Marion, what are you doing in here?"

When Marion hadn't reappeared at the briefing, Jay Omega had gone in search of her. He had checked the coffee shop and the lobby without success, and finally he decided to look in the room to see if she had been taken ill. As he made his way along the second-floor hallway toward their room he had noticed an open door, and when he glanced inside he saw Marion Farley, gazing out the window at the barren expanse of red clay between the pine-topped slopes. She did not turn to face him until he had repeated the question.

When Marion stood up, he could see that she looked ill.

"Are you all right?"

She pointed toward the bathroom. "Pat Malone," she said grimly. "He's dead again."

He looked in the direction she pointed, and for the first time he noticed the blue-robed body sprawled partly inside the bathroom. Jay looked from Marion to the corpse and back again, half expecting everyone to burst out laughing and say "Gotcha!," but the look on Marion's face was solemn and strained, and he was forced to believe that it was true. As he came toward her, he became aware of the smell, and this convinced him beyond any doubt that there had indeed been a death.

"What happened?"

Marion shrugged. "He was like this when I found him. I checked to make sure that he was dead—no pulse—and other than that, I left him alone. The maid was with me when I found him, and she saw to it that the authorities were called. I'm sorry I didn't come back, but I couldn't leave him. I kept thinking to myself, This guy wrote *River of Neptune*. I know that doesn't make him anything extraordinary, but—well, to me it does. I'm an English professor. I'm a *fan*." There was a catch in her voice. "I even wanted to get his autograph."

Jay put his arms around her. "Far be it from me to talk you out of revering writers," said the author of *Bimbos of the Death Sun*. "But there really isn't anything that you can do here."

"I know, Jay. I said I would stay until someone came for the body, though. You understand, don't you?"

Jay sat down in the armchair by the window and motioned for her to sit on the bed. "I'll keep you company," he said. "We'll make it a two-person wake. It's too bad about the old fellow. I think he was looking forward to this. Wonder where he's been all these years."

"I wonder *who* he's been all these years," said Marion. She told

Jay about the medicine bottle issued to someone other than Pat Malone.

Jay looked puzzled. "An alias? That seems strange. I wonder how the police are going to notify his next of kin."

Marion looked sadly at the crumpled figure in the doorway. "I wonder if he has any," she said.

"Didn't that old fanzine of yours say that he had been married?"

"Thirty years ago," said Marion. She gasped. "I wonder if *she* knows he isn't dead. I mean, he is, but I wonder if she knew that he didn't die in 1958."

Jay Omega shrugged. "Won't the police handle all that?"

"I don't know," said Marion. "If it was natural causes, they might not try too hard. And it might take them weeks or months. Damn it, I want to know who Pat Malone was for the last thirty years! I wonder if he had any ties in fandom!"

"I brought my portable computer," said Jay diffidently.

"Of course you did. You never go anywhere without it!" snapped Marion. "So what? Are you going to compose the eulogy?"

"No, but I may be able to find out some things about Pat Malone in a hurry. You remember Joel Schumann?"

"An engineering student of yours? Sort of."

"He gave me a phone number that might be helpful. Joel is known around the department as the Napoleon of hackers."

Marion looked interested. "An FBI of nerds! It might work. When can you start?"

"This evening after the boat trip," said Jay. "The rates go down at five."

Ever a Stormy Petrel Unto Us

> *—Francis Towner Laney's epitaph in fandom. (The term is used figuratively for one whose coming always portends trouble.)*

CHAPTER 11

AT TEN FORTY-THREE in the morning, a gaggle of rubber-booted literary tourists waddled down the red clay slopes of Breedlove Lake and clumped onto the concrete boat ramp, which now stopped two hundred yards from the water's edge. Above them towered hillsides of clay and rubble, once submerged beneath the lake and now forming a desolate canyon beneath the pine-topped hills surrounding it.

Beside the boat ramp, a rocky mountain stream bubbled down the hillside, headed for the distant lake water. Before the drawdown the stream had been swallowed by the expanse of Breedlove Lake, existing only as a current within the reservoir, but now it had been freed to course through its own eroded canyon, through seasons of silt, as it cut its way to the muddy waters of the great Watauga, pulsing again through the heart of the valley.

The concrete of the boat ramp ended twenty feet down the slope, succeeded by a flat graveled plain that might once have been a road. Another hundred yards on—and thirty feet down, had there been a lake—the road fell away into a series of curving rock ridges, spiraling down to a shelf of brown clay that was the new shoreline. Except for deep gullies that had trapped the ebbing lake water, the valley was visible again, and once more the Watauga River, artery of the region, was a discernable confluence, kept within its banks by the release of its overflow through the sluice gates of the TVA dam.

Three boats waited in the shallows of the river. Two of them were outboard motorboats, capable of ferrying five passengers and operated by leathery good old boys in windbreakers and fishing caps. Obviously, they had hired out their private vessels for the day's expedition for a little excitement and some easy money. The third craft was the large, flat-bottomed sightseeing boat on loan from the Breedlove Marina, which, with its red awning, and its Tennessee flag flying, would hold twenty passengers. It was used by the marina for its regularly scheduled tours of the lake area, a particularly popular outing during the warm months of early autumn, when the changing leaves on the oaks and maples turned the surrounding mountains into bands of flame and gold.

Geoff Duke led the party of editors and journalists aboard the sightseeing boat, and Ruben Mistral motioned for the Lanthanides and their guests to climb into the motorboats to begin their quest for the time capsule on Dugger's farm. Mistral, now sporting a gold-braided captain's hat, mounted the newer-looking motorboat that was obviously intended to be the flagship of the expedition. He was joined by Brendan Surn and Lorien, and Jim and Barbara Conyers, all of whom looked as if they were attending a funeral. Mistral patted Conyers' shoulder, and smiled encouragingly at the others, but he received only tentative smiles for his efforts. Jay Omega and Marion Farley, who had made a belated appearance at the point of embarkation, joined Erik Giles, Angela Arbroath, and George Woodard in the second outboard.

When everyone was comfortably seated and, at the helmsmen's insistence, corseted with orange life preservers, Ruben Mistral gave the signal for the boats to cast off, and the journey began. One by one the vessels glided out into the channel of the amber-colored river, heading upstream toward the sunken village of Wall Hollow and the farms beyond it. In the second craft, the boatman, who had introduced himself as Dub, admitted to Marion that this was his first stint as a lake guide, but he allowed as how he was a lifelong resident of the area and was willing to make conversation if anybody had a mind to ask him anything.

"Where is the town?" asked George Woodard, surveying the sea of mud surrounding the channel.

Dub smiled. "This lake is seventeen miles long, buddy. It'll take us a good hour to get there, I reckon."

They rode for a while in silence, past black trees spangled with snagged fishing lines and lures that clung to the dead branches like spiderwebs. There was an eerie stillness about the valley, and the slowness of the churning outboard made their passage seem like a nightmare journey through a surreal landscape. It might have been a deserted battlefield or the scene of some sudden disaster: the overriding feeling in the barren and silent valley was one of death and irreparable loss.

Marion shivered. "It's so eerie in this wasteland. Lines from T. S. Eliot keep running through my head."

"I know," murmured Angela Arbroath. "I've never seen a place so desolate in bright sunshine. It even feels cold. Do you suppose that it's Pat Malone that is making me feel gloomy?"

George Woodard's piggy face became animated with alarm. "Angela!" he hissed. "We aren't supposed to talk about you-know-what."

Marion looked at him with ill-concealed contempt. "I found the body," she said.

"Did Mistral ask you not to tell anyone about Malone's death?" asked Jay.

Angela nodded. "He didn't want the reporters to find out. He thought it would distract them from the reason we're here. I can't believe that Pat Malone is dead."

George Woodard stared at her. "I can't believe he's alive!"

"Yes, it takes some getting used to. I'd said good-bye to him all those years ago, and then suddenly he's back, and—"

"In all my life I have loved but one man, and I have lost him twice," said Marion dreamily. Noting her companions' puzzled looks, Marion hastened to add: "That's from *Cyrano*. It seemed appropriate."

They floated on in silence for a while. When they passed under the concrete arch of the Gene C. Breedlove Bridge, looming half a mile above their heads, envious spectators leaned over and waved at the makeshift flotilla. Its passengers craned their heads to peer at the pink blobs high above them, and a few of them returned the greeting.

George Woodard, lost in thought, barely noticed the bridge at all. He was pondering the death of Pat Malone and envisioning a memorial issue of *Alluvial*. After giving the matter careful consideration, George had decided not to demean himself and his phone bill by activating the S-F grapevine, but he concluded that the prestige of his 'zine depended upon his being the final authority on the Lanthanides reunion and on the Malone affair. He was, after all, both an old comrade of Malone's and an eyewitness. Why should the other 'zine publishers have the story. If he established himself as the authority on it (surely none of the other Lanthanides would bother), he could be invited as Fan Guest of Honor to any number of conventions in the coming year, which would mean that he would have his way paid to these conventions and the really good ones would give him plaques for his wall commemorating his status as Fan Guest. Pat Malone owed him that.

He considered his material for a memorial issue. New eulogies would have to be solicited, of course, and perhaps some samples of Pat's writings could be included. Would Pat's recent undeath affect the copyright laws, he wondered. Would anybody even *believe* that Pat Malone had come back? No one had thought to take any pictures of him. Perhaps it would be best not to mention him at all, but, of course, he had unimpeachable witnesses. And besides, hardly anyone ever questions the veracity of anything in fandom. The memorial issue was sure to be a big seller in fannish circles. He wondered if he could afford to double the number of copies for this issue.

George, for one, was not sorry to see Pat Malone dead. The late Pat's sneering reappearance at the Lanthanides reunion had been a forceful reminder of how little he had missed the scornful, bullying Malone. George was always twice as inept when Malone was present. With painful clarity now, he remembered Pat Malone's old practical jokes at his expense. There was the shaving cream in his bed, and the phony acceptance letter from *Weird Tales,* and the campaign Pat and Curtis had started at a Knoxville con to "cure" George's virginity. Well, perhaps he ought to forgive them that one. Earlene had volunteered to effect the cure, and George had fallen hopelessly in love with her. Sometimes, though, he wondered if she had done it in hopes of getting the attention of Pat Malone.

Had Earlene ever loved him? Were those sadistic jokers from the Fan Farm ever his friends? And did he like who he was; had he ever liked himself?

George looked out at the barren lake bed, wondering if his life had been a mortal version of Breedlove Lake: a pleasant, opaque facade, covering up a whole lot of nothing.

In the bow of the white motorboat Ruben Mistral struck a pose— like stout Cortes silent upon a peak in Darien, the *Times* reporter had quipped. Several of his colleagues scribbled down the phrase, unaware that Keats was being quoted. (*USA Today* reported the phrase as "a mountain in Connecticut.") Mistral's expression of solemn dignity suggested that he was leading an expedition up the Amazon rather than taking a boat ride in conjunction with a business deal. Occasionally, though, he forgot to provide a photo opportunity for the journalists' boat, and he would sit back down beside Brendan Surn and attempt to converse over the noise of the outboard motor.

"Great to see you again, Brendan!" he said, patting the older man's shoulder. "It's been too long! About the only time I get to see you these days is at those damned science fiction cons!"

Lorien Williams raised an eyebrow. "Don't you like cons?"

Mistral's smile wavered, and he glanced at Surn for his cue. "Have you ever been to one?" he asked.

"Of course," said Lorien. "I've been to—"

"I mean, with Brendan. I've never seen you at a con with Brendan."

Lorien shook her head. "No. I haven't had that honor yet."

Mistral snorted. "Honor! Did he tell you about the time he took a manuscript-in-progress to a con so that he could read from it, and one of the fannish bastards stole it? That was in the days before copy machines, too. Or the time one hot little number sneaked into his room with a passkey, and he had to call hotel security? She was underage, of course."

Brendan Surn smiled vaguely in Lorien's direction. "Not all fans are bad, Bunzie. *We* used to be fans."

"We didn't behave the way these punks do today," growled Bunzie. "They've gone a long way past water balloons. The only reason I go to cons these days is to see old friends. This reunion is perfect. Old friends, and no fans."

Lorien Williams studied him thoughtfully while she waited for Brendan to rise to the defense of fandom, but the old man turned away, staring at a rusting oil barrel that lay half buried in the Watauga mud flat.

After an hour's journey upstream, they began to see more skeletal trees in the mire, and the remnants of stone walls loomed ahead of them on the port side. "Yep," said Dub the helmsman in response to the unspoken questions. "That's Wall Hollow coming up on the left there. Not much of it left, is there? That stone building over there was the jail, and next to it was the Azalea Café. It was built out of river rocks cemented together. It has held up real well. Of course, most of the town was made of wood, and it's all gone. You can still see the roads, though." He pointed at the patches of asphalt visible in the plain of red mud. "That would have been Main Street."

"It doesn't look like a town anymore," said Marion, staring at the desolation.

"No, but it puts me in mind of a funny story," said Dub, who seemed to be the least affected by the ruins. "At the time the town was condemned by the TVA to make way for Breedlove Lake, there was a mayoral race going on in Wall Hollow, and strange as it may seem, the election was hotly contested. And one old boy said, 'I don't know what those politicians are getting so het up about. The next mayor of Wall Hollow will be a catfish.' "

The passengers laughed politely, and Angela asked him whether he had gone to the new Wall Hollow, the one that the TVA constructed on the other side of the lake for the refugees.

Dub rubbed his chin and steered for the deepest part of the river. "No, ma'am," he said after a bit. "I moved on over to Labrot Cove, about five miles from here, where I had some kin. I didn't want to lose anything else to that lake there." He shrugged. "Of course, that was a good while ago. Over the years I have got used to it, and now I go fishing over in here without giving it another thought. Why, many's the time I've hauled in a big old channel cat, and said to myself, 'I believe I've done caught the mayor.' "

Erik Giles had been studying the asphalt lines in the mud, trying to get his bearings from the remnants of buildings left as clues. He pointed to a barren hillside in the distance. "Keep going," he said. "Dugger's farm was just up that hollow. The river will take us most of the way."

The trio of boats glided past the ruins of the old train depot and passed within the shadow of the old stone gristmill, a shell of a building still standing against the deluge of pent-up lake water. The only sound for several minutes was the click of camera shutters from the flat-bottomed tourist boat as the photojournalists recorded the occasion.

Once past the wreckage of the old river bridge, the Watauga snaked between smooth red hills that for years had been merely shallow places in the lake. Now they were mounds of rubble, ringed like redwoods with the concentric circles of ebbing waves. The river sank into a narrowing valley, past smooth stretches that must have been pasture land, and at times it flowed only a few feet below the level of the asphalt remnants of a country road. The asphalt gave way to a stretch of pebbles, and then the road vanished altogether into mud the color of rust.

"This used to be a beautiful place," said Erik Giles in a voice that was little more than a whisper. "It was so green and peaceful. And we were such kids then. We thought 'happily ever after' was just a question of waiting long enough. We just didn't understand the randomness of our existence." He laughed bitterly. "Now, of course, we know better. Now, I'd say this is a pretty good metaphor for the way life is: it seems beautiful and endlessly deep while you're young, but little by little the water—the life—slips away, and you are left with nothing."

*   *   *

"Do you know where you are yet?" the pilot of the lead craft asked Ruben Mistral.

Mistral shrugged. "The moon?"

The boatman forced a smile. "Best I can recall, Dugger's farm ought to be in the next quarter mile or so, and you'll be wanting to leave the boat there, I reckon, and do some walking around."

"Yes," said Mistral. "It's just hard to get your bearings in this wasteland. Conyers, can you tell where we are?"

"I think so," said the lawyer. "See that outcrop of rocks up the hill there, just below the pine trees? I've stood on Dale's front porch many a time staring up at that thing. In the twilight—from a certain angle—it looks like an Indian. If the foundations of the farmhouse haven't sunk into the mud, we ought to see them right about now."

A few moments later they rounded a bend, removing a looming sandhill from their line of sight. "Look!" said Lorien Williams, pointing to a swampy plateau partway up the slope. "Is that a chimney?"

It was. There was a gently sloping hollow between two bare hills, and within its basin a pool of lake water had settled, covering the foundations of Dale Dugger's farmhouse with its own riparian shroud. A two-pronged remnant of a locust tree rose out of the shallows, and twenty feet past it, a crumbling rock chimney protruded from the orange water.

"We found it," said Mistral. "Start looking for a place to dock."

The three boatmen maneuvered their vessels toward an outcrop of boulders on the bank of the river. One at a time they were able to drift in close enough so that the passengers could climb out of the boats onto the rocks and make their way up the slope toward the site of Dugger's farm. Ruben Mistral, the first to disembark, repeated his landfall several times for the benefit of the cameramen, and then he created another photo opportunity by assisting Brendan Surn from the boat and pointing solemnly toward the ruined chimney. Together they scrambled up the rocky bank, picking their way along the driest parts of the lake bed, trailing a gaggle of camcorders and journalists in their wake.

The other members of the party were left to clamber up the river bank as best they could, without the encouragement of the media or the editors.

"This is certainly a grim occasion," Marion whispered to Jay. "I feel like a gatecrasher at a funeral."

"Remember that we're here to see that Erik doesn't overdo it," said Jay. "Maybe you can cheer him up. He doesn't seem very happy."

Marion looked about her. "None of them do. Isn't it odd how things broke down so quickly into matters of status? Mistral stays mostly with Surn—the two pros, associating mainly with each other. And Conyers and his wife are talking to Erik—the sober ex-fans in coalition. That leaves Woodard and Angela, who were never anything but fans. But maybe I shouldn't mention this to you, Jay. After all, you're a dirty old pro."

He sighed wearily. "I just accidentally wrote an S-F novel, okay? I didn't mean to apply for citizenship in the Twilight Zone."

"I don't think you can apply, Jay. I think fandom takes hostages."

"Be careful where you step, George," said Angela Arbroath, grabbing his elbow. "That puddle may be deeper than you think."

George Woodard, who hadn't even seen the mud hole he nearly plunged into, blinked out of his reverie and thanked her. "I was just thinking about the time we stayed up all night listening to the plotting of *Starwind Rising*," he said. "The moon was shining low beneath that branch of the locust tree, and it filled the whole horizon. As we listened to that story, I could actually *see* the story happening. I remember picturing one of the heroes looking just like Conyers. You know, he always did have that clean- chiseled all-American look. It was just like a movie going on in our heads. Once I found myself searching the surface of the moon, looking for traces of the domed cities, and I remember checking to see if my helmet was on. My helmet! I'd forgotten I wasn't in a spaceship orbiting the moon."

Angela smiled. "I didn't know Brendan had talked about his books in such detail to you all."

George flushed. "Actually, it was Dale who told that story. But I'm sure he'd discussed it beforehand with Brendan!"

Angela nodded. "I suppose so." She looked around the valley and then at the chimney rising out of muddy water a few yards away. "I guess I remember Pat better than anyone else from the Fan Farm. Sometimes he'd tell me what all of you were up to when he wrote to me."

"Do you still have the letters?" asked George eagerly. "I'm planning a memorial issue of *Alluvial*."

"No, George. I wouldn't let anyone see those letters without first obtaining Pat's permission, and I guess that isn't going to happen, is it?" Seeing his disappointment, she went on. "There isn't much in them that would interest fandom, anyhow, George. Like most men,

Pat talked mostly about himself. And he tried to carry on a long-distance romance with me, which worked better on paper than it did in real life." She smiled ruefully. "Like a lot of things in fandom."

Their conversation stopped when a reporter approached them, tape recorder in hand. "Can you tell me what your thoughts are at this moment?" she asked breathlessly.

George Woodard squinted at her. "Are you from *Locus*?"

After twenty minutes of site inspection, interspersed with photos and interviews, Ruben Mistral signaled for everyone's attention. When the crowd stopped milling around and stood in a respectful huddle around him, he stalked over to the black husk of a tree a few hundred yards from the chimney pool. The tree stood at the foot of a gently sloped mound of red clay, scored by a series of upright posts, each about four feet high.

"This is what remains of the fence," Mistral announced. "The first landmark. And that is the tree that we used as the second marker. This, ladies and gentlemen, is the very spot on which, thirty-six years ago, the Lanthanides buried their time capsule. It is time to resurrect the past. It is time to begin the digging. I will go first."

Mistral's contribution to the retrieval effort was to remove exactly two spadefuls of mud—the second was for good measure, in case someone's first photo did not turn out well. After that, each of the Lanthanides was invited to be filmed wielding the shovel, before the actual work of unearthing the jar was turned over to the three boatmen, under the direction of Geoffrey Duke. All four had donned khaki coveralls for the messy job of excavating a mud hole.

Marion clutched Jay's hand. "What if it isn't there?" she whispered.

He groaned. "Don't even think such a thing!"

"Well, what if it isn't? Everybody in fandom knew it was there, didn't they? Suppose crazed science fiction fans from Knoxville—"

"Hush, Marion!"

"I wonder if anybody will ever make such a big deal over your unpublished stuff."

"I doubt it," said Jay. "They certainly haven't been overly enthusiastic about the *published* stuff."

Several yards away from them, Brendan Surn was leaning on Lorien Williams' arm and smiling benignly at the diggers. "Aren't you excited about this?" asked Lorien, smiling up at him.

"Why, yes," said Brendan Surn mildly. "Yes, thank you. It's very nice."

Lorien's smile froze in place. That was the answer Brendan always gave when he was fading out of the here and now and hadn't the least idea of what was going on. No more interview questions today, she thought. She wondered how she would field the questions for him.

While the digging was going on, Ruben Mistral took up a position a safe distance away from the mudslinging, which he watched with an expression of dignified expectation. A few of the reporters tried to bait him with fanciful questions, such as "What if you find a skeleton?" or "What if the time capsule isn't there?" but he only smiled at them and refused to be drawn into any negative speculation. Privately he was wondering how the authorities were dealing with the problem of the late Pat Malone back at the Mountaineer Lodge, and he was wondering whether he ought to take any steps to suppress the news of his death. So far so good, he told himself. There would be time to worry about damage control later. First, let them find that damned jar.

Digging in mud wasn't easy. The sides of the hole kept collapsing in on it, and water seeped up from the bottom as they dug. The three diggers were soon transformed into identical mud-caked gingerbread men. When fifteen minutes of digging had elapsed, taking the hole to a depth of three feet, several people who obviously knew the Lanthanides' proclivities remarked that none of them were energetic enough to have buried anything so deep. Geoffrey Duke reminded these doubters that mountain streams had carried silt into the lake bed for more than three decades, depositing layer after layer of extra soil on top of the original cache.

The editors, who had grouped together at the back of the crowd, for fear of being invited to dig, eyed the excavation efforts nervously. "Suppose it isn't there?" asked Lily Warren.

Enzio O'Malley shrugged. "You ask them to write their stories from memory and you get better stuff, because now they've been pros for thirty years."

"What about the dead ones?"

"Even better. You get Mistral or Surn to give you a general description of the plot, and then you farm out the story to somebody famous who can really write. I'd like to see Robert McCammon write the Curtis Phillips story. Maybe Michael Moorcock for Deddingfield's stuff. Now that anthology would be worth publishing!"

Lily Warren gave him a sour smile. "So, Enzio, you will actually be disappointed if they find anything?"

"I wouldn't say that. But if I acquire the rights to it, I'll make sure the contract says I get to request some rewriting."

The Del Rey editor heaved a sigh of exasperation. "If Enzio had been given the Ten Commandments on Mount Sinai, he would have had them down to six before he left the summit."

A clink of shovel on metal drew gasps from those nearest the hole, and the crowd surged forward. "We got it!" shouted Geoffrey Duke, wiping his forehead with a mud-stained forearm. "I see a lid down there!"

"Easy, fellas!" said Mistral, elbowing his way to the side of the pit. "Don't break the glass now. That water would completely ruin the contents."

Marion went up and hugged Erik Giles. "They found it!" she cried. "I'm so happy for you!"

"I hope it's worth it," said Giles sadly.

One of the diggers jumped into the rapidly collapsing hole and, knee-deep in muddy water, fastened a rope around the neck of the jar. While he pushed and rocked the jar to free it, the others pulled on the rope, and moments later it gave, sending the digger sprawling into the side of the mud hole as the brown encrusted jar slid to the surface amid cheers from the onlookers. With a triumphant flourish Geoff Duke wrapped the unopened jar in a clean plastic sheet, while the other mud-caked diggers helped their comrade out of the hole and headed for the river to rinse off as best they could.

At Mistral's insistence, the Lanthanides grouped around him, smiling sheepishly into various camera lenses, as their leader held the jar aloft like a recently bagged trophy.

"Here it is!" yelled Mistral. "The Dead Sea Scrolls of Science Fiction!"

"Are you going to open it, Mistral?" asked one of the reporters.

"Not in the middle of this pigsty," he retorted. "It's too valuable for that. Let's go on back to the lodge, and we'll clean this thing up and let you get a look at it."

"When can *we* look at it?" yelled one of the editors.

"Photocopies will be made of the material, and you will have until tomorrow morning to read the contents, and to deliver your sealed bid to Sarah Ashley."

Another reporter waved her hand above the crowd. "Mr. Mistral!" she called out. "One more question! Isn't that the highway up there beyond those trees?"

Mistral looked up, just as a car whizzed past a few hundred yards above their heads. Just past the grove of oak trees up beyond the boundary of the lake, the road curved around the mountain, running parallel to the lake for a stretch before it snaked away again. Mistral grinned ruefully and held up his hands.

"Could you tell us then why we had to take boats to get here?"

Ruben Mistral grinned at her. "I wasn't sure how to recognize Dugger's farm from the road. It isn't always that close to the lake, you know. Besides, honey, the boat trip makes better copy," he told her. "But anybody who wants to hitchhike back has my permission." With that he handed the jar back to Geoffrey Duke for safekeeping, then turned and ambled back down the hill toward the river. After a moment's pause, the entire troop of muddy followers plowed along after him.

He wanted to pound on their doors, call them out
in their housecoats and frowsy pajamas,
and tell them in clear words
that time buries itself like a river under a lake
that river feeds, that though the past is irretrievable,
nothing left down there is gone.

—DON JOHNSON
Watauga Drawdown

CHAPTER 12

JAY OMEGA AND Marion Farley were not invited to the remainder of the afternoon's events. When the three boats had safely moored again at the Mountaineer Lodge boat ramp, Ruben Mistral gave everyone an hour's break to get cleaned up from their muddy trip upriver. At that time, he informed the Lanthanides, they were to assemble in the downstairs conference room to witness the official opening of the time capsule, to be followed by interview sessions with the journalists. The editors who did not want to observe the publicity marathon in action were urged to attend a private screening of Ruben Mistral's latest movie, *Laser Nova,* after which photocopies of the time-capsule contents would be issued to them, and they would be returned to their hotel in Johnson City to prepare for Sunday's auction.

"You ought to try to talk to Ruben Mistral sometime this weekend," Marion told Jay. "Did you bring along a copy of *Bimbos of the Death Sun*? Maybe he could help you sell the movie rights."

Jay shook his head. "Just what I need—to be famous for writing *Bimbos of the Death Sun.* It was bad enough when it was a paperback original that no one could ever find."

"But think of the money, Jay!"

"Think of the dean of engineering, Marion. Try to get tenure with something called *Bimbos of the Death Sun* on your vita!" He smiled at her expression of disappointment.

She sighed. "Tell me about trying to get tenure! My department hires two tenure-track people for every *one* position. I wish I could have become a professor in the good old days, like Erik Giles did. Back then you got tenure more or less automatically, just for hanging

around for a few years without screwing up. I don't know if he's
ever published anything. Whereas I have to spend every waking moment grubbing up some obscure footnote—''

"I see," said Jay. "So you think that if I could make a career out
of science fiction I could escape all that hassle."

"You could. Ask Isaac Asimov about academia some time."

Jay smiled. "Ask practically everybody else about low advances
and an uncertain income. Anyway, thanks for trying so hard to make
me famous, Marion. But it takes more than talent to be Ruben Mistral, and I don't think I've got it. Anyhow, we have more important
things to do. Can you find the hotel manager and see what he knows
about Malone's death?"

"I suppose so. But is this really any business of ours? Shouldn't
we at least consult Erik before we do anything?"

"I talked to Pat Malone late last night after the party. I kind of
liked him." He grinned. "Maybe I'm becoming a Pat Malone fan.
Anyway, this is between me and him. Will you help?"

"I said I would." Her eyes narrowed suspiciously. "What are you
going to do?"

"I'll be up in the room mobilizing the troops."

Marion hesitated. "Look . . . you're not going to get arrested for
breaking into the files of the U.S. government, or AT&T or anything.
Are you?"

"Me? A hacker? Not a chance. Besides, I doubt if government records would be much help. What we need is a lot of people from a lot of
different places to make phone calls for us and ask the pertinent questions."

"And what makes you think that a bunch of fans from all over the
country would be willing to help you out in this investigation?"

Jay grinned. "Are you kidding, Marion? These are people who
will argue for days over the meaning of a phrase in a *Star Trek*
episode, and I'm going to give them a chance to solve a mystery
concerning fandom's greatest nemesis—Pat Malone! If what you've
told me about fandom is correct, I think they'll jump at it."

"They probably will," sighed Marion. "It is, after all, gossip that
can be rationalized as a public service inquiry. Go to it! You'll put
the KGB to shame."

The ceremony for the opening of the time capsule was set for four
o'clock. The small conference room seemed to be lit by lightning, so
frequent were the flashes from the photojournalists' cameras. The
Lanthanides posed separately, together, and in a series of group shots

clustered around the now-unmuddied time capsule. The huge glass jar had been cleaned with a succession of wet Mountaineer Lodge towels before the meeting began, and it now occupied the place of honor on a table in the front, covered in a shining white dropcloth.

"I suppose he couldn't find any red samite," muttered Lily Warren, who was unfavorably reminded of the Grail legends.

Ruben Mistral waited until the flashes dwindled to an erratic few before he took his place as master of ceremonies of the Grand Opening.

"Ladies and gentlemen," he intoned solemnly. "We are about to engage in time travel. Remember that a Greek philosopher—I forget which one—said that time is a river, and that you cannot stop time, because you can never set your foot in the same place twice. But today we found that river of time, just as it was thirty years ago, before the lake was created, and we embarked on that river in search of—" he smiled at his own conceit "—in search of our lost youth. Those were the days when we were fans, idolizing the tale tellers and the dream merchants, and we put all our hopes for the future— our writing, our precious brain children—into this one fragile vessel and sent it forward to the future to wait for us." He patted the lid of the time capsule.

"For thirty-five years it has waited. Through war, and flood, and the untimely deaths of some of our beloved comrades, this little vessel of silicon has held our brightest hopes. And today we went back to get it. The time has come to open it. Ladies and gentlemen, it is a solemn moment when one comes to terms with one's youth. May I have a moment of silence, and the assistance of Brendan Surn, in opening this reposit of our youthful ambition?" He was gratified to see that a number of reporters appeared to be taking down his speech in shorthand. In the back of the room, camcorders were rolling.

After a moment's hesitation, Brendan Surn, assisted by Lorien, made his way to the table where the time capsule sat, gleaming under the camera lights. Mistral removed the cloth, revealing a jumble of papers and other objects crammed into the translucent pickle jar. He motioned for Surn to take hold of the side of the jar, while he gripped the other side. "It may have rusted shut," he explained to the assembled witnesses.

On cue Geoffrey Duke advanced from the sidelines holding a flat rubber mat, which was in fact a large jar opener. He tapped expertly on the top of the lid and then applied the opener, wrenching it with considerable force. After two more tries, the lid opened, amid cheers from the audience. With a little bow to Mistral, Geoffrey made a hasty exit, leaving his boss to tilt the jar forward to give people another view of the contents.

"I suppose I'd better take this stuff out," he murmured. "I hope I can remember what all of it is." He reached into the jar and pulled out a propeller beanie. "I believe that was yours, George." In carefully neutral tones he read the attached tag. "By 1984, all the world's intellectuals will be wearing these."

George Woodard hunkered down under waves of laughter. "We were *kidding*!" he protested.

Mistral reached back into the jar. "Oops, better be careful with this. A movie poster of *War of the Worlds,* liberated from the Bonnie Kate Theatre in Elizabethton. I'll bet that's worth something these days." He looked at the other Lanthanides. "What are we doing with this stuff?"

Jim Conyers smiled. "In 1954 we said we'd donate it to the science fiction hall of fame."

More chuckles from the audience.

Sarah Ashley stood up. "Since the happy day of such a repository has not yet come, perhaps we could use these things as a traveling exhibit, when it's time to publicize the anthology." She smiled as polite applause approved her suggestion.

"Okay," said Mistral. "Thanks, Sarah. Good idea. Now, what else . . . picture of a dog."

"That was to fool the aliens," said Erik Giles.

"Good plan. Here are the manuscripts. I'm afraid they're not in accordance with your submission guidelines, guys." Groans from the editors in the audience. "Geoffrey, if you'll take these away to be photocopied." He peeked at one page of the stack of papers and grinned. "Angela, do you still circle your i's?"

"Sometimes, Bunzie. Do you still misspell weird?"

He sighed. "She knew me when, folks.—What else? There's an envelope in here, addressed to the Lanthanides from John W. Campbell Jr."

"That's right!" cried Woodard. "Remember, we wrote to him and asked for a letter to the future that we could include in our time capsule. And we never read it. Open it! Let's see what he said!"

Mistral began to tear the flap on the yellowed envelope. "John W. Campbell Jr., as many of you may know, was the legendary S-F editor from the Golden Age of Science Fiction. He discovered most of the great ones—"

"Except us."

Mistral forced a laugh. "Well, I think everybody got their share

of rejection slips from Mr. Campbell. Let's see what he has to say
to the future.'' He pulled out the letter and scanned a few lines.

As the silence grew longer, Jim Conyers called out, ''Well, Bunzie? What does he say?''

Mistral reddened. ''It's on Street & Smith letterhead, and it's from
Campbell's secretary, Kay Tarrant. It says: 'Mr. Campbell regrets
that he does not have the time to reply to your request. . . .' '' He
stopped reading amid the shouts of laughter. ''Let's see what else is
in here.''

''A jar of grape jelly in case Claude—that's an old inside joke
from fandom, folks. We might as well skip it. And here's some old
magazines—''

''—Which are very valuable,'' said George Woodard, unable to
contain himself. ''If they go on display, I must insist that every care be
taken—''

''Make it so,'' said Mistral with a smirk. ''Now, let's see. We have
an August 1928 issue of *Amazing,* signed by both E. E. 'Doc' Smith
and Philip Francis Nowlan.''

''Worth four thousand dollars. Minimum,'' said Woodard.

''Some Ray Bradbury fanzines; old comic books, no doubt valuable; copies of *Alluvial,* letters from various people . . . Carl Brandon,
Sgt. Joan Carr.''

''Those people didn't exist,'' Jim Conyers reminded him.

Mistral raised his eyebrows. ''That ought to *really* make them
worth something.''

For the benefit of the press Jim Conyers explained about hoaxes
in fandom, and how a fan might assume several personas in letter
writing, since early fans seldom met.

''Thanks for clearing that up, Jim,'' said Mistral, calling the meeting back to order. ''Here we have Curtis Phillips' beloved copy of
H. P. Lovecraft's *Outsiders,* annotated by himself and Lovecraft
expert Francis Towner Laney.''

Erik Giles spoke up. ''Unfortunately, as I recall, Curtis' comments
were based on his interviews with the demons themselves, and contain their comments about Lovecraft and Laney.''

''They *liked* Laney,'' chuckled Brendan Surn.

''The volume is priceless,'' declared Woodard.

''Well,'' said Mistral. ''That's about all the interesting stuff. Thank
you all for coming to this momentous occasion. The Lanthanides will
hang around up here to chat with the press, and the rest of you can
go and hang out in the bar until the bus comes. Or come look at the
exhibits here.''

''Make sure your hands are clean,'' Woodard warned.

*   *   *

Sarah Ashley heaved a sigh of relief. Her blond hair was still immaculately coiffed and her gray suit was perfect, but there were lines of strain around her eyes, and her face was drawn. The interviews were over now, the exhibits had been removed, and only she and Ruben Mistral were left in the conference room with the empty pickle jar, which now looked very ordinary and unimpressive.

She set down the assortment of papers on the desk in front of Ruben Mistral and began to wipe her soiled fingers with a moist tissue. "Well, you old rogue," she said, smiling at her most audacious client. "You've done it!"

Mistral's eyes widened in mock innocence. "I don't know why you doubt me, Sarah. Isn't it everything I said it was?" He patted the humble pickle jar as if it had just won the Derby.

"Miraculously, yes," she said dryly. "I suppose the handwriting will have to be analyzed, and perhaps the paper tested to certify age. Depending on how picky the purchaser is about authentication. But I shouldn't think there will be any problems whatsoever in going ahead with the auction tomorrow. You really did produce the lost works of the genre. Thank God. I had visions of looking foolish in front of thirty million people."

"The time capsule is absolutely genuine, Sarah. The sleight of hand was in the hype," said Mistral with a feral smile. "I took what is perhaps a mediocre collection of juvenilia and parlayed it into the Dead Sea Scrolls of Science Fiction."

"Yes, I heard that. Nice catch phrase."

"It should be. I paid an ad agency five grand to come up with it." His manner grew conspiratorial. "Incidentally, while we're being candid, there is one little matter I need to discuss with you, Sarah. We had an unexpected visitor turn up last night, and now he's dead."

She listened expressionlessly while Mistral explained the reappearance of Pat Malone and his sudden death some twelve hours later. When he had finished his recital, Sarah Ashley's eyes narrowed. "I do dislike coincidences. It was natural causes, of course?"

Mistral shrugged. "What else? I didn't talk to the police, of course, but nobody has said anything, so I thought it best not to mention the incident to the press."

"Very prudent. Perhaps tomorrow you might tell the story to the winning bidder, in case he wants to use it in publicizing the anthology. By then the news stories we need will have been filed with their respective publications, don't you think?"

Mistral nodded happily. "That's all right, then. I guess it's all over but the photocopying."

"And the bidding. But you must let me worry about that."

Locked in the attic of Ruben Mistral's consciousness, Bunzie pounded and pleaded to be let out, but his chances of having any say-so in the proceedings was nil. He might mourn his old friend in private, and even wonder about the circumstances of his death, but this was business, in which he was never permitted to interfere.

Marion knew that her appearance in the manager's office wasn't going to brighten his day any. The long-suffering hotel official had already endured a peculiar, media-infested science fiction get-together, the murder of one of the guests, and the arrival of police on the scene to disrupt the normal routine and intimidate the other patrons of the lodge. All he needed now was a self-appointed amateur sleuth wasting his time with ingenuous questions. Marion hoped she didn't look too much like a scatterbrained crank.

She phrased her request to the desk clerk with what she hoped was polite authority, and after a few stammered objections and a five-minute wait, the clerk led her back to the office of Coy A. Trivett, manager of the Mountaineer Lodge. It was a small, sparsely furnished room, decorated with framed photographs of mountain scenes and a hardware-store calendar from Elizabethton. The carpeting matched that in the lobby, and the worn chintz loveseat had been salvaged from the lobby seating area during last spring's renovations. Trivett himself, a blond man in his thirties, looked like a high school athlete who was thinking of running to fat. At the moment he wore the tentative smile of one who has resolved to be civil despite all temptations to the contrary.

"Is everything all right?" he asked in the anxious tones of one who knows better.

Marion introduced herself, placing a slight stress on the honorific "doctor" with which she prefaced her name. She found that use of her title helped to prevent people from mistaking her for an idiot. "It was I who found the body," she explained. "And I just wanted to see how the investigation was going. In case the police want to talk to me," she added in an inspired afterthought.

"I believe they will," Trivett told her. She noticed a lingering trace of a local accent in his carefully precise speech. "I had a call from them a little while ago, and they asked whether your group would be staying on through tomorrow. They said they'd be over in the morning to talk to you people."

Marion's eyes widened. "Do they suspect foul play?"

"They didn't say exactly. But they took the fellow's medicine along with them for testing. Were you a friend of his?"

"I had just met him," said Marion. "But he was rather famous. I guess most people in science fiction have heard of Pat Malone."

The hotel manager blinked in surprise. "Who?"

"I suppose he wasn't exactly a celebrity outside the genre, but, believe me, in science fiction, Pat Malone was a name to conjure with."

"Ma'am, who are you talking about?"

"Pat Malone. The gentleman who died here last night."

Trivett frowned in confusion. "Was that his stage name or something?"

"No. Why?"

"Because the dead man was a Mr. Richard Spivey. At least according to his driver's license. I don't know anything about a Pat Malone."

On the editors' bus, en route to the Johnson City Holiday Inn, Enzio O'Malley was complaining loudly to all and sundry. "Some of this stuff is *handwritten*!" he wailed. "I haven't had to read handwriting since I edited the college poetry magazine!"

"Be thankful it's legible," said Lily Warren. "I was afraid they'd find a time capsule filled with muddy water—that is, if they found anything at all."

"This is going to take me hours to read."

"Fortune cookies take him hours to read," muttered the Del Rey editor sotto voce.

"Has anybody looked at any of this stuff?" asked Lily. "I wondered if some of these stories are early drafts of pieces they rewrote and published later. I'd hate to pay six figures for a draft of *Starwind Rising*."

"This story by Dale Dugger is pretty good," said a short dark girl who couldn't have been more than twenty-three. She had recently been transferred from the romance division to science fiction, and she was still unfamiliar with her new territory. "Has he got a back list?"

After a few moments of stifled laughter from her rival editors, Lily Warren said gently, "No, Debbie. Dale Dugger died of alcohol-related disorders in Nashville. He isn't significant."

Enzio O'Malley scowled. "Well, at least we can assume that he wasn't a temperamental old bastard like the famous ones."

"I thought Mr. Conyers was very nice," said Debbie.

Lily Warren sighed. "He's just a lawyer. The famous ones are Surn, Mistral, Phillips, Deddingfield, and possibly Erik Giles, who wrote the C. A. Stormcock book."

"He thinks he's famous," said O'Malley. "I asked him to autograph my photocopy of his time-capsule short story, and he refused point blank."

Lily Warren laughed. "I always suspected you of being a closet fan, O'Malley."

"Are all the authors represented in the manuscript?" someone else asked

Lily flipped through the pages of faint typescript and badly photocopied holograph manuscripts. "I don't see Deddingfield," she said. "Everyone else is there."

Someone from the back of the bus called out, "Has anyone read the story by George Woodard?"

"I'm saving that for late tonight," said O'Malley. "For a sedative."

"All right," said Jay Omega. "I think I can fly this thing."

As soon as Marion had gone, Jay went out to the car and retrieved his Tandy 1400HD laptop from the trunk. At nearly twelve pounds, it was a bit heavy to be a portable machine, at least compared to the latest technology, but Jay was used to it. He liked the keyboard and the backlit screen, and he couldn't see any point in dropping a thousand bucks on a newer model just to save himself a few pounds of luggage. He could write books on it, send faxes with it, and, when he hooked it up to a telephone, he could access the world.

Several minutes later he was back in his room establishing a command center. He had dragged the round worktable over beside the bed, within reach of the telephone wall jack. He unplugged the touch-tone phone on the nightstand, and in its place he plugged in the computer modem. He set up the computer in the center of the worktable and attached it to the modem.

Now all he had to do was make some phone calls.

Jay Omega took out his wallet. Tucked away with his Radio Shack credit card, his SFWA membership, and his frequent flier ID was a cardboard Guinness beer coaster with Joel Schumann's telephone number scribbled on the back. Beneath that was a second number, inscribed: Bulletin Board—J.S., Sysop. It was this second number that he needed. The notation beside that number indicated that Joel Schumann was the systems operator (i.e. sysop) for an electronic bulletin board to which a number of computer enthusiasts in his area subscribed. Through Schumann's bulletin board, users could contact other people on other bulletin boards anywhere in the world, but because everyone wasn't always logged on, it could take days for the right person to receive a message. Jay decided that he needed some advice before proceeding. Although he dutifully paid his twenty-dollar yearly dues to keep the system operating, bulletin board chatting wasn't something he had much time or inclination for. Once a week he checked the messages to see if someone were trying to reach him, and occasionally he scanned the screens of typewritten conversations to see if anything more substantial than *Robocop* was being discussed. Most of the time it wasn't, so he let it go at that. Now, though, he needed some advice, and he was pretty sure that Joel Schumann was the place to start.

Jay dialed the number, hoping that one of the four lines was free. A click told him that it was, and almost instantly his screen lit up with the logo of Joel Schumann's bulletin board. Jay logged on and typed in his password: *Frodo,* which was the name of Marion Farley's cat. He had no idea how she had come up with that name, and it never occurred to him to ask. After a moment's pause the system pronounced him cleared for entry and informed him that he had seventy-two minutes to spend before being disconnected.

"I hope that will be enough," muttered Jay. After a moment's thought, he typed in a message to "ALL": PLEASE ADVISE. I NEED TO CONTACT S-F FANS FROM ALL OVER THE COUNTRY TO TRACK DOWN A MISSING PERSON. URGENT AND IMPORTANT MATTER. TIME IS LIMITED. I'M IN A MOTEL NEAR JOHNSON CITY, TN, USING LAPTOP. PLEASE ADVISE FASTEST AND MOST EFFECTIVE WAY TO CONTACT FANDOM.— J. OMEGA.

After reading through the lines to make sure he hadn't misspelled anything, Jay transmitted the message and logged off. Now he had to wait for somebody to read his message and leave a reply. Because it was a Saturday he knew that it wouldn't take long for an answer. He decided to call back in half an hour. While he waited, he ambled over to the television and began to flip through the channels, testing his theory that at any given hour of the day, *Star Trek* is always playing somewhere. It wasn't, but he did find an old episode of the British series *Blackadder,* a program which Marion ranked somewhere between chocolate and sex. He had settled back on the bed, happily immersed in a parody of court life in the sixteenth century, when Marion burst in.

"You won't believe what the hotel manager said!" she cried.

Jay turned down the volume on the set. "Try me."

"He said the dead man was someone called Richard Spivey."

"He could have changed his name, I suppose. It would have made it harder for fandom to track him down. Did you look in his wallet?"

Marion shivered. "No. I didn't want to search the corpse. That's why I'm an English major. But he did have books autographed by some of the Lanthanides."

"To Spivey or to Pat Malone?"

Marion considered it. "Neither, that I recall. One of them was to Curtis Phillips *from* Pat Malone. Maybe he got it back when Curtis died. It seems strange, though, doesn't it?"

"Everything about Pat Malone is strange. I don't suppose you were able to find out how he died?"

"Mr. Trivett doesn't think they know yet. But he did say that they took his medicine bottle along to be tested."

"What was in it?"

"Elavil. Prescribed to Spivey. And before you ask, I have no idea what that is. *You're* the science person, not me."

"Is there anybody here with any medical background? Maybe we could ask them."

Marion ticked each of the Lanthanides' names off on her fingers. "Angela!" she said. "She works in a hospital, doesn't she? I suppose you want me to see if she knows what Elavil is.'"

Jay Omega glanced at his watch. "I think I can call the bulletin board back now to see if they have any advice for me. You might also ask Angela for any information on Pat Malone's supposed death in 1958. What authority did they have for believing him dead? While you're at it, ask her if she's positive that he was Pat Malone."

"They certainly acted as if he was," said Marion with a grim smile. "He created more stir than Ted Bundy at a beauty pageant."

"I wonder if Ruben Mistral contacted Pat Malone's next of kin about the time capsule. See if you can find the answer to that one, too."

Marion sighed. "This has a familiar ring to it. I talk to people while *you* talk to machines."

"No, Marion," said Jay with wounded innocence. "I'll be talking to people, too. I'm just using machines to do it."

"All right," she sighed. "I'll go and grill the suspects." At the door, Marion hesitated and looked back. "Jay, you don't really think he was murdered, do you?"

He shrugged. "I haven't given it much thought. I'm sure the police will tell us. Right now I just want to know who he was."

*   *   *

When Marion had gone, Jay went to his computer and typed in
Alt-D and then *M* to allow him to manually enter the electronic bulletin board phone number from the Guinness beer mat. He typed in
the number, hit return, and waited while the computer dialed the
number. After two rings the line was answered, and after he typed
in his identification, a welcome screen from the bulletin board asked
him if he wanted to check his electronic mail. He hit *return* and found
that there was one message waiting. He pressed *R Y, return.*

After a moment's pause the message appeared:

TO Dr. Mega—FROM Sysop. SUBJECT: Please Advise. All right, all
right, I'm here. You didn't have to shout. (Don't use all caps next time.)
Remember when I made you subscribe to Delphi? I know that all you
use it for is to snag cheap air fares, but it does have other uses. I hope
you can remember your password. If so, call the Tennessee local
TYMNET number, 615-928-1191, and log into Delphi the way you do at
home. Go to CONFERENCE, then type WHO. This will list current conference conversations. Hopefully you will see a conference name that
looks promising for your line of inquiry. You don't need to join it. You
can issue the command WHO IS <User Name>, and that will give you
a profile of the people currently in the conference: where they live,
what they like, etc. If you want to talk in their conference, type JOIN
<Conference name or number> and then you can barge in and start
asking them questions. If your topic is really offbeat, you can create
your own conference, and let the strange ones find you. (What have
you gotten yourself into now, Dr. Mega?) I'll be around for most of
the evening in case you get in further trouble, need bail money, whatever. May St. Solenoid be with you. JS.

Jay made notes of the instructions in Joel's message, sent a quick
reply of thanks to him, and logged off the bulletin board. Then he
turned off the television, yawned and stretched, and sat down at the
keyboard of his computer. "It's going to be a damn long night in
fandom," he muttered.

Marion found Angela Arbroath in her room recuperating from a
marathon session of nostalgia and journalism. "I hope I'm not disturbing you," said Marion, strolling past Angela into the room as if
she were sure of her welcome. "This must have been quite an exciting day for you!"

Angela, who was wearing a flowered kimono and leather thongs, looked tired. She had scrubbed off her makeup, so that her lips had a bloodless look to them and her wrinkles stood out in high relief against her pale skin. "I guess the news about Pat sort of overshadowed all the rest of it," she said apologetically.

Marion sat down on the unused one of the twin beds, and settled in for a long chat. "I am sorry about what happened to Pat Malone," she said. "I didn't know him, but I found the body, you know, so you can imagine how it has made *me* feel. I wondered, though—are you certain that it *was* Pat Malone?"

The older woman smiled. "He knew things that only one of the Lanthanides could have known. You weren't there, were you, when he turned up at the party last night? Within minutes they were all bickering as if it were more than thirty years ago. He knew just what to say to infuriate them." She sighed. "He always did."

"Can you think of anyone who might have wanted to kill him?"

"Hon, I can't think of anyone who didn't. At one time or another, Pat Malone antagonized every correspondent he ever had, every close friend, every sweetheart. Did you ever read *The Last Fandango*?"

"No. I've certainly heard about it, though. Was it ever actually published?"

"In a manner of speaking. It was mimeographed and distributed by the Fantasy Amateur Press Association. And in the book he severely criticized the Fantasy Amateur Press Association."

Marion nodded. "Yes, I knew about that. I've never seen one, though."

"It was nothing fancy. Just pages and pages of typing. No illustrations, no sophisticated typesetting, nothing to make it visually pleasing. Nothing to make it pleasing, period." She looked away. "I cried when I read it. He said so many awful things about all the people that I knew. And the worst of it was, I couldn't really deny any of it. It's just that he saw them so uncharitably." She smiled bitterly. "And about me? Oh, he said that I lacked only beauty to be a femme fatale. He was most unsparing of people's feelings. But, of course, he was hardest on himself."

"In what way?"

"He wanted people to know what an idiot he thought he had been for succumbing to fandom, so he outlined his whole experience in getting involved in science fiction, and he outlined the disillusionment that made him leave."

Marion tried to temper her excitement. "Did he mention the Lanthanides?"

"Yes, of course. He said that Surn was pompous, and George was a fool, and he was critical of everyone, but the most damning thing he did was simply to chronicle their bickering, and their naïveté, and their youthful arrogance. He made them—and himself, you understand—look like arrogant clowns. And then he proceeded to do the same thing to the rest of fandom as well.''

"Could anyone who read *The Last Fandango* have known the things he talked about last night?''

Angela looked puzzled, but she considered the question. "I don't think so,'' she said. "He mentioned a few pranks that weren't included in his memoir. If he had written down every stupid thing they did, his book would have been longer than *War and Peace*.''

"So he knew a lot of embarrassing secrets?''

"I suppose so. Not that anyone ought to care about who was sleeping with who after so long a time.'' She smiled reflectively. "But I guess Barbara Conyers just might at that. Anyhow, why did you ask me if he knew anything dangerous? He wasn't murdered.''

"Not that we know of,'' Marion admitted. "But it seemed possible. The hotel manager told me that the police took Pat Malone's prescription medicine along with them. It was Elavil. We wondered if you knew what that was.''

Angela Arbroath sat up straight. Her expression became thoughtful. *"Pat Malone* was using Elavil?''

"Apparently so. Or at least he had it in his possession. The name on the bottle said 'Richard Spivey.' What is it?''

"Amitriptyline. It's used to treat depression.'' She seemed to have forgotten Marion's presence. "That would explain a lot. He used to get so caught up in wild schemes—like fandom—and then later he would berate himself for having wasted his time on them. Yes, I suppose he might even have been manic depressive. Although, I have to say that he didn't seem to behave much differently last night from the way he was in the old days, so I don't see that the medicine was doing him much good.''

"I wonder if they've notified his next of kin. Did he have any? I thought you mentioned once that he was married.''

"That was in the fifties,'' Angela reminded her. "And his wife was about ten years older than he was. Don't ask me to explain *that*. I do remember that there was a lot of chauvinistic letter writing in fandom in those days, with those runty little shits asking each other what he saw in *her*. Nobody ever thought to marvel that she'd seen anything in *him*. Well, as I say, it's a long time ago. She may have died.''

"Maybe so. By the way, have you ever heard of Richard Spivey?'' asked Marion, trying to appear casual.

Angela shook her head. "If he's a new writer, don't expect me to know him. I haven't kept up."

"I don't know who he is," Marion admitted. "But I sure do wish I knew what killed Pat Malone so conveniently. Not that the police would confide in me."

"Get Jim Conyers to ask them. He's a lawyer around here, and he's probably old friends with the sheriff."

Marion looked at her with renewed respect. "What a perfectly simple, brilliant idea."

Angela nodded. "Well, I hope you find out something," she said. "As cantankerous as Pat was, I never wanted him to be dead."

There was a soft tapping at the door. "I'll get it," said Marion, eying her hostess' kimono. She went to the door and eased it open. "Yes?"

Lorien Williams stood there, twisting her hands and looking anxious. "Excuse me, is Miss—um—you know, Angela. Could I speak to her, please?"

Marion glanced back at Angela, who waved for her to let the visitor in.

"Is anything the matter?" she asked as Lorien edged past her, head down and slouching. Behind her, Marion looked over at Angela and mouthed: Who knows?

"I wondered if you could take a look at Mr. Surn," she said to Angela. "I think somebody said you were a nurse."

Angela paled. "What's the matter with Brendan?"

Marion said, "Shall I call an ambulance?" She was remembering the huddled form of Pat Malone, slumped on the bathroom floor.

"No. It isn't that bad. I mean, it isn't a heart attack or anything. It's just that sometimes he has . . . well, bad spells. There are times when he doesn't know me, and he gets very angry. I don't blame him, of course. I'd get angry, too, if—" Lorien's voice trailed off uncertainly.

Angela looked from Marion to Lorien and back again. "I'll just go in the bathroom and change," she said.

"I'm going to look for Jim Conyers," said Marion.

Meanwhile, back at the electric Scout meeting, Jay Omega had succeeded in logging on to a nationwide computer chat on Delphi, and he established his own conference, devoted to "a discussion of the Lanthanides." He labeled his file MORE FANDANGO, reasoning that the word "Fandango" would be a red flag to anyone who remembered Pat Malone, and that everyone else would give it a miss.

This was not entirely true; a few people chimed in wanting to discuss the lambada, an association which eluded the sedentary Omega, and a few college-age chemists tried to get up a discussion of the periodic chart, but after a quarter of an hour, someone from Indiana actually did check in, responding with: IS THIS ABOUT P. B. MALONE? AND, IF SO, WHAT ABOUT HIM? HE'S DEAD. The message purported to be from one J. A. Bristol.

Jay typed back: YES, BUT NOT FOR AS LONG AS YOU THINK, PER-HAPS. I NEED TO TALK TO SOMEBODY IN MISSISSIPPI ABOUT VERIFYING P.M.'S 1958 DEMISE.

Meanwhile, other people chimed in with their own opinions of Malone's novel, and of *The Last Fandango*. Jay replied: CAN WE TABLE THESE TOPICS? BIOGRAPHICAL DATA URGENTLY NEEDED. IS ANYONE ON FROM CUPERTINO, CA?

Of course there was. Cupertino, which is in California's Silicon Valley, has more computers than bathtubs. The response to Jay's request was almost immediate. "Kenny," another collegian, said: NEVER HEARD OF THIS MALONE GUY, BUT I LIVE IN CUPERTINO. SO?

Jay consulted the notes he had scribbled down, containing every-thing he could remember about Pat Malone. PLEASE CHECK PHONE DIRECTORY FOR AN ETHEL OR A MRS. PAT/PB MALONE, he told Kenny.

Two other conference crashers were ignoring Jay's line of ques-tioning to pursue an argument of their own about the symbolism that one of them saw in *River of Neptune*.

In exasperation, Jay fired at them: HAVE IT ON GOOD AUTHORITY THAT THE NOVEL PROPHESIES THE COMING OF NINTENDO. YOU HAVE NOW REACHED EQUILIBRIUM. GO AWAY!—HAS ANYONE OUT THERE EVER SEEN PAT MALONE? LATELY?

NO, BUT I SAW ELVIS AT PIZZA HUT LAST WEEK.

Jay was beginning to understand why the police hauled people in for questioning: so that they could hit them. He ignored this last bit of baiting and waited for serious replies. What did he need to know about Malone, anyway? He made notations on one of his data sheets:

"Malone's hometown?" Get Marion to find out.

"Cupertino, Ca—Ethel Malone—Verify." Beside that he wrote: Kenny.

"If dead, what happened to his possessions." He scratched that one out. The book in the dead man's suitcase had belonged to Curtis Phillips. Malone had only autographed it. Jay put in a new item: "Compare handwriting samples."

"Mississippi—Malone's death—Verify."

"Richard Spivey?"

"Malone—Physical description."

"Cause of death."—Marion working on it.

"Elavil." Ditto.

"Washington Med School. Body donated?"

He glanced back at the computer screen. Three messages were waiting for him. One said: MOONFIRE SPEAKING. I THOUGHT PAT MALONE WAS AN IRISH PUNK ROCK GROUP—ALL FEMALE. Another respondent had shot back: NO! HE WAS THE SALMAN RUSHDIE OF FANDOM. The third note was from Kenny: ETHEL IS IN THE PHONE BOOK. NOW WHAT?

It helped that the desk clerk had become convinced that everyone connected with science fiction was crazy. After the barrage of requests she had endured that day (pickle jar cover, corpse removal, indefinite use of a telephone line), Marion's request for a list of all the Lanthanides' room numbers seemed positively reasonable to her. She copied them out on the back of a Sunday Buffet flier and handed it over with a weary sigh. What would they be wanting next? Electric soap? She closed her eyes to check out her headache on the Richter scale. At least she was now psychologically ready for the Tennessee war gamers' convention coming up in September.

Armed with this guide to the other guests' whereabouts, Marion first checked the restaurant to see who was there: nobody she recognized. Either they went to dinner early, or they had called down for room service. As she studied the diners in the restaurant, though, she realized that there was a familiar look about at least a dozen of them. Many of them were bespectacled and heavyset, and they wore T-shirts with slogans on them and hairdos that had never been fashionable. Several of them were reading paperbacks while they ate; the others appeared to be arguing. Fans! Marion backed slowly toward the door before she turned and fled.

"Well," she said to herself as she waited for the elevator, "at least it will give me a pretext for dropping in on people. I can warn them that the fen have arrived." Waving, she caught the attention of the long-suffering desk clerk. "Yoo hoo!" she called as the doors were closing. "Will you please not give out these room numbers to anyone else?"

"Sure," said the desk clerk to the closed elevator doors. "Everybody except *you* is a crank, right?"

Marion tapped gently on the door to the Conyers' room, hoping that they weren't the sort of people who went to bed ridiculously early and were smug about it.

Barbara answered the door, and Marion could see that the room's television was on, tuned to *Star Trek: The Next Generation.* "Hi!" said Marion brightly. "Can I come in? By the way, you want to be careful about opening the door without asking who it is. There's a contingent of fans in the building."

Barbara looked at her husband and smiled. "I'm not used to the idea of Jim having fans."

Marion sighed. "You never get used to it."

Jim Conyers motioned for her to sit down in the armchair by the worktable. "We brought snacks from home," he grinned. "Because Barbara's a skinflint. Want a beer? Diet Coke? Autograph your forehead?"

"Diet Coke," said Marion. "Unless you really need to practice the autograph. Seriously, though, I'm here to talk to you about Pat Malone."

Jim and Barbara looked at each other. "It was a sad business," he said quietly.

"I know," she said. "We also thought it was a very convenient coincidence. Pat Malone shows up, threatening, from what I hear, to do a new *Fandango,* and suddenly he dies."

"I thought of that," said Conyers, scooping ice into a glass and pouring Marion her drink. "But our secrets are pretty small potatoes."

Marion shook her head. "Not with all those reporters hanging around. And the hotel restaurant is full of fans. Any little indiscretion on anybody's part could—just this one week of your lives—easily make the AP, the *Enquirer,* and *Time* magazine. But, of course, that's just idle speculation, until we know how Pat Malone died."

"Presumably we'll find out sooner or later."

"It had better be sooner," said Marion. "Unless you want this to leak to the press. We thought that since you are a local attorney, you might be able to tap some inside sources and find out. We really need to know."

Jim Conyers thought it over carefully. "All right," he said. "I can't see any harm in it. I'll do what I can. I'll call your room when I've found out anything."

Marion gave him a helpless smile. "Could you please call now? Our phone line is kind of tied up."

She sipped her Diet Coke and chatted quietly with Barbara while Jim Conyers consulted the telephone directory and began to make his calls.

"I think it went rather well today, don't you?" asked Barbara. "I was awfully afraid they wouldn't find anything. They weren't terribly organized, you know."

"They'd never misplace their manuscripts," Marion assured her.

"Well, I hope the New York editors like what they read." She lowered her voice to a conspiratorial whisper. "I want to remodel the kitchen."

Jim Conyers was oblivious of his wife's conversation. "Well, that was fast work, Dennis," he was saying into the phone. "Guess we're lucky it's the slow season, huh? Say that again, will you? I need to write it down. How do you spell that? Oh, just like it sounds. M.A.O. And what are you calling it?—Think so, huh?—Okay, Dennis. Keep me posted. Yeah, if I can help you out, I will. Thanks again."

The two women looked up at him expectantly. Conyers set down the phone. His face was grave. He picked up the note pad and held it at arm's length. "According to the medical examiner, he died of having something called an MAO inhibitor mixed with his medication. And they think it was murder, so they'll be back in the morning to talk to all of us." He looked sternly at Marion. "Another thing. According to them, the deceased was one Richard Spivey. Now who the hell was Richard Spivey?"

Marion shook her head. "I wish I knew."

The chief reason I am writing these memoirs is to try to get you, and you, and you to face your own personal problems like men instead of like fans, get you out of the drugging microcosm, and triumph over whatever is keeping you in fandom.

—FRANCIS TOWNER LANEY
"Ah, Sweet Idiocy"

CHAPTER 13

BRENDAN SURN WAS quiet now. For nearly an hour Angela Arbroath had sat with him, held his hand, and talked soothingly of times gone by. At last her soft Southern voice had seemed to penetrate his anger, and tears drifted down his cheeks. Now he was sitting on his bed, clutching his silver NASA jacket, and staring off into nothingness.

Angela patted his hand and eased away from him. "I think he'll be all right for now," she told Lorien Williams.

The girl summoned a grateful smile. "Thank you. I've never been able to calm him down as quickly as that. Mostly when he gets into rages at home, I just leave him alone until he tires himself out." She sat huddled on her twin bed, in a black T-shirt and slacks, looking very small and lost. Dark circles shadowed her eyes.

"I suppose this is more than you bargained for when you took this job," said Angela.

Lorien hesitated. "I was such a fan of Mr. Surn," she said at last. "I had read everything he ever wrote, and all the biographical material I could find on him. He seemed so grandfatherly, somehow. You know, like Yoda. And I wasn't very happy with my parents. They were always hassling me to give up fandom and get some mundane job, like being a stockbroker." She made a moue of distaste. "I thought I'd go and see Brendan Surn. He'd understand me."

Angela sighed. She had heard it all before. Science fiction writers build castles in the air, and the fans move into them. (And the publishers collect the rent.) It was easy to find solace in someone else's storytelling, or in their apparent acceptance of what *you* are, and to build a soul for them. Surely, the fan thinks, he will like me as much as I like him; let me go and see him. It usually leads to disappointment: neither faces nor souls are as pretty in real life as they are on paper.

Angela remembered her own fascination in the fifties with Miranda Cairncross, a woman writer who wrote a wonderful tale about a Danish girl called Gefion who becomes caught up in the Ragnarok, the Norse version of Armageddon. She had found so much wisdom and lyrical beauty in *Ragnarok* that she read it over and over until she had nearly memorized it. She couldn't wait to meet the author, and at a book signing in New Orleans one Christmas she got her chance. Clutching her tattered copy of *Ragnarok,* she stood in line, half expecting to be picked out of the crowd as a soul mate and whisked off to tea with the author. She had even made a green velvet cloak like the one Gefion wore in the novel, so that the author would know of her devotion.

But the magic friendship did not happen. Miranda Cairncross turned out to be a gawky, colorless woman who seemed dismayed at the prospect of talking to the crowd of fans hovering around her table. She signed the books with fierce concentration, as though she were shutting out her surroundings, and when she finished each one, she would look up at the purchaser with a taut, forced smile. Angela could not imagine anyone less like the bold and reckless Gefion of *Ragnarok.* When she reached the head of the line, Angela handed over her book and said, "I really love your writing."

Miranda Cairncross peered at her over the pile of books, took in the sight of the plain young girl in a green velvet cloak, and reddened slightly. "I do what I can," she said. Moments later she returned Angela's copy, inscribed "There is no frigate like a book, M. A. Cairncross." Angela recognized the Emily Dickinson quote (another interest she might have shared with the author), but at the time she was disappointed that Miranda Cairncross' dedication had not been more personal.

Years later, after she had run into Brendan Surn at a few conventions and seen him besieged by soul-starved young strangers, she saw things from the other side, and she realized that touching people through their books was the best that most authors could do. Anything else was a letdown. By then she had also realized that the Dickinson quote about books being frigates was meant perhaps as a gentle warning from the author, telling her not to stray too far from life. She saw Miranda Cairncross years later, a frail old woman who had been brought to Worldcon to receive a plaque. Angela decided that the best way to thank her would be to leave her in peace.

"Yes," she said to Lorien Williams. "So you went to see Brendan Surn, thinking that he would be your friend."

"I guess so." Lorien was close to tears. She glanced over at the staring figure of Surn and continued, "When I got to his house, the place was a mess, and he didn't seem to know how to cook or anything, so I said to myself, I'll just stick around until his household help comes back. But they never did! I think his maid must have quit, and he never got around to advertising for another one."

"So you stayed?"

She nodded. "I didn't know what else to do! I mean, I couldn't leave him. I guess I could have later, after I learned how to manage everything. I could have hired someone, I guess. But he seemed to need me. And I didn't know what else to do with myself anyway." Her voice broke. "But it isn't like I thought it would be! Sometimes, when he's wet the bed again or burned up another teakettle trying to boil water, I'll say to myself, This is the man who wrote *Starwind Rising*. This is a being of greatness. But he isn't! He's just an ordinary, sick old man. And I feel trapped."

"Did you become friends?"

Lorien shook her head. "He's never reacted to me the way he did to you today. I think I'm just a convenience for him, not a person!"

There is no frigate like a book, thought Angela. Aloud she said, "Fans are not friends, dear. It can be dangerous to forget that."

Jay Omega didn't even look up when Marion entered the room. He was staring at the screen of his computer as if it were showing Indiana Jones movies. "Your ferret is reporting in, sir," said Marion, tapping him playfully on the shoulder.

"Shhh!" he said. "I'm talking to somebody."

Marion looked around the otherwise empty room. "Who? Friend of Curtis Phillips?"

He slumped back in his seat and looked up at her. "No. Not a demon. A guy out in California, and one from North Carolina. Whole crowds of people. Look at this." He tapped a block of text on the screen.

Leaning over his shoulder, Marion read aloud: "To J. O. Mega. From Kenny in Cupertino. Called Ethel Malone's number. The woman who answered says Ethel is in a nursing home, and that she's her grandniece. She says her Great-Uncle Pat died in 1958. Thinks they have a death certificate around someplace. Physical description: 6'2" (she thinks); green eyes; black hair; very pale. Says she sometimes gets crank calls from fans. Asks that fans not make pilgrimage to her house, as she barely remembers Great-Uncle Pat. Wants to be left alone. She sounds cute, though. I'm thinking about asking her out.—Kenny.''

"Let me type a reply thanking this guy for his trouble," said Jay. "Then you can tell me what you found out, Marion. By the way, have we eaten dinner?''

Marion reached for the room service menu. "I thought you'd never ask.''

When she came back from ordering a couple of chicken dinners, Marion turned back to Jay. "So, did he fake his death certificate so that he could get rid of his wife as well as his friends?''

"I don't think so," said Jay. "A guy from Mississippi went down to his local library and found an obituary for Pat Malone in an old newspaper on microfilm." He grinned. "Somebody who called himself Jim Hacker offered to break into the records of the University of Washington medical school, but I declined.''

"Good. I'm sure the dean of engineering takes a dim view of professors being wanted by the FBI.''

"I also got some interesting reminiscences from some old-timers that didn't quite square with things here. I get the funny feeling that the Lanthanides are still playing 'you and me against the world.' By the way, can you get me a copy of the time-capsule stories?''

Marion looked smug. "I already did," she said. "I asked Geoffrey Duke to make one for me. I thought it might be useful in case I decide to do an article.''

"Good. Have you read them yet?''

"Of course not. I've been running errands for a certain engineer with delusions of grandeur.''

"Oh. Well, sometime tonight I wish you'd take a look at them.''

"Don't you want to see them?''

Jay shook his head. "No. I need you to read them in that sharklike way that English majors read things. Analytically.''

"I see," said Marion dryly. "I'll try not to mistake that for a compliment. Anything else?''

"You have read the Lanthanides' published work, haven't you?''

"I just finished teaching the early science fiction course, remember? Of course, I have!''

"I thought so. Good. That ought to wrap it up.''

"So what do you think about all this?''

"You first, Marion. Any news?''

Marion nodded. "Angela Arbroath says that Elavil is used to control depression, among other things, and Jim Conyers phoned his friends in law enforcement, and was told that the case is a suspected homicide, and that the investigators will be back sometime tomorrow to question everybody. Something called an MAO inhibitor got added to Malone's medicine. Apparently, a tablet had been crushed and added to his drink.''

"MAO inhibitor. I know what that is. My Uncle Ewen . . . Well, anyway, that's interesting. Anything else?"

"The police have the deceased listed as Richard Spivey."

"Good," said Jay. "And do *they* think he was Pat Malone?"

"The Lanthanides? Yes. Angela says he had to have been. He knew stuff that only one of the Lanthanides would know." She ticked off the members' names. "Dugger's dead, Deddingfield's dead, Curtis Phillips is dead, and all the rest of them are here. Besides, if he wasn't Pat Malone, why would any of them kill him?"

"I wondered that," said Jay Omega. "And I don't know. But I rather think that they do." He looked thoughtful and then embarrassed. "Marion, did you bring my SFWA directory in that rat's nest of bibliographic papers you insisted on packing?"

"Yes. And don't say it was a waste of time, because I still might interview one of the Lanthanides for an analysis of early S-F for one of the journals. Maybe."

"You probably won't, but I'm not complaining about the fact that you brought it. I just need my directory."

Marion retrieved the booklet containing the membership list of the Science Fiction Writers of America and resisted the urge to fling it at him. Jay began to flip through the dog-eared pages. Several entries were marked with comments (e.g. "Sent thank you note") and a few had telephone numbers written after them in pencil. "She's not in here," he muttered.

"What are you up to now?" asked Marion.

Jay continued to thumb through the booklet. "Who is the most famous person I know in science fiction?"

Marion searched her memory. "Well, you shook hands with Arthur C. Clarke once."

"No. I mean the most famous person that I can *impose* upon." He handed her the booklet. "And your choice is limited to the people I have phone numbers for."

Marion began to flip through the pages, going from back to front. "You served on a committee with him once . . . didn't we meet her at a con last spring?" Finally she stopped turning pages, deliberating over one entry.

"Did you find someone?"

She took a deep breath. "John Brunner is an extremely nice person, and he seems to like you," she said carefully. "But since it is about three o'clock in the morning where he lives in Britain, I'd advise against presuming on his benevolence."

"Good point," said Jay. "I suppose I could wait until five A.M. to call him. That would make it ten on a Sunday morning where he is. But I wanted to get this done tonight."

"Get *what* done?"

"Look, if the Lanthanides don't get this solved very quickly, there will be all three rings of a media circus. I think I'd better explain that to them."

"I think they realize it."

"Like hell they do. They're just sitting around playing dumb and hoping it will all go away. But it won't, unless they start cooperating very quickly."

Marion's eyes narrowed. "What does this have to do with John Brunner?"

"Nothing."

"Then why are you going to call him at ten o'clock on a Sunday morning?" She wailed.

"Because I'm hoping that he has Jazzy Holt's phone number, and that he'll give it to me."

"You are going to call Jasmine Holt?" gasped Marion.

"Not unless I have to," said Jay grimly. He looked at his watch and sighed. "I guess we'd better try to settle this thing now. Tomorrow may be too late. Could you round up the Lanthanides and bring them here?"

"Why would they want to do that?" asked Marion. "Most of them hardly know you."

"Tell them that we will meet here at eleven to resolve this thing. If they don't show up, I will consider that permission to report my findings to the police instead. And then I'll call a press conference."

"You're going to do that? *You?* The person who wouldn't even tell the local paper about your award nomination?"

"This is different," said Jay. "Their sense of priorities is beginning to get on my nerves. And besides, I liked the man who was killed."

Ruben Mistral might have objected strenuously to Jay Omega's proposed meeting, except for the fact that his body was still running on California time, so it still seemed the shank of the evening to him, and he wasn't sleepy. Besides, the threat of adverse publicity ap-

pealed to the practical side of Mistral's nature, and he agreed that
some sort of discussion would be prudent. Marion persuaded the
others to come by ending her summons with the statement: ''—And
Ruben Mistral is coming.'' With varying degrees of reluctance,
everyone agreed to turn up at Jay Omega's room in one hour's time.

Jay spent the hour before the meeting online with the Fandango
grapevine he had created in hopes that he might learn more useful
bits of information about Pat Malone. He also made a phone call to
Raleigh, North Carolina to check out a theory of his own. Marion
read the time-capsule stories, with occasional snickers or caustic comments which Jay steadfastly ignored. Finally, though, ten minutes
before the Lanthanides were due to arrive, he logged out of Delphi,
switched off the computer, and turned to Marion. ''Well?'' he said.
''Have you read them all?''

She looked thoughtful. ''Oh, yes.''

''What do you think?''

In most unscholarly terms, Dr. Marion Farley told him.

At five minutes to eleven the Lanthanides began to arrive. Jim and
Barbara Conyers came first, bringing a bottle of wine, as if they were
accepting a dinner invitation. Marion seated them on the double bed
nearest the window, and left Jay to exchange pleasantries with them
while she went to answer another knock at the door. George Woodard
was there in his pajamas and bathrobe, giving a slumber-party air to
the gathering. He was followed by Angela Arbroath, who was arm
in arm with a dazed-looking Brendan Surn. Lorien Williams came in
after them, appearing more tired than nervous. Finally Erik Giles and
Ruben Mistral appeared, bringing along chairs from their own rooms.

''I'm too old to sit on the floor,'' said Erik. ''Met Bunzie in the
hall, and he agreed with me. Here we are. What's this all about?''

The Lanthanides turned expectantly to Jay Omega, who reddened
a bit under their solemn stares. I guess you're wondering why I asked
you here,'' he said softly.

Jim Conyers scowled. ''I'm wondering why we bothered to
come.''

''Well,'' said Jay. ''Believe it or not, I mean well. I know that this
anthology means a lot to most of you, and that you want the time-
capsule retrieval to be remembered as a solemn and meaningful
event—and not as the prologue to a sensational murder story.''

George Woodard yelped. ''Pat Malone was murdered?''

Mistral's response was more pragmatic. ''Who knows this?''

''The police. Maybe some reporters by now, but if you're lucky, they haven't made any connection yet between the deceased and the reunion. They will, though, if this thing goes into investigation. Especially if they find out that Pat Malone had come back to life for this reunion."

"He's right," said Ruben Mistral. "We need to talk about damage control. Jim, you're a lawyer. What can we do?"

Jim Conyers shrugged. "Cooperate, I guess. Once the medical examiner ran that tox screen and found a suspicious substance present in the deceased, there was no chance of stopping the investigation. The longer it drags on, the more publicity there's going to be."

Erik Giles interrupted him. "Could I have some of that wine, Jim?"

The others shushed him and went on talking at once, but Barbara Conyers flashed him a sympathetic smile and handed him the bottle and a plastic glass.

"What if we called a press conference and said we had nothing to do with it?" asked Angela Arbroath.

Jim Conyers shook his head. "People might naturally wonder why you saw fit to call a press conference over the demise of a total stranger. And *then* you'd have to tell them it was Pat Malone, and *then* —"

"Was it?" asked Jay Omega.

"What?"

"Was the dead man really Pat Malone? Can anyone swear to that?"

The Lanthanides looked at each other. "Well, after thirty years . . ." said Angela hesitantly.

"He was still pale," George offered. "And six feet tall."

"I thought Pat looked like a frog in the old days," said Barbara Conyers. "Sort of saucer-eyed, you know, and loose-lipped. But we've all changed so much. I wouldn't have known any of you on sight."

"It hardly matters," said Erik Giles, taking a sip of his wine. "He knew things about us that no one else could have known."

"He enjoyed it, too!" said Woodard indignantly. "He was going to make us all look like fools again. Just like he did to everyone in *The Last Fandango*!"

Ruben Mistral looked from Jay Omega to the laptop computer still set up on the table, and back again. "What are you getting at?" he asked.

"I'm trying to help you people settle this, before we all become suspects for the local police," said Jay. "And I think George Wood-

ard made a key point just now. The man who died was going to make
fools of you all by telling things that you didn't want made public.
I think someone murdered him to prevent that. So, if we knew what
the secrets were, it might help us guess who killed him.''

Erik Giles smiled gently. ''You needn't do all this on my account,
Jay,'' he said. ''I know I invited the both of you here, but you needn't
feel responsible for me. We're not such old fogies that we can't take
care of ourselves.''

''It's the man who died that concerns me. One of your little secrets
caused it.''

Angela Arbroath shook her head. ''The least important secret might
have been the one he was killed over. How could you tell?''

Jim Conyers looked amused. ''You're not suggesting that we confide in *you,* are you? If we didn't trust one of our own, why should
we let you hear our secrets? Assuming, of course, that there are any.''

''Well,'' said Jay Omega, shrugging. ''I thought you might want
to see the murderer punished. Or at least stopped from killing again.
Especially since he killed a total stranger.''

Angela stared. ''What are you saying?''

He spoke slowly and carefully. ''That man was no more Pat Malone than I am.'' He waited for the exclamations of shock and disbelief to subside before he continued. ''The man's driver's license
said that he was Richard Spivey, from a little town near Raleigh,
North Carolina. And I believe that to be true.''

''Richard Spivey!'' cried George Woodard.

''Do you know him, George?'' asked Erik Giles.

''I'd never seen him, but he'd been subscribing to *Alluvial* for
years. Richard Spivey from North Carolina. He didn't write very
often, though. He *never* discussed the Lanthanides, or claimed to be
one of us.''

''What address was used?''

Woodard shrugged. ''A post office box, I think.''

''How do you know he wasn't Pat Malone?'' Angela demanded.

Jay pointed to the computer. ''Because I asked.'' He told them
about the call to Ethel Malone, and about the man in Mississippi who
had found the obituary. ''I think Pat Malone died a long time ago,
and somebody decided to take his place. True, he had information
that only one of the Lanthanides would know. Where would he get
it? I thought the fact that he was on Elavil was an indication. *And*
he was from North Carolina.''

''Curtis!'' cried George Woodard. ''Curtis was in a mental institution in North Carolina.''

"And Elavil is a drug used in psychiatric cases," whispered Angela. "Are you saying that this man was only *pretending* to be Pat Malone?"

"I don't know," said Jay sadly. "I think he may have actually believed it by now. He and Curtis Phillips were both patients in a psychiatric facility outside Raleigh. I know, because I called and asked. I'm pretty sure that he had heard Curtis Phillips talk about the Lanthanides for years and years until it actually became real to him. He remembered it as an experience, the way you visualize a movie you have seen, or a particularly vivid novel."

"But he didn't even know us!" Erik Giles protested. "Why would he want to embarrass us?"

"Because that's what Pat Malone would have done," said Marion. Woodard laughed bitterly. "Another damned fan hoax!"

"It was very convincing," said Jim Conyers. "But I must agree with our host here that we have an obligation both morally and legally to provide any information that we can."

No one spoke. Brendan Surn seemed to have forgotten that they were there. The others glanced at each other nervously.

"If no one wants to confide in us, we could make some guesses," said Jay. "For example, there are sexual goings-on that one might rather forget three decades after the fact." He held up a folded slip of paper. "I have Jasmine Holt's phone number here."

In fact, he had a blank piece of paper, but he counted on the fact that no one would ask to see it, and the bluff worked.

"That business about my wife being promiscuous was totally exaggerated," said Woodard. "We were both believers in free love back then, and I believe she had sexual relations with a good many members of fandom. It was a philosophical statement. I see no reason to be embarrassed by it." Beads of sweat made his skin glow like damp cheese. He pushed a greasy forelock away from his eyes. "Of course, she's not at all like that now."

"Your kids might be less tolerant, though, George," said Jim Conyers. "Mine sure were." He sighed and glanced at his wife. "I guess I'd better tell you about this before you call Jazzy."

"Jim!" said Ruben Mistral warningly.

"The statute of limitations passed long ago, Bunzie," said Jim Conyers. "I checked."

"It was at a con, and we had all had too much to drink," said Mistral. "And we—I wouldn't call it rape, would you, Jim? We didn't know she was underage."

"You guys raped Jasmine Holt?" The question was out of Lorien's mouth before she could think better of it. "Sorry," she muttered, and pretended to read the cable television guide.

The color drained from Barbara Conyers' face. "Oh, Jim," she whispered.

He looked away. "It was before we got engaged," he muttered.

"Come on, no big deal!" said Bunzie jovially. "That was a hundred years ago. By the time she married Curtis we were all pals again. And when she married Peter I gave the bride away."

"I doubt if Pat would have told that story," said Erik. "He was just as involved as we were."

Marion glared at the Lanthanides, looking considerably less sympathetic than she had moments before. "There are some literary secrets here, I think, that might have been worth revealing." She noted with satisfaction that the Lanthanides had begun to look uncomfortable. "Take Dale Dugger's story, for example. It isn't very expertly written, but the atmosphere is wonderful. It's about a Martian soldier coming home from the war to find that he has more in common with the enemy aliens than he does with the people back home. It sounded very familiar."

Lorien Williams blinked in confusion. "But—that scene you described is famous! It's in Brendan's book *The Galactic Watchfires*. That's the chapter when Tarn-yan returns to Qar."

Mistral shrugged. "So what? We lived in each other's pockets in those days. Who's to say that Dale didn't write the scene after hearing Brendan tell the story?"

"And Curtis Phillips wrote about a mad wizard who has sex with a demon. Both those guys were fairly recognizable, too." Marion looked down at her hands, so as not to look at any of the Lanthanides.

"Curtis was crazy," said Erik Giles.

"Yes," spluttered George Woodard. "But I remember he told me—"

"Shut up, George!" said Mistral.

"And you're going to let them publish this anthology?" Jay marveled.

Mistral shrugged. "For a pile of money. We'll write prefaces to all the stories that will take the sting out. And we may do a little judicious editing."

Still blushing, Marion continued. "Why doesn't Peter Deddingfield have a story in the time capsule?"

The Lanthanides looked at each other, but no one spoke.

"Everybody else is there. Angela, Pat, Dale, Curtis, George, Erik,

Reuben Bundshaft, Jim Conyers, and one by C. A. Stormcock. But you always said that you were C. A. Stormcock, Erik!"

He raised his plastic glass to her in a mock toast. "So I was."

"But you aren't, Erik, are you?" she said, looking at the other Lanthanides for confirmation. "Don't bother to lie to me, folks. I read those stories. The Stormcock story is obviously by the guy who wrote *The Golden Gain,* and the story signed 'Erik Giles' is just as obviously written by the person who wrote the *Time Traveler Trilogy.*"

Marion looked at the stricken face of her old friend, and then at Jay Omega. "Maybe we shouldn't discuss this in public," she murmured. "Maybe, Erik, you and I could just—"

He finished the contents of his glass and set it down. "It's all right," he said. "These people all know, my dear. They've known for more than thirty years. We just didn't think that it would ever matter much." He turned to the Lanthanides and smiled. "I can't think why I invited them to come with me. I suppose it serves me right for being a coward. I didn't want to face all this alone. Or perhaps subconsciously I was tired of the pretense."

Angela shook her head. "You couldn't know that Pat Malone would show up. And we would never have given you away, Stormy."

"So you're Peter Deddingfield?" said Jay.

"I was once. But I wasn't the important one. The fellow who married Jazzy, and who wrote all those wonderful books later on— I always think that *that* is the real Peter Deddingfield. I gave up the name when we both left the Fan Farm. When I knew that I did not want to become a professional writer."

"Buy why?" asked Marion. "If you had published as Stormcock, and he hadn't published anything. Had he?"

"No," said George Woodard. "People have always wondered why Pete Deddingfield's first published short story was so bad. It's because the 'old' Pete wrote it. Stormy, I mean."

"So Peter Deddingfield—the famous one—was really Erik Giles. Why switch names?" Marion persisted.

"Can't you guess, Dr. Farley?" asked the professor in a gently mocking tone. "Because my old friend had something that I wanted and he no longer valued. Erik Giles had a doctorate in English."

Marion stared. "You don't have a Ph.D.?"

"No. He didn't need one to be a writer of science fiction, which he had both the talent and the desire to be. I, on the other hand, had written one book that other people liked far more than I did. I was tired of it all: the puerile jokes, the posturing, the financial uncertainty. What I wanted more than anything was a nice soft job on a college campus, where I could teach my classes and be left alone with my dignity." He smiled, remembering. "So Erik Giles said to me, 'Take the damned degree. We'll swap names, and we'll both be happy. Swear the Lanthanides to secrecy, and who'll ever know?' "

"But you taught all those classes!" Marion protested. "You went to conferences!"

"I didn't write very many journal articles," he reminded her. "Tenure was easier twenty years ago. As for the rest of it, impersonating an English professor isn't very difficult. I have a knack for being pretentious."

"But you could have got a degree of your own," said Marion.

"Yes, but by the time I could afford to, I was already employed as Erik Giles, and there seemed little likelihood of ever being caught. By then, I couldn't risk being exposed as a fraud. No university would have hired me after that, regardless of my credentials."

"What about your families?" asked Jay.

"Mine died when I was in my teens, and Erik's mother passed away while we were living in Wall Hollow. It was easy to lose touch with old friends back in Richmond. And as time went on, there were fewer and fewer people who might have known."

"Except Pat Malone," said Jay.

"Yes. When he came back, I knew that he wouldn't keep the old secret. He would revel in exposing the deception. It wouldn't have mattered for my old friend, who died rich and famous. But I enjoy my job at the university, and I wanted my pension in a few years' time."

Angela Arbroath clasped her arms against her body as if she were suddenly very cold. "Oh, Stormy," she whispered. "Did you kill him just for that?"

He considered the question. "I'm not sure," he said at last. "It seemed the most pressing reason at the time. But I think the real reason was that I was so damned disappointed that he wasn't dead I couldn't stand it! I went to his room to reason with him, but I took the medicine with me, so perhaps even then I knew. . . . Anyhow, it's a better world without Pat Malone in it." He looked at Jay Omega. "I suppose the autopsy gave it away?"

"The MAO inhibitor," said Jay. "I knew that it's prescribed for hypertension. If you mix it with Malone's—er, Spivey's—Elavil, it lowers the blood pressure too much, and causes a coma, and then death."

"Yes, I suppose I was lucky that he was taking his own medication, and that he was old. Otherwise he might have survived to enjoy my disgrace. He'd have liked that.''

Jim Conyers interrupted. "You don't have to say anything else, Stormy! You need an attorney. I'll be happy to represent you. When the police get here—''

The once and future Erik Giles waved him away. "It doesn't matter, Jim," he said quietly. "The other thing you must not do with an MAO inhibitor is take alcohol. And I've just about finished that whole bottle of wine by myself. I'll be dead by morning.'' He swayed slightly as he stood up and tottered toward the door. "Now, if you'll excuse me, I will go gently into that good night.''

He could see himself
in six months, afloat on the refilled Watauga
where the drowned swim forever....

—DON JOHNSON
Watauga Drawdown

CHAPTER 14

JAY OMEGA WATCHED the sun rise over the brown wasteland of Breedlove Lake. Beside him in equal silence sat Marion Farley.

Erik Giles (they still thought of him that way) had not gone particularly gently into that good night, as he had wished. The roomful of witnesses to his prospective suicide had been impelled to call the police, or, attorney Jim Conyers warned, they might be considered accessories, since suicide is still a crime. By the time a rescue squad arrived from New Wall Hollow, it was too late. The combination of alcohol and medication had done its work irreversibly, and if Erik Giles had not gone peacefully and with dignity, he had nonetheless gone, despite the application of respirators, injections, and the defibrillator.

When it was over, Jim Conyers talked to the officers in charge of the case and convinced them that there was no point in wasting county money on a murder case when the perpetrator was already dead. They agreed that for official purposes, their report would read that both Richard Spivey and Erik Giles had died of heart conditions in unrelated circumstances. The press would not be told otherwise. No mention of Pat Malone was contained in any summary of the weekend's events.

"I said I'd defend Stormy, and I did," Conyers told the others. "There will be no scandal attached to his death. It was the only defense he wanted."

Marion leafed through the time-capsule manuscripts for the hundredth time. "Did you know it was Erik all along?" she asked Jay.

"No. After we learned that an MAO inhibitor had been used, I knew that the killer would be on medication, but that didn't exclude any of them, really. I thought it might be Brendan Surn because he is a bit unbalanced."

Marion gave him a faint smile. "Pretending to be somebody else," she mused. "The mental illness of fandom. I did it myself once, you know."

Jay looked startled. "Did you?"

She nodded dreamily. "Just for one night. It was back when I was in college. I got a blind date with some guy whose parents were stationed in the Philippines with Voice of America. All he could do was moan about how homesick he was. So to make him happy, I pretended to be Petrice Jones. She was my best friend in high school, and she had lived in the Philippines until her sophomore year. After three years of listening to Petrice, I knew all her classmates by name, her old teachers—everything! The guy had a wonderful evening talking about old times with 'Petrice.' And I took care never to see him again."

"You meant well. I'm not sure Richard Spivey did."

"No. But I think Pat Malone would have been pleased. I can imagine him in some smoke-filled hereafter enjoying the sensation of his unscheduled return. It almost makes me believe in demonic possession."

"Are you going to tell the university about Erik's impersonation?"

Marion sighed. "I've been going over it in my mind for hours. But I always come to the same conclusion: no. It seems to me that it doesn't matter what name Erik used during his adolescence. He was the professor everyone liked and respected, and he wouldn't want to lose that in death. Most of our colleagues have never heard of an S-F writer named Deddingfield, anyway. Why spoil his memory? He was a good teacher."

"That's what I thought," said Jay. "Let him be remembered as the professor. He wanted out of fandom badly enough to kill for it. What's one more secret among the Lanthanides?"

The literary auction for the Lanthanides time capsule took place as scheduled at ten o'clock Sunday morning in the Holiday Inn in Johnson City. Sarah Ashley accepted the sealed bids and promised to reconvene the group at eleven to announce the winner to the press.

Enzio O'Malley was having brunch with Lily Warren on his company's American Express card. "Well," said Lily, toying with her eggs Benedict. "Do you think you got the anthology?"

O'Malley shrugged. "I doubt it," he said, stifling a yawn. "How about you?"

Lily shook her head. "Fifty K was as high as I could go without making a phone call. After reading the manuscripts, I decided not to make it.''

"It'll go high. Those maniacs on Fifth Avenue would pay two grand for a cheeseburger. There's no telling what they'll bid to get this.''

"Too bad,'' said Lily. "Since your company has Surn's back list, I know how much you wanted to acquire this.''

"I got a budget,'' said O'Malley. "If I paid a million for this wad, and it bombed, I'd find myself editing role-playing games in Wisconsin.''

"I thought you said that if they publicized this well, it would sell automatically.''

"Theoretically, yes,'' said O'Malley. "But I wouldn't want to bet my career on it. I'm a schemer, not a gambler.''

"And are you planning any schemes right now?'' asked Lily, smiling.

"It's already done.'' He yawned again. "That's why I'm so tired. I got up at six A.M. this morning to call London. And I got my book deal.'' He grinned as he speared another pancake. "So while some checkbook publishers spend a mint publicizing the Lanthanides to sell their crummy anthology, my company brings out a kiss-and-tell book by the celebrated S-F critic—''

"Jasmine Holt!'' cried Lily. "My God! She was married to two or three of them, wasn't she?''

"Yep. And she hasn't mellowed any with age, either,'' said O'Malley cheerfully. "Dirty laundry! That's what people want to read. Who cares what a bunch of postadolescent nerds actually wrote, for chrissake?''

"But they're writers,'' said Lily. "I thought they had fans.''

O'Malley looked at her. "Would you want to bet a million dollars and your job title that there are enough S-F fans out there to buy fifty thousand copies of the over-the-hill gang's juvenilia in hardcover?''

"I guess not,'' murmured Lily.

"Exactly. I got the Holt memoir for twenty-five K. And we won't have to pay that much to the person who really writes it, either.'' He flashed her a feral smile. "Literary judgment, Lily! That's what it's all about.''

Ruben Mistral was smiling as he put down the phone. The Lanthanides had gathered in the conference room for a catered brunch while they waited for Sarah Ashley to report the results of the auction. "It's over," he announced to the others. "The anthology is sold."

"What's the deal?" asked Woodard eagerly.

"One point two million dollars. It's a hard/soft deal, world rights, fifty/fifty on screen rights."

"What does that mean exactly?" asked Angela.

"And how soon do we get it?" Woodard again.

Mistral smiled at their eagerness. "Sarah will explain the business angles to anyone who is interested. As for the money, you'll get some of it in a few weeks, but don't go on a spending spree. You won't believe the tax bite!"

Jim Conyers stood up. "I guess that's it, then. The reunion has accomplished its goal. We're all free to go, by the way. There will be no further investigation on the two deaths."

"Understood," said Mistral. "And we're all sworn to secrecy. Right, guys?"

"It doesn't feel right to leave it like this," said Angela.

"Not to worry," said Mistral. "We'll do a tribute to Stormy in the anthology. First-class stuff."

Brendan Surn spoke up. "It reminds me of our trip to Worldcon all those years ago. Remember then? We all worked and planned, and we didn't make it out of this valley. Finally, though, one by one, each of us did make it out. Some of us became famous and well off, but we always missed what we had here. Never quite found that anywhere else. And now we all come back for the big reunion and we find that we can't get back in. Not really." He looked out at the red clay scar between wooded hills. "We couldn't get back."

"Yeah, sure, Brendan," said Ruben Mistral. "Can't go home again, right? Well, people, I got a plane to catch." He shook hands with Conyers, hugged Angela, and headed for the door.

George Woodard hurried to catch up with him. "Listen, can I talk to you for a minute?"

Mistral tried to glance at his watch without being too obvious about it. "Sure, George," he said. "Another business question?"

"No. I have a favor to ask," said George, looking nervously about. "You see, in western Maryland we have a little science fiction convention every September. It's called Mason/Dixiecon. We have a few panel discussions, a little art show. We show old movies. You'd really like it, Bunzie. And I was wondering . . ." He took a deep breath. "Would you consider being our guest of honor this year?"

Ruben Mistral winced at the thought of spending an entire weekend in a dreary burg in Maryland, signing autographs and telling high school kids how to make it in Hollywood. But before he could plead a prior commitment, his mouth opened, and he could hear Bunzie saying, "Sure, George. I'd like that. Count me in."

They walked out together, with Woodard prattling happily about *Star Trek* blooper reels and Fifties starlets.

Lorien Williams was packing Brendan's belongings in his old leather suitcase while he stood at the window looking out on the barren shore.

"I heard the drawdown is ending today," she said to him. "The hotel clerk said that the dam is repaired, so next week they'll be letting the lake fill up again."

He did not seem to have heard her. After a moment, she shrugged and went on packing. He was much better today; more alert and in good spirits. She wondered if the time change had bothered him. It was a pity to put him through it again so quickly, but at least she'd know what to expect when they got back to California. She'd have to field all the phone calls until Thursday at least. She looked longingly at the new Bob Cameron paperbacks she had bought to read on the trip. She still hadn't got around to them. Too bad. Bob Cameron was a really great author. She loved his futuristic stories. Lorien sighed and looked back at Brendan.

Someone knocked at the door. Lorien waited a moment to see if Brendan would respond, but he seemed not to have heard. She decided to answer it.

"I'm getting ready to go," said Angela Arbroath, setting her suitcase inside the door. "I thought I'd just stop in and say good-bye." She was dressed in a shapeless brown dress for traveling, and her hair was pulled into an unattractive bun: the invisible woman.

Brendan Surn turned away from the window. "Hello, Beanpole!" he called out. "Good to see you!"

Angela smiled at the look of surprise on Lorien's face. "He means me, all right," she told the girl. "You should have seen me back in '54."

"You're better today, aren't you?" she said to Brendan Surn. She sat down on the bed beside him, reaching up to brush a lock of silver hair away from his face. "You look better this morning."

He sighed. "It comes and goes, Angie. It's like a sea mist. Sometimes my mind can't see a foot ahead in any direction, and at other times it's as clear as it ever was. I just take my pills and hope."

Angela took a deep breath. "Listen, Brendan," she said briskly. "I hear you've got a big fancy house in California, and I have to tell you, I have no interest in even visiting anyplace like that. But I tell you what: I do have the prettiest little white cottage in Mississippi that you ever saw. I have an herb garden, and cats, and the warmest, sunniest kitchen in the world. And I have a guest room.''

He nodded, beginning a smile.

"Brendan, nobody's promising anything right now, but would you like to come and stay with me for a while, and see if you like it? I think maybe Lorien has places of her own to go."

Brendan Surn looked down at her with his wisest, gentlest smile. "Yes, Angela," he said. "I'd like to sit in a garden now. I've seen what there is in the sea. Can I come today?"

Angela motioned for Lorien to come over. "Let's talk it over, Brendan," she said. "All three of us. We have all the time there is."

Jay and Marion were carrying their bags out of the lodge when they met Jim Conyers. He slung a suitcase into the back of his station wagon and followed them to their car.

"Is it over?" asked Marion. Her face was still strained and swollen-eyed.

"Yes," said Conyers. "The police are calling off the investigation on both deaths, and the auction went as planned. A little over a million, Bunzie said."

"I'm sorry about the way it turned out," said Jay Omega. "I was trying to help."

The lawyer nodded. "You were right. A murder investigation wouldn't have made things any better. And I think that when Stormy had found out that it wasn't Pat, it would have ended just the way it did."

"Brendan Surn was the only one who didn't tell lies," mused Marion. "Remember, he kept saying that Pete wasn't dead. We thought he was just senile."

"I wish it could have been a better reunion for you," said Jay.

Jim Conyers looked out at the dead lake. "It was the right reunion," he said at last. "Bickering, posturing, arrogance, and occasional lapses of genuine affection. They were my best friends, God help me." He smiled. "They were the best friends I ever had."

In the office of a small print shop in Cato, Mississippi, an elderly man was reading *People* magazine. He was sitting with his feet propped up on the old oak desk, a few inches away from a computer screen glowing green in the shadows beyond his reading lamp. His black-framed glasses slipped down on his sloping nose, revealing bulging eyes that made him faintly resemble a frog. The top of his head was a hairless dome, but the fringe that remained encircling his ears was still jet black, emphasizing the pallor of his wrinkled skin. He was six feet tall, hollow-cheeked and gaunt, and he possessed an expression of clever malevolence. He was reading about the retrieval of a time capsule in Wall Hollow, Tennessee.

Turning to the photograph of the assembled Lanthanides, mugging for posterity with a mud-caked pickle jar, the old man burst out laughing. "What a bunch of fuggheads!" he snorted, and turned to an article about a New Orleans jazz festival.

The message on the computer screen read: THANK YOU FOR HELPING ME VERIFY THE DEATH OF PAT MALONE BY FINDING THAT OLD OBITUARY COLUMN IN THE LIBRARY. JAY OMEGA.

He glanced at it and laughed again. "Fuggheads."